THE QUEEN OF ZOMBIE HEARTS

THE
QUEEN OF ZOMBIE HEARTS

GENA SHOWALTER

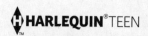

ISBN-13: 978-0-373-21163-0

THE QUEEN OF ZOMBIE HEARTS

Printed in U.S.A.

To Mom and Dad. Just because.

ROSES ARE RED

VIOLETS ARE BLUE

BE VERY AFRAID

WE'RE COMING
FOR YOU.

A NOTE FROM ALI

Are you ready for this?

The romance and sizzle...the betrayal...loss...pain...

The end?

I thought *I* was. I had begun comparing myself to a coin, with life on one side and death on the other. I'd felt as though I'd been tossed in the air, only to tumble down fast and hard. Which side I landed on would be totally up to fate. But I've learned not everything that happens is meant to be.

Think about it. The fact that I ate a bagel with cream cheese for breakfast—not fate but hunger.

The fact that I lost my mother, father and beloved little sister in a car crash—not fate but panic.

The fact that four of my friends were gunned down in one night and two others were killed soon after—NOT FATE! Evil.

Fate and *meant to be* come down to one thing. The tool we've been given to shape our destinies. Choice. Mine...yours...theirs. Good, bad. Ugly.

Here's mine: Months ago, I decided to join a crew of slayers and spend my nights fighting zombies.

Yes. *Zombies*.

These vile creatures live among us, invisible to the ungifted eye. They emerge at nightfall, hungry for human spirits, the essence of life. They feast, and they poison, and if ever you're bitten, *your* spirit will rise, starved and ready to devour.

I considered zombies the worst enemy ever to walk the earth.

I was wrong.

Humans can be more dangerous than monsters.

There's a company out there. Anima Industries. *They* control zombies, and they've decided slayers are a problem with only one solution: extermination.

Now, slayers have a choice. Go underground...or go to war. In other words, hide our coins or toss them ourselves.

We've lost so much already, and there are so few of us left. The smart thing to do is pack up and hide. Live to fight another day.

Screw smart.

We're tossing. One way or another, we will destroy Anima for good—or they will destroy us. But this time, only one group is walking away.

Our choice is made.

Ready or not, here we come.

See you on the other side,

Ali Bell

UP IS DOWN AND DOWN IS UP

"Dude. How about that one?" My best friend, Kat Parker, pointed toward the far corner, to a table occupied by three boys about our age.

One guy was hot enough to melt a polar vortex. One wasn't handsome in the traditional sense, but with his unusual chartreuse eyes, it hardly mattered. The third was amazingly rugged, with a fresh scrape on his cheek and scars on his knuckles.

Well, well. We had finally found a smorgasbord of different flavored man-meat.

"Perfect," I said with a nod.

"I don't know." Reeve Ankh, my other friend, surveyed the boys and chewed on her bottom lip. "I'm getting danger vibes from the one on the right."

The one on the right—Knuckle Scars. Excellent. Her dandar—danger radar—was working at optimal levels.

In our little trio, she'd always been the voice of reason. Or, as Kat would say, "the voice of shut up and live a little."

My darling Kat meant it in the nicest way possible, of course. She simply had no filter. She always spoke her mind, always stood up for what she believed—that her way was the best way—and lived by the motto I'm On Board the Awesome Train and You Can Hop On or Get Run Over.

Was it any wonder I loved her so much?

"This is stupid, you guys."

The grumble came from Mackenzie Love. Once my archenemy, now one of my favorite pet projects.

Most people were surprised by our sudden friendship, but I'd learned life could change in the blink of an eye.

Everything could change in the blink of an eye.

I accepted, and I rolled.

"Suck it up." Trina Brighton, the last member of our group, kicked Mackenzie under the table. "This was *your* idea."

"That's right. You asked for our help, and we agreed to give it to you on one condition. That you do what we say, when we say." Grinning her happy-kitten grin, Kat rubbed her hands together. While I had grown to like Mackenzie, she hadn't. But she *had* softened...ish. "This is gonna be fun. For me!"

Hated to admit it, but...yeah, it was gonna be fun for me, too.

We were at Choco Loco, a chocolate bar where girls picked up treats and boys picked up girls. Not that I wanted to be picked up.

I'd been going out with the drool-worthy Cole Holland—officially...again—for a little over a month. And, okay, yeah, there was a slight problem with our relationship. In the course of that month, we'd been on...give me a second to count them—zero dates. We'd had a total of...let's see, let's see—

zero minutes alone. And we'd kissed...oh, I don't know—zero times.

Here are things that suck worse: _____.

Okay, fine. There *are* a few things that suck worse. Like the time I was an all-you-can-eat dinner buffet for zombies. The time I battled the worst Z-poisoning in the history of ever. And my personal favorite, the time Anima Industries locked me away, electrocuted me, starved me and studied me like a freaking zoo animal.

Considering all I'd been through, my love life should have been a sparkling diamond in a sea of coal. Or a sea of "Cole." Har har. We had tried to get together, like, plan-everything-down-to-the-last-second tried, but each of our sneak-overs had encountered one teensy-weensy problem.

Her name: Nana.

Seriously, my grandmother had morphed into the Make-Out Police, and okay, okay, I didn't really have to rack my brain to figure out why. One night Cole had saved me from a very painful death, and we'd decided to celebrate. Alone. He'd stolen into my bedroom, and we'd done what we always did. (I *refuse* to provide the down-and-dirty deets. But it was. Down and dirty. *Anyway.*) She'd heard us—the horror!—and had busted in.

We'd still had (most of) our clothes on, but yowza, the position she'd caught us in...

Ever since, Nana has been attached to my side. In fact, the only time she detaches is when I'm hanging with my girls, or when I'm prowling the streets, hunting zombies.

Don't get me wrong. I love Nana to pieces. And so does Cole. When the three of us get together, we actually have fun. But I want more. I *need* more. I'm addicted to Cole's hands…and his mouth…and oh, Ali-want, his nipple ring. Withdrawals stink!

"What are you waiting for, love buns?" Kat banged her hand on the table. "Did I not make it clear that you don't get a vote in this? That the tribe has spoken? You know what you gotta do, so, do it."

A waiter stepped up to our table before Mackenzie could respond. He set a mousse shooter in front of each of us.

"Um." Reeve frowned. "We didn't order these."

"Compliments of the hounds in the corner." A wink, and the waiter was off.

In unison, my friends and I gazed at our chocolate-addiction enablers. Hot and Chartreuse lifted their own mousse shooters in a toast. Knuckle Scars just stared.

Reminded me of Cole.

Kat stood and called, "My friend MacLovin' will come over and thank you in person just as soon as her heartbeat settles. You totally rocked her—"

Mackenzie tugged on her arm, both returning her to her seat and silencing her. "Do you have to be so humiliating?"

As the toasters high-fived, Kat slapped Mackenzie on the shoulder. "What are you complaining about? We came here to find you a date, and now, thanks to me, it's practically mission accomplished. I've set the stage, so all you have to do is walk over there and pick your favorite boy toy. You're welcome."

Mackenzie leaned over and bashed her forehead against the table.

"Why are you acting like such a baby?" Kat gave her another slap. "You're, like, some kind of super ninja warrior who spends her nights catching butterflies and—"

"Good glory," I said. "Stop calling it that."

"Seriously." Mackenzie stopped bashing and looked up. "You make us sound like—" she shuddered "—girls."

Though Kat and Reeve were civilians, not slayers, they knew about the dark, secret world in operation around them. And Kat, well, she now liked to refer to slaying zombies as catching butterflies. She was sweet like that.

"I'm fine with calling it catching butterflies," Trina said.

Kat smirked.

Mackenzie gaped at Trina.

"What?" Trina shrugged. "I'm confident in my masculinity."

I snorted. Trina might look like she could lift a bus, but her heart was as soft as marshmallows.

"You should talk to the boys and get it over with, Mac." Reeve ran her finger over the rim of her shooter and licked away the chocolate. "Kat looks ready to drag you over there."

"True story," Kat said with a nod. "Just seconds away."

"If she does," Reeve continued, "the last five minutes will become your happy place."

"Fine." A scowling Mackenzie pushed to her feet. "But I'm not going to try to charm them."

"As if you could," Kat said, and Mackenzie's scowl darkened.

"You've got this in the bag." I truly believed that. Mac wouldn't have to use charm. Not with a face like hers.

All of my friends had model-perfect faces. And yet, each was so different.

Kat, with her straight dark hair and hazel eyes, was girl-next-door lovely. Reeve, with her brown waves and doe eyes, was traffic-stopping stunning. Mackenzie, with her black curls and emerald eyes, was child-of-an-angel exquisite. And Trina, with her short spikes and black-rimmed eyes, was punk-rocker cool. I was the oddball, with pale hair and eyes so blue they were freaky.

As Mackenzie trudged closer to the boys, a shadow fell over our table.

Kat squealed with delight and threw herself into the arms of the culprit.

No need to glance over to figure out who had just arrived. Frosty, her on-again, off-again boyfriend.

They had a weird relationship, because even when they were off, they were on. Like, all-over-each-other on. I'd never seen two people more bat-crap crazy for each other.

She peppered his face with kisses. "You came!"

"And you look amazing."

"Obviously."

Ha! Such a perfect, confident response. Such a *Kat* response. I'd have to remember it the next time Cole complimented me.

"I couldn't stay away." Frosty combed his fingers through Kat's hair. "I believe your last text said, and I quote, 'If you aren't here within the next ten minutes, I will probably forget all about you and fall in love with someone else.'"

My girl had such a poetic way with words.

Lucas, as attractive as ever in a polo with the sleeves rolled up to display his dark arms to perfection, stepped out from behind Frosty. He nodded at Trina, peering at her for several seconds beyond polite. A lance of awareness arced between them. Well, *well*. I'd suspected they were secretly seeing each other, and this just cinched it. Good. They deserved a steamy dose of happiness.

Kat wrapped her fingers around Frosty's wrist and pulled him closer. "I've always believed open lines of communication are the key to making any relationship work. That, and presents. Do you have one for me?"

"Me, too!" Reeve waved her hands expectantly. "Gimme."

Frosty ignored her. As usual, he cared only about his girl. "Shouldn't my exalted presence be present enough? I ditched Cole and Bronx and broke speed records to come snap the spine of anyone who's made a play for you. And since that's surely everyone breathing, I just need you to tell me where you'd like me to start."

My ears perked at the mention of Cole. "Where'd you leave him?"

Of course, Frosty ignored me, too.

"Tatty's Ink," Lucas said. "Bronx is getting Reeve's name inked into his arm. Which, I just remembered, is supposed to be a surprise."

Reeve cooed happily, thrilled with her boyfriend's unexpected gift.

I'd decided to get two new tattoos myself, so...why not drive over there *now*? Cole could hold my hand through the process, and afterward, he'd realize there had never been a more perfect chance for Nana-free time. Two birds, one delectable stone. Afterward, we could...do things. I shivered with anticipation.

Knowing it would have been criminal to leave a single drop of my mousse shooter behind, I downed it and licked the rim, then licked again just to be safe. I knew I wasn't over-hyping the dessert when I muttered, "This is the best thing in the entire world."

"Agreed," Reeve said.

Finally, I made the brave decision to step between Frosty and Kat.

Yes, other people had been donkey-punched in the throat for doing such a thing, but I was willing to risk it. I needed my best friend's full attention.

"I'm leaving, and I'm taking Mackenzie with me." Love bug was my ride. "You're not going to have as much fun without me, but I hope you're willing to make the sacrifice."

Kat pursed her lips. "What about this most special of occasions? Girls' day out."

Honestly? "It crashed and burned the second Frosty and Lucas showed up."

"Hey," Frosty said behind me. "I only crash and burn the people who say I crash and burn things."

"True story." Kat blinked up at me. "But that aside, let's cut through the crap and focus on what you're really saying. I have to choose between him and you."

If it would save me from having to argue about leaving? "Yes."

"Oh. Well, then. I choose you," she said with a sunny smile. "Of course."

Should have seen that coming. As much as she loved Frosty, she loved me. Maybe more. We were sisters of the heart rather than blood, and (almost) always put each other's needs above everyone else's.

"Get lost, Frosty." She made shooing motions over my shoulder. "You can remind me of my affection for you later."

"But, kitten," he said, his tone beseeching. And it was funny, hearing one of the biggest, baddest Z-killers in Birmingham, Alabama, reduced to begging, all because a tiny fluff of nothing had decided not to play with him. "I have a fever, and the only prescription…is more cow-kat."

Kat narrowed her eyes at him. "Cow-kat?"

"Dude," Lucas muttered. "Do you *want* to lose a testicle?"

"Okay," Frosty said, "I'm man enough to admit that might have come out wrong."

I gripped Kat by the shoulders. "You don't have to worry about hurting my feelings. I'm *foaming-at-the-mouth eager* to see Cole."

"You planning to make out with him?"

"Yes," I admitted, even as my cheeks heated.

"That's so cake. And you'll give me every detail?"

Wait. "Cake?"

"My new favorite word, meaning so totally beyond amazeballs."

Well, okay, then. Soon, it would be the world's favorite. "If you insist, I'll give you a play-by-play." I knew she would.

She thought for a moment, sighed. "Fine. Go. We'll reschedule."

"Really?"

"What can I say? I'm a giver."

"Thank you, thank you, a thousand times thank you." I kissed her cheek and raced to Mackenzie's side.

"—must be a light switch, because every time I look at you, I'm turned on," Chartreuse was saying.

No. Just no. Pickup lines were never okay. "We've gotta go," I told her.

Chartreuse frowned. "But she just got here."

Relief radiated from Mackenzie. "Sorry, boys. It's been… Yeah." She said no more as *she* tugged *me* toward the door.

"Hey!" Reeve called. "No one said 'bye to me."

I waved, saying, "'Bye. We love you!" over my shoulder.

She blew me a kiss.

Trina laughed at something Lucas said, unconcerned by our departure.

Mackenzie and I stepped into the wintry afternoon. The sun was shining but the air was chilled. Shoppers wove in and out of nearby boutiques, each lost in their own little worlds.

"Thank you," Mackenzie said with a shudder. "The only guy I had any interest in never spoke a word to me."

"Let me guess. Mr. Knuckle Scars."

"Yeah. How'd you know?"

"We have similar taste." Proof: we'd both dated Cole. "He would have been my choice, too." And not just for his rugged appeal.

Every slayer in the war against Z's had lost loved ones to bites and battle wounds, and the sorrow and grief tended to build barriers around our hearts. More and more, it became clear that the strong had a better chance of survival; Knuckle Scars had definitely been the strongest of the bunch.

Shockingly enough, Frosty—who had lost more than most— was the exception to my theory. He'd fallen for Kat despite her kidney disease. But I wasn't going to think about her illness and the pain she was—and would be—forced to endure. I'd break down and be forced to compartmentalize, shoving the heartbreak into a deep, dark corner of my mind, to be dealt with later.

My compartments were almost full.

I'd told myself I'd stop doing it, stop locking away the hard emotional crap and finally deal with my feelings, but I'd fallen back into the habit…and honestly, I wasn't in any hurry to change.

"Where are we going?" Mackenzie settled behind the wheel of her truck. "It's too early for patrol."

Oh, yeah. We had to patrol for zombies this evening. We'd be with Gavin the man-whore—another one of my pet projects, despite his warped sense of humor—and the mostly silent Bronx. Time was limited.

"We're going to Tatty's," I said and explained why.

"I'd advise you to play a *little* hard to get, but I swear, it doesn't matter what you do. Cole thinks it's the most adorable thing ever. It makes me want to stab you both in the eye."

A few weeks ago, she would have spat those words at me like weapons. Because the moment Cole had displayed an interest in me—which had been at moment one, thank you very much—she'd hated me.

My sparkling personality had eventually won her over.

Fine. Personality had nothing to do with it. We were soldiers in a war, and we were fighting for the same side. A bond had formed.

"If you stab us both in the eye, we will wear matching patches and pretend to be pirates," I said. "You'll wish you'd stabbed *yourself* instead."

She shuddered. "You still have an evil side, I see."

"Yes, and your tears are the food she craves."

Mackenzie almost cracked a smile.

I scanned the parking lot when we reached our destination, fighting disappointment when I couldn't locate Cole's Jeep.

Maybe he'd walked? You know, for exercise. As if he didn't get enough at his gym, running the treadmill, lifting weights and boxing in the ring. But he wasn't inside, and my disappointment intensified.

I could call or text him, I supposed, but this wasn't just girls' day out. It was boys' day out, too. He could still be with Gavin, Bronx and new-to-the-team Justin. Well, new *again*. Long story.

"Do you have a few hours to spare?" I asked Mackenzie.

"Is my other choice heading back to Choco Loco?"

"Yes."

"Then I do."

I headed to the back of the shop with Artist Guy, the man who'd done my other tattoos. There were two, one on each wrist; the reason he already had my permission slip on file. The first one he'd given me was the white rabbit to represent my sister, Emma. She might be dead, but she still came to visit me. The second, a pair of swords in the shape of a cross to represent my parents.

"Tell me what you want," he said as I settled into the seat.

I'd thought about this for quite some time. Everything we felt always found a way to manifest outwardly. Smiles, frowns. Laugh lines. Scowl lines. This was my way of showing my love for the family and friends I'd lost.

"To start, I want a phoenix on the back of my neck." This would represent Cole. I hadn't lost him—and wouldn't!—but he still deserved a place of honor. With his help, I'd risen from the ashes of my past and forged a new future. "Then I want a pair of boxing gloves above the daggers." They would represent Pops, my grandfather, who'd been killed by zombie toxin. As a teenager, he'd trained in the ring, and throughout the rest of his life, he'd taken hard knocks with grace and bravery.

Artist Guy got to work, and though I'd done this before and had known what to expect, it still hurt. *Bad.* By the time he finished, my neck and arm throbbed incessantly.

"Well? What do you think?" he asked.

I studied the boxing gloves and smiled. They looked like they were made of tattered brown leather, with a bowed string holding them together. "Perfection."

"As if I could do anything less."

Men and their egos.

I approached the full-length mirror hanging on the wall. Hand trembling, I lifted my hair and turned to the side while glancing over my shoulder. My breath hitched. The bird's head was light green and came up to my hairline. The wings were a rainbow of colors, each crackling with golden flames, wrapping around both sides of my neck, stretching toward my ears. The belly was a mix of red and gold and centered on the ridges of my spine, while the tail was shaped and shaded like peacock feathers, stopping between my shoulder blades.

"It's...it's..." I gasped. "I don't even have words."

"I know," he replied. "I'm amazing. It's the best work you've ever seen. Blah, blah."

Cole was going to flip out.

"You remember how to prevent infection?" he asked.

"Yes." I paid him and joined Mackenzie in the lobby. Her reaction to the ink was similar to mine. Total shock and awe.

"As much as I'd love to stay and stare, we'd better go." She gestured to the outside world. "Darkness is rolling in."

I glanced out the window, and sure enough, the sunlight was muted. Well, crap. Night came earlier and earlier. We hardly had time for rest and relaxation anymore.

When had we ever?

But we were trying. All slayers—including our mascots, Reeve and Kat—had recently enrolled in a home-study program, leaving the classroom behind. With our schedules, we'd been missing class or, when we had shown up, falling asleep. Our grades had been slipping. Now we had a little control.

Out of habit, I searched the sky for a rabbit-shaped cloud. Anytime my sister noticed zombies stirring in their nests, preparing to brave the wild and hunt a meal, she created one just for me. Right now, there wasn't one. Good.

Tonight I would go through one neighborhood after another, searching for Z's, protecting homes. If all went well—and that's how it was looking—I'd finish around 3:00 a.m. Boys' day out would be officially over.

"Let's go," I said.

We piled into Mackenzie's truck and headed to the gym, where we would begin. Along the way, I texted Cole.

U'll B home 2nite, yeah?

His response came lightning-fast. Yeah. U got plans 4 me?

Me: If there aren't any Z's 2 fight, guess I'll have 2 settle 4 getting my hands on U.

Cole: Settle away. I'll B w8ing.

Me: BTW, I have surprise 4 U.

Cole: Naked surprise?

Me: Better.

Cole: Nothing better.

Me: Prepare to have UR mind blown!

Me: I MEAN CHANGED. CHANGED.

Cole: Hahaha. I prefer blown. & right back at ya, babe.

I stored my phone away.

"You're practically *glowing* with happiness." Mackenzie pretended to gag. "Tell me you're still capable of killing zombies and that you're not considering spraying them with rainbow dust."

As if I'd waste rainbow dust on zombies. "Don't you worry about me, love bug. You want to know why there's no sign of life on Mars? Because I've been there."

She tried to hide her grin. "If you tell me Death once had a near–Ali Bell experience, I think I'll risk a little pirate roleplaying and just go ahead and stab your eye."

"Why would you want to eye-gouge the girl who's counted to infinity—twice? The girl who can win a game of Connect Four in only three moves? The girl who can start a fire by rubbing two ice cubes together?"

"Definitely going to eye-gouge you," she muttered.

I laughed. "All's I'm saying is that I'm ready for tonight… no matter what happens."

2

BY THE SKIN AND THE TEETH

It was 3:04 a.m., and, as expected, there was no sign of zombies. I was now off duty, but not expected home until 7:00 a.m.

Life couldn't get any more perfect.

Oh, wait. It could. Mackenzie and Bronx lived with Cole and his dad, Mr. Tyler Holland, and they'd decided to spend the rest of the night at the gym. I hadn't said a word about my plans with Cole, but my ear-to-ear smile might have given me away.

Gavin offered to take me home. Ever the gentleman, he opened the passenger side of his car for me.

"I've got people to do and things to see." He motioned me inside. "Hop to, cupcake."

"Thank you."

"Don't get used to it."

He meant that with every fiber of his being. *Shouldn't laugh.* I adored the guy, but I wasn't blind to all of his faults.

One of *my* faults: I found every one of his charming.

He settled behind the wheel and gunned the engine, the ice on the window melting. He eased onto the road and said, "So, when do you get your license?"

"Next week." There'd been a time I'd wanted to vomit blood at even the thought of controlling the metal death trap known as *car,* but battling an evil zombie-twin version of my-self—don't ask—kind of put things in perspective. "Why? Are you tired of chauffeuring me around?"

"Nope. Just want to make sure I move to another state in time. You're a tragic accident waiting to happen." He cursed. "Sorry. Didn't mean to go there."

"Don't worry about it. We both know I make the geriatric crowd look like NASCAR champions." I had a love/hate relationship with speed. I loved slow and hated fast.

"Exactly my point," Gavin said. "There's such a thing as road rage, and I has it."

"You has a whole lot of other things, too," I muttered.

"True, and they're all awesome."

I rolled my eyes. "By the way, you're not taking me home. You're taking me to Cole's." At least, I hoped. I texted him, praying he hadn't fallen asleep.

No Z's, I typed. U ready 4 me?

His reply came within seconds. Ready? Ali-gator, U have no idea. Hope UR in the mood 2 play Hungry Zombie & Helpless Human, because I want a nibble. How soon can U get here?

Me, my heart fluttering with excitement: 10 minutes.

Cole: Make it 5.

Me, my heart fluttering a thousand times faster: Done!

Cole: Bro and Mac w/U?

Me: Nope. They love us enough 2 give us nite 2 ourselves.

Cole: Perfect. I'll turn off alarm & unlock my window.

Gavin winked at me. "So tonight's the night, huh? Finally gonna get that cherry popped."

No way. There was just no way he'd gone there. "You are *such* a pig."

"Pigs are cute."

"And filthy."

"The perfect combination."

It was impossible to insult someone who never took offense. "Look, I'm not going to discuss my sex life—or lack of one—with you, of all people."

Undeterred, he said, "Unless you break your neck on the way in, you're diving into that boy's bed the second you get there, and we both know it."

Good glory. He and Nana were a tag team, and I wasn't sure which one had the better right cross.

"So…you want any tips for taking things from ordinary to extraordinary?" he asked. "I'm something of a sex-pert."

"Actually, you're something of a slut-pert."

"Don't be ridiculous. That's not even a word."

I couldn't judo-chop his airway. He would lose control of the car and crash. "Why don't I just cut off my ears and give them to you?" I muttered to myself. "It would hurt less than this conversation."

"Fine. Be that way. Fumble around in the dark. See if I care."

"You totally shouldn't care!"

"Well, I do. You're my cupcake. I happen to think you deserve to be frosted just—"

"Don't you dare finish that sentence or I swear I'll start a douche-bag jar and make you put a fiver in it."

He grinned at me. "It'd be a douche-purse jar, and you know it."

Never going to live that down. Nana and her "teen-speak" would haunt me for the rest of my life. "Why don't you tell me all about your first time, hmm? Was it special? Did you cover your bed in rose petals?"

"It was the most specialest," he answered, deadpan. "And yes."

I rolled my eyes again. I rarely left his presence without giving him five good ones. "Whatever. This subject is closed, Barbie, so you can shut it now or lose your tongue."

He didn't shut it. Of course. "Barbie? *That's* the nickname you pick for me?"

"Hate it?" I asked with a smirk. A girl could only hear "cupcake" so many times before she had to strike back.

"Absolutely *love* it. I've always suspected you want to take me out and play with me."

See! Impossible!

"Anyway," he continued, "how are you going to seduce Cole Has All the Luck Holland?"

I snorted. "Are you serious? Like a girl really needs to do anything more than breathe."

He shook his head and tsked, as if to say *I pity you.* "Listen up, cupcake. I'm about to drop major pearls of wisdom."

"Even though I know how rare wisdom-dropping is for you, please, don't."

"If I want to get a chick into bed, I say one of two things. 'I screwed up.' Or 'let's talk about it.' Boom. Clothes are flying, limbs are tangled and freaky things are happening. But if you say those things to Cole, he's such a pansy he'll be over and done in his jeans before the good stuff even starts."

"Give me a minute to get over my shock that you're still single."

"I know, right. You'll probably need more than a minute, though. It's a real mind puzzler."

"Look, some couples care about more than sex." I thought about the way Cole sometimes looked at me, as if the sun rose and set just for me. "They care about connecting."

"You're proving my point for me. They care about connecting…physically."

"Mentally. Emotionally."

"Honey buns, only one half of the couple cares about the mental and emotional, and here's a hint—it's not the guy. But I digress. You're just going to jump him, aren't you? No muss, no fuss—you'll just tear off his clothes and show him who's boss." He wiggled his brows. "Why, Ali Bell, I didn't know you had it in you."

Question: If I gutted him like a zombie, would anyone actually convict me of a crime?

Answer: No! Everyone would thank me.

"Just…concentrate on the road," I said.

He obeyed, which made me suspicious of his next move. I studied his profile. He could have been plucked straight out of a magazine. An underwear ad. Hence the nickname I'd given him. He was pretty-boy beautiful, with blond hair and sparkling eyes of green and gold.

"You're staring," he said. "Thinking about doing me now?

Well, I hate to break it to you, cupcake, but that ship has sailed."

Third eye-roll. "Trying to figure you out."

"Although," he continued, as if I hadn't spoken, "I could probably be convinced to show you how a real man pleases a woman after Cole screws everything up. You know, as an act of mercy."

"I'd rather a zombie show me. You will never be a candidate." Keeping him humble was a service I offered free of charge—and I still wasn't sure I was getting my money's worth.

He shrugged. "Your loss."

"You're only being so generous—" I nearly choked on the word "—because you don't like being told no."

"Or because chicks are like candy, and it's my mission to taste-test all the different flavors."

Fourth eye-roll. "Roughly four weeks ago, you claimed you wanted to find true love and become part of a meaningful relationship."

"Roughly four weeks ago, I was an idiot," he replied with a shudder.

I shook my head in exasperation. "You're an STD waiting to happen. You know that, don't you?"

"Super talented director?" He hiked his shoulders. "Not sure I want to get into the movie business, but okay."

"Wrong. So totally douchey. And you're already in deep."

He flipped me off, and when I laughed, he pressed his finger against my nose. "I take it Cole's dad has no idea you'll be staying over and corrupting his son."

"That's right." Just to be contrary, I added, "I'm going to corrupt him *so hard*."

Gavin gave a dramatic sigh. "If I didn't like Cole so much, I'd hate him. That prick always gets the rare, limited-time flavors." He eased the car to a stop beside the curb and killed the lights.

My mind instantly switched tracks, my heart drumming with excitement. In less than a minute, I would be in Cole's arms.

"Thanks for the ride, Gavin."

"Anytime, cupcake. Even if it wasn't the ride I wanted to give you."

"Good glory." I removed one of my gloves and threw it at him.

He caught and kissed it.

An-n-nd there went the fifth eye-roll.

There went another answering grin.

I abandoned the warmth of the car for the frigid chill of the night, my boots crunching in ice as I raced toward the spacious one-story with red brick and white wood trim. In my eagerness, I missed the rock in my path and tripped.

A+, self.

Cole's window was in back, the first on the left. It was unlocked, just as he'd promised. I scrambled inside as quietly as possible and closed the glass behind me.

Before I could turn around or adjust to the deeper darkness of the room, I was grabbed.

A hard hand clamped over my mouth, silencing my gasp. Another hand wrapped around me, pinning my arms to my sides to prevent my elbows from doing any damage.

"I said five minutes, Miss Bell." Cole's low, husky voice caressed me, draining the fight right out of me. "You took eight. Do you know what that means?"

I swallowed a giggle. "I need to buy a watch?"

"You're finally getting that spanking I've been promising you." His hands fell away, and I spun to face him, keeping my eyes to the floor out of habit.

Usually, when our eyes met for the first time during any given day, we had a vision of our future. We'd caught a glimpse of each other earlier this morning, saving us the hassle now.

I was glad.

What we'd seen… I hadn't let myself think about it, too afraid I'd break down. Cole, leaning against a tree, crimson streaking his face and chest, soaking his hands, his expression a mix of unequaled pain and immeasurable grief as I walked away from him.

Walked. Away.

There was no reason good enough for that.

How badly was he injured? When would the vision come true? In a few days? Weeks? Months? There had never been any sort of time limit. The only guarantee was that it *would* happen. We'd never managed to stop one.

Red alert! Red alert! Impending emotional breakdown.

I shoved the worry into the mental box, stretching the sides. It was a fight, but I managed to lock the lid.

Better. For now.

"You can look at me," he said. "I won't bite…very hard."

My gaze moved up, up and linked with his, and suddenly I

was trapped by a yearning that had plagued me since the first moment we'd met. For him...for this...for more.

A slow grin lifted the corners of his wicked mouth.

Dude. While Gavin was pretty, Cole was pure, rugged sex appeal. He should totally come with a warning. *Possible panty melting.* Moonlight spilled over him, illuminating him, and for a few seconds, I thought I heard angels singing. His black hair stood out in adorable spikes, as if he'd plowed his hands through the strands one too many times. Eager to see me, perhaps? His gorgeous violet eyes were framed by lashes so thick and black, he always looked like he'd applied eyeliner.

As for the rest of him...

Good glory! I knew the physique hidden by his clothing. Skin bronzed to perfection. Muscles honed to perfection. A perfect chest covered by the most perfect tattoos. One of his nipples was pierced—meow!—and it was, you guessed it, perfect.

His knuckles feathered over my cheek, the slight touch electrifying me. "I missed you."

Shivering, I said, "How much?"

"Why? Do you think you missed me more?"

"Sure of it."

"I will happily prove you wrong. After I see my surprise."

"Get ready for pure awesomeness." I lifted my hair and pivoted, revealing my neck.

Silence descended.

I frowned, suddenly nervous. What if he didn't like it? Ink was permanent.

"Ali." His voice, so husky and deep, was temptation and

silk, stroking over me. "Did I ever tell you all the reasons I love you?"

"No." I licked my lips and shook my head, gathering the courage to face him. His eyes were heavy-lidded, smoldering. He liked the tattoo.

"Tell me now," I commanded softly.

"I'll tell you the top ten. One," he said and kissed my forehead. "You are brutally honest. It's such a rare and precious trait."

Major points for my man: he'd led with personality rather than appearance.

"Two." He kissed my eye. "You have the perfect sense of humor...perfect for me. It's a little warped, and a lot twisted, and you can make me laugh when no one else can."

I almost melted. Almost. I had to hear the rest. "Go on or I'll hurt you." Had I sounded as breathless to him as I had to myself?

He chuckled. "Three." He kissed my other eye, gentle, so gentle. "You're smart. I want to see your brain naked."

Ha!

"Four. You are freaking hot."

"Obviously." And okay, yeah, he got points for that, too. Maybe because I so very rarely *felt* hot. Or maybe because I so desperately wanted another kiss. A harder one. On my lips. With tongue and teeth. And roaming hands. Or maybe because I wanted him to want *all* of me.

"Five." He kissed my cheek, and I moaned. *More.* "You are unbelievably kind." He kissed my other cheek. "Six. You love with your whole heart, nothing held back."

"Come on. Kiss me for real." Did he want me to beg? Because I would…after I made him beg a little, too.

"Seven." He pressed his lips against one side of my jaw, skipping my lips, dang him. "You are such a good fighter, I could stand back and watch you do all the hard work, and I wouldn't feel like a wuss. I'd feel like a genius."

"I'll believe that when I see it."

"Eight." He kissed his way to the other side of my jaw. "The way you sometimes look at me… It's as if I'm the sweetest dessert in the bakery and you are desperate for a bite."

Yes, yes. A big, delicious bite. "At one time," I said, the huskiness of my tone surprising me. I wrapped my arms around his neck. "That look of mine scared you." With good reason. I'd been loaded with zombie toxin and had literally wanted to eat him. Well, not me but my zombie twin. Z.A.

"Nine," he went on and nibbled on my ear. "You're like the world's most perfect drug. One hundred percent pure, guaranteed to addict after the first taste. I can't imagine my life without you in it—don't want to."

My skin tingled, and my blood flashed white-hot. "Cole," I said on another moan. I tangled my hands in his hair, angled his head, trying to take over. "Please. Stop talking, and start acting."

"Ten," he said and finally—blessedly—pressed his lips against mine. Only it was soft, far too soft. "You would die for me, the same way I would die for you."

"Yes, yes, I would." I waited for hard.

He didn't give it to me. His face hovered directly over mine as he…deliberated his next move?

Happy to help with that. "Take off your shirt," I commanded, already pulling at the material. "Now."

He gave me a quick smile. "Impatient?"

"Feral. And don't you dare complain. You're to blame."

"Complain? I'd rather celebrate." He plucked his shirt from my hands. "Take off your coat."

I was only surprised it hadn't already burned off me. I was *that* hot for him.

As he jerked the cotton over his head, I yanked at my coat and sweater, leaving on the tank, jeans and boots...for now. My gaze, controlled by a force greater than myself, traveled all over him—*gold star for this one, God*—before settling on his chest. He'd tattooed my name in bold, black letters that stretched from one nipple to the other.

Breathing him in...*mmm, soap and strawberries*...I traced the design with shaky fingers.

He gave a little moan. "Before we start, Ali-gator, I've got to warn you."

"*Before* we start?"

He fisted a handful of my hair, careful of my sore nape, and tugged me against him. Male strength against feminine softness. His gaze was fierce, unwavering. "I'm not going all the way with you."

The heat in my blood instantly cooled. "But why?" Right after my brush with death, he'd been ready. More than ready.

And I had been, too. Still was. I'd accepted that sex was something I could never take back, that it would change the course of our relationship...and me. While I wasn't a big fan of change, this was Cole. My Cole. I'd deal.

"After your grandmother interrupted us that night," he

said, "I got to thinking." A hard mask fell over his features, making me suspect he'd done more than think. He'd probably listened to a lecture from his dad. "I'm eighteen. You're sixteen."

"Almost seventeen."

"I'm a legal adult. You're not."

"Cole—"

"Let me finish." His tone was now as hard as his features, intractable. "I think we should wait."

I peered up at him. At five-ten, I was tall. At six-four, he was taller. He was wider than me, heavier, and anytime I was near him I felt utterly consumed by him. Usually I adored it. Today, not so much. "Two years is—"

"One year, three months."

"—a long time," I finished.

"Not when we've got a lifetime together."

I opened my mouth to protest. Finally his lips crashed into mine.

Instant inferno. I kissed him with everything I had. We'd discuss the year-and-three-months wait at another time— maybe after I'd taken the edge off. Right now, I was simply going to enjoy him…and whatever he'd give me.

As my nails scraped against his back, and his hands anchored on my bottom, yanking me even closer, a thousand little fires ignited in my belly, spreading through the rest of me. What I'd thought was an inferno before? Not even close.

The flames must have spread through him, too, because he hoisted me up, rubbing himself against me. I wound my legs around his waist, practically melding our bodies together. He walked to the bed and laid me down, half of me hanging over the edge. All the while, the kiss continued. Hotter. Faster.

"We can do other things," he rasped. "Like before."

"Yes. Like before." The things he'd made me feel…

He planted his hands at my temples and raised his head. Panting, he said, "But maybe we'll go a little further this time."

I licked my kiss-swollen lips and uttered a trembling "Why are you still talking?"

His grin was slow and wicked as he played with the clasp of my bra through my tank.

Beyond the bedroom door, glass tinkled.

Cole paused, frowned. "What—"

Multiple footsteps thumped against a wood floor.

Pop.

Pop.

Shocked, we bolted upright together. I knew that sound. Gunshot muffled by a silencer. But…but…

"Someone's here," Cole said, rushing to the nightstand to palm one of the weapons perched on top.

Who would attack the Hollands? And why? *Doesn't make any sense…no sense…*

Cole gave me a sharp look.

Right. Arm up. I shook my head to disperse the fog of stupidity and pulled two daggers from my boots. I never went anywhere without them. But daggers were for up-close-and-personal grab-and-stabs with zombies. Shots had been fired. I wouldn't be dealing with zombies.

I dropped the daggers and grabbed the pistol I had stashed in my coat.

"Cole! Run!" his father shouted—just as the bedroom window shattered.

Cole didn't have a chance to run.

More glass shattered. Something launched him across the room like a rocket-propelled grenade. He smashed into the wall, slid to the floor, leaving a thick, bright red smear of blood behind him.

NO SPILLED GUTS,
NO GLORY

What the heck was going on?

Gasping, I dropped to my knees. "Cole?" I whispered, frantically crawling toward him. The pistol clinked against the floorboards, reminding me of a ticking clock.

I hated ticking clocks. An entire life could be altered in a single second.

I released the weapon and pressed two fingers into his neck, feeling for a pulse. *Don't be dead, don't be dead, please, please, don't be dead.* And yeah, okay, I knew death wasn't the end for us. Look at my sister. But I wasn't ready to lose any part of Cole.

Thump…thump. Thump…

Thank God! Slow, but strong. He was alive.

His eyes fluttered open. "Ali?"

"It's okay," I said. "You're okay. You're going to be okay."

"What happened?"

I surveyed the damage. There was a hole in the shoulder. Blood soaked him.

"Someone just shot you, I think. Right in front of me. That someone could still be out there. We could still be targets." The two halves of my brain were at war—hope versus dread—screwing with my focus. "What should I do?"

"Bind." He spoke softly, the word little more than air. "Shoulder."

Of course. Yes. I knew that. But...binding his shoulder wouldn't do much good. Blood was gushing out of him. He needed fire; it would cauterize.

Slayers could produce fire; it was necessary to kill zombies. *I* could produce fire. When summoned, the flames crackled at the ends of our fingers. We pressed them into zombies, and the heat spread, purified, burning away evil and darkness. Eventually, zombies exploded. For some reason, I could flame from head to toe and only a moment of contact was needed to end a zombie.

When used on humans, the fire healed...sometimes. Sometimes it caused final death, just like with zombies.

It had healed me, and it would heal Cole. We were both slayers, and that was the key distinguishing factor between healing and exploding.

Right?

I had to try. He wouldn't make it otherwise. He was hemorrhaging strength, his head lolling to the side. His lips were starting to turn blue, his skin chalk-white.

Frantic, I closed my eyes. Humans were made of three parts. The spirit, the source of life, was bound to the soul, which consisted of the mind, will and emotions. Both were housed inside the body, the outer shell. With a deep breath in...out...I forced my spirit and body to separate; it was like removing a hand from a glove. Because zombies were spirits, they could only fight other spirits. I'd learned to divide like this at a moment's notice.

Cold air enveloped me. Without the insulation of skin and muscle, my spirit felt the temperature drop what seemed like a thousand degrees.

"What are…you doing?" As a slayer, Cole could see into the spirit realm. Could see *me*.

Couldn't pause to explain. When it came to stuff like this, I was so new I had trouble multitasking.

Light, I thought, and the ends of my fingers heated. I peeked… flames crackled all the way to my wrist. *Good, good.* I reached *inside* Cole's shoulder.

His breath hitched. That was it, his only reaction. Even still, I knew his pain was off the charts. *Been here, done this.* He'd basically just received third-degree burns on his soul. But he hadn't turned to ash, so I would consider this a win.

I dismissed the flames and returned my spirit to its proper place with a simple touch, then studied Cole. His color was back to normal. That quickly. I grabbed the shirt he'd discarded and wrapped the material around the still-bleeding, but now-charring wound.

What next? I didn't know if there were bad guys with guns trained on the open window that was allowing flurries to bluster inside the room. I didn't know how many bad guys were in the house, shooting at Mr. Holland—or if Mr. Holland was still alive.

My insides twisted into a maze of painful knots.

No matter what, we couldn't—wouldn't—leave without him.

"Can you walk?" I asked.

Cole's jaw clenched with determination. "I don't...care if I...can. I will."

Despite the pauses in his speech, his timbre was stronger. Not just because of the emergency cauterization, I was sure, but because his bones were reinforced with iron-hard resolve, and his muscles pumped full of courage.

"I'll find your dad and meet you—"

"No." His tone was inflexible, meant to stop any argument. "We stay together."

"Time is of the essence."

"Don't care. My dad. My decision."

Very well. "We need more weapons." I crawled to the gun he'd dropped and slid it to him. Then I continued on to the nightstand and claimed the minicrossbow he had stashed there.

Cole struggled to his knees. "I'll go through...door first. You stay...on my heels. Got it?" He yanked a backpack from his closet, grimaced.

No, I didn't get it, and I wouldn't do as he'd demanded. The strong led the weak, not the other way around.

"I'll go first."

"Just—" He frowned, then held up a finger for silence.

I paused to listen for suspicious noises. Wind whistled eerily and...ice crunched. Every instinct I possessed shouted *red alert, red alert!*

Someone was coming in hot.

I turned and aimed just as a masked man swung his legs through the window. As he straightened, I squeezed the trigger. An arrow lodged in his throat, shutting off his airway and cutting off a bellow of pain before it could even form.

A kill shot.

I'd done what was necessary. I couldn't regret that.

Keeping my weapon trained on the intruder, I closed the distance. His head was turned to the side, his eyes open, but glazed. No pulse. He had an earpiece anchored to his lobe. I lifted the bud and listened, heard a tangle of voices.

"Hit. I'm hit—"

"—like me to proceed?"

"He's dead—"

There were more of them.

The door wrenched open, and I spun. I registered Mr. Holland's identity at the same time I gave the trigger a second squeeze, barely managing to twist my wrist and send the arrow into the post at his side.

"Get down," Cole commanded with a mixture of concern and relief.

Mr. Holland remained on his feet. One of his eyes was swollen shut; he scanned the room with the other, inhaling sharply when he spotted Cole, exhaling slowly when he spotted me. Crimson streaked his face. "There were four. Three inside, one outside. But it looks like you got him." He stalked to Cole's side and peeled back the soaked cotton to check his wound.

Cole winced.

"Clean shot, all the way through. Edges burned. Bleeding slowing." Mr. Holland threw the shirt aside, removed the one he wore and rebound his son. "We don't have much time. One got away. He'll come back with others."

"I've already heard others," I said. "On the dead guy's earpiece."

"Those men aren't here. They're at Ankh's."

Mr. Ankh, Reeve's father. He wasn't a slayer, but he funded our cause and allowed Nana and me to live at his house.

"Nana," I rasped. "Kat." She'd planned to stay the night with Reeve. Were they hurt?

Not knowing...

I should have been there, should have protected them.

"I'm sorry," Mr. Holland said, "but I don't know the outcome. This was a planned attack, meant to take us all down at once."

All? "You mean—" *No. No, no, no.* I didn't like where my thoughts were headed.

"Ankh called me. Someone shut down his security system. I was getting dressed, intending to go over there and help, when another call came in. Frosty. Soon after, Bronx rang. But I didn't have a chance to answer either boy. Two men busted through our back door. So, yes. I suspect every slayer on our team was targeted tonight."

Frosty. Bronx. Trina. Lucas. Cruz. Collins. Gavin. Veronica. Mackenzie. Justin. Jaclyn. If anything had happened to any of them... Different emotions hit me with the force of a baseball bat. Pain, regret, worry and a sharp lance of rage.

A to-do list took shape in my mind. *Compartmentalize. Get Cole to a doctor. Find everyone else. Destroy the people responsible.*

I didn't have to wonder about the culprit. Anima Industries. No question.

"The Ankhs have multiple secret passages meant for quick getaways," Cole said, his expression fierce. "Ankh got everyone out, Ali-gator. I guarantee it."

Like me, he abhorred lies. I believed him.

I confiscated the backpack, and he winced. "Sorry," I muttered as I anchored the strap over my shoulder. Whatever he'd stuffed inside weighed a million pounds. At least. "Let's get out of here."

We made it to the garage without incident, and I uttered a quiet prayer of thanks. Cole climbed into the passenger seat of his Jeep, and I set the backpack at his feet.

Mr. Holland tossed me a set of keys. "You're driving."

"Yes." A license wasn't important right now.

"Take him to Holy Trinity Church. Pastor's office. Bookshelf." Mr. Holland looked to Cole. "Like the shelter we built for your mom."

Cole stiffened. Any mention of his mother always had that effect. She'd been a slayer, and she might have had a shelter, but she'd still died during a zombie attack.

Mr. Holland met my gaze. "That's where Ankh and your grandmother will be if—"

They survived, I finished for him and would have flown straight into a panic if not for a whispering replay of Cole's assurance. *Ankh got everyone out, Ali-gator.*

"Just make sure my boy gets there," Mr. Holland said.

Nothing would stop me. "What about you?"

"I won't be far behind."

What did he have to do? Bury the bodies?

Oh, glory. Probably.

Trembling, I took my place behind the wheel. My palms sweat. My blood ran hot, but my skin iced over. Acid poured through me, stinging. As the garage door lifted, Cole reached over and squeezed my hand, offering what comfort he could. His skin was colder than mine and clammy.

"I won't let anything happen to you," I vowed, put the

pedal to the metal and jetted onto the road. I braced myself, expecting a hail of bullets to pepper the vehicle. As seconds ticked into minutes, I began to relax.

If only the reprieve could have lasted. I turned a corner and spotted Gavin's car wrapped around a pole. Steam curled from the crumpled hood. The driver-side door was open, but no one was behind the wheel.

"No," I gasped out.

"He's tough," Cole said. "He's smart, and he's been through hell and back and survived."

Tears welled as I parked in front of the wreckage. If Gavin survived, he was definitely injured. He would be nearby, hiding in the surrounding trees, waiting...unless he'd been carted somewhere else.

Searching for him could waste precious time. Time Cole didn't have.

I had a choice to make.

Knowing how my mind worked, Cole said, "I'm wounded. Not dead. Stop worrying about me...and do what you have to do...for Gavin." The more he spoke, the more labored his breathing became.

"I don't want to leave you," I admitted. "You need medical attention ASAP and—"

"Reason eleven," he said, and it took me a moment to catch up. All the reasons he loved me. "You're willing to risk... everything for your...friends. Besides, you won't...be alone. Where you go...I go."

What! "No. You're staying in the car."

"Ali."

"Cole. You're already panting. You're still bleeding. Movement has increased the flow of blood. And you're wearing shorts."

His gaze raked over me. "Ali-gator. You're wearing a tank."

Again with the iron-hard resolve. "You'll slow me down. And no, no more arguing. We're sitting ducks here."

He scowled. "Fine. Be careful...or I'll be mad."

I kissed him, hard and fast. Cold air cut at my exposed skin as I emerged. My feet had somehow morphed into heavy boulders, but I managed to maintain a swift pace, tracking a blood trail from the car to a tree that had scratches in the bark. From there I discovered a set of footprints that were the right size, with a depth consistent with Gavin's muscled weight.

The prints stopped abruptly.

"Gavin," I called, willing to chance Anima's notice. Anything to help my friend. "It's Ali."

No response. Not even the call of insects.

The silence...*killing me.*

"Gavin. Please."

Again, silence.

A well of tears. There wasn't anything more I could do. I raced to the car. Cole was paler, and what little strength he'd gained had clearly abandoned him.

"Any...sign?" he asked.

"He was definitely here, but whether he's unconscious or elsewhere, I don't know. I'll get you to Mr. Ankh and come back." Before he could comment about the danger I'd be facing, I said, "How are you holding up?"

"Baby, we just got back together." His teeth chattered. "There's no way I'm dying right now."

I wanted to turn on the heat, but didn't. The low temperature was his best friend right now, helping to slow the bleeding. *Thank you, old episodes of* Scrubs.

"Do you promise?" I asked.

"Promise."

I eased past the church. A beautiful three-story brownstone, shaped like an M. In the center, steep concrete steps led to the main door. Both sides were raised at the roof, coming to a point in the form of an intricate iron cross. I counted ten stained-glass windows, and all were intact. The parking lot was empty, illuminated by a single street lamp.

I searched the surrounding area for any sign that Mr. Ankh—or Anima—was nearby. As late as it was, the shops and cafés were closed. No one seemed to be huddling in the shadows. Only two cars were in the lot across the street, and both were empty. Neither belonged to anyone I knew.

I parked in a neighborhood two blocks away. Anima clearly knew where we lived. They also had to know what we drove. If they sent someone after us, I didn't want the vehicle near the church.

"We'll stick to the shadows and hoof it," I said.

Cole grimaced as he swiped up the backpack. "You were... right. I'm slower. If trouble comes...don't hang around...to help me. Get yourself...inside that building."

No way. "We stay together, remember?"

"Only when...convenient for you."

"Exactly." I got out before he could respond, the cold sucking the air right out of my lungs.

When he stood beside me, mist dancing in front of his face, I tried to take the pack, but he scowled at me. "Reason twelve. Stubborn. But as long as…I'm breathing…I will protect you…carry what burden I can."

That. That was one of the many reasons *I'd* fallen in love with *him*. "Cole—"

"Me man. You woman." Everything about him was as hard as granite. He motioned forward with a tilt of his chin. "Walk."

"Getting shot makes us cranky, I see." On the lookout, I launched into action. The night had secrets hidden in its shadows, and if I wasn't careful I could be bitten by one.

Cole stumbled several times but managed to keep up.

Coming to a small brick fence built for decoration rather than security, I crouched. No one loomed ahead; we scaled the obstruction with only minor difficulty and worked our way to the back of the church. While I used the skill I'd picked up from Frosty and jimmied the lock on the door, Cole leaned against the wall. His breathing was even more labored now. Should I use the fire again?

No time. Hinges squeaked as I shouldered my way inside the building. All the lights were out, pitch black greeting us with open arms. I used the flashlight app on my phone— there was an app for everything—chasing away the shadows. We were in a kitchen. It was small, but clean. We were alone. Ahead, a hallway branched in three different directions.

"This way." Cole took the lead, his steps shuffling, his gait slower by the minute.

I made sure the light illuminated the way as we bypassed each of the doorways and entered the sanctuary. I muttered a prayer for strength and peace. Was Nana here? Were my friends? Or—

Borrowing trouble.

Right. We sailed through the sound room, a storage over-flowing with choir robes, and finally entered the pastor's office. Cole, who was wobbling on his feet, flipped on the overhead lamp, and I stuffed my phone in my pocket. I blinked in an effort to adjust to the added brightness and saw a book-case, desk, computer, file cabinet and a few chairs.

"I'm missing something," I said. "Where's the shelter?"

"Here." He squatted and scooped out the things inside the bottom cubby of the bookcase. Reaching back, he lifted a hidden hatch, revealing a tunnel just big enough for an adult male to crawl through.

"Down," he said. "Hurry." His lids closed…then snapped back open.

How close was he to passing out?

I practically flew through the hole—found a ladder. Dark-ness enveloped me as I descended. Like a real-life Alice in Wonderland, I thought with a nervous laugh. My palms began to sweat all over again, and I had to squash images of Cole losing his grip and tumbling to his death.

Trickles of light filtered in. At the bottom, I hopped to the cement floor. With my help, Cole was able to do the same with minimal pain.

"Anima will pay for this," I vowed.

"Yes, and they'll…pay…in blood."

A lot of blood.

We were in a small, dim box of a room, but voices rose beyond the far right wall. Voices I recognized.

I bounded forward. "Nana!"

"Ali?" she responded.

Light brightened around the corner, and I quickened my pace, soon entering a spacious room loaded with gurneys, medical equipment and weapons. Nana, dressed in her favorite nightgown, headed straight for me. I gathered her in my arms and hugged her tight, doing my best not to snot-cry all over her.

"Thank God! You're alive." She was the only family I had left, and I would rather die than lose her. "You're really alive."

"I'm telling you, I had to be surrounded by angels tonight. There's no other explanation for my survival."

"I'm so sorry I wasn't with you."

"I was glad you weren't. I would have hated knowing you witnessed the violence we did. You've seen too much already." A shudder rocked her small frame, and I couldn't bring myself to admit I had witnessed more than my fair share tonight, too. "I took comfort knowing you were out there and safe."

Behind me, I caught the soft sound of shambling footsteps and pulled from Nana's embrace. "I'll be right back." Cole had just passed the threshold, and I raced to his side.

His features were pinched, his skin pallid. He managed a small smile when I reached him. At this point, I think he was running on pure adrenaline. "Told you...she'd be...all right."

"Gloat all you want." *Just live!* I shoved the backpack from his shoulder, the heavy weight thumping against the floor. "Let's get you to a gurney."

"Ali, you have to know...not afraid...to die."

Jolt! And not the good kind. "I know that." A person afraid of dying could never really live, and Cole Holland definitely *lived*. "Why are you telling me this now? You made a promise to me and I expect you to keep it."

He leaned against me in an effort to remain on his feet.

I wound my arm snug around his waist. "Mr. Ankh," I called. "Help."

The male stalked around a curtain. He was shirtless and stacked with as much muscle as the slayers; it looked like he'd been in the process of sewing his own wound back together, because a needle and thread hung from a thick, seeping gash on his clavicle. His usually dark skin was almost as pallid as Cole's and was now marked with cuts and bruises.

He spotted us, quickened his pace. Together, we hefted Cole onto a gurney. Which was a big-time struggle. He passed out halfway up, becoming a dead weight. Mr. Ankh shouldered me out of the way to clean him up and patch the wound on his shoulder.

Mr. Ankh is a surgeon, I reminded myself. *He knows what to do.*

"He's going to be okay, right?" I asked.

A tic below Mr. Ankh's eye. He remained silent.

I pressed my lips together.

Compartmentalize.

Yes, but how much more could the compartments take?

Nana came up beside me, squeezed my hand.

"How did you get here?" I asked.

"One of the tunnels in Mr. Ankh's house leads straight here."

"Where are the others?" I scanned the room and answered my own question. Kat reclined on one of the gurneys, her dark hair tangled around her pale face, her expression...odd. Blank.

I frowned. Something—more than the obvious—was wrong with her.

Reeve sprawled on the gurney beside her, her hair just as tangled. Her eyes were closed, and she was so still she could only be…

No! "Tell me she's okay."

"She is. She had to be sedated." Nana released a shuddering breath. "So did Kat."

Okay. Okay. I could guess the reason. Reeve had probably tried to leave to find Bronx, and Kat had probably screamed bloody murder, desperate to get to Frosty.

"I have something to tell you, dear," Nana said, sorrow practically dripping from her.

I stiffened. "No." I could guess what was coming.

"You need to know. Two of the…" She sniffled. "Two slayers were…are…"

"No," I repeated.

"Lucas and Trina. Beautiful Trina. They…"

I shook my head violently. *Don't want to hear this.*

"Lucas called. Trina was with him. They were being chased. Ankh told them where to go. Then he and I… We left the girls here, sleeping in a safe room, and went to get the others."

I focused on that—that Mr. Ankh had taken my grandmother from safety and placed her in danger—and not the words to come. Not… *Don't say it. Please, don't say it.*

"He suspected he would need my help. That he'd have to tend to their wounds while I drove. I wish he'd been right. It would have been—" She cleared her throat. "We arrived first. The two came running around the corner."

She was. She was going to say it. "Nana, stop. Just don't." If she didn't say it, and I didn't hear it, it wouldn't be real.

More sniffles, before she added, "Ankh tried. He tried so hard to kill their pursuers. And he did. But not before both kids were gunned down. They never made it to the car. I'm so sorry, dear. So very sorry."

Not prepared.

Lucas and Trina. Dead.

Dead!

Two friends. Gone. Because Anima had decided to stop watching us, stop threatening us, and act. Because we'd become so caught up in our own little world, we hadn't realized someone was about to unleash a maelstrom of pain.

I hadn't gotten to say goodbye.

Just like that, the compartments burst at the seams and every emotion I'd managed to stave off came rising to the surface. Regret, worry and guilt, now mixed with grief, anguish and fury, created a tidal wave and flooded me.

Drowning…

I fell to my knees and sobbed.

BRAINS ARE OVERRATED (AND SALTY)

I had the strangest dream. A little girl, probably three, maybe four, was strapped to a chair, a plain but elegant woman sitting at her side, holding her hand. The woman had such a slender bone structure she looked like some kind of fairy princess from a storybook. She had wavy, shoulder-length hair the color of wheat and eyes so pale they were freaky.

I'd seen those eyes before. Many times before.

Like, every time I'd looked in a mirror.

They were rare. And yet, the little girl had those eyes, too.

Were they mother and daughter? Relatives I'd never met?

It was possible, I supposed. But why was I dreaming about them?

And why was I assuming this was real, just because it felt that way? Dreams were just that. Dreams. They weren't fact.

"Don't worry," the woman said with a quaver. "Once they finish, I'll take you home and make your favorite cookies."

"I want to go home now. I don't care about cookies."

"I know you want to go, sweetie, I know. But you can't. Not yet. This is necessary."

"Why?" Tears fell in earnest. "They hurt me, Momma."

The mother began to cry, as well. "You're such a special little girl. You can do things no one else can. Through you, they can help other people. *Save* other people."

They? Who were *they*?

"—not leaving her." Nana's voice registered, as did her concern.

The dream vanished in a puff of smoke.

I tried to open my eyes, didn't have the strength. Lethargy made my skull feel as if it had been hollowed out and stuffed with boulders.

"You are."

Mr. Holland's voice now. He said something else, but a high-pitched ring invaded my ears, distorting the rest of the conversation. "—bry mand take see."

"Moo bought I cast soon loo."

I bit the side of my tongue, tasted the copper tang of blood. The ensuing pain must have set off a chemical reaction, releasing all kinds of goodies, because I received the boost I needed. The ringing faded, and tendrils of strength wound through me.

"—at war right now, and that makes you a target. Ali won't be the fighter I know she can be, *needs* to be, if she's worried about you." Mr. Holland possessed the same iron-hard determination as his son, making the words sound as though they'd been chiseled from ice. "You're going and that's final."

I cracked open my eyelids, then blinked rapidly to clear the blur. Meanwhile, memories banged at the door of my mind, demanding entrance. Before I could decide whether to accept or decline, the door splintered and I was bombarded. Cole, shot. Gavin, missing. Kat and Reeve, sedated. Trina and Lucas—

No.

No!

But there was no erasing the knowledge. They were dead. Shot and killed. Gone forever.

My mind shied away from the devastation. I couldn't allow myself to grieve. Not now. Later, though…

Yes, later.

Right now, it was time to start compartmentalizing again. Nine of my friends were out there, targets to the madmen running Anima, and they had to be found.

Moaning, I sat up. Dizziness struck, as if it had been waiting for me.

Another memory took root. I'd broken down and cried. Mr. Ankh had approached my side and, while cooing comforting words at me, withdrew a syringe from his pocket and injected me with something. A sedative, I thought now, my jaw clenching with irritation.

"Easy, dear." The sweet scent of Nana's perfume teased me as a gentle arm wrapped around my shoulders to keep me upright.

My hands quaked as I rubbed my gritty eyes. The dizziness faded, the room and the people in it coming into perfect view. Nana, with her black bob brushed and gleaming, her nightgown replaced by an oversize T-shirt and a pair of sweatpants. Mr. Holland, standing beside her, his face cleaned and bandaged.

Beyond them, Kat and Reeve paced inside a small room surrounded by glass. Probably two-way mirrors. I met Kat's gaze, but she looked away, as if she had no idea I was there.

"Are they confined?" I asked, and a second later Reeve beat at one of the walls.

"Yes. Frosty and Bronx have yet to be found, and the girls are determined to hunt them," Mr. Holland said. "They tried to sneak out."

Of course they did. "Release them," I commanded. "Now. Kat's not even a target. We can send her home." Where she'd stay safe.

He gave a single shake of his head. "She is Frosty's biggest weakness and one of yours. Of course she's a target. And we both know she won't go home. She'll go after her boyfriend, no matter what we tell her. Reeve, too. And while both girls have had some training in self-defense, they aren't ready for an all-out war, which is exactly what they'll get. They stay."

Stay, yes, I conceded. Locked away? No. But we'd come back to that. "Where's Cole?"

Nana squeezed me tight. "Don't you worry about him. He's doing well. Better than any of us expected. Ankh hauled him to the house to feed him."

Relief was, oh, so sweet. "So it's safe to go back?"

"Safer by the minute," Mr. Holland said with a nod. "When Ankh isn't playing doctor, he's working on the security. As soon as he's satisfied there are no other hidden vulnerabilities, we'll be able to go in and out the front door. Until then, we are to sneak through the tunnel."

"What about the other slayers?"

The vim and vigor seeped out of him, and his shoulders slumped. He looked away from me, no longer able to hold my gaze. "We don't know where they are."

But he knew *something*. He just didn't want to tell me what it was. Hands beginning to sweat, I said, "Text them. Tell them to come here and—"

"I want to," he interjected with a shake of his head, "but I won't. Anima could have their phones."

He was right. Dang it!

He scrubbed his fingers through his hair. "Every news station has been running a story about last night's eruption of 'gang violence.' They claim Cole is the leader of one gang, and his rival, a street thug named River Marks, decided to get rid of him and his crew."

"Wait. How did they know Cole was any kind of leader?" And did the police know I'd shot and killed someone in his home?

I sucked in a fiery breath. Oh, glory, I'd shot and killed someone.

Compartmentalize.

"No." Mr. Holland's features softened as he computed the direction my thoughts had taken. "I snuck back to the house this morning. Someone had come by and cleared away the, uh, collateral damage. The cops saw that the house was broken into, and Cole's blood was on the wall, but nothing more."

Anima had gone back, then.

"For now," he added, "we lay low. We let Anima wonder who survived."

And who didn't, I finished for him, taking a few seconds to breathe. The problem with such a plan was that we had to wonder, too.

"Again," I said, "I'm unsure how the police connected the dots to Cole. They should have just assumed he was a victim."

Mr. Holland worked his jaw. "Apparently, a mysterious source called in the information."

Mysterious. In other words, Anima.

Nana rested her head on my shoulder. "Tell her the rest, Tyler. Better it come from you than someone else."

My heart dropped. "What is it?"

He closed his eyes, but not before I caught a flash of grief. "Cruz is… He's dead, too. He was found in his bed, a bullet in his brain."

No. No, no, no. Another friend lost. A beautiful life ended far too soon.

Compartmentalize!

"I'm going after the others," I announced. They were out there. They were alive.

They had to be alive.

I was going to find them and bring them back.

Mr. Holland didn't hesitate. He nodded, surprising me.

"I'm taking Kat and Reeve with me," I added. They weren't ready for war, no, but I couldn't drive *and* search *and* defend myself *and* patch injured slayers.

Even superheroes needed sidekicks.

"God save me," he muttered, scrubbing a hand over his face. "After what happened with Ethan, Ankh will never allow you to put Reeve in Anima's path."

Ethan. My hands curled into fists. Reeve had dated Ethan before she'd started dating Bronx. He'd secretly worked for Anima, gleaning her secrets, *our* secrets, and ultimately leading to her kidnapping and my torture.

"I hate to break it to you," I announced, "but what you said about Kat is true of Reeve, as well. She's already in their path. Whether she's with me or not, she's in danger."

He flashed a quick smile. "Save the arguments for Ankh."

Mr. Ankh, the world's most stubborn male. And that was saying something, considering Cole was in the running. "I will." Now, to circle back to the start of our conversation.

"Free the girls. I'll take them to the house, and the three of us will do whatever's necessary to get through to boss-man."

"Free them yourself." He pulled a chain from around his neck, a key dangling at the end, and tossed it at me. "I just came from the house, and I'm not going back." His gaze swung to Nana. "I'm taking your grandmother out of state. For her protection," he added with more volume.

Ah. Their earlier fight suddenly made sense.

Nana morphed from calm to practically spewing fire in the snap of fingers. "I told you before, but I'll tell you again, because you are obviously hard of hearing. I'm not going any-where. Did you understand that time? *Anywhere.*"

We'd see about that, too.

I cupped her cheeks, and stared into dark eyes so like my mother's and little sister's—eyes that both broke me and made me stronger. "You must," I said gently. "For me."

Astonishment wafted from her. She shook her head, utter-ing one succinct word. "No."

"These people are ruthless, Nana. They kidnapped me, tortured me, and when they finished with me, they would have killed me in the most painful way possible. Yesterday, they *did* kill three of my friends." Hot tears suddenly streaked down my cheeks. "They must be destroyed."

"But—"

I cut her off with a firm "I know these people. They won't hesitate to hurt you to get to me. So please. Please! Go with Mr. Holland. Stay safe so that I can stay focused."

A beat of silence…another…each crackling with tension.

"I will go with him," she said, surprising me. Then she added, "But only if you'll come with us." I heard the despair in her tone. "My husband is dead. My daughter is dead. My only other grandchild is dead. I can't lose you, too."

Destroying me. "Nana. If I don't do this, you'll lose me anyway. I won't be...me." I'd been born for this. I wasn't afraid. I was ready.

"At least let me *try* to protect you."

From the corner of my eye, I saw Mr. Holland pull a syringe from his pocket. Going to drug her like Mr. Ankh had drugged me? Oh, man. When she woke up, she would be *tee-icked.*

Worth it. I clasped her hands in mine. "I'm needed here," I said, and she once again shook her head. "Only slayers can fight Anima *and* zombies. And you know we'll be facing both."

He gently struck.

Her eyes widened, and she gasped.

"Please understand," I whispered, "and know that I'm truly sorry."

"Ali...together..." Her lids closed, her head slumping forward. Her knees buckled.

Mr. Holland caught her before she hit the ground and cradled her against his chest.

"Stay with her," I commanded, shoving a new wave of guilt in that mental box. "Take care of her. Guard her with your life."

"I will." His eyes were diamond-hard, cold and almost cruel. "I don't want to go. I would be of help here. But I can't fight the zombies. Plus, I'm out of practice, and you're not, and I know Cole. I know he'd want your grandmother safe at any cost. Besides, I can work from the sidelines and text you anything I learn."

"I won't let anything happen to your son," I replied softly.

He nodded, satisfied. "I'm not going to tell you where we're going. It'll be better if you don't know."

"Agreed."

"This morning, I bought ten burner phones and gave them to Cole. He has my new number, and I have his. If anything happens, you call me."

"You have my word." I placed a soft kiss on Nana's cheek and smoothed the hair from her brow. "Tell her I'll call her at least once a day."

He turned and stalked out of sight.

I missed her already.

I strode to the back room and unlocked the girls. The door was open only a crack when they bum-rushed me, pushing their way out. I stumbled backward as their gazes found me.

Reeve had been ready to fight, her hands balled into fists. Now she breathed a sigh of relief. "Ali. You're all right."

Kat had been ready to fight, as well, her eyes narrowed, her teeth bared in a fierce scowl. Her cheeks were paler than they'd been last night, the stress of the situation hell on her malformed kidneys.

"Ali!" she cried.

Before I could blink, the two were on me, hugging me, kissing my cheeks, crying on my shoulders.

"I'm so freaking scared," Kat admitted. "This situation is *so* not cake. Mr. Ankh told us slayers were attacked last night, that Lucas and Trina… They were—" She gulped, unable to finish the sentence.

"I know," I said, somehow speaking past my own trembling. I brought her hand to my cheek, needing to feel her skin against mine. She was here, and she was okay. "Cruz was… He was… He's gone, too."

Both girls tensed, and I knew they were wondering how many others had been taken from us…and how much loss we were going to suffer before this war ended.

"Have you seen Bronx?" Reeve asked.

"No. I'm sorry," I replied, and her shoulders drooped. Then I gave her the comforting words Cole had given me. "He's tough. He's smart, and he's been through hell and back and survived. This? This is nothing."

"What about Frosty?" Kat said, shaking me. Her emotions were too much for her small figure to contain.

"I haven't seen him, either," I admitted. But if I knew the boys, and I did, they were frantic for news about their girls. They wouldn't have gone far. "Don't worry. We'll find them."

"Together," she insisted. "Don't try to send me home. I won't go. I won't! I've already called my dad, told him I'm spending the next few weeks with Reeve. Maybe even longer."

Something wonderful about her father: he let her do anything she wanted.

"If you guys are in danger," she continued, "*I'm* in danger, and I don't want my dad caught up in it. Besides, if I stay, I can cancel my dialysis at the hospital and Mr. Ankh can do it here."

I held up my hands, a gesture of acceptance. "I agree with you. Now let's put on our big-girl panties and go convince Mr. Always Right that he's seriously wrong."

IMPOSSIBLE?
ONLY IMPOSSIBLE-ISH!

Reeve drove a golf cart through the dark, damp tunnel, all the way to the basement of her mansion. A place we'd often referred to as "the dungeon." I expected Cole to be there, lying atop one of the many gurneys, feasting on egg whites and turkey bacon—that was healthy, right?—but he wasn't. I ignored my twinge of disappointment.

A fingerprint ID allowed Reeve through another door and into the house itself. On our feet now, Kat and I followed her up a flight of creaky stairs we'd traversed too many times to count. Usually, at the top, all vestiges of dungeon vanished, replaced by the luxuries of massive wealth. Rich mahogany-trimmed walls. Plush carpets probably woven by enchanted fairies. Glossy antique furniture. Not today. Graffiti decorated the walls in a collage of every color imaginable.

Somewhere, a rainbow was weeping.

There were rips and holes in the carpets, and several pieces of the furniture were in pieces.

Had Anima trashed the place to give credence to the supposed gang war?

Yeah. Probably. *Just one more crime to add to their ever-growing list.*

Reeve pressed a button on the intercom. "Daddy. Where are you?" she asked, an edge to her tone.

"My office, princess," he returned, his voice weary. "Ali, Cole's in your bedroom and he's been asking for you. I suggest you visit him before I'm forced to restrain him."

I gave Kat and Reeve a hug and said, "Don't tell Mr. Ankh what we're planning. I'll lead the conversation after I've seen Cole." I pulled away.

I think they nodded. I was moving down the hall already, too quickly to keep track.

I flew up another flight of stairs, darted down a hallway, snaked a corner and raced into the bedroom. Instant surge of relief. The other piece of my soul was propped against the bed's headboard, embraced by fluffy white pillows. His skin had a healthy tint, and the violet eyes I so adored were no longer glazed with pain, but bright and alert. His left arm was in a sling and his right had IV tubing running through his vein. His chest was half-covered by bandages.

"Ali." His gaze heated as it locked with mine, and I would have sworn the earth tilted.

A second later, my surroundings faded—

—and suddenly Cole was stalking down a narrow corridor. Blood trickled from his lip.

I was slung over his shoulder, my fists beating at his back, my knees digging into his torso. "Let go," I demanded.

"Never again," he countered.

"You keep saying that. What do you want with me? What

do you want *from* me?" As if I didn't know him, sometimes better than I knew myself.

"I want what I've always wanted. Everything—"

—as suddenly as it had begun, the vision ended.

Because the world *was* tilting. I was falling, hitting my knees.

"Ali!" Cole threw his legs over the side of the bed.

"Stay where you are or you'll rip out your IV! I'm okay." I stood, shaking off the momentary flash of dizziness that had taken me down. Lingering effects of the sedative, I was sure.

Cole didn't listen. He made to rise. I rushed to his side, easing onto the mattress, pressing my hip against his and pushing him to his back. For now, I didn't care about the vision. We'd seen it weeks before, and we would see it again. We'd figure it out then.

"You should be used to girls falling at your feet," I said.

He cracked the barest hint of a smile. "I'd rather have one girl standing beside me."

Sweet-talker. "How are you?"

He twined his fingers with mine, lifted our joined hands and kissed my knuckles. "I'm better now that you're here."

Six little words, and yet my heart swelled with love. Were all guys so open about their feelings? So willing to admit when they needed, when they wanted…when they had to have or else?

"How's your recovery?" I asked.

"Better than it should be. Nearly burning me alive was a good call."

I donned a haughty air. "Did you ever doubt it?"

"Only all night and a little this morning."

"So hardly at all."

He cracked another smile. "Last night I was getting weaker, so I performed the fire trick on myself. Charged me right up. But had it not been for you, I wouldn't have known to do it."

"So you owe me."

"Exactly. I pay in kisses."

"Good thing I accept that currency." I adored this playful side of him—and hated knowing it wouldn't last. "Have you been told about Trina, Lucas and Cruz?" I asked softly.

"Yeah." He scoured his other hand over his face. "But that's not all. The gym burned down."

Horror sped through me at full throttle. "Bronx. Mackenzie. They were there."

He gave a clipped nod. "The good news is, no bodies were found inside."

Okay. Okay, then. They'd either gotten away or been captured. Just like all the others.

Stomach cramp.

"We haven't heard from anyone. News stations have been blasting stories about the attacks, but besides Cruz, no other murders have been reported." I paused, mentally preparing myself for a fight. "I'm taking Kat and Reeve, and we're going on a hunt."

He surprised me by giving another nod. "That's great." Of course, he just had to add, "I'm going with you," which deflated me.

"You need to stay in your sickbed for at least a month, the way you made me stay in mine." I'd been recovering from a stab wound—one *he* had given me.

Don't worry. It wasn't domestic abuse or anything. He hadn't done it on purpose.

"Try to keep me here. I dare you," he said, then winked. A challenge? "You'll end up beside me."

"Oh, no. Not that. Anything but that," I responded with a mock shudder.

"Smarty." He tweaked the end of my nose. "Even on my worst day, with both hands tied behind my back, and no gun, I can shoot better than you."

"Maybe so," I said, practically dripping sweetness. "But you have no control over your swords."

His eyes narrowed. "Low blow, Miss Bell. Very low blow."

"I thought so." I fluffed my hair.

"Does Ankh know what you're planning with his precious?"

"Not yet."

"Are you actually going to ask him for permission?"

"Well, yeah." The girls and I could leave without his knowledge, sure. I was good at sneaking. But he would panic and go looking for his daughter, maybe get himself killed. I didn't need the added guilt.

"He won't just say no," Cole said. "He'll try to sedate you and lock you up."

Yeah. Probably. "I've seen his work firsthand. But I'm onto his tricks now." He wouldn't catch me off guard a second time. "He's just going to have to trust me and stop trying to surround Reeve with bubble wrap."

"I get where he's coming from," Cole said, everything about him softening. "To Ankh, she is a reason for getting up in the morning, and there's nothing more important to him. Without her, he might as well just curl up and die. And that, Miss Bell, is exactly how I feel about you."

Oh, glory. Nana had destroyed me with her declaration, but Cole...Cole was utterly *slaying* me....

"There's a difference between you and Mr. Ankh," I said with a soft smile. "You know I can defend myself, and you trust me to make smart decisions. Isn't that right, Mr. Holland?" Eew. No way I'd use the name reserved for his father. Backtrack. "Mr. Cole."

He tugged on a lock of my hair. "That's right. Therefore, I will girl up, as Kat likes to say, since that's apparently better than manning up, and I will let you go—"

"Wait. You'll *let* me?" I interjected with attitude.

"—without a fight," he finished. "Besides, I wasn't asking if I could come with you. I was telling you I'd be by your side."

Le sigh. His determination was kicking up a fuss again. "What's your blood pressure? Do you have a temperature? Are you even steady on your feet?"

He smiled and said, "Reason number thirteen. You always ask way too many questions."

Of all the things I'd expected him to say, that didn't even come close. He definitely had to be feverish. "*That's* a reason you love me?"

"See? Another question. But yes, it is. It's charming."

Well, he was the only one who thought so. Other people found it off-putting. And that was being kind!

I leaned over and kissed his brow, careful not to brush against his injury, then pressed my brow into his. "Don't think the fact that you avoided discussing your condition has escaped my notice. But I'll let it slide...and I'll *let* you come with me. As long as you stay in the car."

"Let me?"

"Oh, good. Your ears are working."

The softness faded from his expression, fierce protectiveness taking its place—as well as cold-blooded aggression.

The aggression wasn't directed at me, I knew, but at Anima.

"Let's play a little game I like to call Cole's in Charge and Ali's Not."

"Pass! Played it before, hated every second."

The flash of another grin. "You know I think you hung the moon, right?"

"Right. Just like I know you held the ladder and looked up my skirt."

"But you're not going to talk me out of this," he continued. "So, go down, speak with Ankh. I'll get dressed."

Stubborn boy. "I'd offer to take out your IV, but that would make me an enabler."

"Won't be the first time I've removed one myself."

The Care and Feeding of an Alpha Male 101. Sometimes, you just had to humor them. "Fine. Have fun with that."

"Don't leave without me," he commanded as I stood. "I mean it."

"Fine, fine." I held up my hands, all innocence. "I'll wait for you to come downstairs."

Moving as fast as lightning, he leaned forward and hooked me by the nape, tugging my face to his. He kissed me hard and fast—no innocent forehead peck for this boy, not this time—and I moaned at his ferocity. "Also, don't even think about sedating me."

"Fine," I snapped. He was severely limiting my options.

I left the room and stalked down the stairs, texting Nana along the way. I just couldn't help myself.

I love U. So much. One day, I hope U'll 4give me.

She'd wake up…wherever, and the note would be waiting for her.

I sent her a second message. 1st update. I've seen Cole & he's back 2 his bossy self. I've set Kat & Reeve free, & now I'm going 2 chat w/Ankh then find rest of slayers. I'll B careful, swear!

Mr. Ankh and the girls were in the kitchen, eating sandwiches.

Not one to waste time, I explained my search and rescue plan while slapping together a PB&J. The conversation went better—and worse—than I'd hoped. Before I'd even finished, Mr. Ankh was shaking his head. I didn't let that stop me, however. The fact was, I didn't just need Kat and Reeve. *They* needed *me*. They'd rather die than stay behind.

"No," he said. "You're too recognizable. Anima will see you, follow you and then kill you all."

I could suggest we spend a few hours dyeing our hair, altering our appearance, but even that wasn't a guarantee we'd escape notice. "With this supposed increase of gang violence, the police will be everywhere. Anima wouldn't dare try anything in public." I hoped.

"It's too dangerous," he insisted. "Kat is sick. She needs rest and relaxation, not—"

"Hey! Don't make me pimp-slap you, Dr. Jekyll and Mr. A. Because I will." Kat raised her hand to prove she meant business. "I'm ready to roll."

He pursed his lips, as if he'd just sucked on a lemon. "I'm not an unreasonable man."

Ha!

"And I know the others need to be found. So, *I'll* go with Ali, and you girls will stay here."

Uh, that would be a big fat no. He played by the rules. We

made our own. "Don't worry. We'll have a bodyguard. Cole is coming with us."

"Cole? Hardly." Mr. Ankh rubbed his forehead. To ward off an ache? "That boy needs rest just as much as Miss Parker does."

"So he doesn't need any, and he's good to go?" Kat quipped.

"Tell that to him," I said to Mr. Ankh, then hiked my thumb at Kat. "And her."

He threw his arms up, all *I'm the last sane man in the universe.* "Why do I even bother? No one ever does as I recommend anyway."

All right. I'd try this from a different angle. Hopefully one that wouldn't give him a coronary. "Had you told everyone about the church," I said, "this could have been avoided. But you didn't." *Throwing blame. Maybe not the best route.* But the truth was the truth, and I wasn't going to sugarcoat it.

He glared at me. "After Justin betrayed us, I wasn't sure who I could trust, and I wanted Reeve to have an escape that no one else knew about. You can't fault me for that."

I heard the guilt in his tone. The self-recrimination. "No. I can't."

I hadn't been part of the group back when Justin started sharing slayer secrets with Anima. But I *had* been part of the group when his equally culpable twin sister was captured and tortured right alongside me, and he'd realized just how badly he'd screwed up. He'd helped us destroy an entire contingent of Anima soldiers.

"If you have a better idea for finding the others," I said, after devouring the last of my sandwich, "I'll do it."

"Hey," both girls bellowed in unison.

Mr. Ankh glared at me.

"Daddy," Reeve said, "I've been training. I'm not helpless. And I want to help. I *need* to help. Don't stand in my way. Let me act like the girl you raised me to be. Strong. Courageous. The girl you wished Momma had been."

Her mother hadn't been able to see the zombies, but still she'd feared them. That fear had grown…and grown…until she'd committed suicide.

My mind drifted to my own mother. Her family had come from a line of slayers, but she herself hadn't been able to see the zombies, either. She'd been so beautiful. Short, with dark hair, eyes and skin. Just like my sweet Emma. When people had seen the three of us together, they'd assumed tall, fair me was adopted.

"Very well," Mr. Ankh finally croaked. "Do what you think is best. But I want you back within these walls by ten. No later."

I nodded, flabbergasted by his acceptance. I hadn't even had to beg.

"If you're saying yes just so you can blindside me with a sedative before I walk out the door," Reeve said, deflating some of my triumph, "you should know that this is the last time I will ever trust you."

He held her gaze for a long while, his eyelids slits, and I knew what he was thinking. First: *Crap, she figured out my plan.* Second: *She's not ready for this.*

And he was right. She wasn't.

In training, it was best to start with something easy, win and move on to something harder. Build your confidence and your skills. Reeve was still in the "easy" phase, and yet I expected her to remove her training wheels and slay a dragon?

So, I totally got Mr. Ankh's fear. I simply wasn't going to cave to it. We had a choice. Give up and let the enemy do worse, or rise up with what we had and go balls to the wall.

I was going balls to the wall. And if I lost, at least I'd go out in a blaze of glory.

"Fine," he said, releasing a breath of defeat. He flattened his hands on the table—in an effort to avoid his needles, I was sure. "Go with Ali. Search." His dark gaze slid to me and narrowed. "I'm holding you responsible for her safety. Kat's, too."

He wasn't the only one.

Jaw clenched, he said, "There's a car in the church parking lot you can use. It's beaten up on the outside, but the engine purrs with more than a hundred ponies ready to run."

Typical guy description.

I gave him a jaunty salute.

He marched off to his office, mumbling under his breath, and we marched to the armory.

By the time the girls and I finished loading up with weapons—daggers in our boots, sedatives in our purses, guns sheathed at our waists, extra bullets in our pockets, brass knuckles on our hands—Cole was dressed and ready, the IV nowhere in sight.

His cheeks were paler than before, indicative of the strain he'd just put himself through, as he handed each of us one of the burners. "My new number is already programmed in."

"Sweet sling, Cole," Kat said with her patented smile. "It only knocks three points off your alpha-male card."

His response was dry. "I'm sure spanking a naughty little girl like you will return my number to its original glory."

Kat's wide gaze immediately swung to me. "You didn't tell me that your boyfriend had a pain-and-punishment fetish."

"You didn't ask. But yeah, he does. I'm threatened with a spanking daily."

"Lucky," she whispered, skipping past me, heading toward the entrance to the secret passage.

We climbed in the golf cart, Reeve at the wheel.

"Where do you want to go first?" she asked. "When we're topside, I mean."

"I...don't know," I said. There were too many options. Gavin's car. Was it still there? Frosty's house. Justin and Jaclyn's house. Actually, *any* of the slayers' homes.

"Then it doesn't matter which road we take," Kat pointed out. "With nowhere to go, we'll never reach a destination."

A nice way of saying *make a decision already, dummy.*

"We'll go to Cole's gym." Or what was left of it. Any slayers on the run might have gone there. Might have stuck close by after the fire had died, hoping other slayers would show up.

Reeve parked at the back of the room, the one with the gurneys, and we walked to the ladder.

"What happens if we get separated?" she asked.

Hope for the best, plan for the worst. "If you can, get your butts back here. If you can't, hide and call me. If you lose your phones, don't panic. I'll find you. Whatever it takes."

But I couldn't help wondering if I'd just made the worst decision of my life.

EAT your HEART OUT

The gym was a pile of charred rubble, as expected, but the sight of it made my heart fester and ooze with an infected wound in need of tending. *Shouldn't be this way.* The air, heavy with smoke, painted the surrounding landscape an eerie gray. There was something very postapocalyptic about it. As if we were the only survivors and we now had to figure out how to navigate a new world.

At least there wasn't a rabbit cloud.

The authorities had already come and gone, leaving barricades behind.

Reeve hid our car at the side of another house. The gym was—had been—a large red barn planted in the middle of a neighborhood with homes spaced apart by acres of wheat and surrounded by a forest.

Any one of my friends could be waiting in the forest. Possibly injured.

Possibly being hunted.

"Reeve, you're with Cole," I said, taking charge. "Kat, you're with me."

"Prison rules?" Kat asked. "Kill first and ask questions later?" She withdrew a .38 revolver. It had no safety, but it did have a laser at the end to help her sight whatever she wanted to hit. Plus, the trigger was coiled tighter to prevent her from shooting accidentally.

Yeah. It had happened. She startled easily.

Reeve pulled a .22 from her purse. The gun had very little backlash, was more likely to irritate a target than kill it, but with halfway decent aim, she would be able to slow even the biggest of men.

"Actually, we're going by Holland rules," Cole said. "The best safety is this." He wiggled his index finger in front of their faces. "Don't put yours near the trigger unless you're ready to fire. Side note. You aren't ready to fire unless Ali or I say you're ready."

"But keep your weapons out and ready," I added.

Cole kissed me before we disembarked, sending a warm pulse through me. With the girls at our sides, we ran toward the forest, tree limbs seeming to go out of their way to slap us. When we were deep enough inside that we were concealed from prying eyes, everyone slowed and moved in the direction of the gym.

"Ready to split up?" I asked. "You guys come in from the west, and we'll come in from the east. We'll cover more ground."

"Sounds good." Cole held out his arm, stopping me. Which in turn stopped the girls. His gaze pierced me. "Don't get hurt. I mean it."

"As if I'd dare. But you'd better be careful, too. You aren't just a pretty decoration for the world to enjoy, you know. You're *my* decoration."

"And you're my toy."

We shared a look ripe with amusement and promise before branching apart.

"You guys are weird," Kat said, "but the good news is, Cole is probably stronger than ninety-nine percent of the population, even with his arm in a sling."

"A perfect description for Frosty, too."

"True story." Worry in her eyes, quickly extinguished.

With every exhalation, mist formed in front of my face. A signal trained trackers would pick up on, but it couldn't be helped. We made our way to the east side of the gym and… saw footprints! Excitement mingled with hope, filling me up and giving me new purpose. Who had made them? Bronx or Mackenzie?

But…why not both? Why was there only one set?

Some of my excitement drained.

"Come on." We followed the prints for a few yards. They were big. Too big to belong to Mackenzie. One—the right one—dragged. And there was a drop of blood beside that one…and that one. Bronx, if that's who had left these, was injured.

I stepped through one line of bush after another, remaining on alert, my .44 at the ready. The drops were getting thicker, and I thought the person responsible must have begun to drag his other foot, too…only to stop. I looked around. Saw nothing. Up. Down. Left. Right. Where the heck—

"There!"

My excitement returned in an instant. He'd camouflaged

himself with mud and leaves, and if not for the green of his eyes, I would have missed him. He was leaning against the tree, and "he" wasn't Bronx. He was Gavin.

Kat and I rushed to his side. He didn't respond. He was still, too still, his head resting on his shoulder. On closer inspection, blood was clearly mixed with the dirt, and my heart sank. His mouth was tinted blue, and, despite the cold, his teeth weren't chattering.

My hand shook as I felt for his pulse....

"Please, tell me he's alive," Kat pleaded.

"Yes," I nearly shouted. "He is."

"Thank God!" She exhaled with relief. But she was paler than she'd been a moment ago, and I wasn't sure if the problem was stress or her kidneys. Or both.

"Gavin," I said, gently patting his cheeks, willing my warmth into him. "You've got to help us get you to your feet. We may be strong, but we're not strong enough to carry you to safety fireman-style, so you've got to walk. Come on, Barbie. Please. Do it for your favorite cupcake."

He didn't even blink.

Very well. We'd do this the hard way. The riskier way. The same way I'd helped Cole.

"Watch my back," I told Kat. "In a few seconds, Gavin might grunt or scream. Don't touch him. Don't touch me." She wasn't a slayer. She wouldn't be able to see me in spirit form, and she wouldn't be able to feel my fire—until it was too late, and she was dead.

She didn't bother asking questions. Trusting me, she got into position behind Gavin, on the alert for any signs of an ambush.

I closed my eyes, drew in a deep breath. Held it, held. As I exhaled, my spirit emerged. I quaked from the newest increase of cold, ice crystals buying prime real estate in my chest.

"Light," I commanded my hand.

This time, it did not obey.

Okay. So. Starting a fire was going to be difficult this go-round. Noted.

But I didn't give up. Strength to summon the flames came by faith. A spiritual weapon for a spiritual power source. I didn't allow myself to worry, either. Worry actually weakened faith.

"I can do this," I said. "I *will* do this. Now. Now! *Now!*"

Words were another spiritual weapon. They could be used for my good or my bad. Positive or negative. Today, I focused on the positive and flames sprang from the ends of my fingers, slowly spreading to my wrist. Slow. Not what I was used to, but okay. I could work with this.

Unsure of Gavin's injuries, I pressed my hand into his chest—his sluggish heart.

He didn't ash, thank God, but he did unleash a broken scream, his back bowing. At any other time, the sound of his pain might have made me flinch. Now? I smiled.

I maintained the contact for several seconds before withdrawing, dismissing the flames and returning to my body.

"You can touch us now," I told Kat.

Gavin groaned.

"Good boy," I said, wanting to dance and sing. I hadn't lost him. "I know it hurts, but you're stronger than a little pain, right? And if not, well, you'll soon get to enjoy Mr. Ankh's vast array of drugs, so it won't matter."

He tried to focus on me, but his eyes were rocking back and forth, unable to stay locked on any one object. A sign of dizziness. "Ali?"

"Yeah, I'm here."

"Kat, too." She moved to his left, squeezed his hand.

"Kat, I need you to text Cole," I said. "Tell him to return to the car, that we've found Gavin, and he's hurt pretty bad."

"On it," she said, withdrawing her phone.

Now for the hard part. "We can help you, Barbie, but we need you to stand."

He didn't act as if he'd heard me. "Wreck...was chased, shot at...ran, lost tail...got to gym...fire..."

"I know. Everyone but Cole is missing," I said as gently as possible. I'd tell him about the deaths after he was stabilized.

"Frosty," he said, then grimaced and clutched his side.

Kat pocketed her phone and pinched his chin, forcing him to face her. "What about him? Have you seen him?"

"Ali," he repeated, as if he hadn't heard her. "Help."

Disappointment could have felled her, but my friend squared her shoulders, determined to motor on.

I was beyond proud of her. "Let's get him to Mr. Ankh."

With a major effort from both of us, we finally maneuvered him to his feet. As he swayed, we positioned ourselves under his arms, becoming his crutches. Had to be a comical sight, two sticks trying to balance a grade-A manimal. My legs juddered under his weight, and I'm sure Kat's did, too.

As we lumbered forward, Gavin said, "Saw...Frosty. He came to gym...men chased us...he led them away...from me... but not before he told me...meet him...Wok and Roll."

Kat practically bubbled over with exhilaration, and I didn't have to wonder what she was thinking. The Wok and Roll was a twenty-four-hour Chinese buffet only a few blocks from here, and if Frosty was still there, waiting for Gavin, she could be in his arms within the next half hour.

Cole and Reeve paced beside the car. Spotting my ragtag trio, Cole rushed over and took Kat's place. Reeve opened the back.

"Any sign of Anima on your end?" I asked.

"Not one."

Together, we got Gavin settled inside. I straightened, stepped back and said, "Take him directly to your house, Reeve, rather than the church." Gavin might blow an artery if he had to climb into the tunnel. "But call your dad on the way and let him know you're coming. He'll do something to ensure Anima isn't nearby, watching."

She nodded. "Done and done."

Kat took my hand, tugged. "Ali and I are heading to the Wok and Roll. Frosty might be there, waiting for Gavin."

"Uh, Kat." I planted my heels. Hello tricky, sticky situation. "You're going with Reeve."

"What? No." She gave a shake of her head, drawing attention to the fact that she was paler than before. "No way. No how."

Yes way. Yes how. "You're not objective when it comes to Frosty." More than that, he'd had Anima on his tail. Could be with Anima right now. Not only would Mr. Ankh disapprove of me taking her into a situation far more dangerous than this one, but Frosty would also. "I need you to listen—"

"No." She stomped her foot. "*You* listen. I'm going!"

O-kay. I suddenly understood why Cole was as hard-core

as he was. Arguing with your allies wasted precious time. "Kat. Please. Be reasonable."

Cole didn't give her a chance to respond. "Two choices. You'll do what she says." In full commander mode, he added, "Or you'll do what she says. Feel me?"

Her eyes narrowed to tiny slits, the patent stillness of a predator coming over her. "Oh, I feel you all right. Now *you're* about to feel *me*."

He flattened his good hand on the car, caging her against the metal, leaning down to get into her face. "You want to try something? Go ahead."

Ding, ding. Round one of The Bloodbath has begun.

"Gavin could be bleeding out right this minute." I glared at one, then the other. "We could have targets on our backs. Get in the car and go, Kat."

Still she shook her head, stubborn to the bitter end. "I'm going after Frosty. That's final."

I looked to Cole. He was practically hemorrhaging determination. Hard decisions came with hard consequences—he was getting ready to make one. One of us would have to go with her, and we both knew it.

"It's time for you to prove number seven." That he would stand back and let me fight. "You're injured. I'm not. I'll be the one to find Frosty."

I expected an argument. Instead, he gave me a clipped nod and grabbed Kat by the waist, hauling her inside the car, holding her down. She fought like, well, an alley cat, hissing, clawing, scratching, and it tore me up inside. Every fiber of my being screamed to help her, to stop this, to give her what she wanted, but I didn't. Sometimes what we wanted wasn't what we needed. I would apologize later, and she would have to forgive me…because Frosty would be with me.

Please, let him be with me.

I stored my .44 at my waist (safety on). As the car sped away from the curb, tires squealing, my gaze collided with Cole's, and through the window, we experienced a moment of total understanding. He'd do whatever was necessary to protect the girls. Even at the cost of his own life.

It had better not come to that.

The second the vehicle was out of sight, I sprinted into the forest, heading toward the shopping center where the Wok and Roll was located. The activity helped loosen my regret, and I began to warm, my blood rushing faster and faster through my veins.

Eventually, gnarled trees gave way to a paved road. I went up a hill, down a hill, through another neighborhood, careful to study every passing car, before finally reaching my destination. My lungs burned. Despite the cold, beads of sweat rolled down my spine.

It was Saturday, and shoppers were out in droves. Building after building stretched on both sides of me, each peppered with stores and restaurants. Being around so many people unnerved me. Anyone could be with Anima, just waiting to strike.

Strike and die.

A bell tinkled over the door as I entered the buffet. The scent of fried meat immediately assaulted me, and I almost hurled.

Only one other customer was there. A middle-aged man who definitely wasn't Frosty, and I highly doubted he was with Anima. He had to be one egg roll away from a heart attack.

Frustration cut at me. *Enraged Kat for nothing.*

No, no. Maybe Frosty had taken off, but had plans to return.

There was still hope.

A bright-eyed hostess approached me, smiling a smile that didn't quite reach her eyes. "How many?"

Could *she* be with Anima? "Just one."

She led me to a table in the center of the room.

"In back, please."

Shoulders stiff, she moved to the booth hidden by a huge aquarium and arched a brow, a silent *is this good enough for princess?*

"Perfect." I scooted into my seat, accidentally on purpose brushing against her to feel for weapons. Nothing. "Thank you."

Her lips compressed as she set a menu in front of me and took off.

I pulled out my phone and texted Cole. Frosty isn't here. Gonna wait N case he comes back. Has Kat calmed down?

Cole: Kat—no. U—DON'T WAIT LIKE SWEET LITTLE TARGET, GO HOME.

Swear I heard his irritated voice reverberating through my mind. He'd let me do this, and now he regretted it. Figured.

Me: News flash, Holland. ALL CAPS DOES NOT INTIMIDATE ME.

Cole: IT SHOULD. THE WRATH OF C.H. IS NOT A PRETTY THING.

Me: Bite me.

Cole: This just in—I will. W/pleasure. But I want U 2 come back & get me. Currently there R no other cars available. BTW this is nonnegotiable.

Me: Sorry, babe, but this was an FYI exchange & not a solicitation 4 orders. U can use the time apart 2 negotiate this. (I used an emoticon to flip him off.)

Cole: So that's a soft yes?

Good glory. I put the phone away, before he distracted me from my purpose. More than he already had.

Think! Even if Frosty had plans to come back to the Wok and Roll, he wouldn't have gone very far. Unless he was forced. He would probably move from shop to shop, where he could watch the restaurant's front door for Gavin without allowing anyone to get a lock on him.

But…if that was true, he would have spotted me and come racing over.

"Know what you want to order?" asked the hostess—waitress now—when she reappeared at my table.

"Hey, was there a fight in here today? Any kind of yelling match?" Any hint that my friend had been spotted?

Her brow furrowed with confusion. "No. Why?"

Rather than answer, I threw a twenty on the table. "Never mind. I've got to go."

She didn't try to stop me as I stalked outside. I leaned against the brick wall, as if taking a moment to warm myself against the cutting breeze. Really, I was scanning the shops across the way. Clothes. Clothes. Coffee. Shoes. Bakery. Cloth—

Coffee.

He could stay there longest, without drawing notice.

I rushed over and entered the warmth and deliciousness of

the caffeine-scented shop. I studied the occupants, my nerves about to reach the breaking point, and—

Found him!

Joy. Such profound joy. He was in the corner, looking out the glass window. He'd hidden his pale hair under a hat. The coat he wore had to be stolen, because I'd never seen him wear it, and it wasn't his size. It was also pink with purple flowers.

I walked to Frosty's table, pulled out a chair.

"Get lost—" Relief eroded all hints of anger. He leaned toward me. "Thank God it's you. Tell me everything you know. Start with information about Kat."

"She's alive and well and desperate to see you."

He closed his eyes, one of which was black, and sagged against the table. "You have no idea how badly I want to see her, too, but when I searched Ankh's place last night, she was gone."

"There's a secret passage that leads from Ankh's to an underground facility," I said. "She was staying there."

"Was?"

"As of this morning, she's back at Ankh's. He's refortified the security."

Frosty's hand curled into a fist. "I've been so worried…."

"I know," I said, patting that fist. "Why didn't you come to the Wok and Roll when I arrived?"

He frowned. "I didn't see you."

"But you were supposed to meet Gavin there."

"No. I was supposed to meet him at the coffee shop *across* from the Wok and Roll."

I'd blame Gavin's confusion on blood loss.

"Is he okay?" Frosty asked, an edge to his tone.

He expected bad news. "He will be," I said, determined. "Right now, he's in pretty bad shape. Cole, too, though he's doing much better. He was shot." *Keep it together.* "They're both with Mr. Ankh."

"Good. That's good." A grim cast overshadowed his expression. "Cruz is—"

"Yeah. I know." The sting of tears. *Shut down the waterworks. Now.* "Trina and Lucas, too."

He ground his fists into his eyes. "What about the others?"

"I wish I knew. You haven't heard or seen anything?"

"Only that Justin and Jaclyn are missing."

Had the twins been kidnapped? Or were they dead?

Jaclyn and I weren't the best of friends, but we were no longer enemies. I hated the thought of her out there, suffering— or worse.

"I planned to give Gavin five more minutes," Frosty said. "Then I was going to head out and start searching for the others."

More proof that ticking clocks sucked. Had I arrived a few minutes later, I would have missed him. "What happened last night? With you, I mean."

Bleakly, he said, "I was at home, in bed but still awake. I heard a squeak and tried to sit up. A hard hand slapped over my mouth, and a needle jabbed into my neck. It was an instant mind-screw. I was dizzy. I was weak and compliant. The guy must have drugged my guardians, too, because he was able to get me downstairs and out the front door without their interference. Then he made the mistake of putting me in the front seat of his car. The moment the dizziness eased,

I was able to force him off the side of the road, get out and head for the gym."

"But it was already burning to the ground," I confirmed.

"I noticed armed men chasing an injured Gavin and did my best to gain their attention. I succeeded, but it took almost two hours to lose them and another two to make it to Ankh's. I kept passing out. Then I came here."

So. Anima hadn't wanted to kill Frosty. But they'd certainly wanted to kill Cole. Why?

What was their plan? Their purpose?

"Do you know where any of the others might have hidden?" Bronx. Mackenzie. Veronica. Collins.

"Bronx...maybe. I was going to check a meeting place of ours when I left here."

"I'll go with you. Just need to tell Cole what's going on."

"He micromanaging?"

"Something like that."

I texted Cole and Kat at the same time. Found Frosty. He's alive & well. We have lead on Bronx. More soon. & Kat...I'm sorry. I will make it up 2 U, swear!

Cole's response came seconds later. Keep me updated.

Kat's came a few seconds after that, and only after I'd read it did I chill. Bring my boy toy home & all will B 4given.

Oh, how I loved that girl. She wasn't going to hold a grudge or even yell at me.

"So," Frosty said as we stood. "I have to ask you a personal question, because our next move hinges on your answer."

I tensed, unsure about what he could possibly want to know. "Ask."

"How do you feel about stealing cars?"

KEEP CALM AND CARRY A GUN

Fact: life is a giant classroom and every day is an opportunity to learn something new.

Fact: you have to be prepared for pop quizzes, because they can come from anywhere or anyone.

Also fact: I wished I'd called in sick today.

What I learned from Professor Frosty? How to properly boost cars. The guy could do wicked things with a single piece of wire.

"I'm a criminal now," I lamented as we soared down the highway. Killing in self-defense didn't count. "I'm an accomplice. A thief."

"Actually," he said smoothly, "you're a freelance valet. All you're doing is moving a car from one location to another. There's nothing wrong with that, now, is there?"

I snorted, humor momentarily overcoming my reservations. "Freelance valet?"

He hiked his shoulders. "Just go with it."

Why not? "So, how'd you learn to do it, anyway?"

"I'll tell you, but you can't ball like a baby. You'll want to, because it's tragic. Like, break your heart and—"

"I get it. No one has ever suffered like you. Go on."

He huffed and puffed for a minute. "Does Cole know you're made of ice?"

"Yes. He likes to melt me."

"*Anyway.* It's like this. I've been able to see zombies since birth. I cried all the time. After a while, my dad couldn't take it and left. My mom was on her own and had to be the one to calm me down every time I screamed about monsters. It freaked her out, and she put me through all kinds of medical and psychiatric tests she couldn't afford. No one could figure out what was wrong with me, and by the time she had a new boyfriend, she couldn't take the constant stress anymore, so she gave me to my aunt and uncle. I started hanging with the wrong crowd." He studied my face longer than necessary, considering he was behind the wheel of a car. Checking for tears?

I admit, I was tempted to offer one or two in supplication. He'd been abandoned. Forgotten. But I held them back and lifted my chin. "I'm sorry you went through that. I am. But everyone comes with baggage. Did I ever tell you about the time I lost my entire family in a car crash?"

He barked out a laugh. "You and Kat, man. You're, like, the only girls on the planet capable of surprising me. I expect sympathy, you give me lip service. It's kind of nice."

A bit of a backhanded compliment, sure, but I'd take it. "So, what happened to your mom?"

His fingers tightened on the wheel, a testament to his discomfort. "She visited me a few times, and now that I can drive, I have an open invitation to visit her, but she has a new family now, so…"

Even more heartbreaking. I threw him a bone and changed the subject. "How'd you meet Cole?"

Now his lips curved into a naughty smile. "You familiar with prison rules, Ali-gator?"

Stupid nicknames. They were the equivalent of verbal fungus. You couldn't ever get rid of them. "Somewhat. According to Kat, there's only one. Kill now, ask questions later."

"Actually, there are ten. But the first and most important is this—whenever you're the new kid, flat-out annihilate the current king, and no one will ever mess with you. Well, when I moved to Cole's district, he was the current king, so I challenged him in front of everyone. He knocked me out flat, then helped me up. We've been friends ever since."

"Brothers at first punch," I said, and he nodded.

"Something like that."

I wondered how many other kids were out there, able to see zombies but uneducated about the truth.

My dad had been able to see zombies, though he hadn't known what they were. As a boy, he'd watched one murder his mother. Over the years, his fear of them had only grown… and grown…until he'd later turned to alcohol and locked my little sister and me away.

But then, that's what fear did. That's the destructive power it wielded, and that's why I was so determined to resist it, no matter what was going on.

Sometimes, though, my determination wavered—and it usually revolved around one person.

"Can I ask you a question?" I said.

"Isn't that what you've been doing?"

Har har. "Kat's kidney disease."

A beat of taut silence. "Waiting for the question."

"Is there anything we can do?"

"You think I haven't researched? Made appointments just to talk to specialists about her?"

"And there's nothing?"

"Nothing," he repeated hollowly.

I peered out the window, silent. Basically, Kat's death was just a waiting game. A ticking clock that would soon zero out.

"Let's talk about something else," he said, taking a corner faster than I liked. "Like the current sitch. Anima has had multiple opportunities to come after us like this, but they never have. I mean, the time they had you, Kat and Reeve locked up we wouldn't have fought to kill, because we would have been afraid they'd hurt you girls in retaliation. So, I have to ask myself. Why now?"

Good question. "Let's take a look at what we know. They've been working on ways to control the zombies, to steer the creatures to attack anyone standing in the way of their research. And they hope to use the zombie toxin to create a serum for eternal life, without consequences, and supposedly save mankind from disease and death, but in the meantime, they don't mind experimenting on and killing innocent people."

Frosty thought for a moment. "What if they've succeeded?"

"You suspect…what? That they want us out of the picture, so that there will be no one able to stop what they're doing, because no one will know about it."

"Exactly."

Then the situation did not bode well for us. Because Anima would strike again. And soon, while we were injured and weakened.

I could almost hear a countdown in my head. The *tick tock, tick tock* I could never escape.

My hands curled into fists. *Calm. Steady.*

No fear, remember?

Frosty stopped in the school parking lot. Asher High. Home of the Tigers. (Go Tigers!) I frowned. There were several other vehicles there, so ours didn't stand out. But…

"You think Bronx came here?" I asked.

"Maybe."

Well, okay, then. That was good enough for me.

We entered the building—the doors were unlocked, saving us from committing another crime. We stuck to the shadows as we wandered down the halls. I kept a hand on the inside of my purse, my fingers curled around the hilt of one of my daggers. Just in case. No one jumped out at us and we were able to enter room 213 without incident.

But…dang it! There was no sign of Bronx. I wanted to stomp my foot.

"You contemplating throwing a hissy?" Frosty closed in on the chalkboard. "There's no need. I was right. He's been here."

I looked left, right. Saw nothing. "How do you know?"

Frosty motioned to the chalkboard. "He left me a message."

I read the words scribbled across it. *Love me. Hurt me. At midnight. Party like rock stars.*

O-kay. "What does it mean?"

"Take the first word of each sentence. *Love hurt. At party.* Meaning, Mackenzie Love is hurt and he's got her…where?"

Crap. How bad were her injuries?

"They're at…a party-supply warehouse? Doubtful." He was mumbling now, clearly talking to himself, trying to reason things out. "A place we partied? More likely. But he wouldn't have picked just any place. He would have… Someplace I'd remember… The last place? Yes, yes, yes. I know where he is!"

My heart drummed with excitement. "Then let's go."

We ended up in a run-down neighborhood about fifteen miles out of Birmingham. After wiping our prints, we ditched the car—maybe someone else would decide to do a little free-lance valeting, moving it out of the area entirely—and hiked to the worst house of the lot.

It had peeling paint, broken shutters and cracked windows. Pieces of shingle hung from the side of the roof. The planks of wood on the porch released a death rattle as we walked to the door.

Frosty knocked. A shadow soon crept over the bottom of the door, and I knew someone was looking out the peephole.

"About time," an unfamiliar voice said. Hinges released a high-pitched whine as the dilapidated entrance swung open. A petite brunette with a patchwork of pink scars on one side of her face moved out of the way, allowing Frosty to sail past her.

"Where are they?" he demanded.

"Back room."

I started to follow after him, but the girl stepped into my path, blocking me. I had to look down…down…down…. She barely topped five feet. She was young, no more than four-teen. And she was spunky cute, with dark green eyes gleam-ing with fierce protectiveness.

"Who the hell's your friend?" she called to Frosty. Her narrowed gaze never left me.

"That's Ali. Let her in."

Her features pinched with distaste. "So you're the infamous Ali Bell, are you?"

Great. What had she been told about me? Her sneering tone suggested I was so evil, the devil had actually sold his soul to *me*.

I nodded. "I am. And you are?"

"Juliana, Veronica's younger sister. What of it?" All attitude, no finesse.

My chest clenched with nearly unbearable longing to see my own little sister. Emma hadn't visited me in weeks. Where was she?

The last time we'd spoken, she'd told me our connection was thinning and we would be seeing each other less often. I'd taken that to mean once, maybe twice, a week. I wish I'd known "less often" could actually mean "never again." I would have hugged her harder, longer. Perhaps never let go.

"May I come in?" I asked softly.

"Whatever." Juliana stiffly angled to the side. I entered the house and took stock.

No pictures hung on the walls. The furniture was well used, but patched and polished. There wasn't a TV or computer, but a vase containing fresh flowers sat on the coffee table. A sweet, floral scent perfumed air that would have been musty otherwise.

I'd had no idea Veronica, my greatest frenemy, had a younger sister. Or that they were, apparently, living in abject poverty. Poverty, and yet, Bronx had felt it was safe to come here, even though it wasn't safe to be at any other slayer's house. So, this house must have escaped Anima's notice. But how?

And what about the party Frosty had mentioned? It had been held here? Why? And when? Had Cole attended?

Why hadn't I been invited?

Ugh. The last was asked in a disgusting whine. As if any of that crap mattered in the wake of such devastation.

"Where are your parents?" I asked. Voices seeped from the hall. I would give Juliana a few more minutes to invite me back, and then I was going on my own, rude or not.

"Dead," she said in a snippy tone.

"I'm sorry."

"Sure you are. For an encore, why don't you ask me how I got the scars?"

Okay. "How'd you get the scars?"

She blinked in astonishment, her mouth hanging open. Clearly, she hadn't expected me to do it. "I was burned." Her words lashed like a whip. "Not that it's any of your businesses."

"Hey," I said, palms up in a gesture of innocence, "you offered." And wow, I suddenly felt guilty for treating Veronica so craptastically when I'd first met her. She hadn't exactly had an easy life.

But then, like I'd told Frosty, none of us had. We were all hurting in some way.

Juliana glanced at her feet, shifted from one side to the other, then looked up at me. "Have you heard from Cole?" she asked, her tone now grudging.

"He was shot, but he's on the mend."

Relief she couldn't hide; it was clear she genuinely cared for him.

Get in line.

All right, so, it was time to check on my friends. Without another word, I stalked down the hall.

"Hey! You can't go back there." Juliana stayed close to my heels. "This isn't your house."

I opened one door, found it empty save for a single twin mattress and a blanket and kept going. There was only one other room…and that's where I found everyone. Three twin-size mattresses were propped on the floor. Mackenzie was sprawled across the one on the left, Bronx the one in the center and Veronica the one on the right.

Mackenzie was asleep. Dark curls spilled around pallid skin. Her lips were raw from being chewed, and there were several abrasions on her face. The hem of her shirt bunched over her middle, and I could see the bandage wrapped around her waist.

Bronx and Veronica were awake and alert.

He looked healthy, propped up against the wall, one hand cupping the back of his neck, the other resting at his side. His dark hair, died green at the tips, was mussed. The piercings in his eyebrow and lower lip gleamed in the light. No visible cuts or bruises.

"She was stabbed," he said, his teeth clenched with anger. Anima should be very afraid. Of all the slayers, he was the most uncivilized, and I'd always suspected humanity had become a facade he sometimes wore. "I don't think our attackers expected anyone to be at the gym. There were two of them, and when they broke in, we heard them. We moved to the shadows, watching, waiting. When we realized they were pouring gasoline on everything, we tackled them. She was stabbed, a match was lit and one of the guys was able to run away."

I walked to her bed and sat at the edge, my hip touching

hers. Gently I smoothed a hand down her cheek. Tremors struck me. My limbs were growing heavier by the minute. My adrenaline must be crashing. I might not have the strength to push out my spirit and light up.

"Frosty," I said. "Can you light up?"

"Yeah. Why?"

"Because you're going to put your fire inside Mackenzie's wound."

In unison, everyone in the room belted out a refusal.

"Like hell he is!"

"Are you insane? The answer is no!"

"That's so not happening."

"Zip it," I said, and miracle of miracles, they obeyed. "Remember when I was sick? You guys healed me with your fire."

"Yeah, but you were part zombie," Bronx said. "She isn't. The fire will help her spirit and harm everything else."

"Not true. The two are connected. What injury one sustains, the other sustains. So why can't the opposite be true?"

Silence.

"Look, I've done it to Cole. He's even done it to himself, and he's now on his feet. Just a little while ago, I did it to Gavin. He strengthened almost instantly."

"Hold up." Veronica's tone was as hard as granite. "You're telling us you put Cole and Gavin at risk? That you weren't a hundred percent certain what would happen, but you did it anyway?"

In a nutshell, yes. But… "They were already at risk," I pointed out.

Mackenzie moaned, as if the argument had disturbed whatever restful state she'd managed to achieve.

"Do it, Frosty," I commanded.

"You ain't his boss," Juliana barked.

He rubbed his knuckles in the crown of the girl's head. "Thanks for the backup, squirt, but I've got this one." He strode to Mackenzie's bed.

Juliana's gaze threw daggers laced with hate at me.

I dismissed her, saying to Frosty, "Don't wuss out. Do it."

"You better be right about this," he muttered. Out flowed his spirit, flames crackling at the end of his fingers.

He touched Mackenzie, and she gasped, clearly pained. He tensed to draw back.

"Don't," I said. "Don't sever contact until she screams."

He bared his teeth in a fierce scowl.

A moan slipped from Mackenzie...another. Her head thrashed against the pillow.

"Ali," Frosty groaned.

"Just a little longer."

Then Mackenzie opened her mouth and screamed. She batted at Frosty's hand, but because he was a spirit, and she wasn't, she couldn't touch him. Couldn't stop him.

He stepped back, and she sagged against the mattress. I leaned over her, looking for any change. Her color was returning, pink flooding into her cheeks, and the dark circles under her eyes were fading.

That. Quickly.

A lady never smirks.

Since when have I ever been a lady?

I smirked.

Frosty rolled his eyes. "We get it. You told us so."

And don't you forget it! I looked to Bronx. "Are you hurt?"
Should Frosty torch him, too?

"I've got a few bumps," he said, "but I'm fine."

My gaze shifted to Veronica.

"I'm fine, too," she said.

Her green eyes were bright with worry. Her dark hair was
tangled, grass and twigs woven into the strands. Even still,
she was a beautiful sight. Physically flawless—Cole's perfect
counterpart. Which was probably why they'd dated.

Yes. Cole had gotten around...and around.

"Someone clue me in," I said. "How is this place a secret?"

Veronica ran her tongue over her teeth. "Jules and me are
off grid. I don't buy or rent anything under my own name.
Only the guys here...and Cole...know where we live." Like a
guilty suspect during interrogation, she looked away from me.

Cole had known and hadn't told me. Me, his girlfriend.
His one and only.

I had no words.

No, that wasn't actually true. I had a lot of words—for myself. I wasn't a jealous girl. Either Cole was mine or he wasn't.
End of story. Either I trusted him or I didn't.

But he'd broken up with me for several weeks, and he'd
spent those bachelor days with Veronica. He hadn't cheated
on me, considering we'd been over, but it had certainly felt
like it. Because they'd done things. Things I didn't like to
think about.

Things he now refused to do with me.

So, yeah, I kind of wanted to claw her face off and spit in her
skull.

Graphic much? Straitlaced Ali piped up.

Not graphic enough, Bloodthirsty Ali quipped.

Hello, new personalities. So nice to meet you.

So, going full circle. Cole was mine. There was no question about that, and I did trust him. Totally and completely. And I knew he wasn't interested in anyone else. Not even Veronica. But…yeah. This omission hurt.

Get over it. People are allowed to keep secrets. And it's not like this is important right now anyway.

And there was Pragmatic Ali. I knew her well.

"I was out last night," Veronica continued. "I'm a regular at Hearts, and I went home with… Well." Her cheeks flushed, and she cleared her throat.

Didn't want her little sister to know she'd left the nightclub to get a little some-some from a stranger?

"It's okay," Juliana said, glaring at me. As if everything wrong with the world was my fault.

I wasn't judging, jeez.

"He tried to drug my drink," Veronica said, her voice trembling. "He didn't realize I'm the untrustworthy type and switched our glasses the moment his back was turned. He went down, and another guy came rushing into the room, clearly expecting me to be the one on the floor. We fought. I won. Barely. I raced home on foot and had no idea what was going on, just assumed it was a date-rape thing, until Bronx started banging on my door a few hours ago."

Anima was smart. They knew how to track. The time she'd spent here concerned me. "I don't think you guys are safe. You're hard to find, yes, but not impossible. Sooner or later Anima will show up, and we all know what will happen then."

She blanched but said, "I can take care of myself and my sister, thank you. I've been doing it for a long time."

"Don't play the pride card," Frosty said. "You and Juliana need to be behind Mr. Ankh's walls, and that's that. He has cameras and a system to alert him if anyone steps foot on his property. You don't. He also has secret passageways if there's a problem."

Veronica sighed. "Okay, okay. I get it. My place sucks. His doesn't."

Listen to him but not me. Awesome.

"I'd like to see what *you* could afford, Ali Bell," Juliana snapped, marching to her sister's bed. The two joined hands in a show of support.

Once again, my chest constricted. I'd had that kind of unity with Emma, and I missed it almost as much as I missed her.

"Cat fight later," Bronx said. "I'm ready to go. I need to see Reeve."

Need was far stronger than *want,* but I knew he wasn't overstating. The same bond existed between Cole and me. Invisible but fierce.

"If Kat isn't in my arms within the hour," Frosty said, checking the safety on his gun, "I'm going to get cranky."

First: that was a scary thought. A cranky Frosty was a murderous Frosty.

Second: if we were going to stay together, we'd need an SUV.

Fabulous. "Looks like we're all about to become freelance valets."

BONKERS TODAY,
BONKERS TOMORROW

On the drive to Mr. Ankh's, I texted Cole to let him know Mackenzie was in need of medical help.

His response took a while, but it did come. Ankh says he'll B ready.

I also texted Kat and Reeve to let them know their men were on the way and good to go. Close to thirty replies came in.

The highlights?

Kat: Cake! CRAZMAZING! Knew U could do it, Ali me girl!

Kat: WAIT. I know U said he's good 2 go, but does he still have all his parts? I need 2 know if I can knee his man junk. HE MADE ME WORRY ABOUT HIS WELL-BEING!

Reeve: Is Bronx speaking, or has he gone silent? Tell me! Please! I have 2 know which side of him I'll B dealing w/ so I'll know which Reeve 2 let greet him—the lover or the he-woman street fighter (yes, I fight. Sue me!).

Kat: Would now B a horrible time 2 break up w/him? Who

cares! I'm gonna do it. Causing a girlfriend untold worry is a crime punishable by death!

Kat: BTW how many people did he have 2 kill 2 survive? & is that why U left me behind (& almost earned an alley kat experience U would never 4get)? B honest. U didn't want me 2 C the bodies, did U?

Reeve: WHY AREN'T U HERE??? I'll street fight YOU if U don't hurry.

Kat: Is it bad that I'm turned on right now?

When we got there, it was no surprise to see Mr. Ankh, Reeve and Kat waiting on the front porch. Kat should have been flushed, considering her excitement, but she was still pale. I didn't like that. And where was Cole?

Unfortunately, the couples weren't given a chance to hug and kiss—and whatever else. Mr. Ankh began barking orders the moment the car doors opened, demanding Frosty carry Mackenzie to the room next to Gavin's and that Bronx clear the way. The girls could only walk next to their boys, talking a mile a minute.

"—get a reward for surviving," Kat was saying. "You can start by taking off all your clothes and—"

"I don't need to hear this, Miss Parker," Mr. Ankh snapped.

"—showering," she finished. "Alone. Of course. I like my men clean."

"How's Gavin doing?" I asked, trailing behind.

"Far better than I anticipated." Mr. Ankh stopped, forcing me to do the same. He glanced over his shoulder. "He'll survive."

Relief poured through me, sweet and welcome.

"Two boys. Two wounds. Two miracle recoveries. Any clue how that's happening?" he asked, catching me off guard.

"Slayer fire," I admitted.

His eyes glazed for a moment, his medical mind probably assessing the pros and cons. Then he leaped forward to catch up with Frosty and Bronx. I took a step, intending to follow, but Kat came flying out the door. She propelled into me, wrapping her arms around me. Her grip was weaker than usual.

"Thank you, Ali. Thank you, thank you, thank you."

I hugged her back, tears burning my eyes. "I'm so, so sorry, Mad Dog. I know I apologized over text and you said all was forgiven, but I had to say it in person. I couldn't take the chance that we'd find him and he'd be injured, and you'd freak, and I'd have to try and cart both of you—"

"I know. Cole explained on the way home." She pulled back and gave me a watery smile. "Besides, you brought him back, and that's all that matters."

With that, she was gone, chasing after her man.

"Have Mr. Ankh check you out," I called, trudging forward. Prickles on the back of my neck stopped me. Something was going on around me, and my spirit sensed it. My mind just hadn't caught up yet.

Trying to act nonchalant, I spun slowly, eyeing the grounds. Big, thick bushes circled the edge of the property, hiding the residents from prying eyes. There was no—

There! A fall of wheat-colored hair surrounded a pale face. For a second, only a second, light blue eyes met mine, before the woman—somehow familiar, though I was certain I'd never met her—turned away from me and disappeared in the foliage.

Palming a dagger, I rushed after her. Who was she? Why was she here? To spy for Anima?

Surely not. There was no way she could have gotten past Mr. Ankh's security. Right? So, Mr. Ankh had to know she was here. *Right?*

Just before I reached the spot where I'd first seen her, I ground to a halt. What if he didn't know? What if this was some kind of ambush? I focused on the sounds around me. There was a whistle of wind. In the distance, a car's engine purred and a dog barked. No voices. No snapping limbs. No shuffling footsteps.

Like every girl in every horror movie ever made—a specialty of mine—I did not turn back. I inched forward, quietly working my way through the branches and leaves.... I found her standing a few yards away, next to one of the tallest trees on the property. Waiting for me. Though it was freezing out, she wore a black tank top, no coat, and seemed unfazed by the cold. At least her legs were covered by camo pants and her feet with combat boots.

"Who are you?" I asked, letting her see the knife.

"Samantha," she said, and there was so much longing radiating from her, my heart actually shuddered. "Sami."

"Sami." An odd throb started up in my chest. "That's your name?"

"No. Not mine." She offered me a sad smile, and her identity instantly crystallized. The woman from my dream. The one with the little girl.

The two were real.

Part of my family?

Surely. Those eyes...

"Who is Sami? Who are you?" I repeated more sharply.

"I have a gift for you," she said, holding out her hand.

Accepting the gift, whatever it was, would be stupid. I didn't know her, not really, and I certainly didn't trust her. But that didn't stop me from closing the distance. What can I say? Curiosity owned me.

"Make an aggressive move," I said, "and I will gut you. I won't think twice about it."

Her gaze met mine—the longing and sadness so much stronger now. Breaking my heart. But there was also…pride. Why?

I found myself asking, "What's the gift? And are you related to Phillip Bell?" My dad. Did I want her to be? "What about Miranda Bradley?"

"Time is short, and the gift is necessary." She waved me even closer. "It will help you defeat your enemy."

True or false?

Could this be a trick? Yes. But deep down, where instinct overpowered logic, refusing seemed…foolish.

Test her.

I reached out, letting my hand hover over hers, ready to draw back at a moment's notice—or stab, as promised. She shut her eyes. Tendrils of warmth drifted from her and seeped into me. It wasn't long before it surrounded me, consumed me and grew hotter…so danged hot. It was like being set on fire from the inside. Yet, she wasn't even touching me.

True or false—I now had my answer. False. Totally false. I tried to pull away but couldn't. I was stuck. My head fell back as a scream traveled up my throat, ready for release.

Suddenly she dropped her arm to the side. The scream died. The burning faded.

"Wh-what did you do to me?" My skin tingled. My blood fizzed.

Silent now, she pointed to a spot on the tree, turned her back and glided away, disappearing behind another bush.

"Hey!" I shouted, pursuing her. "I'm not done with you." But when I crossed the bush, she wasn't there. In fact, there was no sign of her. No footprints. No lingering scent in the breeze.

I searched...and searched...but came up with nothing.

Frustrated, I returned to the tree, to where she'd pointed. Several vines ran down the side and—

I frowned, moved closer and ran my fingers through them. They weren't vines. They were too firm, too warm.

Cords? Wires?

"What are you doing?"

The voice came from behind me.

I spun and met Cole's gaze. What progress! He was already out of the sling and clearly ready for action.

"Come here," I said.

He moved to my side. His heat instantly enveloped me, sweet tingles pricking at me. I ignored them and pointed to the wires.

He went from zero to sixty in less than a second, his calm shattered. "Those aren't Ankh's, but I bet they're hooked into his system, which would explain how Anima was able to get inside his house." He confiscated my knife, sliced through each one. "How did you find them?"

"A woman," I admitted, saying nothing of the burn she'd caused in me. No reason to alarm him when I wasn't clear about what had been done.

"What woman?"

"Her name may or may not have been Sami. Or Samantha." *And she gave me a gift. Said she wanted to "help" me.*

"She called and told you about the wires? Or she was actually here?"

"Here."

Violet eyes narrowed on me with laser-sharp focus. "You saw a stranger on this land, a day after we endured a massive attack that led to the deaths of three of our friends, and rather than shouting for help, you thought you'd follow her?"

Ugh. Put that way, I sounded like the world's biggest idiot. I *felt* like the world's biggest idiot. Still, I said, "That about sums it up, yes."

His eyes narrowed further. "Where is she now?"

"Don't know. She got away."

He took my hand and dragged me back to the house. "We'll watch camera footage and track her down. I'd like to chat with her."

No one waited in the foyer, saving us from having to answer any questions about where we'd been or what we'd been doing. Cole shut us inside Mr. Ankh's office and claimed the desk chair. Clearly, he knew all the computer codes, because his fingers danced over the keyboard without hesitation. I stood over his shoulder, suitably impressed.

The front porch appeared on screen, Mr. Ankh, Kat and Reeve there and waiting. The SUV Frosty had temporarily borrowed pulled up, and everything played out like I remembered. Bronx leading the way. Frosty carrying Mackenzie. My little conversation with Mr. Ankh. My hug session with Kat. My stopping and looking around.

When I leaped into motion, Cole pressed a few more keys, and the entire front lawn came into view.

Only, there was no sign of the mystery blonde.

"But...she was there," I said, confused. "I saw her."

Cole leaned back in the chair and ran two fingers along his jaw. "Ali-gator. You're tired, stressed. Maybe you—"

"I did *not* hallucinate. How could I? She showed me the wires. Which I previously knew nothing about! Consciously or subconsciously."

He thought for a moment. "I'll tell Mr. Ankh about the wires, but for now, we'll keep quiet about the woman."

"But you believe me, right?"

"Of course," he said, as if the answer had never been in doubt. "Weird stuff happens to you. It's part of the package. I've accepted it." He stood and gathered me in his arms, and I leaned my head against his shoulder, taking comfort in the racing beat of his heart.

"Thank you."

"Save your thanks, because I'm about to start yelling."

Uh-oh.

"Do not ever—*ever*—follow after a stranger like that. Do you hear me?" He wasn't actually yelling, but it was pretty darn close. "She could have led you into an ambush."

"Duh. I had the same thought."

He stiffened, saying softly but menacingly, "You had the same thought, and yet you trailed her anyway?"

Had to learn when to zip my lips. "Don't forget number seven. I'm such a good fighter, you could stand back and watch while I take care of business."

"That doesn't mean you're invincible." His sigh caused several strands of hair to dance over my forehead. "I'm going to regret number seven for the rest of my life, aren't I?"

"And probably part of your afterlife, too."

He snorted. "Come on. It's my turn to show something to you." He led me upstairs and into the first room on the left.

A lump on the mattress shifted, and I paused. Who—

"Jaclyn," I said, nearly buckling with relief. Another slayer had been found.

Even in her sleep, she recognized me, turning her head toward the sound of my voice. Tangled hair surrounded a beat-up face. One of her eyes was black-and-blue, swollen, and her lip was split in the center. Skin usually a healthy olive was now pallid. She looked terrible, but she was alive. Alive meant she'd heal.

"Where's Justin?" I asked. Her twin brother was never far behind.

"Still missing."

From the highest high to the lowest low.

"Coley-poley!" a girl called.

I pivoted as Juliana threw herself into Cole's open arms. His expression softened, becoming almost…tender.

I still wasn't jealous. Maybe. He had girl friends, and I had boy friends, and there was nothing romantic about it. Nothing wrong with it. But there was something between these two. A definite bond.

A definite bond he'd kept secret from me. Why?

Once, Veronica had bragged about an "ace in the hole," something guaranteed to break up my relationship with Cole. At the time, I hadn't given it much thought. Ace? Please. Now I didn't think I'd be pondering much else.

At least Juliana was too old to be Cole's kid. (Yeah, I admit it. A secret baby had been my first guess.)

A whispered conversation ensued between the pair, and I hesitated to join. I didn't want to interrupt, but I didn't like standing on the outside, either.

Cole brushed his knuckles over Juliana's scars. She grinned, not the least bit self-conscious with him. She knew she was loved and accepted, just the way she was.

I headed toward the bed, intending to sit beside Jaclyn. But Cole had been aware of me, even though he'd seemed utterly absorbed by Juliana, because he returned me to his side with a gentle tug. His arm wrapped around my waist, and I found myself tucked firmly against him. He gave off more heat than usual and it cast a net around me, ensnaring me. But then, I was a willing captive. I gladly breathed in the sweet scent of him—the fruit candies he ate when no one was looking— and cuddled against him, this boy who'd become my shield against the rest of the world, my shelter in any storm, but also my anchor. He kept me grounded.

"Have you met my girlfriend, Ali?" he asked Juliana.

She transformed from sweet to sour in a snap. "Yeah, I've had the displeasure. And I shouldn't have to remind you that you're not usually into blondes. I mean, weren't you and Gavin boinking your way through the brunette population? What happened with that? Everyone needs a goal."

O-kay. Wow.

"Mouth," Cole said on a sigh.

"Yes," Juliana said, nodding. "I have one."

He wagged a finger in front of her face. "You shouldn't talk about boinking. You don't even need to think about it."

"I'm fourteen, not a damn baby." She planted her hands on her hips. "Would you rather I used the word *fu*—"

"No!" Cole released me to slap a hand over her mouth. "Never."

She blinked up at him innocently.

"Just so you know, I'm all about the blondes now." He tweaked her nose and dropped his arm. "This blonde in particular."

Juliana made a face, said, "Whatever. You guys are gross" and flitted away, but not before looking back at me and sticking out her tongue.

"Real mature." Clearly the girl had a crush on Cole. Just as clearly, he had no idea her feelings veered in a romantic direction. "She makes me feel like I've showered with sunlight and rainbows."

"Don't worry. She'll grow on you."

"Like fungus?"

Grinning, he grabbed me in a headlock with one hand and rubbed his knuckles into the crown of my head with the other. "No. Not like fungus."

"Like mold?" I managed to say through my giggles.

He released me and as I straightened, framed my face, peering into my eyes, the intensity of his expression draining my mirth, making my insides tingle all over again. I'd missed him. Missed this. Us.

"Thank you, Ali."

I blinked, the new direction of the conversation lost. "For what?"

"For finding my friends. For bringing them here."

"They're my friends, too."

"I know, but you could have returned here and stayed safe, like part of me really wanted you to do. But you didn't. You put my needs before my wants, your needs before your wants, and even above your own life, and I will be forever grateful."

I rested my palms on the girth of his shoulders. Oh, the burdens these babies had always had to carry. But he wasn't alone, not any longer. "That's what love does. It gives."

His gaze dipped to my lips. "Well, I want to give *you* something." His voice was low, husky. "Reason fourteen. You are one smoking blonde. All this hair... I like it wrapped around my fists."

"Yeah?" I asked, breathless.

"Oh, yeah. I like to have you under my control." He fisted the strands, as he'd described, and angled my head the way he wanted it. "It's the only time you do what I tell you."

The sheer dominance of the action excited me. "I could say the same."

On the battlefield, we were as tough as armor. In a fight, we never backed down. But when we were in each other's arms, we could give and take and demand...beg...and it just made the moment sweeter.

Jaclyn moaned, capturing our attention, fragmenting the moment.

I moved to the bed, away from the temptation of Cole. Jaclyn hadn't yet woken. Her dreams must have been plaguing her.

"She needs fire," I said.

"That's what I was doing when you arrived."

His absence now made sense. "How did you find her?"

"I didn't. She came to us. She says two guys broke into her

home and drugged Justin. When she tried to stop them from leaving with him, she was thrown across the room. She pretended to be unconscious as Justin was carried to a van. She hot-wired a neighbor's car and followed."

"And?" I prompted.

"And she passed out before she could explain the rest."

Dang. "If she knows where Anima took Justin, we can go in and get him."

"And destroy Anima once and for all." He moved beside me, pinched a lock of my hair. "I got sidetracked when everyone but you came upstairs."

"That's when you decided to go total Animal Planet and track me, right?"

His lips quirked at the corners. "That's right. The hungry lion and the gimpy gazelle."

"Please. You're the one with the injury."

"Not anymore."

"You mean it's gone completely?" Excited, I pushed back the collar of his shirt. A bandage was taped to his chest; it was white, without a single speck of blood. I lifted it to peek at his wound—or rather, his baby scratch. The center was already closed, without the aid of stitches, the edges pink and irritated rather than raw and angry.

"I just… I can't… The fire works so quickly."

What if we'd gotten to Lucas, Trina and Cruz in time? Could they have been saved, their lives spared?

Oh, glory. I loved the answer as much as I hated it. Yes. They could have been saved.

Guilt…so much guilt. The dark companion to "what if."

It choked me, made me feel like the one who'd pulled the trigger, the one who'd ended them.

"We can't look back. We'll never get anywhere," Cole said, a catch in his voice. His mind must have traveled the same road as mine. "We can only move forward, learn from our mistakes."

Jaclyn moaned again, her eyes now rolling rapidly behind her lids. Sleeping Beauty was close to waking up.

I gave Cole a swift, hard kiss. "I want to talk to Jaclyn alone." Men had attacked her, so Cole might scare her.

He could have refused or fired off a thousand questions. Instead, he said, "All right" and gave me a swift, hard kiss in return. He left, shutting the door behind him—leaving me trembling.

Would he always affect me this strongly?

I sat at the edge of the bed and patted the top of Jaclyn's hand. Her skin was cold and clammy. "You're safe now. I'm not going to let anything happen to you."

Gasping, she jolted upright. Her good eye was wide and wild, and she couldn't quite catch her breath.

"You're safe now," I repeated. "You made it to Mr. Ankh's."

"Ankh's," she repeated, falling back on the bed. Her expression shuttered with agonizing pain. "Justin."

"Where is he, Jaclyn? Do you know where the men took him?"

"Justin," she said again, then rolled to her side and sobbed. "I couldn't save him. I tried, but I couldn't fight both intruders, so I waited for them to leave with Justin and tracked them. They're going to hurt him. Hurt him so bad. I need him safe. Ali, I need him safe."

"I know." I brushed the hair from her sweat-dampened

forehead. "I know. That's why you've got to calm down and think. Talk to me. Tell me the rest."

She latched on to my hand. "I stole my neighbor's car. Ours had been disabled. I found the van easily enough and trailed it to a warehouse about an hour away." She rattled off the address. "There was no one outside, but there were a lot of men inside, and they had a lot of weapons. I snuck through the building, but couldn't find Justin. I knew I needed help, so I drove to Cole's, saw the state of the house and drove to Ankh's." Her gaze beseeched me. "Who's out looking for Justin?"

Never one to lie, I said, "No one."

"What! Why—"

"You passed out," I said. "We didn't know where to start."

She croaked, "How long have I been here?"

Judging only by the time I'd been gone… "About six hours."

"No!" She threw her legs over the side of the bed. "The longer he's there, the greater chance they've…" Tears streaked down her cheeks and as she stood, her knees buckled. "I have to help him."

I caught her and let her use me as a crutch. I didn't lead her to the door, but circled back to the bed. "Listen to me. You're in no condition to travel. I will gather the other slayers, the ones who haven't been shot, stabbed or beaten, and we will go to the warehouse. We will find Justin. You have my word."

I never offered a promise lightly. I would do this or die trying.

"I'll go with you," she said, once again trying to stand.

I pushed her back down. Gently, but firmly. "You'd only get in our way, and you know it."

"No. I feel better by the second," she said.

Truth? Or exaggeration? Her color *was* better, and the swelling in her eye had already gone down.

"Alice."

The sweet voice came from the entryway, yet I hadn't heard the door open. I twisted, and my heart nearly jumped out of my mouth. Finally! My eight-year-old little sister, Emma—or rather, her spirit—had arrived. She stepped from an almost blinding ray of light, her straight-as-a-pen hair hanging in two dark ponytails. She wore a pink leotard, a pink tutu and pink ballet slippers. The outfit she'd died in.

I wanted to rush over and hug her more than I wanted to take my next breath, but she was a spirit, and just like with zombies, spirit could not tangle with flesh.

I winked at her instead.

The dark eyes she'd gotten from our mother beseeched me. "Alice," she said again. Almost a moan.

Something was wrong.

My grin fell.

"Ali?" Jaclyn asked. She couldn't see Emma. Only Cole and I could. I'd always thought it was because I was connected to my sister and Cole was connected to me.

"I'll be in the hall," Emma whispered and vanished.

A sense of urgency overcame me. "Stay here," I said to Jaclyn. "I mean it. I can take care of Justin, or I can take care of you. Your choice."

She sighed. "Justin."

"I'll keep you updated." I practically sprinted into the hall. Thankfully Emma was the only person in sight, and all the bedroom doors were closed.

"I'm so happy to see you." And I was. Even if she'd come bearing bad news.

Her hands twisted together as she said, "I heard what happened. Four of your friends were killed and—"

"Four?" I interjected and shook my head. "There were only three."

She peered down at her ballet slippers. "No. There were four."

"You're certain?" Of course she was. When had she ever been wrong? I closed my eyes and let the knowledge sink in. Another life lost. Another friend taken from us.

Only two slayers were still missing. Justin and Collins. So, which one was it?

The urge to fall on my knees and scream, "That's it! I've had enough! No more!" hit me, but I somehow found the strength to remain in place, quiet, another storm of tears on lockdown. There was too much to do. Starting with my promise to Jaclyn.

Compartmentalize.

"Anima is planning something else," Emma said. "Something big."

I'd figured, but confirmation managed to rip me apart. "Do you know what?"

She nibbled on her bottom lip, shook her head. "All I know is this—what happened last night was only the beginning."

PREY FOR ME

I told Cole what I'd learned from Jaclyn, and what I'd learned from Emma, and his reaction was similar to mine. Shock, anger…agony. It was hard, watching him suffer. Worse than dealing with my own riotous emotions.

He fisted a handful of his own hair, yanking at the strands as if he meant to pull them out, and stalked around my bedroom. His boots thumped against wood, then rug, then wood again. He stopped in front of the wall and, with an animalistic growl, punched a hole in the plaster.

He'd done that before, the day he'd broken up with me. His emotions had been too strong to contain.

"We can't lose another guy, Ali. We just can't."

I'd had the same thought, but in reality we'd deal with whatever we had to deal with. That was life.

"There's a good chance we'll see them again," I said, hoping to console him…and myself. "They're Witnesses now, just like Emma." Dead, but not gone.

He punched another hole in the wall, standing in the dust of the aftermath, panting.

"Cole," I said gently. "C'mere."

He stalked to the bed, plopped beside me. He was like the lion with the thorn in its paw, and I had to proceed carefully.

Bleak violet eyes lifted as he said, "Remind me that I'm alive."

Without hesitation, I climbed onto his lap, braced my knees at his sides and pressed my lips against his. "You're here. You're mine. And I'm yours."

He opened his mouth to let me in, and our tongues thrust together. It wasn't an easy kiss. Or a gentle one. But then, comfort didn't have to come that way. This wasn't even a slow build to something more. It was hard, and it was harsh. It was a conflagration.

He clung to me as if I was a lifeline.

Actually, no. That wasn't true. We clung to each other, reveling in the moment, the sensations…the pleasure. Losing sight of the world and its pain.

He twisted, taking me with him, and pushed me against the mattress; his muscled weight pinned me down, but he didn't give me another kiss. He lifted his head. His panting grew worse, his nostrils flaring with every deep inhalation. A thin sheen of sweat covered his brow. Tension branched from his eyes.

"Ali. I have a present for you."

I wanted to cry out in denial—I knew he wasn't talking about the present I really wanted. Him. I knew how his mind worked. He'd stopped the make-out session before it could reach a point of no return and had no intention of starting up again. But I didn't cry out. This wasn't about me, but us.

"Show me," I managed to say.

He leaned forward, slid his hands under the pillows and brushed against me. Wicked sensation sent me into a tailspin.

Maybe I'd cry out after all.

He straightened with a snap. Our gazes locked.

I remained silent. *Good Ali.* But I did lick my lips in wicked invitation. *Bad. Bad!*

He watched, tensing, and leaned down—only to straighten with a snap again. A growl rose from his chest. "You are too much of a temptation."

Clearly, I wasn't enough of one. *Whine, pout.*

"These are for you." He spit the words like weapons. Which was kind of funny, considering the fact that he was actually holding weapons. In each of his hands was a small ax. The dark metal gleamed in the light, and I could see words etched into the bellies.

I sat up, taking the weapons to study them more intently.

One read There Is No Place Darkness Can Hide When Light Shines.

Okay. That was seriously beautiful.

The other read Cole Belongs to Ali, Now and Always.

And that, well, was seriously *beyond* beautiful.

"Oh, Cole." I met his now-unsure gaze, and my heart absolutely melted.

"I had them made for you. They arrived a week ago, and I've been waiting for the right moment to give them to you."

"But...how...? Your house."

"They were in the backpack."

The million-pound backpack he'd refused to leave behind. Tears beaded in my eyes.

"Thank you," I whispered and clutched the weapons to my chest before setting them aside. I wrapped my arms around him and hugged him tight.

The hug led to another kiss—yes!—and I suspected the kiss would have led to something more if a knock hadn't sounded at my door. He wouldn't have been able to resist, not again…surely.

"Meeting. Ankh's office. Five minutes," Frosty called.

Sighing, Cole clasped my hands and helped me up. "It's probably for the best."

"Not *my* best," I grumbled.

He gave me a small smile.

As we trudged to the door, my cell phone beeped, signaling a text had just come in. I checked while I walked.

Nana: I'm safe.

Thank God!

Me: I'm sorry 4 what I did 2 U, but I'm happy UR safe. I luv U.

Nana: You are forgiven. I would have done the same thing to you—drugged you and sent you away—but you beat me to it. Kick some zombie butt, dear. For sheezie.

I laughed. Nana and her "hip teen-speak" always brightened my day.

Another text arrived on the heels of that one. By the way, I noticed your new tattoos. They are lovely. But I thought you were going to wait until I could go with you?

Uh-oh.

Sorry. My bad. An opportunity arose & I took it.

As distracted as I was, I almost collided with a wall. *Another A+ for me.*

Cole grabbed my shoulders and steered me in the right direction.

"Thanks."

"Anytime." His phone beeped. He checked the screen, brightened, then scowled. "My dad says he and your grandmother are safe. He also says he's going to run down some contacts he has and see if they know anything about Anima's future plans, and that I'm to remember that just because he isn't around doesn't mean I can ride the carnal carousel with my girlfriend."

I gasped. "He did not say that."

Cole showed me the text.

My cheeks heated.

We strode into Mr. Ankh's office, where everyone else was already situated. Mr. Ankh gave a speech about eating properly and resting. We needed to stay strong. Then, he said, we'd put a strategy together in the morning. He talked about making time for our home-studies program and always turning in our schoolwork. This war didn't mean our responsibilities ended.

Cole explained what Jaclyn had witnessed, leaving out the part about a fourth victim. I knew why. Distraction was the number one cause of death among slayers. Well, that and zombie toxin, Anima plots and not asking for help when it was needed. But that was beside the point.

After a little debate, we decided—in the nicest way possible—*screw Mr. Ankh's wait-for-tomorrow plan.* We'd raid the warehouse now. Time wasn't our friend, and it just might be Justin's...or Collins's...worst enemy.

Cole, Frosty, Bronx, Veronica and I loaded up with weapons. I packed my new, awesome axes! Ready, eager, we settled

in Mr. Ankh's SUV. (The one we'd stolen…I mean, *valeted*…
had already been wiped and moved.)

As Frosty gunned the engine, Jaclyn came rushing out of
the house.

I sighed.

"I'm coming," she said, claiming the only available seat in
back, glaring at me, all *try to stop me.*

Why do I bother?

Great. Now I sounded like Mr. Ankh.

Kat, Reeve and Juliana watched us speed from the driveway, each radiating a different emotion. Kat: concern. Reeve:
determination. Juliana, a slayer-in-training: anger.

They were staying behind to help Mr. Ankh with Mackenzie and Gavin. At least, that was the story they'd been fed.
Only Juliana had complained.

"I can help. I'm ready!" she'd shouted.

But how could *she* be ready when I was pretty sure *we*
weren't?

Frosty parked in an abandoned alley several blocks from
our target destination. We stepped into the daylight, barely
noticing the cold air blustering around us. We looked like six
normal teenagers, easily overlooked and forgotten. Hoods hid
our identities, and jackets covered our weapons.

"We're splitting up and hitting the warehouse from three
sides," Cole said, taking charge. That's what he did best. "Stay
in pairs. Jaclyn and Bronx, you take the north. Frosty and
Veronica, you take south. Ali and I will take the west."

Everyone nodded and branched off.

Cole and I rounded the alleyway corner, entering the flow

of pedestrian traffic. He twined his fingers with mine and
kept a laid-back pace to avoid unwanted notice. The warehouse was in the middle of industrial workplaces, clothing
shops, restaurants and apartments. Some of the buildings were
old and crumbling, and some were brand-new, the chrome
sparkling in the sunlight.

Why would Anima have a warehouse in such a public place?

What would happen when we got inside it?

Best-case scenario: revenge.

Worst: we'd lose more slayers.

Not on my watch. "I'm bringing my A game tonight," I
announced. I thought about the "gift" the woman had given
me. What was it? Something…nothing? Right now, I could
use any possible advantage.

"You aren't the only one."

"Yeah?"

"Oh, yeah."

I smiled. "The thought of Anima's destruction is my new
happy place."

"Not my bed? I've been usurped?"

Was that a pout I heard in his voice? "You aren't interested
in going all the way. So yes, you've been usurped."

"Ali Bell." His free hand fluttered over his heart. "Are you
pressuring me to have sex with you?"

"Yes!"

He tsked. "And here I thought you were having fun with
me anyway. I guess we'll have to practice more often."

Oh, sweet glory. He better not be kidding! I was about to
reply—was "we will start tonight" too demanding?—when he
swung me to the side and pinned me to the side of a building.

Suddenly tense, I whispered, "What's wrong?"

"I see the warehouse, and I need a moment to study it without letting anyone know that's what I'm doing." He leaned down and nuzzled my cheek, the angle of his head allowing his gaze to focus on the warehouse.

The tension left me…and with its absence, I couldn't stop my riotous reaction to the boy in front of me. I began to tingle, burn. *Ignore! Focus!*

"I don't see any cameras," he said, "or any shadows over the windows to indicate movement inside." He paused. How could he act so calm? "There's a For Lease sign in the window."

"Maybe they used the building for the attacks, but it's not really theirs?"

"There's only one way to find out." He straightened, drawing me to the west side of the building.

We came to a garage door secured by a big metal lock. A careful study proved no one on the street was looking our way. I dug through the purse draped over my torso, grabbing a small bolt cutter to snap the lock in two. The metal fell, clanking on the dirty concrete.

"Nice," Cole said.

"B and E is just one of my many new skills. Thank Frosty."

I exchanged the cutter for the axes and nodded to let Cole know I was ready. He gripped his minicrossbow in one hand and lifted the door with the other; cogs rolled and squeaked, announcing our presence. My heart pounded against my ribs in a fast, unsteady rhythm. But as light from the outside spilled into the building, illuminating a small, dusty entryway, no one demanded to know what we were doing. There was only an eerie, terrible silence.

I stepped deeper inside, the smell of old pennies making me cringe.

Blood.

"There's no one here." Cole reached out and flipped a switch on the wall. Light flooded the entire building, highlighting… nothing. There was no equipment. No car. No people. No… anything. Not even blood. The only thing out of place was the thick pile of sand on the floor.

It was disappointing. And creepy.

"I don't understand," I said.

Frosty dropped in from a window, a dagger in hand, and Veronica came in behind him, clutching two short swords. Bronx and Jaclyn bolted through the front door. He had a police baton, and she had a SIG Sauer.

"No," Jaclyn said, violently shaking her head. She spun, taking everything in. "This isn't right. They couldn't have cleared out so quickly. There were cars and shelves and boxes."

"Maybe you misremembered the address," Frosty suggested.

"No!" She stomped her foot, and the floor made a strange clank. "No."

"You were out of it," Veronica reminded her. "Maybe—"

"No, I—"

"Be quiet," I demanded, marching forward. I stopped in front of Jaclyn and gently pushed her out of the way. Once, twice, I stomped my foot and heard the same *clank, clank*. Even felt a slight vibration.

It was a hatch. Had to be.

I dropped to my knees, frantically brushing the sand from the ground, searching for a handle.

"What'cha doing?" Frosty asked, crouching beside me—to watch.

"Cole," I said. *A little help, please.*

"Uh, I happen to know you're not doing him," Frosty replied.

Cole settled beside me and dusted wide sweeps with the long length of his arms. "Go wider."

I did. The others joined me. More and more sand flung out of the way…and then I saw it. A small, finger-sized hole. A mix of excitement, dread and hope filled me.

Everyone gathered around.

"Reason fifteen. Intrepid," Cole said, and I grinned at him. "Open it and step back."

Five different weapons were suddenly trained on me. Well, trained on the door. I just happened to be in the line of fire.

What were we going to find? For the second time this week, I felt like Alice in Wonderland, about to fall down a pit, a new adventure forced upon me. I gulped. My hand shook as I hooked a finger in the hole and tried to lift. Nearly pulled a muscle, but the door remained firmly in place.

"Slide it," Bronx suggested, his tone strained, as if he was fighting a laugh.

I glared at him. Then I pushed, and sure enough, the lid slid out of the way. I performed a backward somersault, but nothing jumped out and tried to snag me.

"I see stairs," Bronx said.

The scent of old pennies grew stronger. A lot stronger. And I heard several distinct sounds. The rattle of chains. The shuffle of feet. Moans of unending hunger.

I shared a wide-eyed look with Cole. Zombies.

He raised the crossbow, the faint scent of string wax blending with the rising stink of rot. Taking the lead, he eased down the stairs. I claimed the spot behind him, the others staying close to me. Small lamps hung from the wall, but they were few and far between; they weren't very bright anyway, so our path never had anything more than a dim illumination.

Then Cole stopped abruptly. Tension radiated from him.

I peered around his shoulder and found—

Collins.

I cut off a sorrowful cry. No one needed to hear me lose control. Collins had always kept his hair shaved, and I could see a large gash on his crown. His back was propped against the wall, his eyes open but blank. Blood streaked his face and chest—a chest that wasn't rising, wasn't falling; it was still, so very still. Bones stuck out in his arms and legs, and I wondered if he'd been tossed down the hull alive and suffering, abandoned and forgotten.

I couldn't stop my next cry in time.

A chorus of "What's wrong?" erupted behind us.

I shouldered my way past Cole and crouched in front of Collins. I patted his face. He didn't blink, didn't flinch. Desperate, I slapped him.

"No," someone croaked. "No!"

"Not Collins, too."

"I can't…can't deal…"

"Tell me he's all right!"

I pressed my forehead against Collins's and blindly felt for a pulse in his neck. A minute passed as I waited, hoping, praying; it was the longest minute of my life. Of all our lives. But…no. I never felt a beat.

"He's...he's dead." There. I'd said it. Made it real. Stinging tears brimmed in my eyes. "But maybe all he needs is a little fire to get him going." We didn't know everything the fire could do. "Let's put our hands on him."

"Ali," Cole croaked.

I looked up. The anguish in his eyes...the regret...the hate, a mirror of mine. "We have to try."

And we did. Each of us. All at the same time. But again, there was no change.

I punched his chest, once, twice, my every emotion worsening, wild. Cole pinned my arms to my sides.

"Enough, love."

But...but...this wasn't fair, wasn't right. "We can't—"

The rattling of chains cranked up the volume; the moans of hunger became more frenzied.

"We have to deal with the zombies," he said.

I laughed bitterly. Had Anima made a list of all the ways to torture us before ending us? *Kill their friends one by one. Pit them against zombies while they're mourning.*

What would they do next?

No. Here was a better question: What would *I* do next? I was still in this game, still a force to be reckoned with—still capable of doing damage to their forces. I straightened, palmed my axes.

Cole pounded down the remaining steps, a .44 in one hand, a dagger in the other. The rest of us weren't far behind, our determination a palpable force. Today, it wasn't kill or be killed. It was simply KILL.

We hit the bottom and turned the corner. And there they were, an extension of the greater enemy. I took stock. At least a hundred sets of bloodred eyes watched us. Each zombie had sagging, paper-thin skin that was grayer than I was used to seeing. Not a single creature had a full set of hair, and very few had more than a handful of strands. They were older, then. Stronger.

Time to catch a few butterflies.

I braced my feet on the floor and prepared to separate the two halves of myself—to go total mad hatter. The zombies darted toward us...only to stop several feet away, as if they'd hit an invisible wall.

My mind whirled with questions as I searched the room. Why would... Ah. That was why. While slayers used chemicals that caused inanimate objects to become solid in the spirit realm—Blood Lines—to prevent the zombies from being able to enter homes or cross into specific areas, Anima used electric pulses. A poor imitation, but an imitation nonetheless. There was a stand on each side of the room, both with small red dots glowing in the center.

We had a moment to breathe and decide the best course of action.

"I don't care about the pulses," Bronx snarled. "I'm going to kill each and every zombie."

"We don't have time for you to go on a rampage," Jaclyn said. "Justin is out there. He needs our help."

"We can't leave the zombies here." Cole rolled his shoulders. He was pure aggression, ready to be unleashed. "You know that."

We all did. Anima would only use them against us later. "The pulses could weaken, and the zombies could escape, kill innocents, create even more creatures for us to fight."

While the Z's preferred slayers—we were tastier, I guess—they wouldn't refuse an average citizen, especially if they were starving. And these zombies were definitely starving. "We could pour a Blood Line in front of the door, but someone could come along and wipe it away."

"This is happening." Frosty stared at the zombies and licked his lips, as if he could already taste their second deaths.

"Don't be foolish. There isn't enough room to do what we need to do to win," Veronica said.

"We can even the odds." Cole released the safety on his gun.

Zombies clawed and kicked at the invisible wall. It must have shocked them, because the first line fell back...only to have the second line march over them and do the same. The pattern repeated again and again, but one thing stayed the same. Black saliva oozed out of their mouths. They'd scented a meal and wouldn't rest until they'd gotten one.

Boom, boom, boom. Cole fired into the crowd of Z's, and one by one they dropped. "Enough talking. More doing."

We shot and injured as many as possible, until we ran out of bullets. But there were still too many red eyes trained on us.

Jaclyn shook her head, dark memories dancing behind her eyes. "I can't... The pain..."

I wasn't sure what Anima had done to her all those months she'd been locked up, but after what they'd done to me, I knew it had been horrifying. Since our escape, she had barricaded herself inside her house, afraid of the world.

"You don't have to fight," I told her. "You can go up and wait."

She was too far gone for my words to penetrate.

I looked to Frosty. "She can't stay here. Will you carry her out? Maybe pour a Blood Line in front of the door?" That way, zombies wouldn't be able to leave the room and get to her. But then, we wouldn't be able to leave in spirit form, either.

"Done and done." He jumped into action.

The moment he returned, I said, "I'll light up. You guys concentrate on throwing the zombies at me." We could shoot, stab and even decapitate the creatures, slowing them down, but none of that would lead to death. As our hail of gunfire had just proved. We had to ash them.

Cole met my gaze. "I won't be far from you."

"I know."

"If your fire dies out..."

Which had happened. Multiple times. "Don't worry. I still know how to fight."

"Of course you do. I taught you."

Arrogant sexy beast.

"Let's do this." Frosty stepped out of his body.

The others did the same. A miracle made flesh—or spirit. One version of my friends shimmered; the other remained frozen, no longer capable of movement.

I rose to my tiptoes and kissed Cole. "I love you, and you had better come out of this alive."

"I will. We *all* will."

Trusting him, I kicked over one of the stands.

WAR AND PIECES

Zombies surged forward en masse, a gruesome, fearsome sight.

The real me emerged, leaving flesh and blood behind, a shell the zombies would ignore. They cared nothing for literal brains and meat. They wanted the good stuff. The essence of me. The source of my every breath. My spirit.

Well, they wouldn't get it.

The spirit wore and carried whatever the body wore and carried, so I remained loaded down with weapons. I disregarded the colder air, the chilling sounds—now louder—the brighter lights, the ranker smells, and hacked through a zombie's chest.

Turned. Slashed through a Z-head. Turned. Swiped a Z-throat. Turned. My blade cut through a Z's mouth. Black goo oozed and splattered over my hands, burning. I disregarded the pain, too. I had to remain in a constant state of motion as the creatures surrounded me and closed in—or else.

I swung the axes and arced back to avoid snapping teeth,

then circled back around to nail the culprit in the throat. He fell to the floor, minus his head. Hands reached for me—I removed them. More teeth snapped at me—I knocked jaws together, grinding already decaying enamel into powder. Then I finished one creature's fight with metal through the brain.

I cursed my inability to properly multitask. I needed to light up. Now, now, now. My light was our only hope for victory. But one thing became clear. I wasn't going to get a moment of peace.

Work with what you've got.

Light up, I commanded, even as I swung at another zombie. *Light—*

One of the creatures tangled his fingers in my hair and yanked. There was a sharp sting in my scalp, but I ignored it just like everything else and went low, twisting and raking one of my blades across his middle. Rotted guts spilled on the floor, making it slippery.

Steady.

Because the crowd of zombies had separated us, Cole had to work his way back to my side. His features were strained, and I suspected his injury, though healed on the outside, was sensitive and tender inside. But still he motored on, protecting me here and now, protecting others later.

Frosty worked his way beside Cole, the two forming a wall of muscle in front of me. Then Bronx was there, another wall. Then Veronica. Suddenly I was surrounded. These slayers, my friends, were giving me that moment of peace.

I stilled, closed my eyes. Breathed deeply. Told myself I could do this, building my faith.

I straightened my fingers, curled them. *I can…light up…now!*

But there was nothing. No heat.

Come on. Light up!

Again, nothing.

Worry tried to sneak in and break me down. This might be the one time the ability failed me. The rest of my friends would die and it would be my fault.

Shut up, Downer Ali!

I held fast to my faith, knowing I had to believe I could do this, despite my feelings, despite the circumstances, despite what seemed to be happening—or *not* happening—before I could actually do it. Because that's how faith worked. If everything came easily, I would never be tested or exercised, would never grow stronger.

Like working out at a gym. At first, my puny limbs had been able to lift only the baby weights. The more I'd trained, the stronger I'd gotten. The longer I held on now, the hotter and brighter my fire would be when it finally arrived.

And it *would* arrive.

"You can do it," Cole urged.

My eyelids flipped open as he broke a zombie's neck.

"You've got this, Als." Frosty swiped his sword across a zombie's middle.

Yes. Yes, I thought, reminded that words were a weapon right now. Whatever a slayer said while in this form, this realm, he received.

Well…as long as he believed it.

Thank God the others believed what they were saying; a lance of strength shot through me.

I closed my eyes, concentrated. *Light up.*

"You can do it," Veronica repeated.

"This?" Bronx said. "This is nothing for Ali Bell."

Their faith hooked with mine, undergirding me, shielding me from any more worry. *You will light up, Ali Bell!* Right... now!

At the ends of my fingers, flames flickered to life, quickly spreading to my wrists, elbows and shoulders.

Time for a good old-fashioned butt kicking.

I basked in the heat now stroking higher...lower...everywhere, and focused on the battle.

But...how... In just a few seconds, everything had changed. A zombie had Veronica pinned on the floor, and he was chomping on her neck. Bronx was trying to pull the creature off her, but the thing was like a dog with a bone, its teeth sinking in deeper as it shook its head. Finally, though, Bronx succeeded... but three others quickly took its place. He fought, but four others jumped on his back, tossing him to the floor in a tangle of limbs.

I rushed over and touched the creatures with my fingertips. Instant ash. But the small victory wasn't as sweet as it should have been. Veronica and Bronx were out for the count, already overcome by toxin and writhing in pain.

I touched them, too, and both screamed. It hurt worse to burn out evil than it did to heal a wound, but it had to be done.

Frosty rushed to their sides, intent on helping, but a horde of zombies seemed to come out of nowhere and he collided with them midway, ricocheting backward. Another pair tackled him while he was off balance and pinioned him to the ground, where the entire group gnawed all over him.

Again I rushed over and swiped my fingertips over the creatures. Again they ashed, and again I saw one of my friends writhing on the floor.

I touched him, and like Veronica and Bronx, he screamed. Only, he cursed me, too.

He would thank me later.

"There," Bronx groaned, pointing to a group of zombies that were dog-piled in the corner.

I sprinted over. Swipe, swipe. Ash, ash. Swipe, swipe. Ash, ash. Jaclyn! She'd come back to help us, only to be overcome. Now, she wasn't moving. As I pressed my palm against her chest, a growl sounded behind me. I whipped around. A female zombie lunged at me, ready for dinner. I punched her, and she ashed.

Where was Cole? I combed the room… There! On the other side. He had no bites and remained steady on his feet, good, good, but his motions were slow, sluggish.

A zombie clawed at his cheek. I raced over, determined to help. Or tried to race over. Other zombies moved into my path.

A second creature snuck up behind him.

"Cole," I shouted.

A mistake.

He looked my way, what was happening behind him forgotten.

I wasn't going to reach him in time. The zombie was able to grab hold of his arm, lower its head and bare its teeth, ready to feast on his spirit.

"No!" I stretched out my arms, willing to take the bite for him. But, dang it, I still wasn't close enough to do it.

Then the distance ceased to matter. A bolt of electrified

power shot out of me, the air actually crackling with tiny zings of lightning.

Every zombie in the room catapulted into the air…and they stayed there.

What the heck had just happened? How? I tripped over my own feet and fell to my knees. Panting, shocked, I jumped up and spun. Slayers were on the floor, and zombies were still floating above us.

Impossible.

Reeling, I finished the journey to Cole and gripped his arm. My fire seeped past his clothing, past his skin, and did its healing thing inside him. He hissed in a breath, collapsing, crashing hard, but didn't stay down long. He leaped up. Sweat trickled down his temples as he looked at the zombies, then me, then at the zombies again, probably trying to make sense of what he was seeing.

Good luck. I hadn't yet managed it.

"Heal any slayers in need of fire." I wasn't sure how much longer the Z's would remain suspended in the air. "And I'll kill these suckers." But…how? I couldn't reach them.

As he hurried over to our friends, zombies kicked at him, but couldn't make contact. They were too high up. He clasped Jaclyn's hand with his fiery one and helped her to her feet. She hissed, as he had done, but remained upright.

I breathed a sigh of relief. She would be all right.

Then, knowing Cole would be taking care of the others, too, I focused on my opponents. I stretched out my still-glowing hands toward the one closest to me…and gaped as the others twirled.

I rubbed at my eyes…and the entire nest of zombies crashed

into the floor, slamming into slayers, knocking them down, and curses erupted throughout the room. I threw my arms into the air, and back up the zombies went.

Seriously! What had…how did…

Zombies shadowed the movements of my hands? As if the bolt of power I'd felt leave me had created some kind of link between us?

Testing my theory, I rotated my wrists. Zombies spun, mimicking the motion. I rotated my wrists in the opposite direction. Again, zombies spun.

There *was* a link.

Could this be another ability? Maybe. Probably. Who was I kidding? Definitely. I'd never heard of anything like it, but that hardly mattered.

I made a mental note to check the journal I had at home. Written in some sort of spiritual code by one of my ancestors, a slayer. Through an ability of his own, he'd known secrets about our kind, our talents.

Beads of fatigue collected in my shoulders, snapping together, growing bigger and stronger, before rolling all the way to my fingertips; suddenly my arms felt as if they weighed a hundred pounds each. My hands began to sink down… down… The zombies inched toward the floor.

"Not yet," Cole shouted, helping Veronica to her feet.

I gritted my teeth, focusing on one zombie in particular. I crooked my finger at him. If I truly controlled these creatures, I could end their torment—and my own. He flailed and fought…but actually inched closer to me. Excited, I jumped up and touched him.

He burst into ash—white ash, like snow, and good glory, it was beautiful, glistening as it descended.

Why such a significant change?

Did it really matter? *I'm Super Ali.*

I grinned and skipped to one creature after another, touching, ashing, touching, ashing, utterly enjoying my job.

Finally, there were no zombies left.

Can't pout.

The fire in my hands died, and my tired arms dropped to my sides.

"You have to be careful with this particular skill."

The voice jolted me. It shouldn't be here, in this room. Baffled, I spun and came face-to-face with the mysterious blonde.

"You," I gasped out. "How'd you get here? Did you follow us?"

"Ali," Cole said, his voice dripping with confusion. "You want to tell me who it is you're talking to?"

"Her." I pointed. "Sami."

"Ali," he said, gently now. "There's no one there."

Wait. He couldn't see her? But...she was right there. I knew she was there.

I reminded myself that he hadn't seen Zombie Ali anytime she'd separated from me, either. But this wasn't Zombie Ali, a spirit capable of shielding her presence.

Was this woman a spirit, though? A Witness, like Emma? That would certainly explain why Mr. Ankh's security cameras hadn't recorded her presence.

But Cole could see Emma. Why not this woman?

"I gave you my ability to push out streams of power," she said.

Gave it? Racked my brain, came up empty. "I don't understand."

"You have visions with the boy, Cole. You can light up from the top of your head to the soles of your feet. One bite of your spirit, and the zombies sicken."

True. True. And true. "And?"

"*And* a spirit doesn't lose his or her supernatural abilities through death—they spring from the spirit, after all. But those abilities can be passed. Meaning, you can give your abilities to someone else, and other slayers can give you theirs, but what you give, you can no longer use."

So…she'd given me her ability, knowing she would no longer be able to use it herself. Why?

"Or abilities can be stolen. But that's a lesson for another day." Her eyebrows drew together. "Anima knows all of this. Why don't you?"

Good question. "How did you do it, Sami? Pass it to me, I mean. *Why* did you do it?"

She squared her shoulders, as if expecting a blow. "My name isn't Sami. I'm…" Her light blue gaze flicked to Cole. "Helen."

"Helen," I repeated and heard several gasps of horror.

She gulped. "What they'll tell you about me——"

"Don't worry about them. Concentrate on me. Who's Sami?" I asked.

A hard hand gripped my shoulder, and before I knew what was happening, I was being dragged across the room. The moment the two parts of me connected, they snapped back together; I sucked in a breath, looked for the woman—Helen—but she was gone.

Who was she? Why was she helping me?

And she was. Helping me. Clearly. I had no doubts about that now.

Slayers lined up in front of me, demanding my full attention. Cut and bleeding, they stared at me with differing degrees of rage.

"What?" I demanded.

"Do not talk to that woman again." Cole leaned down, putting us nose to nose. "I don't know how you're seeing a dead woman you've got no connection to and I'm not, but if she visits you again, walk away. Don't listen to her. Don't even look at her."

Wait. "So you know her?" I asked, baffled by the intensity of his aggression.

"*Of* her," he barked. "Now, this subject is closed."

Wow. I'd never seen him like this. Not with me. "Why?"

"Closed," he repeated.

Fine. For now. But the moment I had him alone...

Frosty scrubbed a hand down his face. "The last time Ali exhibited a strange ability, she almost killed us all."

Thanks for the reminder. Jerk. I blew him a sugary kiss.

"She saved us today," Jaclyn announced. "So why don't you leave her the hell alone."

I offered her a small, grateful smile.

Frosty held up his hands, palms out. "I wasn't complaining. Just stating a fact."

Sure. "Was anyone bitten and not touched with fire?" For years, slayers had been forced to rely on an antidote to combat Z-toxin. But the antidote had one major flaw: with continuous use, it eventually stopped working, which meant, we had to stop fighting. For-freaking-ever.

For me, it had stopped working.

The fire had saved me from more than death.

My question received a denial from each slayer.

Cole snapped, "All right. Let's get out of here." He was still like a live wire. "Anima could come back, and we're in no shape to fight. We should—"

"Wait! What about Justin?" Jaclyn interjected.

"He's not here," Bronx said, his voice achingly gentle. "They must have moved him."

"No." She shook, shook, shook her head, hair slapping at her cheeks. "He has to be here. I saw him."

I moved in front of her, holding her gaze. "Remember what I told you. We're going to find him. We're not going to stop until he's with us." One way or another. "But we need time to recover, or we'll be no good to him."

Tears spilled from her eyes, but she nodded.

We left the warehouse and, sadly, left Collins behind. There was no way we could carry him out of the building without drawing unwanted attention. However, we planned to drive the SUV inside the warehouse and load him up. Give him a proper burial.

I know, I know. It wasn't ideal. His family deserved closure.

Thing was, they'd have to get it another way. We couldn't call the cops. Maybe they would believe we had inadvertently found him; maybe they wouldn't. With our fingerprints all over the place, we couldn't take the chance.

When we reached the back alley, Bronx cursed. Frosty kicked over a trash can. Litter went flying in every direction.

Mr. Ankh's SUV was gone. Stolen...or moved by a free-lance valet.

Karma sucked.

Frosty gave the trash can another vicious kick. "When I catch the filthy piece of sh—"

"We have bigger worries," Veronica said, motioning to the sky. The sun was going down in a hurry, the horizon a kaleidoscope of ever-darkening colors.

Would zombies walk the streets tonight?

If we weren't up for a fight with Anima, we definitely weren't up for another fight with zombies. Not even if I used my cool new ability to push power. Which I'd gotten from the mysterious, and obviously hated, Helen. I wasn't sure I had the strength to use it. Wasn't even sure how I'd used it in the first place.

I searched for a rabbit cloud...relaxed when I spied only shapeless puffs of white.

"I'll call Ankh," Cole said. "He'll send a van for us. Until then, we'll walk around like good little tourists, so that we're not perfect targets. Then we'll pick up Collins."

Sobering reminder.

Hello, crickets.

At least they covered the sound of my breaking heart.

"All right, then." He twined his fingers with mine. "Let's go."

Our group started down the street, everyone lost in their own thoughts...their misery over Collins's loss. There were more cars out now than when we'd first arrived, and even more people, but at least we blended in even better with the evening crowd.

Desperate for a moment of happiness, I wished Cole and I were simply out on a date. A normal date—our first.

As long as we'd been a couple, we'd never gone to dinner together.

So, I went with it. All of our friends were alive. We were happy. He was just a boy, and I was just a girl. He liked me, and I liked him, and the only thing we had to worry about was how far we'd go when we reached my door.

Answer: as far as he'd allow!

Hey. This was my fantasy. We'd go *further*.

Cole brought my hand to his mouth and kissed my knuckles, bringing me back to the present...the pain. I'd never be able to wish Lucas, Trina, Cruz and Collins back to life.

"I'm sorry I snapped at you. I was thrown off guard."

I'd be the biggest tool ever if I made him beg for my forgiveness after Nana and Kat had so freely given me theirs. "You can make it up to me with a victory massage. But who is—"

Anguished violet eyes brushed over me, before skittering away. "Don't say her name. Please."

"I won't." But now my curiosity was a living thing.

"I don't even know if the woman you saw is the one I'm thinking about. There are thousands of people with the same name. But if she is, you can't trust her. You just can't. She's evil in every way. The worst of the worst. A liar and a betrayer."

O-kay. Did that mean she'd once been a slayer?

Had Cole worked with her?

Probably not. He'd said he knew "of" her, nothing more.

"Whatever happened back there," he said, "we'll figure it out. We always do."

Why wasn't his hope contagious? "What if it's something

bad?" I couldn't hide the tremor in my voice. "Like when my zombie twin was living inside me."

His grip tightened. "Are you asking me if I'll break up with you?"

"Yes." He had before. And a girl never forgot that kind of despair.

"I deserve that," he muttered. "The answer is no. Never again. Not for any reason. You're my girl, Ali. That's never going to change. There's no one else I've ever wanted more— no one else I ever will. You're it for me, and if it takes the rest of my life, I'm going to prove it to you."

The fierceness he projected…

I believed him. I also melted against him. "I'm looking forward to that."

"You should. I have plans."

Goose bumps broke out over my skin. "Plans, huh?"

"Oh, yeah. Get ready to learn about reasons sixteen through nineteen."

Before I could respond—*tell me now!*—Frosty strode up to Cole's side, keeping pace. "Hate to break up the foreplay party, but I think we've got a tail."

Stiffening, Cole said, "How many?"

"Only four. Three guys, one girl."

Anima?

"We'll split up." Cole expelled a breath, mist dancing in front of his face. "Divide their efforts and make it harder for them to track us."

Another chase. Great!

"Where do you want to meet?" Frosty asked.

Cole thought for a moment. "Ankh's. They already know we're staying there, and if they make it that far, his cameras will snap pictures of their faces and we can start IDing these people."

I'd opened my mouth to protest, only to press it closed. He was right. We needed IDs. "I like the way your brain works," I said. It was as sexy as the rest of him.

"Me, too. Consider it done. See you two on the flip side." Frosty fell back to take Veronica's hand. "You're with me, Ron. And guess what? Team Fronica is about to…"

I didn't hear the rest. They were already motoring down the road.

Cole nodded to Bronx, who took Jaclyn's hand. They, too, moved away from us.

My adrenaline spiked, and surprisingly enough, it was all systems go. These people could be the ones who had killed my friends. If they wanted to chase me, fine. Have at it. But it would not end well—for them.

"You ready for this?" Cole asked.

"I am, but I can promise you *they* are not."

IT'S YOU, NOT ME

As nonchalantly as possible, Cole ushered me into one of the stores. A bell jingled. Hello, racks of clothing. Hello, line of mannequins. We picked up the pace, darting past the counter.

As a salesgirl shouted, "Hey!" we snaked an employee-only corner. A small narrow hallway provided three doorways. We opted for the one on the right, the break room, heading for the door in back. The word *EXIT* glowed overhead.

Two employees sat at the table. One jumped to his feet and frowned.

"Customers can't be back here."

"Good thing we're not customers," I said as we breezed by.

We shouldered our way outside, the door slamming behind us. As we ran down a darkened alley, the door slammed a second time. We were being followed. Good. I glanced over my shoulder, cataloging our opponents. A male, our age, a knife hilt sticking out the waist of his leather pants. A female, slightly older, with her weapon already in hand. Both were dressed in black.

Anima must have sent them to make it look like gang members had finished the job.

Anger ignited. Another alley loomed ahead. We took a corner at top speed, always staying in the shadows of the buildings. My heart beat against my ribs, a war drum I wasn't going to deny. *Kill…kill…kill…*

"Maybe I can stop them," I said. I might have had reservations about my new ability, but I wanted our pursuers at my mercy, mine to do with as I pleased. However necessary.

You have to be careful with this particular skill, Helen had said.

Why? Right now I couldn't see a downside.

"Like you did with zombies?" Cole said. "Maybe, maybe not. You didn't lift any slayers, so I'm not sure you'd be able to lift an actual person now. Besides, we're too public."

Well, crap. He just had to go and be the voice of reason, didn't he?

I could guess how civilians would react to people being tossed into the air by nothing but, well, air. They would panic, and chaos would ensue. Worse, Anima would learn what I could do, and we'd lose a major advantage.

I filed the new ability in the back of my mind under the heading: *Favorite toy.* Subtitle: *Zombies go boom, boom. Humans? Not sure.*

With a flick of his wrist, Cole lifted the lid of a Dumpster, and for a second, I thought he actually expected me to climb inside. But he jerked me around another corner and finally stopped, pressing me against the wall, acting as my shield. As always. I heard the Dumpster's lid fall back into place and realized what he was planning.

Here's hoping it worked.

As his warm breath fanned over my face, I reached in my purse and withdrew the Judge, a small revolver that used the same ammo as rifles. This thing could do serious damage.

I was in a mood to do damage.

Footsteps echoed…slowing the closer they got to the Dumpster.

Cole and I shared a look rife with anticipation. He tensed, waiting.

Then the footsteps ceased altogether. The pair responsible hadn't reached us, so they must have paused at the receptacle, thinking we were dumb enough to hide inside. The moment we heard the hinges on the lid creak, Cole whipped around the corner and aimed his .44.

"Drop your weapons," he commanded.

Dark curses rang out. There was a rustle of clothing, a thud.

"I know who you are." The female. "You won't kill me."

"Try me," Cole said.

"You can't shoot us both," she taunted. "You can kill one, but by the time you're ready to aim at the other, you'll be dead and I'll get to hunt down your friend. She's a civilian, isn't she? Oh, the things I'll do to her. Maybe I'll even go after your girlfriend when I'm done. I hear she's a hulking he-beast…. I've always wanted to slay one of those."

Time for bad cop/worse cop. I stepped around the corner with my own weapon aimed and ready. "I've never been described that way, but I approve. Oh, and if you make a move on him, *you'll* get slain."

Cole had managed to get the guy on his knees, the butt of a gun pressed against his skull. The girl stood at Cole's side, her gun aimed at his chest.

She scowled at me. One heartbeat passed. Two. Three. The tension between us thickened.

"*You're* the he-beast?" she asked.

"The one and only."

She grappled for a response, finally settling on "Well, you won't squeeze that trigger."

My smile was ice and menace. "Try me," I said, mimicking Cole. "Please. All I need is an excuse."

Another heartbeat passed. Ultimately, she dropped her weapon and kicked it toward me. Smart.

"On your knees," I demanded. "Put your hands behind your head."

"Watch one too many cop dramas?" she mocked.

"Now!"

Though she hesitated, she obeyed.

Would it be wrong to pat myself on the back?

I studied our pursuers more intently. The girl had a short crop of bleached hair. There were two silver hoops in her eyebrows and a stud in her upper lip. The collar of her black leather jacket gaped open, revealing a shirt that plunged to her navel in a deep vee. Every bit of visible skin had been marked by black and white tattoos.

The boy was short and stocky, with a shadow beard that gave him a kind of wolfish look. He had so many muscles he could probably lift a Mack truck over his head without breaking a sweat.

"Trust me, kiddies," Stocky said, his grin as cold as mine. "You don't want to do this."

"Wrong," I replied. "I love doing this. It's fun."

"You're playing with fire, and you have no idea." Tattoos

raked her golden gaze over me. "But how could a delicate little thing like you know?" she said, sneering. "You think you want to walk on the dark side, but one step over and you'd crumble."

Okay, I admit it. My cheeks heated. In our world, "delicate little thing" was the equivalent to a slap in the face.

"But you," she continued, looking Cole over. "You're a big slice of sexy, aren't you?"

I pressed my tongue to the roof of my mouth. It didn't matter where we were, or what we were doing, Cole always garnered female appreciation. He was honey, and women were flies.

I guess that made me the flyswatter.

"I'd stop if I were you." I smiled a little too sweetly, my grip on the gun never wavering. "My trigger finger is developing a twitch."

Cole cocked the hammer on his and pressed the barrel more firmly against Stocky's head. "Enough. Tell us who you are."

I loved watching him in action. He was fearless. Steady. A rock that wouldn't be moved. "Admit you're with Anima."

Stocky spit on the ground. "Hell, no, we aren't with Anima. We heard about what they did to your crew and how they're trying to blame us for their work."

Plausible.

"Who are you?" I asked.

His chest puffed up. "River's best."

Maybe. But that didn't make him an ally. Cole never lowered his weapon.

On a roll, Stocky said, "Anima's pitting us against each other, probably hoping we'll destroy each other and save them the hassle."

"If I don't like your next few answers," I said, "they'll get

their wish. Why were you following us? And what about the
other two? If our friends are hurt…"

"Our orders weren't to hurt," Tattoos retorted. "Just to de-
tain. Lookit, we saw the news. We know we're being blamed
for the death of some of your people. We thought you were
here to seek revenge, but I'm guessing that's not the case because you haven't blown our faces off. You know Anima's at
fault, right?"

Cole finally removed his finger from the trigger and sheathed
the gun at the waist of his pants. Here's the amazing thing. He
was still just as menacing.

I wasn't quite so trusting, though, and while I put the gun
back in my purse, I also palmed a dagger.

"Did you see Anima in action the night my friends were
killed?" Cole helped Stocky to his feet. "They still have one
of our boys."

"We didn't see anything." Tattoos stood on her own. "But
River did."

"Well, then, I want to talk to River." If the edge in Cole's
tone hadn't scared her, the determination in his eyes should
have done the trick.

"He wants to speak with you, too. Maybe even join forces.
You do good work." Her predatory gaze gave him another
once-over, and she licked her lips. "Real good work."

I stepped toward her, ready to charge. Cole held out his
arm, stopping me. Tattoos grinned, and then she and Stocky
gathered their weapons from the ground.

"This way." Stocky motioned for us to follow.

We didn't, not right away. I pretended to enjoy the beauty
around me. The moon, high though it was, was nothing more

than a hook. Stars glowed like diamonds scattered across a sea of black velvet. The perfect backdrop for betrayal.

Okay. Enough of that.

With the pair far enough ahead, I whispered to Cole, "This could be a trap."

He traced his knuckles over my cheek. "Trust me, love. It's not. I know a little about River. He's not the most moral slayer out there, because he follows no rules but his own— and sometimes even breaks those—but he hates zombies as much as we do. He won't want to stop us from doing our job."

I leaned into his touch, savored the endearment he'd used. "Okay. But if he threatens you, I can't be held responsible for my actions."

"You coming or not?" Tattoos snapped from across the distance.

Cole pressed a soft kiss against my lips. "If he threatens *you*, he'll be dead before the night's over."

I had to be a bloodthirsty wench, because I smiled.

We kicked into motion, sticking to the shadows and alleys, constantly glancing over our shoulders. I expected another tail. Or a nest of zombies. It was just one of those nights.

Along the way, I received a text from Frosty, and then a text from Bronx, each telling me they'd lost their tails and all was well. I let them know our situation and that we would contact them as soon as we could.

Finally, we reached a tall, crumbling building of red brick— an apartment complex. The lobby's best feature was the thread-bare carpet; to the side, a girl with tic-tac-toe games etched all over her forearms manned a counter teetering on unsteady legs.

As we passed, Stocky and Tattoos threw their jackets at her. She caught them without a word of complaint, as if she deserved to be treated like a coatrack. My reaction might have been a wee bit different. I wouldn't have complained, either, but I would have set those jackets on fire.

We turned a corner, and the interior experienced an immediate change. From shabby to chic. The walls were freshly painted and decorated with professional portraits. There was Stocky, and Tattoos, and at least twenty others I didn't recognize. The carpets were plush, the furniture obviously antique, with cherubs and birds carved into the wood.

We marched through a state-of-the-art kitchen, with stainless-steel appliances and at least ten kids bustling around stoves and steaming pots. The scent of spicy chicken filled the air, soon joined by the fragrance of cherry cream. My mouth watered. I was tempted to grab a handful of pastries in the five-foot-tall warmer by the back door; they were just sitting there, practically begging me to do it.

But I didn't...take more than one.

I devoured the treat as we stepped into a courtyard. Frenzied cheers, loud and boisterous, assailed my ears. On a sudden sugar high, I scanned the crowd. Another fifty kids were here, male and female, ranging in age from twelve to twenty-five.

What had we walked into?

Silence descended the moment we were noticed. The throng parted down the center, and I felt like Moses at the Red Sea. More than one guy looked me up and down, and to be honest, it kind of gave me the creeps. I was all for being admired—who didn't like to feel wanted?—but these guys weren't sizing me up as a potential girlfriend; they were sizing me up as a potential dinner buffet.

One guy actually made an obscene gesture with his tongue and two fingers.

I guess Cole noticed, because he switched gears and performed a sweet little chest-bump I'd call "your only warning."

"If you want to keep your tongue, you won't do that again," he said quietly. Menacingly.

The guy fronted, squaring his shoulders, trying to stare down a brick wall, but Cole wasn't one to back down—ever—and soon the guy lost his nerve and moved his gaze to his feet.

Cole, vibrating with challenge, took a moment to glare at the other guys. "Anyone else want to insult my girl?"

I know the situation was heated and it was all kinds of wrong to focus on this, but...testosterone overload was magically delicious.

"Well, well," a male voice called, all amusement and snark. "For once the rumors are true. Cole Holland actually *is* an animal in human skin."

I pivoted just in time to watch a Greek god saunter down the part in the sea. Wow. He was as tall as Cole, with hair so pale it was as pure as newly fallen snow. His eyes were dark, almost black, and he was shirtless, his skin inked as heavily as Tattoos, all black and white.

He couldn't have been much older than us. Nineteen. Maybe twenty.

A boy I recognized kept pace at his side. Knuckle Scars, from Choco Loco. *Should have known.*

Greek spread his arms and grinned. "Welcome to my home."

Cole didn't say a word.

*Awk*ward.

"Thanks for the invite," I said. "Maybe next time rethink sending the four horsemen of the apocalypse as escorts. They aren't exactly a welcoming first act."

He looked me over and carefully blanked his expression. "I'm told you're Ali Bell, but…" He frowned. "Don't take this the wrong way, Pop-Tart, but you aren't even close to what I expected."

Pop-Tart? Because I'm packed with fruit and super tasty? Thanks. "And that is?"

"Someone…" He thought for a moment, shrugged. "Not out of a kid's storybook."

And that, ladies and gentlemen, is what you call a third-degree burn.

Why did people always compare me to some fainting, animal-whispering princess too weak to save herself? Would it have killed someone to call me the nasty, village-destroying dragon? I had bite, dang it!

Cole stiffened. "Apologize." That single word came with a wealth of fury. "Now."

"But I didn't do anything," I pointed out.

He rolled his eyes. "Not you. Him."

"For speaking the truth?" Greek asked, genuinely curious.

"There's truth, and there's the delivery of the truth. I didn't like your delivery."

Now Greek was the one to roll his eyes. "Please tell me you aren't one of those people who subscribes to the 'say something nice or stay silent' philosophy."

"I'm one of those people who comes in peace…until it's time to leave everyone in pieces."

Greek pressed his lips into a thin line. He'd just been threatened in his own backyard. Frosty's prison rules, which all boys seemed to know instinctively, probably had a correct way to respond—and I had a feeling I was about to see it firsthand.

"You want a fight?" Greek said. "Done. But you won't emerge unscathed."

Yep. That.

"I want that apology," Cole said. "To start."

Greek looked from Cole to me, me to Cole, different emotions pulsing from him. My spirit recognized them and informed my brain. Anger, amusement, affront, remorse, envy.

Why envy? Had he lost someone he loved? Someone he'd once defended?

Surprisingly enough, he settled on amusement. "Very well. My apologies, Miss Ali. Next time, there will be no references to princesses. Only wicked witches."

"Appreciate it." Now, then. I brought us back to the proper track. "You must be River. I've heard so little about you, and to be honest, even that is starting to seem like too much."

He grinned. "Well, there's a little fire in you after all. That's good."

A little? "Baby, you have no idea."

The grin slowly widened. "You have questions for me, I'm sure, just as I have answers for you. But first, you're going to have to prove you are who you say you are."

Big shocker. "I'm sure you're not referring to a driver's license."

"Correct."

"You called me by name. You know who we are," I pointed out, "or we wouldn't be here."

He shrugged. "You're still going to have to prove it."

"We've got this," Cole whispered to me.

"I know just the thing." River rubbed his hands together and said, "You're going to experience a little something we call Fright Night."

MY ZOMBIE ATE YOUR HONOR STUDENT

The sea of people parted again, revealing a round chain-link fence with a dome overtop. Curiosity and dread competed for dominance as I trudged forward, Cole at my side. We stopped at the edge of the circle, looking down…down…into a pit.

There was no one inside it. But there *was* blood on the walls.

I frowned. "Do you make your crew members fight each other?"

River claimed the spot at my other side. "Every so often. For punishment. Mostly, though, slayers fight zombies."

Then some of those slayer-versus-zombie battles were physical rather than spiritual. Which was totally possible. For Anima.

"You're working with the enemy." They were the only ones who'd found a way to make the zombies solid to flesh, using collars that emitted those electrical pulses.

Hisses all around me.

"No," River said, and for the first time there was a dangerous bite to his tone. "We'd like to burn the company and all of its employees to the ground. So work with them? I'd rather let crows eat my internal organs."

Nice. "You hate Anima that fiercely, but you don't mind using their technology?"

He patted me on the head. "Using their technology is smart, angel cakes. It helps us understand what they're doing and how we can better defeat them."

Okay. That, I understood.

"She isn't your angel cake, or your Pop-Tart," Cole snapped. "She's mine."

Don't laugh. Or snicker.

"Yeah," I said. "I'm his." And okay, I snickered. But only a little!

Cole flicked me an irritated glance. I batted my lashes at him, all *what did I do now?*

"I could have her if I wanted her," River said, his ego bared for everyone to see, "but I don't, so this argument is pointless."

Could he, perhaps, be related to Gavin?

And, seriously. He could suck it.

"Only an idiot wouldn't want her." Uh-oh. Cole was getting worked into another rage. "Are you saying you're an idiot?"

River's brow wrinkled. "Now you're trying to talk me into making a move?"

Boys!

I clapped my hands to gain their attention. "All right, everyone. Get-to-know-you time is over. What's next?"

River put two fingers in his mouth and whistled; in the

pit, doorways I hadn't noticed opened up. Ten collared zombies spilled into the center, the crowd sneering and catcalling.

"Hey, baby. You wanna have me for dinner?"

"You're a cute little maggot bag. Yes, you are. Oh, yes, you are."

"You need a hand? Huh? Huh? How about I give you a finger?"

Noticing the humans above them, the zombies reached up. Black stained lips pulled back from even blacker teeth, saliva dripping down dislocated jaws.

Fighting this many zombies for the entertainment of others wouldn't be the most awful thing in the world. I genuinely enjoyed making a Z-kill. But I wasn't at my best right now. Since I'd realized we were safe, my strength had crashed and burned, taking the rest of my anticipation with it. All I had left was dread and fatigue.

Made sense. I'd been on the go for forty-eight hours plus. My only sleep had come courtesy of drugs. My last meal had been the pastry I'd freelance-valeted. I'd lost four friends, used enough adrenaline to kill a rhino (probably) and had just been chased through the streets.

Even still, I said, "I'll do it. I'll fight." I didn't see any way around it. Cole and I could battle our way through the slayers instead and leave, but we wouldn't get the answers we wanted.

"Aw, how sweet." Everything about River mocked me. "Thing is, sweetness, I don't remember asking. You're going in that cage whether you want to or not."

Anger stiffened my spine. *Oh, no, he didn't.*

"You're right," Cole said, the ease of his acceptance astonishing me. "But we're not doing it because you ordered it. We're doing it because I want you to watch and know the beast you're provoking."

Voices rose. Bets were placed.

River's smile was slow and cool. "I like you more with every second that passes, Holland, I really do." He nodded at two of his crew members, and the boys opened a section of the dome.

Pep-Talk Ali raced in with a vengeance. *Buck up, girl. This one's in the bag.*

An-n-nd… Downer Ali arrived with a rebuttal. *There's so much at stake. You could ruin everything.*

One day I was going to find a way to strangle Downer Ali with my bare hands.

I squared my shoulders and met Cole's anticipatory gaze. Anticipatory. Good. He hadn't lost his desire to fight. He could take care of this even if he had both hands tied behind his back. I could observe.

"Remember reason number seven?" he asked.

Good glory. Not reason seven! Not now. "Yes," I said and tried not to whimper.

"That," he said.

No way. Just no way he was going to stand back and let me do all the work—please!

He wound a lock of my hair around his finger. "This is going to be fun."

Oh, crap. He was, wasn't he? But…but…why? I knew it wasn't because of his injury. As he'd proved, he could be dying and still want to act as my shield. So, that had to mean… what? That he didn't want River to know what he was capable of, allowing him to launch a surprise attack later? Perhaps. Or maybe he was tired of the snide remarks directed my way and wanted me to show these people I was a force to be reckoned with.

Know the beast you're provoking....

Yeah. That one.

And okay, he seriously rocked.

Can't let him down. I stood on my tiptoes and kissed him, uncaring of our audience. "I hope you're ready to be impressed."

"I live ready." He gripped my nape, holding me steady, and kissed me harder.

When we pulled away and grinned at each other, the crowd was oddly silent. I wondered why—shock? disgust?—but honestly, I didn't care. As Cole led me to the opening of the cage, I realized bets were still being placed.

"Ten on the Z with the bow tie."

"Twenty says Ali Bell gets bitten within the first five seconds."

Cole winked at me and waved a hand to indicate the zombies. "After you."

"Why, thank you, kind sir." I searched for a ladder, didn't find one. Great. I'd have to jump.

Whatever.

I didn't give myself time to think, or lament, but stepped off the ledge and tumbled down. Landing jarred me, but I managed to straighten without pause and turn one Ali into two. Zombies swarmed me. I punched one, then another, drew in a deep breath, held...held...gathering what strength I had into the center of my being, summoning the fire I needed to kill these things...and despite my ragged condition, it came.

My faith had been exercised earlier and was still pumped up despite my condition, so the flames were bright and hot.

I heated…and heated…and heated, until I was nearly burning alive, every inch of me engulfed. All I had to do was stand there and let the creatures touch me. One ashed. Then another. Touch, touch, touch. Ash, ash, ash, until no creatures were left standing.

That. Easily.

Better than I could have hoped.

I stopped and looked up. Slayers could see other slayers when they were in spirit form, even when the watchers weren't in spirit form themselves, and vice versa. Every face in the crowd gaped at me.

Smiling, smug, I joined the two halves of me. But my flames hadn't died down, and they flickered over my skin. I didn't disintegrate, but my clothes were a different story. They vanished in a puff of smoke.

Crap! This had happened once before, when Zombie Ali launched her final attack against me. My spirit had gone a little wonky, struggling to survive. I must be on the fritz again, must have pushed myself too far.

At least Cole was in the pit with me. He leaned against the wall, polishing one of his daggers, as if he hadn't a care.

"Um, problem," I said.

He met my gaze, frowned. "Come here," he said and motioned me over. "Don't get rid of the flames."

As if! Right now, those flames were the only thing preventing me from giving a full-on peep show to our audience. Mortified, I beat feet over to Cole, and though he hissed when he clasped my wrist, he drew me against the wall and shielded me from prying eyes.

"I'm going to give you my fire," he said.

"But that'll just make everything worse!"

"Or better. Mine might give you the strength you need to control yours."

Risky, but okay. I didn't have a better idea.

He split only long enough to press his fiery hand into my chest. I *felt* it, despite my condition, which shocked me, and met a new part of myself. Sailor Ali. She had a few things to say about the pain it caused.

But my fire *did* begin to wane.

"Don't put it out yet," Cole said, rejoining. "I'm going to take off my jacket and shirt. The moment I'm free of them, *then* you douse the flames. I'll dress you."

I kind of wished I'd died in the zombie fight.

"Ready?" He waited for my nod, then dropped his jacket and jerked off his T-shirt. "Now."

I closed my eyes to shut off the heat—*shut off, shut off, freaking shut off.* Success! Cole tugged the shirt over my head and fit my arms through the holes. The material hit me midthigh. He then tied the jacket around my waist, letting it double as a skirt. And, humiliatingly enough, underwear.

"All covered," he said and kissed the tip of my nose. Short and sweet. An offer of comfort. "You did good, Ali-gator. Real good."

"Th-thank you," I said, my teeth now chattering.

He wrapped his arms around me, holding me close. "And now," he said with more volume, turning and facing the crowd, zeroing in on River, "we talk."

A dumbfounded River crossed his arms over his chest. "How did she do that?"

"Here's a better question," I said, just to be contrary. "Why can't *you* do it?"

He flicked his tongue over an incisor, and for a moment, I was certain he would vow to leave us in the pit until his curiosity was satisfied. But he nodded to one of his boys, and a ladder was dropped inside. Cole climbed out first, then helped me over the ledge, making sure all my girlie parts stayed covered.

"She needs clothes," Cole said, his command unmistakable.

"She'll get them." River reached out and pinched a lock of my hair. "Impressive work down there."

I jerked away at the same time Cole pushed him back.

"No touching."

Unfazed, River grinned. "This way." He pivoted on his heel and strode into the building.

Tattoos and Knuckle Scars flanked him, both casting curious glances my way. How wonderful. I was now a circus freak.

Wouldn't be the first time.

Inside, the warm air still managed to prickle against my exposed skin, and I broke out in goose bumps. Cole kept me tucked in tight, and that helped, but it also undermined my image as a cold-blooded Z-killer.

Oh, what did I care?

The journey ended inside a spacious sitting room. There were several couches and chairs in varying colors. The coffee table was scattered with weapons and various parts to weapons. I saw the makings of a .44, a .22 and some kind of spiked sword.

Tattoos took off but returned quickly with a stack of clothes. "Here," she said, thrusting the bundle at me.

"Be courteous to our guests," River admonished. To me, he said, "Please, forgive my sister. Milla doesn't make new friends easily."

I snorted. "Really? Hardly noticed." But in a snap, I realized something important. River was shrewd. The zombie cage fight had nothing to do with proving our loyalty or our dislike of zombies and Anima. He'd wanted to know what we could do—if we were worth aligning with or better off culled. He'd clearly decided we were, in fact, worthy, because he was pure sweetness now.

"Take her to your room," he said to Tattoos—Milla. A delicate name for such a hard-core girl. "She can change there."

Milla shook her head in protest, only to nod when River glared at her.

Cole squeezed my hand before releasing me. Indecision warred within me. Leave, and miss out on some interesting conversation, or stay, and possibly flash everyone in the room.

In the end, I trailed after Milla.

"How did you do that?" she asked. "Can all of Cole's slayers do it? What else can you do?"

"I don't know you, and I don't trust you. Watch me as I don't answer those questions."

"Fine." She opened a bedroom door and glared at me. "Touch my things, and I'll kill you."

You could try. "Same to you, Milla." If she read between the lines, she'd know I'd just made a declaration. Cole was mine.

Up went her nose. "My friends call me Milla, and as you pointed out, we aren't friends. You will call me Camilla. Or better yet, Miss Marks." With that, she sealed me inside the room with a hard slam of the door.

Whatever. I hurriedly pulled on a pair of shorts for underwear and sweatpants, looking around. The room was small, but clean. Nothing was out of place. The twin bed was made, the comforter a princess-pink. *I'm not the only storybook character in town.*

"Over here," a voice whispered.

I stiffened as the speaker's identity registered.

Helen.

Arrows of dread and excitement hit me. She stood at the side of the desk, still dressed in the black tank and jeans. Her features were pale, and she was wringing her hands together nervously.

Expecting me to blast her?

"Why do you keep appearing?" I asked softly. "No. You know what? Don't answer. I wouldn't believe you anyway." Maybe. Probably.

Ugh. I would, wouldn't I? And Cole would be beyond ticked about it.

Ignoring me, Helen pointed to a stack of papers and said, "Read." Then she vanished.

I took a step forward, stopped. Took a step, stopped. To invade Milla's privacy or not?

If Helen was a liar, like Cole thought, she could be setting me up for a fall. But…if not…

My heart galloped. As I tugged on my socks, I hopped my way to the desk. I read the top page and realized it was written in code. Lines, numbers and symbols all woven together. The same code my five-greats grandfather on my mother's side had used to write his journal. This paper was crisp and fresh, obviously a copy of something. But it couldn't be a copy of the journal—that had been buried in boxes of my mother's childhood things for years.

Why did Camilla have these?

A thousand possibilities rushed through my mind all at once. The one I couldn't get past: my five-greats grandfather could have taught other slayers how to write in code, and the skill could have been passed down from generation to generation.

This paper could have come from anyone.

Why would Helen want me to see it?

I was taking pictures with my phone, when a hard knock sounded at the door.

"Hurry up," Camilla commanded.

"Sure, sure." I snapped a final photo, raced over and opened the door before she could burst inside and catch me in action. I tried not to pant.

She gave me a once-over as I pulled on the boots and scowled. Why? The clothes weren't hers, I knew that much. She was way short, and these items were actually a little big on me.

"Those belong to River," she informed me. "You'll have to return them. *After* you've had them dry-cleaned."

Such a sweet girl. "What's your problem with me, anyway?"

She stared into my eyes for a long while and finally sighed. "Lookit. It's just like you said. I don't know you, so I don't trust you, and I'm leery of things I don't trust. It's nothing personal."

I could hardly argue with her—especially since she'd just quoted me! "Well, one thing you'll learn about me is that I never lie. I don't care what it costs me, I always tell the truth."

She flipped her hair over her shoulder. "So easy to say, so impossible to do."

"I agree that it's easy to say, but I disagree that it's impossible. It's a challenge, and I happen to like challenges. Never have run from one, never will."

She studied me again, some of her animosity draining. Then she nodded, as if she'd just made a decision. "River has his faults, but he's a good guy. You better not do anything to harm him."

"I won't—unless he messes with me and mine."

"Fair enough." She motioned me forward. "Let's get back and make sure our boys haven't killed each other."

GREAT MINDS
TASTE ALIKE

I returned to the sitting room to find Cole on a couch, River settled comfortably in the chair across from him. Knuckle Scars had taken off.

"—your problem. You play by their rules," River was saying.

"I don't put my people in unnecessary danger, you mean," Cole countered.

"Some risks are worth taking."

"No life is worth losing."

Tone wry, River said, "Then you haven't met the right people."

Camilla cleared her throat. Neither boy displayed an ounce of surprise as they glanced over at us, proving they'd never lost awareness of their surroundings.

I smiled at Cole, and he smiled back, the air between us crackling with electricity. There'd always been an undeniable awareness between us, like calling to like.

"Well. This isn't awkward at all," River quipped.

Cole waved me over; I walked to him, wanting to tell him about the papers, and when we were alone, I would, but I wasn't sure what to say about Helen. If she was, in fact, helping me, I couldn't allow him to discount the papers just because she'd been the one to point them out.

What a mess.

He tugged me beside him and anchored his arm around my shoulders. Once again his warmth enveloped me, and this time, it was like a drug. I had to fight the urge to lean closer... closer... Heck, why not just climb into his lap?

Camilla moved behind River, forgoing the empty chair and choosing to stand. She was unwilling to give up the advantage of height, I was sure, because she so rarely had it.

"So," I said, taking over the conversation, "what do you know about our friend Justin?" Camilla and Stocky had mentioned River had some inside info.

"She's all business, this one." River grinned at Cole. "I like that."

"Justin," Cole prompted.

Leaning back in his chair, River sipped at a glass of amber liquid. Something alcoholic, judging by the potent scent. "I have spies inside Anima, and while they didn't know what the powers that be were planning, they knew something big was about to go down. We've been watching their warehouses."

Plural. Not singular. "We will want the address of every warehouse you know about."

He nodded. "Of course. But they've already been emptied out. All of them, not just the one you checked out."

So agreeable now. He'd want something in return, guaranteed.

"You should have given me a heads-up," Cole said.

"Would you have given *me* a heads-up?" River asked, brows lifted.

"No," Cole admitted. "But that's something we should change, isn't it." A statement, not a question. "We're on the same side of this war."

River blinked in astonishment. He'd clearly thought Cole would be unreasonable. "Over the past week, activity increased at all four warehouses, but we saw nothing else out of the ordinary. Until two nights ago."

I tensed, not really wanting to hear the gory details of Collins's death, but knowing I needed to. *We* needed to.

Cole was as tense as I was.

"They brought in the guy with the shaved head first," River began.

"Collins," I whispered.

"Where were you, that you saw this?" Cole asked.

I blinked back tears.

"In the rafters," River said.

I pictured the warehouse, looking at it through the eyes of memory. The ceiling...had thick wooden rafters, I realized.

"They took him to the center of the warehouse," the slayer continued, his tone grimmer by the second, "and forced him to his knees. The other one, the dark-haired one, arrived a few minutes later. He was so drugged he couldn't stand, so they dumped him beside the other guy—Collins, you called him."

Stay strong.

"The Anima men talked amongst themselves for a bit. They decided they only needed one slayer." It was like River flipped some sort of switch. One second he was animated and the next he was utterly emotionless. "They took out a gun and shot your boy point-blank, then dumped him in a hole in the ground. I'm sorry."

Cole sucked in a breath.

I knew he'd been picturing everything River explained; I knew, because I'd been doing the same thing. We would forever have a mental video of Collins jerking from the force of the bullet. Gray matter exploding through a hole in the back of his head. He collapsed to the floor.

No wonder there'd been sand. They'd used it to absorb the blood.

What a cruel and horrific death. Wrong on every level.

My nails bit into my thighs. I wished I could comfort Cole, but I couldn't even comfort myself. It took every ounce of strength I had not to curl into a ball and sob.

"They loaded the dark-haired boy in a car and drove off," River said. "I had a slayer on the road, waiting, and he followed, but I haven't heard from him since. A few of my guys are out looking for him."

As much as I hated to think it…River's guy was probably dead. Otherwise, he would have checked in.

"We'll want to know the moment he's found," Cole said.

"Of course." There was a pause before River added, "But I'll expect something in return."

Cole nodded, flipping the same switch, going emotionless.

Had I not known him so well, I would have thought him heartless. But I did know him, and I knew he was struggling to hold it together, just like me. I leaned my head against his shoulder. My eyelids instantly grew heavy, and I had to blink faster than usual to keep them open.

"Normally I charge a very steep price for this type of info," River said, "but all I want from you is an equal exchange. Whatever you learn, I want to know."

Please. He'd want more, and soon, no question. He had *gimme* written all over him.

"Done," Cole agreed. "What about your spies on the inside? Have they learned anything else?"

"Not really. They aren't all that high on the totem yet, but they're digging for information, and they're not going to stop until they've got something. Because here's the thing. Anima hurt your people, hurt them bad, but they blamed my people, which means they're determined to take us both out, and fast."

"And if they can't do it," Cole said, rubbing his fingers over his jaw stubble, "they'll be satisfied if we take each other out."

River nodded. "Exactly. By the way, the second you cleared the warehouse, I had a team go through it, as well as the alleyways, and wipe your prints. They'll move your boy and bury him here with our slayers. If that's agreeable to you."

Had they gotten up and walked away from me? They sounded faraway, as if they'd moved to the other side of the room. I tried to open my eyes, to no avail. And then even their voices were lost to me. I was floating...drifting away...

And, oh, wow, there was Helen and the little girl. They were inside a small bedroom. The girl, perhaps five now, sat at the edge of an unmade bed while Helen shoved toys and clothing inside a bag.

"I don't want to leave you, Momma. Please."

"I'm sorry, sweetheart, but you must."

Tears ran down the girl's cheeks.

"Mommy's made so many mistakes. This is the only way to make things right, to give you the life you deserve."

"I don't want a life I deserve. I want you."

Helen froze. Her back was to the little girl, but I could see her face. She was choking back quiet sobs, and it was breaking my already tattered heart. Her inner pain was so staggering, I didn't know how she would be able to bear it much longer.

But she pulled herself together somehow, wiped her eyes and turned to give her daughter a faux bright smile. "Think of this as an adventure."

"No," the girl said, petulant.

"You'll finally get to meet your father. I told him about you, and he's excited to see you."

"Don't care."

Helen crouched in front of her. "Listen to me. I know you hate when we visit the people in the lab coats. Right? They stick you with needles. They strap you to tables, and no matter how hard you fight, you can't get free."

The little girl shuddered.

I had to look away. My attention snagged on a calendar hanging on the wall. According to it, this had happened eleven years ago. The girl had to be a year older than I'd been at the time.

"Well, they want to keep you now. They want to take you away from me forever."

A continuous shake of that white-blond head.

"I don't want that for you. That's why you have to go away. Your daddy will keep you safe."

"Come with me. Stay with me and my daddy. Please, Momma. Please."

Pain…desperation…so strong even *I* felt them soul-deep. *Don't send her away,* I thought. *She needs you, just as you need her.*

But Helen was made of sterner stuff and returned to her packing. "I've already made the arrangements. I've planned everything, down to the last detail. They'll think that you're… Well, all you need to know is that you'll never have to worry about them again."

The scene faded and I floated away. I fought to stay, grabbing at walls, digging in my nails.

"Ali, love, wake up."

Cole's voice startled me, yanking me the rest of the way out, and I jolted upright with a gasp.

Strong arms banded around me, tugging me back down, forcing me to lie against a warm, strong chest. Familiar. Cole's chest. I sagged against him.

"You were thrashing. You okay?" he asked, tracing his fingertips along the ridges of my spine.

A tremor swept through me. "Nightmare." For Helen and the little girl.

Why was I seeing them in my dreams?

"I happen to be a very good nightmare slayer," Cole said. "Want to tell me about it?"

Not even a little. "Where are we?" I asked. Moonlight spilled into a small room I didn't recognize. There was a desk, a dresser and a bed. Wallpaper covered the walls in patches, and the dark shag carpet sported several bald spots.

"We're at River's place," he said gently. "Remember? He gave us a room for the night."

That was all well and good, but… "We trust him enough to stay?"

"Right now, we don't really have a choice. We need his help."

"And he needs ours," I reminded us both.

"Yes. In the morning, he and Milla are going with us to Ankh's. We've seen their base of operation, and now they want to see ours."

First: Cole got to call River's sister by her nickname, but I didn't?

That blew chunks!

Second: River's desire to see Mr. Ankh's place would have been suspicious if not so understandable. I couldn't fault him for it.

"I can't believe I fell asleep and missed the rest of the conversation," I grumbled.

"I can. You've been running on empty for too long. You needed rest." He caressed my cheek, my jaw…my neck. Each stroke took him lower, until he was drawing a line in the center of my chest. "But you're awake now," he whispered huskily. "Clearly in need of a distraction."

Another tremor swept over me; this time, it sprang from a sweeter, hotter emotion. "You going to do something about that?"

"Definitely." He lowered his head, pressing his lips against mine.

I opened, welcoming him, and his tongue played inside my mouth, rolling against mine, almost lazily, tasting me, adoring me. My arms wrapped around him of their own accord, drawing him more firmly against me. He maneuvered me to my back, giving me all of his weight. He was heavy, but there was something truly magnificent about having him pressed against me like this. He was my shield. I was safe from fear and regret and sorrow, pain. Nothing but pleasure could reach me here.

He lifted his head to peer into my eyes. His lips were pink and kiss-swollen.

"Don't stop," I implored.

His thumbs traced the rise of my cheeks. "You are so beautiful."

When he looked at me like that, I felt it. I combed my fingers through his hair and, with the slightest bit of pressure, drew him back down. "Give me more."

Maybe he sensed my desperation. Maybe my plea had revved him from simmer to boil. But the tone of the kiss changed in a snap, and there was no longer anything lazy about it. He thrust his tongue with determined force, demanding a response, and I gave it, holding nothing back. As if I could. My blood heated, every inch of me tingling.

He didn't remove my shirt, just lifted it and bunched the material under my arms. Camilla hadn't given me a bra, so I wasn't wearing one.

He pulled from the kiss. I whimpered with disappointment. Then he lowered his head and kissed the skin he'd bared. And it was…it was…*so good*. Lance after lance of pleasure shot through me. He used lips, teeth and tongue, and it wasn't long before I was writhing on top of the mattress.

"Cole," I said on a moan. "You better…follow through…."

Oh! Yes!

"Will."

Finally!

I clutched at his shoulders. "You'll give me everything?" Had those breathless, pleading words really come from me?

"Not everything." His lids were heavy and hooded as his tortured gaze met mine. If he wanted me with the same fervency that I wanted him, his control was hanging on by the barest thread. "First time won't be here. But I'll give you more."

More. Yes. "Do it!"

He dived in for another kiss to my lips. It was hard, and it was hot. It was a little wanton, and a lot dirty, and I loved every second of it. His hands were all over me…*all* over me. Everywhere I ached. He'd never touched me like this before.

As I clutched at him and mumbled incoherently, arching against him, the connection I felt to him deepened, like I wasn't just Ali Bell anymore, but now had Property of Cole Holland stamped on my soul. Like I wasn't alone and would never be alone again. Like even if Cole and I were on different sides of the world, a part of him would always be with me.

"Let me know when I hit the right—" he began.

I gasped, my hips shooting off the bed.

"—spot," he finished.

My mind was utterly taken over with bliss, my thoughts burning up before they could fully form. I was laboring for breath, sweating. Everything he made me feel…it was too much…what he was doing…it was too much but not enough… and…and…the pressure was building…and building…

Then…

Something broke inside me. Not just broke, but shattered. It was wonderful, glorious, but also life-changing, as if every part of me was laid bare. I was vulnerable in a way I'd never been before. Like this, I had no secrets. No barriers. No form of protection.

Just Cole.

The sense of connection...*even deeper*. Propelled to a new level. One I hadn't even known I possessed. I realized I wasn't just trusting Cole with my life, but with my future. To treasure me and not forsake me. To always be honest. To consider my feelings and well-being with every new decision.

I was still panting, now dotted with perspiration from head to toe, but I didn't care. I wanted to laugh. "That was amazing."

"Yes," Cole groaned.

Clearly, he wasn't as happy as I was. His pupils were dilated, and tension tightened his features, and it didn't take a genius to figure out what the problem was. He needed to feel what I had just felt. Needed to...break.

"Tell me what to do," I said.

His pupils widened, eclipsing nearly all of the violet. "Are you sure?"

"Yes." *Oh, yes.*

Voice rough, he offered instruction. I obeyed, adding my own spin here and there.

He gripped my hair, then the sheets. "Ali." My name was nothing more than a luscious rasp.

Even though this round wasn't about me, I was just as affected. Just as connected to him. Knowing that he was feeling what I had felt, that I was the one responsible, the one making him feel that way, that he might just have a Property of Ali Bell stamped on every part of *him,* was sweet and heady.

"Ali!"

A roar this time.

The perfect end.

Afterward, we snuggled together on the bed, with my head resting on his chest. His heart raced.

"Is it always like that?" I asked. We hadn't gone all the way, but still. I'd check off this experience as *close*.

"Being in love makes all the difference in the world."

I believed that. I also knew he hadn't loved the other girls— hadn't claimed to, ever. And yet, I was still jealous in a way I didn't understand.

"I know you know this, but I'll repeat it," he said, probably noticing the way I'd stiffened. "When we're in bed together, there's no one else with us. It's just you and me. I'm not comparing you to anyone. How could I? No one could compare to *you*."

He plucked the thunder right out of my jealousy, and I didn't know whether to be thrilled or ticked. Why not both? I tugged his nipple ring with my teeth.

"For a big, tough guy, you're kind of whipped," I teased.

"Are you complaining?" He twirled a lock of my hair around his finger. Habit, I supposed. "Because I haven't forgotten I owe you a spanking."

I snorted and laughed at the same time, and the sound I made as a result was not pretty.

Cole grinned. "I wish my mother was alive. She would have adored you."

A girl could hope. "She was a slayer," I said, remembering what he'd once told me. She'd been attacked by a horde of zombies and bitten. The antidote hadn't worked on her, and she'd later risen from her grave as a zombie.

Later attacked Cole.

Mr. Holland was forced to kill her—again.

"Yeah, and a good one, too. But she was better at recruiting new members to the team. She was the one who brought in Veronica's mom, a former Anima employee."

He had more history with Veronica than I'd realized. No wonder he and Juliana were so tight. They'd probably grown up together.

Well, hello. The jealousy had returned.

After everything he and I had just done, and shared, that shouldn't have bugged me. Key word: *shouldn't*.

"How does that work? Trusting a former Anima employee?" I asked. "Didn't your mom and dad fear she was there as a spy?"

"At first. But she was in some kind of fugue state for a while, and that kind of thing can't be easily faked. When she came out of it, her memory was gone, but she earned their loyalty by saving my mom's life."

Yeah, but even that could have been a trick. A setup. Not that it had been, but yeah. "How did your parents react when you and Veronica started dating?"

"By that time, my mom was already dead."

Duh! I should have known that. He'd been too young to date when she'd passed away. "I'm sorry."

"But she would have loved it," he admitted softly, and I stiffened all over again. "Veronica's mom wasn't interested in her kids, so mine kind of took over their care for a while. Mom favored her."

Poor Veronica. Poor Juliana. I'd known they hadn't had an easy childhood, but it seemed to get worse every time I heard about it. And yet, I couldn't help but wonder—even as I yawned—if the relationship between the two women was Veronica's "ace in the hole."

Cole kissed my forehead. "Go to sleep, love. Big day to-morrow."

"Not yet. Gotta show you something." Yawning wider, I grabbed my phone—saw a million texts from Kat, and one from Nana, and made a mental note to contact them as I opened my photos. "I found this in Camilla's room." I decided not to mention Helen. Not yet. "Can you decipher it?"

The stronger our spirits were, the easier the code opened up for us. Right now, he was stronger than me.

He propped himself against the headboard, intently studying each photo. I sat up, too, enraptured by him. He could have been the poster child for concentration. Then…oh, good glory, *then* liquid silver spilled into his eyes, overshadowing the violet completely.

More than windows. Mirrors. It was creepy.

It was also freaking awesome.

"'At the right time, in the right place, the sacrifice of one will lead to the liberation of many,'" he read. "'Be ready. You have to be ready. Soon. She's coming soon. Be ready.'" He paused. "Those words are repeated again and again."

Prickles of dread, like thousands of needles in my skin. The journal I'd read had been written in past tense, yet this one spoke of the future. Who had written it? And how had the author known what would happen? A slayer ability? Like, say, a vision?

"Who is she?" I asked, thinking out loud. "This *one* to be sacrificed?"

"I don't know."

"Maybe…" When I yawned a third time, Cole brushed his fingertips over my eyes, forcing them to close.

"Go to sleep," he repeated, pulling me down on the pillows. "See you in the morning, Ali-gator."

"But I've got texts...." I knew nothing more.

Sunlight poured over the bed, waking me. I blinked open my eyes, saw that I was cradled in Cole's arms and smiled. He hadn't let me go all night, had kept me close, as if he couldn't bear the thought of being without me, even for a second.

I kissed him and sat up, my hair tumbling around my shoulders.

"Sleep longer," he muttered, trying to pull me back down.

Chuckling, I faced him. His eyelids were at half-mast, but it was enough. Our gazes locked, and the bedroom melted away—

—we were in a forest, the moon high, full and golden. The ice was mostly gone, but it must have melted only recently, because the ground was wet and muddy. Cole was on his knees in front of a thick tree trunk. Blood smeared his cheeks and shirt and soaked both of his hands. Hands he was staring at, as if he couldn't believe what he was seeing.

I walked past him, as if I didn't really see him.

He looked up at me, a lone tear rolling down his cheek. "I tried," he croaked. "I tried so hard—"

—a hard knock sounded at the door, jolting us out of the vision.

Dang it! Stupid interruption! What had brought Cole so low? Had he been injured? What had caused my glazed look?

Can't let myself worry.

But a lone tear rolled down *my* cheek.

"It'll be okay," he said, cupping my cheeks.

Another knock.

To whoever was on the other side of the door, he snapped, "We're up."

"We're heading out in twenty minutes. Be ready or be left behind."

Milla. *Not a morning person, I see.* "Good luck getting into Mr. Ankh's house without us," I called.

Cole kissed my forehead and stood—and I stared at him openmouthed. He was naked, and he didn't care that I had a perfect view of his perfect butt.

"Shower and take care of business," he said, pulling on a pair of boxer briefs.

Boo, hiss.

"Do whatever you need to do," he added. "I'll do the same when you're done."

We weren't going to talk any more about the vision.

The vision.

Reminded of what I'd seen, I rushed to the bathroom and barricaded myself inside. Not that it would help. If Cole wanted in, he'd get in. Locked doors had never stopped him before. I just... I didn't want him to see me cry.

Compartmentalize.

I tried. I really did. But the walls were trembling, about to fall again. Tears rained down my cheeks, burning. We'd endured so much lately, and knowing we had even more to endure...

I turned on the shower to conceal the sound of my sobs.

If the saying "what doesn't kill you makes you stronger" is really true, I'm going to be the strongest girl in the whole freaking world.

Right now, every decision I made was critical. What I did, what I said, who I trusted, would either help me or hurt me—help Cole or hurt him. Would either guide us out of the storm or take us deeper into it. And I know, sometimes storms were necessary. Even flowers needed to be watered. But...yeah.

As the tears continued to rain, I stepped into the shower and cleaned up. Finally calm, I patted myself dry, dressed in the clothes I'd worn into the bathroom—ugh, the dirty clothes. T-shirt, no bra. Shorts pretending to be panties. I had to be all kinds of hobo hideous.

A steam cloud escaped as I exited. Cole often knew what I needed before I ever said a word, and this was one of those times. He had placed a new pair of sweatpants and a jacket on the bed.

Every girl should have a Cole Holland of her own. Just not mine!

"My dad texted," he said. "He tracked down a man who used to work for Anima. One of the higher-ups. Guy says Anima is one of many agencies owned by an umbrella company that makes the bulk of its money on medical patents and is run by a woman named Rebecca Smith."

Smith. "How Matrixy," I muttered.

"Yeah. Name is probably fake, but it's something. Dad's looking into it and will let us know if he learns anything more." He held a bundle of clothes in one hand and, as he passed me, brushed his fingertips over my jaw with the other; I knew he'd noticed the pink tear tracks. "We'll be okay," he said again and closed himself in the bathroom.

I dressed in the new clothes, dried my hair with the towel and entertained Pep-Talk Ali. *In the vision, he's covered in blood, yes, but he isn't dead. That's something, right?*

Very right.

Knowing Downer Ali was only a few heartbeats away, I sang "la la la" inside my head as I tugged on the socks and boots also waiting for me. *La la la la, today's gonna be a good day. I will protect Cole. I will find a clue about Justin.*

I swiped my phone from the nightstand and checked the text messages Kat and Nana had sent me last night.

Kat: Hear UR w/other slayers. Catching butterflies? Or do I need 2 race over there w/a crowbar & an alibi? Never hurts 2 B prepared!!!

Kat: BTW, U owe me a girls' day out. Let's put 1 on the books 4 the sec U get home!

Nana: Just got to missing my girl. Hope all is well with you. I love you!

Kat: Stop me if U've heard this 1. What did the zombie say 2 his date?

Kat: I just love a woman w/BRAAAINS.

I grinned and fired off a round of responses. I told Kat no crowbar or alibi was needed, but the girls' day out was as good as done. I told Nana how much I loved and missed her and that all really was well.

Cole emerged from the bathroom dressed in the same clothes he'd worn yesterday. His hair was damp, making the black strands appear blue. A few water droplets slid from his temple to his jaw and fell to the floor. I moved in front of him to rub my towel through his hair.

He wrapped his arms around me, holding me against him, just breathing me in for several moments. "Do you want to hear reason sixteen?"

"So much I'll probably rearrange your spinal cord if you

refuse to tell me." The reasons he loved me were just as important to me as breathing.

Smiling, he said, "Even if you know the end is coming, you refuse to let me go."

The end? No, no, no, we weren't going there. "We're just getting started," I said and dropped the towel to beat at his shoulders. "There will be no end." Not for decades to come. "You said we'd be okay."

"I know, love. I know. I'm not talking about the vision."

I relaxed, but only slightly. "Then what?"

"When we had the vision of you making out with Gavin—"

"Hey now! We weren't making out. Z.A. was trying to eat him."

Cole kissed the crown of my head. "I know. But the point is, I stopped trusting you, and what I knew about you, instead trusting in what my eyes, or mind, had seen. But you didn't. You loved me, and you were willing to fight for me. Well, I need you to trust me again. Trust that I'm not going anywhere."

Trust. He was right.

Last night I'd trusted him with my body. Today, I would trust him with this.

"Like I said before, I just won you back. Nothing and no one will be able to take me away from you, Ali. Not ever again."

THERE'S NO PLACE LIKE BONES

During the hour-long drive to Mr. Ankh's house, I created a mental decision tree.

Root question: Where had Camilla and River gotten the coded papers?

Trunk: to ask or not to ask.

The branches: if I asked, they would know I'd seen them. If I didn't ask, I wouldn't get an answer.

Would their knowing be such a bad thing?

Not really. What was the worst they could do? Accuse me of snooping?

So I did it. I asked.

"How dare you!" Camilla snarled. "You went through my things."

"Actually, I didn't." Maybe I should have charted the branches a littler farther and picked a better place to have this conversation. A crowded car—bad decision. "Is it my fault you left the papers on your desk for anyone and everyone to see? Wait. Let me answer that for you, since I'll be honest. No. Now, who wrote the code and do you have any idea what it says?"

The question I really wanted to ask: *Do you know who "she" is?*

River scowled at me. "One of our spies saw the document at an Anima facility and made copies. And no, we haven't been able to decode it."

Truth or a lie? Trust him or doubt him? I couldn't do both.

"Can *you?*" Camilla demanded. "Decode it, I mean?"

Well, heck. No matter what it cost me, I couldn't—wouldn't—lie. Isn't that what I'd told her? "Yes," I said. "They talk about the sacrifice of one leading to the liberation of many and a 'she' that is coming. What they don't say is who she is or what she's supposed to do."

"How were you able to decode it?" River asked.

I pressed my lips together, refusing to mention the journal.

"It's a spirit thing." Cole drummed his fingers against the wheel of Mr. Ankh's SUV. River's crew had been the ones to take it but had given it back as a gesture of goodwill. "You have to look at the pages through the eyes of your spirit, not your mind."

My phone beeped, the sound almost like a trumpet in the sudden quiet.

I looked at the screen. Another text from Kat.

RED ALERT. Cops R here asking Q's about Trina & Lucas & Cruz. Like what we were doing other nite, & Ankh is being honestish, just not mentioning Cole's injury, the Z's or Anima. He even told them U guys were on UR way. Oh, & FYI, he said Cole's dad is away on business, & UR Nana went w/him—she's like his new assistant, I guess. Now, back in the lion's den 4 me. I told them I had 2 pee, & I don't want them 2 think I ran away. Or, U know, had 2 do #2. C U when I C U. Good luck!

"Guys," I said with a sigh. Like we really needed another dose of trouble. Legal, at that. "We've got a bit of a problem." I read the text aloud. Well, most of it.

River and Camilla cursed.

"They've already come knocking at my door," River said.

Cole stopped drumming. "What did you tell them?"

"That I had nothing to do with what happened. Then I gave a rock-solid alibi."

I bet his alibi involved his crew, which meant the police probably hadn't bought it. And if they ever found Collins... "Will showing up together hurt us or help us?"

"Help," Cole said, at the same time River said, "Hurt."

Great.

Cole added, "Why not let them know we're working together to find the people trying to take us both down? Because if they ever put a tail on us, and I'm sure they will, they'll see us together and wonder why we kept quiet about our association."

River thought for a moment, nodded. "All right. But if you sell me out, I'll kill you."

Oh, heck no. Death threats weren't allowed. "Say that again, and I will do horrible things to your intestines."

River gave a mock shudder.

Cole reached over and tugged on my earlobe—I'd claimed the passenger seat. "That's sweet of you, love. A part of me kind of hopes he repeats himself. Later. For now, everyone will put on a cheerful face. We're here."

The iron gate blocking Mr. Ankh's property from the rest of the world opened automatically, responding to the sensor on the dash of the car. Neither River nor Camilla looked particularly impressed by the sprawling mansion with alabaster columns and wraparound balconies, and I wondered if pride had anything to do with it. They seemed to have more than most.

There was an unmarked sedan parked in the circle driveway. Cole stopped behind it, and we each removed our weapons, hiding them under seats and in cubbyholes, leaving nothing out in the open.

I finished first and stepped into the cold morning, exhaling deeply. Mist plumed in front of my face. I think my damp hair turned into icicles as I searched for a rabbit cloud. When I spotted one, my heart tangoed with my ribs. So, on top of everything else, we'd be fighting zombies tonight.

Great! We didn't have time for this.

Um. A slayer without time for zombies? I should finally get that spanking, because dang, I was being *so* dumb.

Cole came up beside me. We walked inside hand in hand, with River and Camilla trailing behind us.

"There's a rabbit cloud," I whispered.

He stiffened but said, "We'll be ready. Don't worry."

The moment we were ensconced inside, warm air embraced me, but it wasn't very welcoming. What kind of interrogation awaited us?

"Cole?" Mr. Ankh called.

"Yeah," he returned, as if he hadn't a care.

"Come to my office, please. And bring Miss Bell."

Okay. This was it.

Game on.

The four of us trekked to the office, our boots thumping against the marble tile. The doors were open, allowing us to see inside before we entered. There were two detectives. A man and a woman. The man looked to be in his thirties, and the woman looked to be in her forties. Neither smiled in welcome, but both twisted in their seats to assess us.

Mr. Ankh introduced everyone but River and Camilla. I nodded at Detective Gautier, the male, then Detective Verra, the female. "They have some questions about the night of the shooting," he said. "Your friends should probably wait—"

"No," Gautier said. "They're a part of this. They can stay."

Everyone but Mackenzie, Veronica and Juliana was present. Kat and Reeve, sitting together on the couch, gave me terse waves. Frosty and Bronx stood beside Mr. Ankh, who sat behind the desk. Jaclyn and Gavin perched at the edges of the desk. So awesome seeing him on his feet.

Gavin noticed me staring at him and winked, and I had to curb the urge to run over and hug him. He didn't look like a guy who'd just suffered a mortal injury. He looked healthy, whole…and thank God, like a major pain in my butt once again.

Cole took the only remaining space on the couch and pulled me onto his lap. River sat on the arm of the couch, and I expected Camilla to claim the other side, but she settled at his feet.

"Tell us what happened the night of the attack," Verra said, peering at Cole. Everything about her was no-nonsense. "And then explain why you're with your biggest rival."

Cole just blinked at her. "Rival?"

Gautier tapped his pen against his thigh. "You two are feuding, are you not?"

"You seriously believe what the stations are reporting? That we're part of rival gangs?" Cole scoffed. "Sorry, but that's probably the stupidest thing I've ever heard."

Both detectives scowled at him.

"I have a group of friends," he continued. "We hang out together. That's it."

"We've been over this," Mr. Ankh said.

"The way we hear it," Verra said, never looking away from Cole, "you and your friends constantly show up to school cut up and bruised."

"And that's a crime?" I asked.

Now the detectives focused on me. I think they assumed I would squirm, but I'd faced worse without backing down.

Before either one could say anything, Cole jumped in and said, "Look. I was watching TV when Ali texted me. She asked if she could come over. I said yes."

"What time?" Gautier asked, making notes in a small pad. "And what were you watching?"

"It was right around 3:00 a.m. *Duck Dynasty* was playing."

"Even though it wasn't airing?" Verra asked, no doubt thinking she'd caught him in a lie.

"Netflix," he said with a shrug.

A barely perceptible flash of irritation, before she turned to me. "And you? What were you doing? Why did you text him so late?"

If they could get hold of our text exchanges—and according to *Castle,* they totally could—there would be problems. I had to circumvent things *now.*

"I was hunting zombies," I said, earning shocked glares

from most of my friends. "Kids like to play video games, you know?" All true.

A collective sigh of relief was released.

"Why did you text Mr. Holland so late?" the detective repeated.

I hiked my shoulders. "I was up, and I couldn't sleep." It was the truth, with a few of the more pertinent details left out.

"She came over," Cole said. "We…" His violet gaze circled the room, narrowed. I knew he hated discussing personal things in front of other people. Especially strangers. "We were distracted. Someone fired a shot. Shattered my window."

Gautier started tapping his pen again. "We've been to your house. Someone tried to clean your bedroom, but just because something can't be seen doesn't mean it's not there. We found blood on your floor."

"The bullet grazed my shoulder. I've already recovered."

Nice. The bullet had grazed his shoulder all right…as it had cut through skin and muscle and come out the other side.

"The blood is mine," he continued, "and you can feel free to take a sample to compare with what you found. And yes, my dad tried to clean it up. He didn't want me living in a cesspool of broken glass and congealed blood. I didn't know that was a crime."

"Obstruction is always a crime." Verra took notes of her own and said, "You'd been shot. Why not go to the police? Or at least call? Why not go to the hospital?"

Cole rested his chin on my shoulder. "As you can see, I'm fine. I didn't need to go to a hospital and spend thousands of dollars on a bandage and a couple Advil. And I didn't call the police, because I didn't know what had happened at first, didn't know about the others. When I did, well, I didn't know who I could trust."

Honest and inarguable.

"Where's your dad now?" Gautier asked.

"He's a travel writer, and I'm not sure where he is most of the time. I'm staying with the Ankhs while he's gone."

Mr. Holland was a travel writer? Was that for real?

"Seems odd that he'd leave his son the day after he'd been shot," Verra said.

Cole offered a small, pitying smile. "I'm a legal adult very capable of taking care of myself. He knows that."

Gautier had another follow-up. "Do you have his flight info? We have a few questions for him."

"I don't," Cole replied. "Last I'd heard, he was going to drive."

"I see." Verra turned her attention to me. "And your grandmother left, too?"

"Yes," I said. "I'm staying with Mr. Ankh, as well."

Now her attention shot to Mr. Ankh. "You're responsible for a lot of kids."

"Not all of them are kids. But, anyway, they're safe here," he said, hands forming a steeple on his desk. "I have security most people can only dream about."

"And you need this security because…"

Wasn't gonna let up, was she.

"I get that you're doing your job," Cole said before Mr. Ankh had time to answer. "That you want to find out who killed my friends and tried to kill me. I'm glad. I want you to find the people responsible, too. I want you to make them pay. But my dad wasn't responsible, and neither was Ankh.

Of course he needs security. Look at this house and all the valuables inside it."

He didn't give them time to respond, adding, "Also, River isn't responsible for this. Yeah, I heard the news reports, too, so I was eager to chat with him. But he's convinced me he didn't do it, that he was set up, so I suggest you do a better job of detecting, before we beat you to the truth."

Gautier straightened in the chair as if his spine had been pulled on by an invisible wire. "Don't even think about seeking revenge, son. You get in the way of our investigation, and you'll find yourself behind bars."

None of us made any promises.

As if on cue, both detectives stood.

"I think that's enough for now. Thank you for your time," Verra said. "We'll be in touch."

I'm sure they would.

Footsteps echoed as they marched to the door. *Clink.* A minute later, their car's engine purred to life. Only then did everyone breathe another sigh of relief.

Cole gave me a bear hug, whispering, "Do me a solid and get the girls out of here. I'm going to have River tell the slayers about Collins and Justin."

Poor Cole. He'd have to relive the horror all over again.

I'd make up for it later. I kissed him and stood. "Kat, Reeve, why don't you come with me? I'm starved, and while I'm devouring half the contents of the pantry, you can give me an update about everything that happened while I was gone. Or grill me with questions about what happened on my end."

Both girls hopped to their feet, eager.

"First," River said, his attention riveted on Kat, "introduce me. Please."

Uh-oh. Someone was about to wake Papa Bear.

"All you need to know about this one—" Frosty said, proving Papa Bear had done been woken as he stomped over to Kat to clasp her by the back of the neck and pull her close for a swift, hard kiss "—is that she's mine, and I don't share."

To Kat he said, "Miss me while you're gone."

"Never."

"Harsh. *I'll* miss *you*."

"That's because you love me more than I love you."

He barked out a laugh and spanked her on the bottom. "Everyone knows you love me more than I love you. Now get out of here before I make you prove it."

She was grinning as she skipped from the office.

"You don't talk to or even look at the other one," Bronx said, hitching his thumb in Reeve's direction. "She happens to be mine."

Reeve waved.

Mr. Ankh dropped his head into his upraised hands.

"Possessive little buggers, aren't they?" River said to Camilla. "What happened to friends sharing with friends?"

She was too busy staring at Cole to answer.

I rolled my eyes. After hooking my arm through Reeve's, I drew her out of the room. Kat was already in the kitchen, making me a peanut butter and jelly sandwich. Owed her big-time! I claimed a chair at the table.

"Thank you," I said, beyond grateful as she set the plate in front of me. "How are you feeling?"

"Better," she said.

She looked it.

"So, where are Veronica and Juliana?" I asked.

"Holed up in their room," Reeve said, taking the chair at my left. "My dad wanted them out of sight. He also told us not to mention them to the police."

They really were off the grid, then. I wondered why.

"Um, Ali," Kat began, claiming the chair at my right.

Uh-oh. "What?" I said, the bite I'd just taken settling like a lead ball. "What's happened?"

They shared a look laden with dread.

"The boys were talking about some new ability you have," Kat said, twisting her fingers together. "They said it's, like, as un-cake-like as possible."

To zombies, sure. "And?" I prompted, relaxing.

"Well," Reeve said, picking up where Kat had left off, "when my dad heard about it, he paled. He fell into his chair, and I swear I thought he was going to vomit the dinner I'd spent an hour preparing."

"And?" I asked. Getting answers from these two was worse than pulling teeth.

Kat nibbled on her bottom lip. "He said he knew of only one other person who could do what you did, and her name was Helen Conway."

Helen Conway.

Helen.

My Helen.

That... Well, it proved what Helen had said that day in the forest. Had it really happened yesterday, even though it felt like forever ago? Her hand had hovered over mine as warmth had flowed through me, passing her ability to me. A gift.

"Ali," Kat continued, her voice wobbling. "Ten years ago, Helen died doing a job...for Anima."

GOT BRAIN?

Helen died doing a job for Anima.

The words tumbled through my mind, making me buzz with equal parts bewilderment and frustration. If she had worked for the enemy, why was she helping me now? To lure me in, just to trick me more easily later?

Smart, yes. But not likely.

First, she was a Witness, and Witnesses worked for Team Good, never Team Evil. Second, a monster wouldn't have cared about giving up her little girl.

But her remorse...a dream, nothing more.

No. I didn't think so. Not anymore. The emotions had been real, the scene vivid. It had happened, no doubt about it. My heart accepted what my mind couldn't yet understand. Somehow, I'd seen into someone else's past.

Yet, here was another conundrum. Helen died ten years ago, roughly twelve months after giving up her little girl. So, where was the little girl? Well, not so little anymore. I remembered the calendar, knew she'd be seventeen…maybe eighteen.

What was she to me? Because she had to be something. No one else had eyes like ours. I'd always thought I'd inherited mine from my dad, even though his were dark blue. Apples and oranges, I admitted now.

How was Cole going to react to this?

I peered at Kat. "Would you hate me if I skipped out on another girls' day?"

"Only for a minute. Then I'll get over myself."

I smiled. "If I was into girls…"

"I know! You'd be all over me. You wouldn't be able to help yourself. But that's true of every person on the planet."

Healthy ego intact? Check. I kissed her cheek and gave Reeve a hug. "Thanks, guys."

"I notice you didn't ask about *my* hate," Reeve quipped.

"You're not likely to claw my face off in a fit of pique."

She nodded. "That's fair."

I paced outside Mr. Ankh's office for ten…fifteen minutes, but the conversation remained on business, and I couldn't interrupt. I finally gave up and holed up in my room to pore over the journal and compare its pages to the pictures on my phone.

The effort paid off. I found a missing page in the journal, the paper ripped close to the binding. My mind leaped from one thought to the next. The copied page had come from Anima. Helen had worked for them. If she came from my mother's side, she could have had access to the journal. *She* could have ripped out a page and handed it over.

That would make her the traitor Cole was certain she was.

No time to process. Cole strode into my room and shut the door. Gasping, guilty, I shut the journal and jolted to my feet.

"You're here," I said and gulped.

He frowned. "Do you not want me to be?"

Yes. No. Maybe. "Will you..." *crap* "...tell me what you know about Helen Conway." I couldn't avoid this topic anymore, didn't want to. "Please."

"What do you want to know?"

Everything. "Anything."

"Why?"

"Tell me. Then I'll outline my reasons."

He scrubbed a hand down his face. "She worked for Anima with Veronica's mom. They were roommates, friends. Then Veronica's mom abandoned ship. She didn't."

"How did she die?"

"My dad killed her."

Okay. *That,* I couldn't have predicted. "Because she worked for Anima?"

His eyes narrowed, hate swimming in their depths. "Zombies might have been the smoking gun that killed my mother, but *she* pulled the trigger. *She* sent them. Then she collared my mother's spirit and sent her after me and my dad."

And I was most likely related to her? *Might vomit.* "Cole. I'm so sorry."

He waved away my sympathy, too upset to accept it.

"How do you know she was responsible?" I asked.

"She cornered my dad about a week before, bragged about what she was going to do."

Wait. I shook my head, unsure. Bragged—or warned?

I don't want to think the worst about her, do I? No matter the evidence stacked against her.

"After…just after, my dad went after her," he said, gritting his teeth. "He shot her. And if you want to know any more than that, I'll have to ask him."

This had to be a nightmare for him, like ripping scabs off old wounds, and I hated that—but it didn't stop me. "Yes, please." I had to know the truth. "Ask him."

He stalked across the room to make the call. I dialed Nana.

"Ali!" Hearing her voice warmed some of the chill that had taken root inside me. "How are you?"

"I'm…okay."

"Okay? Well, that's not very banging, is it?"

Banging? *Oh, Nana. Not that word. Please, no.* "What are you up to?" I thought I heard waves lapping in the background.

"Strangely enough, I'm chillaxing. I hate to admit this, but…it's nice. Since your pops died, I've been… Well, you know. I didn't realize I needed this. And that makes me feel so guilty! Especially because you're there, doing I don't know what, and I probably don't want to know what."

True. "You don't need to worry about me. I am kicking butt and not bothering with names."

"Oh, sweetheart. That's wonderful. But are you eating properly? Resting? Doing the horizontal hokey pokey with Cole?"

I nearly choked on my own tongue. "Nana!"

"It's a legitimate question, dear. One that deserves an answer."

"No!" I blurted, certain I was a nice shade of lobster-red.

"I'm not." Not technically. I cleared my throat, then, changing the subject, asked, "Are you safe?"

"Never been safer."

"Good. That's good." I paused. "Nana," I said, launching into an urgent, back-and-forth pace, "am I related to a girl named Helen Conway?"

Silence.

Such heavy silence.

"Nana?"

"Ali," she said. She cleared her throat. "She's my niece. Your mother's cousin. Why?" Gone was her joviality.

So. There *was* a familial connection. Which meant I had a relative who'd (1) worked for Anima and (2) killed Cole's mom. Awesome.

"Why have I never heard of her before? You've never talked about her. Mom never talked about her. Why?"

Again, silence, and I wasn't sure what to think.

Then she said, "She took off right after high-school graduation. I never heard from her again."

"What of her parents?"

"They're dead," Nana added, "just as Helen is."

"What about—"

"Ali. Let's drop this, all right? Please." Her desperation tugged at my heartstrings, and if I'd been made of weaker stuff, I would have done as she'd asked.

But I wasn't. "I can't. I won't." None of her family—*my* family—had known Helen worked for Anima. Otherwise, they would have known about the zombies, and none of them had. "I have to know everything. I deserve to know."

Cole stepped in front of me. The muscles in his face were

like stone, or ice, carved from a blade surely honed in the fires of rage, and it kind of scared me. He'd never looked at me like that.

"Nana," I said. "It's your lucky day. You're gonna get the reprieve you want. But I'm calling you tomorrow, and I expect you to answer all of my questions."

"All right," she said and sighed. "Tomorrow. Just know that, no matter what, I love you. So much. Never forget that."

What wasn't she telling me? Whatever it was, it frightened her. Badly. Made her think I'd grow to…what? Hate her? *Not gonna happen.* "I love you, too. I'll always love you."

Trembling, I set my phone aside. I opened my mouth to ask Cole what was wrong, but he just handed me his phone.

"Mr. Holland?" I asked.

He didn't waste time with pleasantries. "I graduated a year before your parents."

Um, okay. "That's…nice?"

"Just listen," he barked, startling me. "I kept track of the students in the grades behind me, always on the lookout for new recruits. I was especially interested in your dad. But you know that already. You also know he wasn't interested in me."

"I don't—"

"He started dating Helen his senior year."

Wait.

What? My dad and *Helen?*

"I tried to recruit them both, in fact. Unlike your dad, she was interested. Then, from what I've been able to piece together, your dad met your mom at some family get-together and dumped Helen that same night. He and Miranda started dating the next day. A few months later, all three graduated.

Your dad and mom got married almost right away, and Helen took off. I'm not sure when she started working for Anima. All I know is that she returned to Birmingham six years later. There were rumors she'd had a daughter, but the little girl, Samantha, had died."

Wait, wait, wait. Back up. That sweet little girl was dead? *Reeling.* "Died how?"

"Zombie bite."

I didn't like that, wouldn't believe it until I had proof. Rumors weren't always true. If they were, Cole would have horns, fangs and a forked tail and I would, apparently, look like a he-man. What if the girl, Samantha, was out there?

Could she be my...sister?

What did I know about her?

Helen had packed a bag for her. Had planned to send her to her dad.

"Who's the girl's father?" I asked, then froze, ice actually crystallizing in my veins. Dark suspicions were like a cascade of wind. What if she wasn't my sister, but I was...

"Don't know that, either," he said.

Nana's reaction to my questions...

Helen saying, "They'll think that you're..." to the little girl.

Dead, I finished now and knew I was right.

And Mr. Holland had called the little girl Samantha. Sami. The name Helen spoke the first time she appeared to me. At the time, I thought she was telling me *her* name. But she'd clearly been saying *her daughter's* name...while looking at me. Calling *me*—

No!

I vividly remembered my mom—my real mom—telling

me she'd named me after my dad's mother *at birth*. So, why was I even traveling this path? It was impossible. I had no memories of Helen.

Well, except for the dreams.

I struggled to breathe. The truth was, I had no memories of the first five years of my life.

Five, not six.

The difference mattered. I couldn't be Sami. I'd gotten it right the first time. Sister.

But…two facts niggled at me. One, there were very few pictures of my early years, and those we had were of me. Just me. I'd never thought that strange before.

I thought it strange now.

Two, I'd always felt like the odd man out at my grand-parents' house. Like they'd seen something in Emma they hadn't seen in me.

I pushed out a breath.

Time to break down the facts. Helen had dated my dad. Probably slept with him. She'd disappeared soon after grad-uation. To escape the pain of seeing my mom and dad to-gether—to hide a pregnancy?

Then, after her death, she'd come back to help a long-lost second cousin, the daughter of the man who'd betrayed her, and not the company she'd worked for? No. But someone with a closer connection to her? Far more likely.

And really, birthdays could be changed as easily as names.

If she was… If it was true… *Can't possibly be true.* Why wait so long to reveal herself? Why come to me now and not, say, when I first lost my parents? Or when I battled Zombie Ali?

Questions, questions. So many questions.

"There you have it," Mr. Holland said, drawing me back to our conversation. "Everything I know. Now. I want you to tell me why this information is so important to you."

Did he suspect what I did?

I shook my head, even though I knew he couldn't see the action. My gaze found Cole. He wasn't looking at me, but over my shoulder, his eyes narrowed, his lips compressed into a thin line. If Helen was…my mother—no, she couldn't be my mother; I refused to believe it—then the woman who had given birth to me had helped kill the woman who had given birth to him, and in a bid for revenge, his dad had murdered her for it.

It was a sick, twisted history. How could two people in a romantic relationship ever hope to recover?

I walked to the window and peered out into the dwindling light. The sun was hidden, the sky gray. The rabbit cloud was still there, only darker. Menacing, like my mood.

"I'm going to go now, Mr. Holland," I said softly. I had a lot to think about—a lot I didn't want to think about.

He sighed. "I understand. But we're going to talk. Soon."

"Soon." I hung up.

Right now, I needed Emma. She would tell me how silly I was to worry. And that's exactly what I was doing. What I'd told myself I'd never do. Worse, I was probably doing it for nothing.

"You are related to my mother's killer," Cole said, "and I'm related to your mom's cousin's killer, but we'll get through it."

He didn't understand. Didn't know what I suspected. Would he change his mind then?

My gaze snagged on the gate that circled the entire property line and widened. "No." But the image didn't change. Zombies were already out, and they were here.

"We'll put the work in," he said.

Hundreds of the creatures gripped the iron, shaking it. It had been doused in the Blood Lines and was solid to them, even though they were in spirit form. They couldn't bypass it, but they *could* grow tired of waiting and turn their attention to the other homes in the area, killing innocents.

How had they gotten past Mr. Ankh's reinforced security? He had monitors capable of seeing zombie evil—on screen, they glowed as red as their eyes—to alert him whenever a zombie horde approached. But right now, he had no idea. Otherwise, an alarm would have been blasting.

"Cole," I choked. "Zombies. They're here."

He joined me at the window and peered out. He stiffened, saying, "We have to warn the others."

As we hurried down the hall, he banged on every door, shouting, "We've got visitors. More Z's than we've ever fought before."

Behind the doors, footsteps pounded. Hinges squeaked and then our friends rushed out, dressing along the way, River and Camilla among them.

We congregated in the dungeon, where Mr. Ankh kept a stash of weapons.

"I thought you guys were boring," River said, his tone jovial, "but you certainly know how to liven things up."

"Yeah," Gavin said with a nod. "We're good like that. You're welcome."

Ignoring them, Kat said to Frosty, "Don't go catching butterflies," as he strapped a pair of short swords to his back. "Go to the roof and clip their wings with a rifle or something."

"If bullets killed them, Kitty, that would be a great plan," he replied. "But it takes the fire in my hands."

"Not just yours. Other slayers have fire."

"Yes, and those other slayers need someone guarding their backs."

"Why are you being so logical?" Kat beat at his arms, only to stop and sigh. "I know, I know. You're right. I don't like it, but I do understand." She chewed on her bottom lip. "I hate that I can't see them. That I can't help you in some way."

"Knowing you're in here waiting for me helps." He placed a swift kiss on the tip of her nose, like Cole often did to me. "Trust me. I'm not going to let anything stop me from getting back to you."

Reeve was silent as she slammed the clip in a SIG and handed it to Bronx. Jaclyn stared at a sword, unmoving. Everyone else was murmuring about what I'd wondered—how was this possible?

Mr. Ankh sat at a long desk covered by multiple computers, the wall in front of him shrouded by monitors. He was typing furiously at a keyboard. The fact that so many zombies were here at the same time told me Anima had sent them, was probably controlling them with the collars.

But...I don't recall seeing collars on very many of them.

"What are you doing?" Cole demanded, nudging me. "Arm up."

"Sir, yes, sir."

He glared at me before stomping to Frosty to develop a game plan.

"You're a freaking ray of sunshine, you know that," I called. He didn't even glance at me.

I grabbed my axes, a sword and two guns, and a grinning River approached me.

"I hear you're something special on the battlefield," he said. "Better than what I witnessed in the pit."

"I have my moments," I acknowledged, glad for the distraction.

"Well, you're in for a treat. I have moments, too. Practically every single one I live. So let's do ourselves a favor and make things interesting."

"Are you challenging me to a Zombie Kill-off?"

"Person who slays more evil spirits wins?" He nodded. "Done."

"Not done. There's no way to keep track. I ash them a horde at a time."

His grin widened. "Smack talk already."

"Truth talk."

"If you aren't good enough to count your kills, well, you've already lost. At least try to redeem yourself." He patted my shoulder before striding to Camilla's side.

"I didn't agree to anything," I called.

"Did I hear we're having a kill-off?" Gavin asked, coming up beside me.

Seriously?

Incorrigible adrenaline junkies.

As the rest of the slayers ran out of the dungeon, heading outside, Cole returned to me and held me back.

"I love you more than fictional zombies love brains," he said. "Tell me you know that."

I licked my lips and whispered, "I know that. I do."

"No matter what."

I really hoped so. "No matter what," I agreed.

He nodded. "Good." To Mr. Ankh, he said, "I'm guessing you'll be able to see us on the monitors, that the problem isn't your system but something Anima has done to the zombies. So, when you see us, turn on the halogens." With a final glance to me, he strode out of the room.

"Stay here," I said to Kat and Reeve before rushing after Cole. I didn't see him, but did run into Mackenzie along the way. She was steady on her feet, headed for the dungeon, her color high and healthy. "You're fighting?"

"Not this time. I'm better, but not all systems go yet." She lifted the hem of her shirt to reveal a patchwork of black scabs. "A few more days, and look out, zombies."

Our world might be going down the crapper, but at least we could heal each other. "Do me a solid and guard the girls. They could try something sneaky."

She motioned behind me with a wave of her chin. "That's why I'm here. To babysit."

Mr. Ankh must have heard her voice, because he called her over. "My text said *now,* Miss Love, not five minutes from now."

"Suck it," she muttered.

"I heard that, Miss Love."

"Just as I intended you to, Mr. Ankh."

As I continued on, Kat called, "Ali!"

I paused to look back.

"Whatever you have to do, protect my boy."

In other words, do whatever was necessary to use my new

ability. The one Helen had warned me to be careful with. The one Cole didn't want me to use, not because we didn't know a lot about it, I realized now, but because it might have come from the woman who'd killed his mother.

What a mess.

I continued on my way without replying. Nothing about this was business as usual anymore. This was personal, and I had no idea what to do about it.

ZOMBIES ATE
MY HOMEWORK

Rather than continuing on to the tunnel that led outside the Blood Lines and thus the gate, the slayers stopped a few feet away. I came up beside them, Cole on my right, River on my left. The air was thick with the stink of rot, and moans and grunts of hunger created an eerie song—as far from a lullaby as you could get.

I scanned the gruesome creatures drooling over the possibility of eating us. A few were collared. Most weren't. All were as ugly as—

"Trina?" Horror filled me.

Like all undead, the once beautiful Trina wore what she'd died in. Her forever outfit happened to be a black tank and a pair of gray sweatpants—what she'd practiced fighting zombies in. She'd loved to slick back her short hair, but tonight it stuck out in spikes. Soon, it would fall out, leaving her bald. Her skin had a grayish tint, and her once lovely eyes were now red and drooping at the corners.

I...I...

I had loved this girl. Loved her still. When Cole and I had broken up, and I'd been at my lowest, she'd done everything in her power to pick me up. I had trained with her. She had taught me how to drive. And now...

This was her life. Her un-life. Endless hunger. Until she experienced a second death—brought about by her dearest friends. By us.

We had to end her.

I had no words.

No, that wasn't true. I had these: *pain, guilt, regret, remorse, sadness, torment.*

Yes, that one. *Torment.* I was shredded inside. Wasn't sure I'd be able to put myself back together this time.

"She's not the only one." Cole pointed.

As Trina—*not Trina, not anymore, just a shell*—swiped her arm through the slats in the gate, desperate to reach us, two other zombies shoved her out of the way, and I lost my breath all over again. Lucas and Collins were zombies, too.

I covered my mouth with shaky hands. Anima hadn't just sent a horde after us; they'd sent our slain friends, knowing how terribly it would hurt us to forever end them, probably thinking we would hesitate to deliver the deathblow, allowing other zombies to swoop in and end *us.*

Can't give them the satisfaction. "Keep moving," I demanded. The longer we stayed here, staring, the harder it would be to act. Grief would overtake us, hinder us. "Now!"

We launched into motion and finally arrived at the entrance of the tunnel, hidden behind the wall of the gazebo.

Like good little soldiers, we navigated the dank, narrow corridor single file.

At the exit, a monitor with images of the surrounding yard
waited. No zombies seemed to be within reach, but then, the
screens inside the house hadn't shown any zombies, either.

"Here's what we're going to do," Cole announced. "Jaclyn,
you will stay here and watch the bodies. If someone receives
a mortal injury, call Ankh. I'll go out first. Frosty, you'll be
last. You'll shut the door and guard it. The rest of you will
come in from behind and injure as many zombies as possible, tossing them at Ali as soon as she's lit." He turned to me.
"Your only job is to light up."

I nodded, already combating nerves. *No pressure, right?*

Everyone pressed against the wall, leaving the walkway
clear so Mr. Ankh would have room to work if necessary.
I closed my eyes and separated, air blustering against small
patches of exposed skin.

Cole climbed the ladder and flipped the lid, both of which
had been doused in Blood Lines, making them tangible. He
tossed out a minigrenade. *Boom!* Grunts sounded. A leg fell
through the opening, the shoeless foot still twitching. The
bomb wouldn't have hurt the zombies in collars. They weren't
in the spirit realm, where the bomb detonated, but in the
physical realm. We'd have to fight them another way.

As Frosty crouched and placed his now-glowing hand over
it, the rest of us scaled the ladder.

We entered a bona fide war zone.

The forest surrounding Mr. Ankh's house teemed with
zombies. The bomb had killed the ones in the immediate

area, but hordes of others weren't very many yards away. They scented us and rushed over en masse.

My friends met them in the middle.

I remained in place. I had one job, and I would do it. *Light up.*

A small flicker…gone.

Come on, come on. I can do this. I shook my arms. *Light!*

Another flicker, another vanishing act.

I didn't have to rack my brain for answers. Deep down, I really didn't want to do this. Trina, Lucas and Collins were out here. Was I really going to ash them?

You have to. They're already dead.

Uh-oh. Incoming! I withdrew a gun and fired, nailing a zombie in the neck. The creature hit the ground but swiftly climbed to his feet. I fired again and again, nailing him in both kneecaps to hamper his steps. He went down, and though he stayed down, he crawled toward me.

More zombies focused on me. I shot three before my gun jammed. *Can't panic.* I pulled back the slide and tried again. *Click, click.* I cursed. This kind of thing rarely happened; we didn't keep cheap weapons around. Why here, why now? I tossed the useless piece of crap to the ground and withdrew the axes, then launched forward, decapitating the zombie already on the ground as I passed.

Slash. A head rolled.

Hack. Another head rolled.

Thump. The blade of the ax cut through a zombie's chest, but got stuck.

I swung up with my left hand to hack at the zombie behind him with the remaining ax, but he blocked me. At the same time, I released the one that was stuck and palmed a blade to slice through a spine. To a human, it would have been a killing blow. The zombie leaned forward and tried to bite me. I ducked, spun and hacked at both of my opponents at the same time. One lost his head; the other lost the lower part of his jaw and some tongue.

I stomped on the chest of the zombie who was still wearing my ax, breaking his sternum and ribs, freeing the weapon.

Light up. Now!

Again, the meager flicker vanished. Exasperation…irritation—zombies had the upper hand, because of me.

I needed time. Time Helen's ability could give me.

Can't waste precious seconds with indecision. Use it!

Gonna get your wish, Kat.

I held out my arms…waited…but nothing happened. Exactly how was I supposed to push energy out of my spirit?

I gave my hands a shake. Tried again, with the same abysmal results. How had I done it last time?

Figure it out. Fast! In the distance, more and more zombies swarmed Cole. He was somehow using a crossbow and samurai sword in unison, shooting off arrows while remaining in a constant state of motion, slicing away at different parts of the enemy. Severed limbs piled up around him. One wrong move, though…

A few feet away, Camilla grabbed a zombie by the arm and tossed him at River. Then she grabbed another and another and another, as if they were in an assembly line, and tossed them, too. A grinning River decapitated each one. Nice tag-teaming.

I couldn't find Bronx. Gavin was working his way through

a horde of zombies, using his daggers to stab one in the eyes...
then the genitals. Nearby, a zombie managed to tangle his fingers in Veronica's hair and jerk her to the ground, but Gavin
was too preoccupied to notice.

I raced over, and because I was in spirit form, I could move
at a speed natural feet never could. Between one heartbeat and
the next, I reached my destination. But my presence wasn't
necessary. Veronica kicked the zombie in the face, rolled over,
punched another zombie and jumped to a stand, whipping
out a sword from the sheath anchored to her back. Then she
just started chopping.

Warm breath fanned over my neck, and a hungry grunt
sounded in my ear. I spun, swinging my axes. I cut through a
zombie's open mouth just before he bit me. Black ooze spurted
from him as he fell. Steam rose from the wound.

Camilla jumped in my path, her sword raised as if she
meant to kill me. I ducked, instinct demanding I attack her
first. Just before I obeyed it, her blade sliced through another
zombie that had been sneaking up behind me, and I paused.
Goo splattered me, stinging.

"Light up," she demanded.

"I'm trying!" I swung to decapitate the zombie coming in
hot at my right.

"Try harder."

"You don't understand," I said.

"Oh, I understand. I understand you're new, and you need
a little encouragement to help your abilities kick in. Well,
allow me to provide it." She fought her way to Cole.

As I sliced and diced the zombies around me, I did my best
to keep an eye on her. It wasn't wise, dividing my attention

like that, but what else could I do? She withdrew two guns and shot the zombies surrounding Cole point-blank. They tripped about in circles, unable to see, to bite, their faces in pieces.

Cole turned toward her, probably to say thanks, but she aimed the gun—at him. At his chest. Then she looked to me, as if to say, *What are you going to do about it, huh?*

His eyes widened as he lifted his weapons. To kill her before she could kill him? Maybe. But he would be too late.

"No!" I screamed. The surge of desperation did what I had been unable to, shoving a huge blast of power out of me. Little zaps of lightning pulsed through the air. All around, zombies suddenly catapulted upward.

Camilla lowered her gun and gaped. She'd never seen me use this particular skill.

Cole stilled.

I stood in place, breathing heavily, my hands raised and clenched into fists. I'd finally succeeded. But I didn't care. Camilla had endangered the love of my life. Unacceptable! She hadn't intended to follow through, I knew that, but accidents happened.

Rage poured through me, out of me…as if the intense surge of power had left some kind of hole inside me. One by one, the collared zombies began to explode, their bodies bursting apart at the seams, spraying more black goo in every direction. I never touched them.

I spotted Trina, flailing for some kind of anchor, and suddenly my rage was overshadowed by unending sorrow. I tried to switch off the power. Maybe we could capture and cage her. Maybe, one day, we would find a Z-cure. If we did, she could live, like Emma and Helen, as a Witness. Except…

Trina exploded.

I shouted a denial. My knees threatened to collapse. *Stop, have to stop.*

There went Lucas.

No, no, no! I scanned the remaining zombies...still exploding... *Turn it off, freaking turn it off...*

But there went Collins, too.

In seconds, uncollared zombies were gone, as well, leaving nothing but white ash. My knees finally made good on their threat and collapsed. I hit the ground, my brain rattling against my skull. But I was too weak to hold myself up and quickly tumbled to my face.

Can't move... Something's wrong... What's wrong?

"Ali." Footsteps. Cole crouched at my side.

I wanted to turn my head, to meet his gaze, but couldn't. Was this why Helen had warned me to be careful? The more energy I used, the more useless I'd be afterward?

A second later, I was floating. No, being carried. Strong arms were banded around me, a heartbeat racing beneath my ear. Strawberries teased my nose. I was jostled as Cole...descended the ladder? Probably. I didn't even have the strength to open my eyes and check.

Jostled more as... I don't know what.

"Her spirit isn't bonding with her body," Cole said, clearly dismayed.

Ah. But he had to be wrong. With one touch, a spirit always returned to its shell. Its home.

He manipulated my arm, moving it forward and back, shaking it, but nothing happening.

"Let's align her from top to bottom." River's voice registered.

I was forced into a vertical position, multiple sets of hands holding me up. One of those sets must have still been on fire—no, two sets, one up high, one down low—because a tide of warmth swept over me, filling me up, welding me together, and suddenly it was all systems go. I could breathe. I could move.

"Going to be okay," a soft voice whispered.

Helen?

My eyelids popped open. I sprawled on the floor of the tunnel, slayers in motion all around me.

I heard Jaclyn. "—says there's a guy out there, south side of property, and he's not a zombie."

"Spy?" Bronx and Frosty asked in unison.

"Let's find out," Cole said, ice-cold with determination.

He wasn't worried about me anymore, wasn't hovering; must mean I was going to be okay.

"I'll help." River buzzed past me, practically shoving Frosty out of the way to climb the ladder.

I managed to lumber upright—and did, in fact, catch sight of Helen. She sat next to me, her color waxen, her image fading.

"Going to be okay," she repeated. "I took care of the problem."

She'd sealed the leak in my spirit and given me strength the same way she'd given me her ability, hadn't she? By sacrificing her own.

She offered me a small smile before vanishing altogether.

I'M STILL DIGESTING YOUR FRIENDS

"Ali. Good. You're up." Bronx motioned me over. "Gavin could use some help."

Yes, he most certainly could. He'd been bitten, his neck a mess of blood, meat and black ooze.

I pushed to my feet without any problem and rushed to his side. Along the way, spirit and body separated. The moment I reached him I was able to press both hands inside Gavin's wound. For once, I didn't have to tell myself to light up. The fire came of its own accord. Was this thanks to Helen, too?

My heart squeezed. I desperately wanted to speak with her.

Gavin jolted up and would have punched me, I'm sure—he wasn't in his right mind—if Bronx hadn't grabbed him and shoved down. As the flames moved through him, he spewed the darkest curses I'd ever heard. Some were quite inventive, suggesting I have sex with a few of my weapons. In any other situation, I would have laughed.

Camilla stood back, watching me with wide eyes. "The things you do…I don't understand."

And I wasn't going to explain.

I kept my attention on Gavin. The wound began to close right before my eyes. By the time two Alis became one, the skin had already woven back together. That quickly?

Why such a change?

Jaclyn held out a hand, intending to help Gavin stand.

He scowled up at her, even slapped her hand away. "You came out of the tunnel against orders!"

"Because you needed help."

"You let yourself be cornered by zombies," he continued, unfazed by her outburst. "I came over to assist you, and you decided to use me as a human shield. What's worse, you would have left me there to die if they hadn't cornered you again. So accept your help now, Bambi? No." He stood on his own.

Bambi. Cute and insulting at the same time.

"I didn't mean… It was an accident…and when I realized you were down, I fought my way toward you."

He dismissed her words as unimportant and stepped into his body.

"Please," she said, again holding out her hand, intending to clasp his. "You have to believe me."

His gaze raked over her, somehow more scathing than a rebuke, and she dropped her arm. "I don't *have* to do any-thing. I don't even have to like you. Proof—I never fantasize about doing you, and I fantasize about doing *everyone*. You're too flat-chested for me."

Okay. Enough. "Gavin," I snapped.

"What?" he asked, as if he hadn't a clue about what he'd done wrong.

Had he not realized how fragile Jaclyn was? For months, she'd worn a little-girl-lost air like a second skin.

"At least my balls are bigger than yours," she sneered, shocking me.

O-kay. Not so lost anymore.

"You sure about that?" Gavin sneered right back, and I couldn't be sure, but it kind of looked like he was fighting a...smile? "Take off your pants and show me."

"The only way I'll ever take off my pants in your presence is to use the material to choke you to death."

"Children, please." Bronx clapped his hands. "Your verbal foreplay isn't fun for the rest of us."

Jaclyn flipped him off.

Gavin shrugged, his gaze remaining on the object of his anger...lust?

"Maybe we should go back to the house," I said. Tempers were too high to wait patiently for Cole, River and Frosty to return. More important, we needed to be checked out by Mr. Ankh.

"Good idea. Move it," Bronx commanded.

As everyone marched down the tunnel, I glanced back at Cole's motionless form. I hated to leave it behind. *Get everyone situated, go back.*

Kat launched into my arms the moment I slipped through the door. "You survived! As if there was any doubt. Butterflies don't stand a chance against the Ali-nator. But where's Frosty? He's okay, right?" She pulled back to shake me. "Tell me he's okay."

"He's better than okay. He's tying up loose ends." Truth, without admitting he was on the hunt for a possible spy.

She beamed. "That's my boy."

"Ali. This way." Mr. Ankh escorted me to a gurney and tested my vitals.

Meanwhile, Reeve stepped into Bronx's open arms, and Juliana pulled Veronica aside to whisper something in her ear.

"What's this I hear about your spirit not being able to join your body?" Mr. Ankh asked.

"Could have been due to exhaustion," I said, unwilling to discuss Helen.

His winged brows seemed to throw a thousand questions at me.

"But someone lit up and I strengthened," I added, giving him just enough info to pacify.

It worked, and he moved on to check out the others. Using everyone's distraction to my advantage, I snuck out without another word. Well, almost snuck out.

"Hold up," Veronica called.

I wasn't in the mood to deal with her right now. She and her sister thought the world would be a better place without me. Already noted. Didn't need a repeat.

"Where are you headed?" she asked, coming up beside me.

"Back to the tunnel." I would stand guard, and woe to anyone who tried to hurt Cole.

"I'll go with you."

My new dilemma: hint that I wanted to be alone or flat-out say it?

I'd never been one for hinting. "Look, I don't want—"

"Me to go with you? Yeah. I know. But that's too bad. It's happening. There's something we need to discuss."

"Pass."

She flicked me an irritated glance. "I'd follow you into hell right now."

Well, crap. There was no way to fight that kind of determination. "Fine. Whatever. Do what you want."

"Planned on it."

"Planned on it," I mocked.

We reached the end of the tunnel. I sat at Cole's feet, resting my head on the wall behind me. Veronica paced in front of me.

"Just say it, whatever it is," I prompted. "I can take it." Maybe. Probably. "Then you can go."

She ran a hand down her ponytail. "Do you remember when I told you I had an ace that would break up you and Cole?"

No. I'd forgotten. "Veronica, I sincerely hope you take this the way it's intended—an insult. That's one of the dumbest questions I've ever heard."

"Whatever. My ace was Helen."

I stiffened, my back going ramrod-straight. "What do you know about her?"

"I know she's… Look, this is going to be hard to take, but there's no way to drop a bomb like this gently. I just have to blurt it out. Helen is… Ali, she's your birth mother."

Birth mother. The words echoed in my mind.

I wanted to laugh at her.

I couldn't laugh at her.

I'd entertained the thought myself, yes. But to have Veronica state it so baldly, so confidently…

A bomb of anger detonated inside me. "You don't know anything."

Emerald gaze grim, she said, "I know a lot more than you do."

"Apparently not. Her kid died."

"Which is exactly what she wanted Anima to think."

A punch in the gut. "I agree. But I'm not her." I couldn't be. "The ages don't match."

I'm grasping.

"You are." She offered me a sad smile. "And they do. Your birthday is not your birthday. You're Samantha."

Samantha. Sami. Another punch, this one harder, stealing my breath. "Not me. I would remember."

"Isn't that what you're doing?"

Was it? I wasn't sure of anything anymore.

"After Cole gave me his famous brush-off and got back together with you," she said, "I started digging into your past, looking for something to bury you. The pieces fell into place, and I almost told him. I wanted to, so bad. Helen didn't just betray his mother—she betrayed mine. They worked for Anima, were planning to leave together. Only, Helen turned on Erin, my mom. They fought, and Erin ended up with a concussion and no memory."

No memory…

The words taunted me.

Veronica quickened her pace. "I'm not sure how it happened, but my family ended up on Cole's porch. His family took us in, but my mom was never the same. Never remembered Jules or me. Never again cared about us."

"Stop talking," I said. This was too much. I needed time to process.

She ignored me, forging ahead. "For all I knew, you were exactly like Helen, a traitor. I planned to catch you doing something awful. But the more I got to know you, the more I realized you were completely ignorant of her, and you weren't hurting the group. You were helping."

I stood and swayed as dizziness swept through me. "Stop, Veronica. Please."

"You don't want to hear the truth?" she asked. "You, who abhor lies, don't want to admit you've been trapped in one all your life?"

"For all I know, you're saying this simply to break up Cole and me, as planned, thinking there's no way he'd want to date the daughter of his mother's executioner."

I'm grasping again.

Her lashes lowered, as if she couldn't force herself to look at me right now—couldn't deal with seeing her reflection in my eyes. "I saw how he was with you tonight. He knows, or at least he suspects, but still he's protective of you. Actually, he's more than that. He's adoring." A beat of surprised silence. "I never really knew him at all, did I? He was never going to leave you. My ace never mattered."

A tremor nearly rocked me to my butt. "What makes you so sure Helen is...that I could possibly be...?"

"Erin and Helen didn't just work together. They lived together. Two single women with daughters about the same age. I remember playing trucks with Sami. We'd fill them with dirt and crash them. Sami was blonde, beautiful...with unforgettable eyes. Your eyes. But she was always sad, rarely smiled. Never laughed. We used to make up stories about our dads."

A lump rose in my throat, and I swallowed hard.

"Erin and Helen used to talk about them. Erin would tell horror stories about the abusive Todd, while Helen would wax poetic about the one that got away. Phillip."

Phillip.

Phillip Bell.

My father.

I sank to the ground before I could fall. I shook my head. "I would remember." In more than just my dreams.

Veronica took no pity on me. "I have pictures of the two of us. Helen thought she destroyed everything we owned, but she didn't."

No way to prove it's me in those pictures.

But if Helen really had staged Sami's death and given the girl to her father, bits and pieces of my past would make sense. How my dad had prowled through our house every night, a gun in hand. I'd assumed he was watching for monsters, even though the gun wouldn't have hurt them, but maybe he'd been watching for *people*. Those who might be coming after his little girl.

Rebuttal: he hadn't known about Anima, slayers and zombies, and Helen would have told him, would have wanted him informed.

Of course, she could have told him, and he could have refused to believe.

And why had she gone back to Anima? Why not leave, as planned? Why turn on Erin?

Only one answer made any sense, and it was the glue that held the entire sordid story together. To protect the daughter she loved.

To protect...me?

Part of me wanted to accept it. To bask in the knowledge that my mother was out there, helping me. The other part still screamed in denial.

"Show me the pictures," I said.

Veronica nodded. "While we were out fighting, Jules put them in your room for Cole to find. She wants the two of you broken up for good, so he and I can get back together." Bitterness blended with self-deprecation. "She doesn't realize it's never going to happen, but then, she loves him. He saved her life, you know, after Todd purposely burned her and left her for dead. Because yes, he is our dad, and when Erin decided she didn't want us, he had legal rights to us. He still has them over Jules. He's the reason we're off grid."

The hatch to the tunnel flew open, and something fell through. Heart racing, I wiped my face.

The "something" moaned.

I rushed over...and breathed a sigh of relief when I realized it wasn't Cole, Frosty or River. It was one of Anima's best assassins. The guy who'd once shot and killed an innocent man in front of me.

The guy who'd tried to kill *me*.

Instinctively, I palmed a dagger. He was unconscious, or at least, he was pretending to be. He was wily, this one, and couldn't be trusted.

River dropped inside, landing and straightening in one

fluid motion. He pressed a booted foot into the guy's neck, grinning over at me. "I win."

Cole came in next and looked me over. "Everything okay?"

His first concern was for me, always for me. I wanted to cry. No, I wanted to hug him and never let go.

Could lose him over this... "Everyone survived," I managed to say.

His narrowed gaze leveled on Veronica. "If you said something to hurt her, Ronnie, I—" A muscle ticked in his jaw. "Veronica. If you said something to hurt her, I will—"

"It's not what you're thinking," I interrupted, taking hope in the fact that he'd stopped calling her Ronnie, just because I'd once mentioned how much it bothered me. "We'll talk about it when we're alone." Or never. I voted for never.

He looked from me to Veronica, Veronica to me. Comprehension dawned, and he stiffened. "Helen."

Sometimes smart boys were a pain.

I bit the side of my tongue, nodded.

Cole turned away, and my heartbeat finally slowed, the organ withering in my chest.

"You should have seen us," River said, unaware—or uncaring—of the sudden tension in the air. "Guy was fast, but not fast enough. We were able to introduce him to our fists."

"And our elbows," Cole said.

"And our knees and boots," River added. "He didn't stand a chance."

"How'd he get past Ankh's security?" Veronica asked.

Cole massaged the back of his neck. "That's a good question. One I intend to investigate."

"Well, let's get him locked up." And me to my room, where I could pore over those pictures.

"After that, let's talk about what you did out there," River said to me. His gaze moved to Veronica, got caught, and his grin returned. "How about you join the chat, honey?"

The rough-and-tumble Veronica Lane, who seemed to know more about me than I knew about myself, had no defense against a little flirting and freaking blushed. Unreal. "All right. Sure."

Ugh. This day!

Cole and River each grabbed one of the assassin's arms and dragged him forward. Veronica and I trailed behind.

"The real fun starts when he wakes up," River remarked.

"I told you," Cole said on a sigh. "We're not going to kill him."

"I didn't say anything about killing him, did I? I just figured we were going to torture him for information."

"That's not how we do things."

River looked over his shoulder and winked at Veronica. "You're about to start."

THIS WAY. NO, THAT WAY.
OOPS, DEAD END.

Here's what we already knew: the assassin was twenty-year-old Benjamin Ostrander Jr. We'd caught him a few weeks before and let him go. Our mistake. Before freeing him, Mr. Ankh and Mr. Holland had run his fingerprints through some kind of database. Apparently, good ole Benji had run away from home at the age of thirteen and had been arrested a few times for breaking and entering, as well as assault and battery. Right after his fifteenth birthday, he'd dropped off the map.

That must have been when Anima recruited him.

Now we hoped to find out what else his employers were planning and where Justin was being held. But hours passed and Benjamin never woke up, even when prodded.

Too tired to wait any longer, among other things, I strode out of the dungeon.

Cole shadowed me.

"Can we not do this tonight?" I asked, ready to beg.

"Sorry, Ali-gator. We can. We will."

Stubborn boy.

He stopped me at the top of the stairs, fingers deep in my hair so that I had to meet his fiery gaze. "You're upset, I'm upset, so, let's hash this out. It's not good to go to bed this way. It'll just be worse in the morning."

I tried to look away. He increased the pressure, keeping my attention on him. I sighed. "Okay. Fine. We'll go to my room. But I want it noted that you're acting like the girl, getting all talky-feely and crap."

Far from shamed, he said, "Noted." He wound his arm around my shoulders, tucking me against him. A protective stance, an intractable hold.

I'd have to fight to get free. But honestly, the action was both sexy and…majorly sexy.

Cole reached for the knob on my door and frowned. Giggles seeped from the crack at the bottom. "Expecting company?"

"No." I stepped inside to find Kat and Reeve sitting on my bed.

They spotted me and leaped to their feet.

"Ali!" Kat ran over and hugged me. Her grip was weaker than it had been the past few days, and I cursed her disease. "Reeve and I are locking horns over a joke. I say it's wonderful, and she says it's lame. We need a final ruling."

That, I could do. "Let's hear it."

"What did the zombie say during a wrestling match?"

Um… "What?"

"Do you want a piece of me?" she said and burst into laughter.

Cole snorted.

"See!" Kat stuck her tongue out at Reeve. "Even the stick-in-the-mud likes it."

The verdict? "I think it's wonderful *and* lame."

"I'll take that as a victory." She wagged a finger in Cole's face. "By the way, this is a girls-only slumber party. Boys are not invited. You've got to go."

He stood his ground. "Actually, *you've* got to go. Ali and I are going to talk."

"Cole," she said, batting her lashes at him. "I'm seconds away from bringing your penis into this conversation. Are you sure you want to stick around for that?"

He sighed. "You're about to threaten it, aren't you?"

A new round of laughter from the girls.

"Threaten?" Kat shook her head. "No, darling Cole. Remove? Yes."

Reeve walked over and gave him a little push into the hall. "You can talk to your Ali-gator tomorrow, King Cole. Tonight it's besties before testes, and if you don't hit the bricks, I will literally rip off those testes and feed them to you."

"I'm sure Bronx would love to hear you've contemplated putting your hands on my junk," he said, digging in his heels. "I'm staying *and* keeping my private property. Ali likes me intact."

I shrugged. Honestly, what could I really say? Truer words had never been spoken.

"Recognize a losing battle, Cole," Kat said. "It's been a rough couple of days, and we need a break. Let us have this one night. We'll be generous and let you have our girl tomorrow. Maybe." And then she shut the door in his face.

I expected him to burst back in, but he didn't. I almost

laughed as I crawled to the middle of the bed. I'd gotten my reprieve after all.

"I figured you guys would be with Frosty and Bronx," I said.

I spotted a large envelope on my nightstand. The pictures! I hurriedly stuffed the envelope in the top drawer, not wanting to look at the supposed evidence with anyone else around. I wasn't sure how I'd react.

"Frosty is already addicted to me." Kat flipped her hair over her shoulder. "If I spend any more time with him, he'll become a babbling idiot. And really, I like to keep him craving more. Besides, I wasn't lying to Cole. I need a one-night stand with you to just...I don't know, breathe. To be normal kids."

Yeah. That sounded all kinds of awesome.

Reeve threw herself beside me, the mattress bouncing us both. "I wish I could say the same about Bronx. He's in a mood. A horrible, terrible mood, and I don't know what to do about him. He's distant. He's snippy. Do you think he wants to break up with me?"

"Of course not." Bronx wasn't the love-'em-and-leave-'em type. He was the she's-mine-and-that's-that type. "But you have to remember, he just lost four of his friends. In one night." And then he'd watched me explode them only a few hours ago. *Oh, glory.* The memory would forever haunt me. "Another one is still missing. Bronx is grieving."

"I'm sure he's also worried about keeping you safe," Kat said, claiming a spot at the edge of the bed and crisscrossing her legs. "I know Frosty gets a little crazy when we're under attack. And let's face it. The danger level has never been higher."

"I know, but still!" Reeve beat her fists into the pillows.

"I just wish Bronx would talk to me about this stuff, you know? We're a couple. We're supposed to help each other. And I want to help him, I do, but he won't even give me the opportunity."

Guilt sparked, burning me. I'd done the same thing to Cole. Well, no more. Tomorrow, I'd tell him everything. Whatever happened, happened. I'd be a big girl and deal.

"Hunt down Bronx and explain how you feel," I said. "This isn't working for you. Something is broken and you need to fix it. Right away. If you wait, something else will need fixing soon enough, and then something else, until there's too much to do and both parties walk away depressed, defeated."

"Yeah. Okay," she said, but she still sounded miserable.

She'd do what I suggested or not. I couldn't force her.

"Let's shelve the discussion about our boys." Kat lifted her phone to snap a photo of Reeve. "It's selfie time!"

I made a face at her, and she snapped one of me.

"That's it," she praised, *click-click-clicking* away. "Make love to the camera."

She turned the phone on herself and grinned so wide she unveiled a mouthful of pearly whites. *Click, click.* "Dude! I think me and the camera just made a baby."

I snorted, reminded all over again why I loved her so danged much.

"Enough," Reeve said with a laugh, taking the phone away from her.

"Fine," Kat said. "So get this, guys. I got a call from Wren a few hours ago."

"What! That should have been the headline." Wren had been Kat's friend for years, only to ditch her—and by association, ditch me—so that we wouldn't draw her into our crazy and ruin her future. Not that she'd had any idea what our particular crazy happened to be. Then she'd started dating Justin, not realizing he was just as deeply ensconced as we were. "What'd she say?"

"Hear for yourself. She left a message." Kat reclaimed her phone, pressed a few buttons.

"Kat, it's Wren." The device practically vibrated with the volume. "Look, I know I'm not your favorite person, and that's fine. But Justin is missing. Jaclyn, too. Their parents are, like, totally freaking. The cops came and asked me all kinds of questions, but I didn't say anything about it, I swear. I'm just worried something's happened. Have you seen them? Heard from them? Call me back. *Please.*"

Kat sighed. "I haven't called her back. I don't know what to say."

I thought for a moment. "Let me discuss it with Cole before you do. Because honestly? We don't know if she's for real, or if the police have convinced her to try and trap us into saying something we shouldn't, or even if Anima has her phone tapped."

Kat wedged between Reeve and me. "That's such a good point it's almost as if I thought of it myself. And not to switch topics, but...I'm going to switch topics. To me! I've decided to stop waiting to die, stop letting worry ruin the days I do have and start planning an actual future."

I rested my head on her shoulder. "As long as you keep doing your dialysis, I'm happy for you."

"Dude. No worries on that score."

"Then tell me everything. Even the smallest details."

"Well," she said, getting more comfortable, "here's what I've got so far. I'm going to college and getting a Ph.D. in being awesome. That's a thing, right? Everyone will call me Dr. Kitten and pay me megabucks to diagnose all their problems. Because, of course, I will have all the answers."

The trials of the day caught up to me. My eyelids grew heavy. I struggled to keep them open, her voice the sweetest lullaby.

"I'm going to live with Frosty, and he's going to cater to my every whim. When I've decided he's earned the right to be Mr. Kat Parker, I will marry him. You two will be maids of honor, of course. I'm going to force you to wear the most hideous gowns ever created. Can't have anyone thinking you're prettier than the bride."

It was, in a word, perfect.

I wondered about my own future plans. Or tried to. I couldn't see past this war with Anima. I was...

Mmm, so warm...

As Kat talked about her honeymoon, I drifted away....

It was the saddest day of my life.

The whispering voice penetrated my awareness. It didn't belong to me. Didn't belong to Kat or Reeve, either....

The next thing I knew, I was outside. Helen and Sami stood hand in hand on a dirt road, a dark sedan parked behind them. Looked to be empty. Another sedan pulled up and stopped alongside it. Hinges on the door squeaked as— shock hit me—my dad emerged.

He was so young. There were no lines around his eyes. His skin wasn't sallow from years of hard drinking, and his eyes weren't bloodshot. He was handsome, radiating health— and anger.

He stomped to Helen, his gaze continuously flicking to the little girl. "How could you keep her from me?"

Helen raised her chin. "Would you have done anything differently if you'd known? No. You would have married Miranda, and we both know it."

He flinched, and the little girl darted behind Helen's leg.

My dad softened. He crouched in an effort to meet the girl eye to eye. "Hello," he said. "I'm Ph—your dad."

Sami stayed right where she was.

"She's not to know who I am," Helen said. "You're never to speak of me. As far as the world is concerned, Miranda gave birth to her, and there will be paperwork to prove it. Do you understand?"

"No. I don't understand. I don't understand any of this. She needs us both. She—"

"If you can't agree to my terms, you can't have her." Helen grabbed Sami's hand to tug her away.

"I'll do it," he promised, and Helen stilled. "What do I tell her when she asks about you?"

"She won't. She won't remember me."

He frowned, but didn't question her further.

"She's in danger. People want her. Bad people. If they get her, they will hurt her." Tears splashed down Helen's cheeks. "Only one person knows you're her father, and I'm going to— Well, it doesn't matter. She won't matter. You'll have to change Sami's name. Something significant to your family. Give her a new past, and then live as if every word of that past is true. You speak as if it's true."

My dad straightened, nodded. "I'll do everything you've asked. So will Miranda. I won't let anything happen to her."

Helen stood there for several seconds, a war obviously waging in her mind. Finally she said, "Go back to your car. I'll bring her to you in a minute."

She waited until he'd done as commanded before turning and kneeling in front of Sami, taking her by the shoulders. "I love you. *So much*. That's never going to change."

"Don't go," Sami whispered, agonized. "Please."

"It has to be this way. You'll never know how sorry I am." Helen's chin lifted again. She moved her hands to the little girl's temples. It didn't look as if she was doing anything. Just holding her daughter. But in seconds, the terror and desperation faded from Sami's eyes. Her features smoothed out.

"Do you know who you are?" Helen asked, arms falling to her sides. "Do you know who I am?"

Sami thought for a moment, paled. "I… No." The terror and desperation returned in a blink. She spun, searching for something, anything familiar. "Where am I? Who are you?"

Tears once again streaming, Helen took her hand. "Come on. Your father is waiting for you. And so is…your mother."

The next day, I tried to compartmentalize the dream—memory—with zero success. Maybe because I couldn't get past a single thought: I was Sami. Me. There was no denying the truth in the bright light of the morning.

Helen the Slayer Killer was my mother. And I liked her.

Was that wrong? Was it a betrayal of Cole?

Leaving Kat and Reeve sleeping in bed, I showered, dressed and went in search of him, ready to have our chat. He wasn't in his room. The next most likely place was the dungeon, but he wasn't there, either. River was finally having his fun with Benjamin, with, surprisingly enough, help from Frosty. The two had the assassin strapped to a chair and were taking turns introducing his face to their fists.

"Guys," I said. "This isn't the way."

River looked over at me, frowned.

"When you think of another way, *then* we'll talk." Frosty closed the distance and shut the door in my face.

I could have protested. But he was right—I didn't know another way.

I'd talk to Cole about it—I just had to find him first. I tried the gym. Bronx and Gavin were working out, but again, my boyfriend wasn't anywhere nearby. No one knew where he'd gone.

Great!

I turned my efforts to Nana. Standing in the foyer, I typed up a text.

I know about Helen. I know who she is 2 me. U should have told me.

I waited one minute…two…

Finally my phone rang. She was calling. But of course, the doorbell had to buzz a second later. From my vantage point, I had a direct view of the smoked-glass doors.

The detectives were back.

Mr. Ankh strode out of his office, his features pinched. "This is going to be fun."

I let my phone roll to voice mail.

Mr. Ankh did not invite the detectives inside, just stood

in the entryway, a pillar of calm. "All further inquiries are to be directed to my lawyer."

"We're not here with questions," Verra said in her no-nonsense way. "We're here for Jaclyn Silverstone. She's sixteen and therefore underage. Someone called her parents and told them she was here."

Someone from Anima?

Mr. Ankh stood still and quiet for several prolonged seconds. "I'll get her." He shut the door. His bleak gaze met mine. "We have to do it."

"I know." I also knew I couldn't be the one to tell her. She'd fight me, and I might help her run. Already my heart was breaking for her.

Mr. Ankh stomped up the stairs, reappearing five minutes later with a crying Jaclyn at his side. A scowling Gavin strode behind him.

I wanted so badly to barricade the door. Maybe Gavin wanted it, too. He stopped at my side, his hands fisted.

Was he actually *angry* about her eviction?

We moved to the porch. Jaclyn cried even harder as the detectives helped her inside their sedan.

The car's engine purred to life.

She looked out the window, met my gaze.

"Remember my promise," I said.

A tormented nod. The car pulled away, soon vanishing beyond the gate.

Can't react.

"She and I had a vision, you know," Gavin said, as we sealed ourselves inside the house. "In it, we were in bed together."

"What! You did? How? When?"

He scrubbed a hand down his face. "Yes, we did. And I don't know how. I've only ever had a vision with you and Cole, and I thought it was because all of our parents were slayers, so we got a little something extra. Well, neither of her parents are slayers, and yet still, when I saw her this morning, time stopped and we were suddenly... Let's just say she was the recipient of my best moves."

Weird did not even begin to scratch the surface of this development. "Are you attracted to her? Is that why you were so hard on her before?"

Amusement twinkled down at me. "Why, yes, cupcake. That's why I was so *hard* on her."

Dirty-minded gutter rat. "Are you sure this vision wasn't just a fantasy of yours? Even though you claimed not to have them about her."

He tweaked the end of my nose. "I'm sure. Trust me. This slut-spert knows the difference."

Well, wasn't that just wonderful. We had yet another mystery to solve. "I need to think about this."

"You do that. Meanwhile, I'm going upstairs and giving myself a new tattoo. One that says 'Women suck, and not always in a good way.' The reminder might help calm me down."

"Alice."

I had just trudged upstairs, determined to search every room for Cole—still hadn't found him—and discuss this latest mystery. At the top landing, a bright light glowed, Emma in the center of it.

As always, my heart swelled with love for her, and I grinned, everything else momentarily forgotten. A quick look left and right proved no one else was in the hallway. "I'm so glad you're here."

She shifted from one slipper-covered foot to the other. "Even though I'm usually the Bad News Bear?"

"Even though."

She cracked a grin of her own. "Well, today, I've got good news…and, okay, bad news, too."

I didn't allow myself to groan. Didn't want to make her feel any worse. "Lay it on me, little sis. Bad news first."

She nibbled on her bottom lip before admitting, "Justin is hurt. Like, horribly hurt. We've heard his moans of pain echo throughout eternity."

Suspected. Poor Justin. "What's the good news?"

"He's not dead yet."

Yet. The time limit tainted the sweetness of the update. "Do you know where Anima's keeping him?"

"No. There's some kind of block surrounding him."

Of course there was.

If I believed in luck, I'd say ours was the worst.

"Come to my room," I said. "I want you with me while I look through pictures that are probably going to change the course of my life."

Thankfully, Kat and Reeve had left, saving me from having to evict them. I sat at the edge of my bed and placed Juliana's envelope of pictures on my lap. Emma took a place at the windowsill.

Her head tilted to the side, and she frowned. "Nana's worried about you. You should call her back."

"Can you sense our emotions?"

"Not as strongly as I could at first, but yes."

"Then you know I'm upset. She kept secrets from me."

"So did Mom and Dad, but they aren't alive to blame, so you're focusing on her."

I was, wasn't I? "When did you become so wise?"

"The fact that you haven't realized I've always been this wise does not speak well of *your* intelligence."

I threw a pillow, but it ghosted through her. I picked up the phone and dialed Nana's new number.

When she answered, I got straight to the point. "I have two questions for you, and I need you to be totally and completely honest with me this time."

"I will," she said with resolve.

"Is Helen Conway my birth mother? Did Miranda have to adopt me?"

Silence.

"Ali," she finally said. I imagined her sitting somewhere, alone in the dark, her eyes closed as she fought tears.

Stay strong. "That's not an answer."

"Yes," Nana whispered. "Helen is. But Miranda couldn't adopt you, not legally. Your dad said you couldn't be brought to anyone's attention, so he somehow arranged a new identity for you. New name, new birthday, new biological mother."

Well. There it was. Indisputable proof. Helen was my mother. My birth name was Samantha. I'd spent my first few years acting as Anima's favorite pincushion.

Betrayal—check.

Anguish—check.

The people claiming to love me most had hurt me more

than anyone else ever had, but they were dead. I couldn't yell at them. I couldn't demand answers. Though I already knew their reasons. I couldn't tell them how their actions had affected me.

"But that doesn't mean I love you any less," Nana added.

"No, it means you lied to me for most of my life. It means my parents lied to me."

"Ali, dear, I'm sorry, I am, but it was your parents' decision to make. To even be allowed to see you, I had to promise never to breathe a word."

"You've been my guardian for ten months," I said. "All this time, it's been your decision."

"You, my honest one, know the value of a promise."

Low blow.

Also true.

"But I *am* sorry," she repeated. "I chose not to let you know because you'd been through so much already. I didn't want you to have to go through anything else. And honestly, I don't think of it much. You're my granddaughter. Always have been, always will be."

My chest felt like it had been doused in acid. "I'm going to go. I—"

"No! Don't you dare hang up on me," she said, her voice rising to a yell. "If you do, I'll be on the first plane back to Alabama. I might anyway. I want to hold you and answer any other questions you have. I don't know a lot about it—your parents refused to talk about it—but I'll answer what I can."

I sighed. "No. Stay with Mr. Holland. I'm not mad at you, not really, I just need time to deal with everything. I'll call you when I'm ready. Okay?"

"Okay. All right. Just tell me that you know I love you."

"I do. I know. And I love you, too."

We said our goodbyes and hung up. I stood, the packet of pictures falling to the floor. In a daze, I tripped my way to my little sister and just kind of fell at her feet. She wasn't solid to me, and I wasn't solid to her, but still she traced her fingers through my hair.

"You're only my half sister," I said softly.

"And that makes you adore me less?" she asked.

"Never!"

"Well, it's the same for me."

"But the woman who gave birth to me was evil. Awful." Except to me. "She turned on her best friend. She helped kill Cole's mother."

"Well, then, I've got another bit of good news for you. *You* are not *her*. You're the one and only Alice, perfect in every way."

Hardly. "I have her push-ability, Em. I'm *a lot* like her."

"Well, the other slayers are about to be a lot like her, too."

Um...what? "Explain."

Sighing, she said, "When Helen passed her ability to you, it broke through some kind of defensive shield and changed you."

"That, I know."

"Changed you more than you've realized," she said. "More than *she* realized. Now whenever you use your fire on a slayer, you share your abilities with them."

I wanted to deny it, but there was already proof to the contrary. I'd used my fire on both Gavin and Jaclyn, and they'd had a vision for the first time. "Helen said that once an ability is passed, the original possessor no longer has it. I'm still in possession of mine."

"Maybe it was the testing you endured as a child. Maybe it was the drugs and toxins you were injected with when you were tortured. Whatever the reason, you *are* different."

Who else had I healed? Would they develop new abilities, too? If so, would they thank me—or curse me?

Emma pointed to the packet of pictures. "Why don't you look them over? I think you'll be surprised by what you find."

OFF WITH YOUR MESSED UP HEAD

I riffled through the photos of Helen, Sami, Erin and Veronica, my hands trembling. It was odd, seeing the strong, determined woman from my dreams—and the few times she'd appeared to me—relaxed, almost happy.

But Veronica was right. Sami—*I*—had rarely smiled.

In all but one of the photos, I was sullen, clinging to Helen. In the single exception, I was in a sandbox with the slightly older Veronica; I knew it was her. Those dark curls were unmistakable.

A tear rolled down my check, hot and stinging, and just like that, a dam broke, ushering in an uncontrollable storm. A sob erupted, soon joined by another…and another. Everything I'd compartmentalized, planned to deal with later, burst free of its prison.

"Oh, Alice," Emma said, then spoke no more.

Sorrow. Trina, Lucas, Collins and Cruz—dead, ashed.

Heartache. Me, the girl who valued truth above almost anything, lived in a tangled web of lies.

Shock. My mother wasn't my mother.

More heartache. What would happen when Cole was hurt in the woods, like our vision predicted? Would I lose him?

Guilt. I was keeping a secret from Cole.

Though I wanted to wallow in all that I was feeling, I knew I had to let the emotions go. Finally. Once and for all. They were part of the past, and I couldn't move forward if I was always looking back.

I'd never needed to move forward more than I did now. But all I really knew how to do was stuff the emotions back in their compartments. And I might have done it, except the walls hadn't just crumbled—they'd exposed a wound, and if I rebuilt over it, I'd find myself back in this tragic place one day.

"Ali? Emma said something was wrong." Suddenly Cole was sitting beside me, drawing me into the warmth and strength of his embrace.

I sagged against him, burrowing my face in the hollow of his neck and crying. Crying so hard I convulsed. He never let go, just held tighter, running his fingers through my hair and whispering soft words of comfort into my ear.

Things like "I love you, Ali-gator" and "We'll get through this" and "This isn't going to break us" and "We're stronger than that."

When finally I quieted, he picked me up and carried me out of the room, away from the pictures and the pain. My eyes were swollen; they burned as if they'd brushed up against actual flames. My nose was so stuffy I could barely breathe, and every ounce of energy had abandoned me. Just then, I was nothing more than a melted puddle of goo. Embarrassed goo, at that. I'd probably left snot on Cole's shirt.

He entered another bedroom; one glowing with candles. It was spacious, with two separate parts. The bed, and the entertainment area, with a plush couch and a coffee table piled high with food. Some of my favorites. Fettuccine Alfredo. Stuffed mushrooms. Fried cheese. Chocolate-chip cookies topped with vanilla ice cream.

"I put together a hideaway for us," he said, easing me to the edge of the bed. Soft music played in the background. "Thought we could finally have our first date."

A lance through my acid-ruined chest. "You shouldn't have done it. Not for me. Cole, Helen is—"

"I know, love. I know."

Did he? Really? I had to say the words out loud. "She's my mother."

His nod was slow and easy. "Veronica confirmed what I'd begun to suspect."

Sparks of anger. *Not her story to tell.* "My birthday was changed. I'm older than we realized."

"Good to know."

"I dream about Helen. She appears to me."

He crouched in front of me and braced his hands on my thighs. "Ignore the dreams, ignore the woman."

But...I didn't want to. "She helps me."

"She's a liar. She'll betray you, hurt you."

"No, she—"

"Is. She will." His expression hardened, becoming granite. "But who she is and what she does doesn't change who you are—mine."

His assurance did just what it was supposed to. Assured me. And yet, my nerves began to fray at the edges. He saw one side of a coin. I saw the other. She was evil to him, but good to me. He wanted me to forget her. I wanted a relationship with her—wanted whatever I could get.

Would he be able to come to grips with that? "I'm tired of letting Anima run things," I said, switching tracks. "They make a move, and we struggle to recover. That's old. So, in the morning, I'm searching for Justin. I promised Jaclyn."

"While I like your enthusiasm," he said, "you don't really have a place to start your search."

"Yes, I do. We know Justin was driven out of that warehouse. Well, there's an apartment building across the street from it. Maybe someone was watching from a window. I'll go door-to-door, if necessary, and ask. I'll also call Ethan. He used to work for Anima and knows how they operate."

"He might still be working for them."

"There's really only one way to find out."

Silence. A sigh. "Okay," Cole said. "I'll help.

Those words took me full circle, right back to the beginning of our conversation—to the crux of my fears. "If I talk to Helen, learn what *she* knows, will you think *I* am working with Anima?"

Peering at me, voice firm, he said, "Okay, that's it. Spanking time." He sat beside me and tugged me over his lap.

I yelped when he flattened his big hand against my bottom, but rather than smack, he rubbed.

"Do I have your attention?" he asked. "Good. I want you to listen to me, and listen closely. Have I been fooled by Anima before? Yes. But I learned from my mistakes, and I don't make the same one twice. Give me a little credit. And give yourself a little credit, too. You care about your friends. You are kind and honest and as close to perfect as humanly possible. You hate Anima as much as we do. You would never help them, not even for her." He spat that last word. "When the shock of her connection to you wears off, you'll realize she's a monster with an angel's face. That's all."

That's what he wanted. Maybe what he needed.

But I wasn't sure it would happen, and that scared me.

Stupid fear!

He helped me straighten.

"You keep promising me a spanking and not delivering," I said.

"It's your eyes. They can talk me out of anything."

"What is it, exactly, that they say?"

"Usually 'you're so amazing, Cole.' And 'I want to be your slave, Cole.'"

Ha!

"Now how about that date?" he asked.

"Please."

We ate. We talked and laughed and even watched a movie. We were lost in our own little world. But the intimate time together made me...itchy. I wanted more.

Wanted him. Finally.

Guess my eyes would have to talk him out of his clothes.

I straddled his lap, wrapping my arms around his neck and my legs around his waist. "I'm so used to seeing you without a shirt. If you feel uncomfortable wearing one, just go ahead and take it off. I mean, I'm only thinking of you."

Snorting, he stood with me wound around him like a boa constrictor and walked to the bathroom. After placing me on the marble countertop, he removed his shirt—cheer, clap—

and hunted down a washrag. After turning on the faucet, he wet the rag and gently cleaned my face.

Oh, crap! "I must look hideous," I mumbled. No wonder he'd stopped me before I'd even gotten started. "My earlier blubbering has ruined our date."

"Hey. Your blubbering was a highlight for me."

A small laugh escaped me. "Has anyone ever called you sweet? No? Good."

"You've told me I *taste* sweet." He tossed the washrag to the floor. "You ready for phase two of the evening?"

"Depends on what, exactly, phase two is."

"The kiss at the door. Or, in our case, the *shower* door." His heavy-lidded gaze swept over me. "I wasn't going to go this far, not tonight, but you're dirty. Like, really, really dirty. Filthy, even. I've got to do my gentlemanly duty and clean the rest of you up."

My heart skittered into a frenzied beat. "Underclothes on or off?"

"Ladies' choice."

Sucked for him, because he wasn't going to like my answer. Or rather, he was going to like it way too much. "Off."

He moaned as he fussed with the knobs inside the shower. "You're trying to kill me, aren't you?"

"Kill your *resistance*, yes. You'll thank me later."

"I'm sure."

Water rained, and steam thickened the air. He stripped out of his boots, jeans and weapons. Lots and lots of weapons. Daggers. Throwing stars. More daggers. A gun. Another gun. Ammo. The famous minicrossbow. More daggers. Metal clanged against metal, his every movement fascinating me.

"Your turn," he said, his voice a mix of need and command.

I toyed with the ends of my hair. "Can I ask you a question first?"

"You just did. Strip."

Funny man. I eased to my feet. "Would you have waited one year and three months for your other girlfriends?"

He crossed his arms over his chest. "Either way I answer that, I'm going to sound like a douche-purse."

See? That word was going to follow me forever. "So don't add 'knocked into a coma' to the description, and give me the truth."

"Fine. No. No, I wouldn't have. I would have moved on. And before you rapid-fire more questions, no, I won't get tired of waiting for you, and no, I won't move on from you."

Reason number seventeen was about to come into play. "Why wait with me?" My gaze raked over him, and my cheeks heated. "It's clear you'd rather not."

"Because you're mine. Not just now but always. I want to do what's right by you. I *will* do what's right."

"The others were yours, too," I said. Steam continued to thicken the air, creating a dreamlike haze. "Once."

"They weren't mine. They were...practice."

Pretty words. They almost melted me. Almost. "How do you know I won't become practice for some other girl?"

He stepped forward, pressing me against the bathroom counter, the hardest part of him nestling against the softest part of me. He tugged my shirt over my head. "You're just going to have to trust me." His fingers settled on the waist of my pants, unfastened the button. "Do you?"

"Yes."

"Good." He returned me to the counter and removed my boots.

I leaned back, bracing my weight on my elbows and lifting my hips to help him tug off my pants. I was sweet like that.

Once the denim cleared my feet, I was left in my bra, panties and arsenal. One by one, he discarded each of the weapons. I had just as many daggers, but no guns. He looked me over, then looked me over again, as if he couldn't *not* do it.

"Does it bother you that I'm flat-chested?" I asked, the question slipping out before receiving permission from my brain.

His gaze jerked up, meeting mine. "You're perfect. Why would you wonder something like that?"

"Something Gavin said—"

"Gavin commented on your chest?" Cole swiped up one of the daggers. "I will kill him. Will brutally murder him."

I grabbed his wrist, pried the weapon from his kung-fu grip and laughed. "He didn't say it to me. Or even about me."

My very possessive, very protective boyfriend relaxed, but only slightly. "Fine. He can live."

I stripped the rest of the way, and Cole urged me into the shower. He came in behind me, closing the door, sealing us inside, letting the steam thicken around us.

"I will be insanely mad if you ever come home with implants," he said, maneuvering me under the spray of water. "I know I'm repeating myself, but you're perfect."

"Thank you."

But he wasn't done. "Any guy who makes a girl feel like she needs a bigger rack isn't worth shi—crap."

"Shi-crap?" I asked with another laugh, loving him more

with every second that passed. He couldn't be any cuter. "Sounds like something we should keep in our douche-purse."

"*Anyway.* Someone should tell Gavin to get a penile implant," Cole grumbled.

"Jaclyn is one step ahead of you. She told him to grow bigger balls."

"Well, that's a good start."

Remaining behind me, Cole soaped me up...slowly...his hands lingering here, there. He washed and conditioned my hair, his body flush against mine, and it wasn't long before the water wasn't the only thing steaming up the walls.

"Your new tattoos have healed," he said, kissing the base of my neck.

A shiver stole through me. "You still like?"

"Definitely." His thumb traced the top ridges of my spine in a sensuous caress. "But you never told me what the phoenix means."

"You can't guess?"

"I can," he said, nibbling my earlobe, "but I'd also like to hear it."

It was difficult to get my brain to work, but I somehow managed to explain my thought process—that he'd stood in the fire with me, holding my hand, helping me rise from the ashes of my other life. When I finished, he turned me and pressed a soft kiss onto my lips.

"You make me happy," he said.

"Let's see if I can make you even happier." I took the soap from his hands and cleaned him as slowly and thoroughly as he'd cleaned me, adoring every inch of him.

After I rinsed him off, I massaged shoulders granite-hard

with tension and moved my attention to his chest, tracing each of his tattoos…delving lower, to his stomach. A stomach that quivered, making my breath catch—and *my* stomach quiver.

"This was a bad, bad idea." Eyes blazing, he backed me into the wall. "One of the worst we've ever had."

The cool tile made me gasp. "Or the best."

"Maybe I was testing my resolve. I got an F, by the way." He lowered his head and fed me a hard, hot kiss. A deep kiss. A soul-shattering kiss. A kiss sweetened by the water on our lips.

As I wound my arms around his neck, he rubbed against me. "Every time I'm with you like this," he said, "I feel like I've finally found my way home."

I moaned. The things this boy said to me…as potent as his touch, heating me up, liquefying my insides. "Cole."

"Want to do more…shouldn't."

"Should! I'm older, remember?"

"Yeah, but I need time to wrap my head around that." He lifted his head, frowned. A few seconds later, he straightened, severing contact. "Something's wrong."

Yes, something was. He was no longer concentrating on me. "How do you know?"

"I feel like I'm having a vision. Only, I'm not seeing any-thing. Just feeling."

I didn't ask any more questions. Sensing danger was a specialty of his. Jumping from the stall, I quickly toweled off and dressed. Cole did the same, and we both palmed a weapon. Crossbow for him and a .44 for me. I screwed the silencer on the end.

"Zombies?" I asked.

His violet eyes were grim. "No. Something worse."

DROP DEAD GORGEOUS

We abandoned the intimacy of the moment, the agony of wanting, and quietly moved out of the bathroom, letting the water continue to run. I shut the door behind me, though not all the way. The candles in the room still glowed softly, casting muted beams of light. Cole blew out the ones on the dresser and crouched beside it, then motioned for me to settle in beside him.

The grandfather clock adjacent to us struck midnight, bells chiming, and I stiffened. A new day. From this point on, I could not peer into Cole's eyes without having a vision.

Distraction was dangerous in a situation like this.

Not that I knew what, exactly, was going on.

The room was so hushed, the blood pumping through me so swiftly, my ears rang. No wonder I never heard the door to the bedroom open or the footsteps of the man dressed in black; he eased his way toward the bathroom, stepping into my line of vision. Shock lanced through me.

Benjamin, with a .44 of his own clutched in his hand. Like mine, the weapon had a silencer.

Cole didn't waste time with conversation. He raised his crossbow and fired off a shot.

The arrow sank into Benjamin's shoulder, impact pushing him into the bathroom door, which swung open, dragging him inside. He tripped over the weapons we'd left behind, but as he fell, he spun and aimed the gun right at us.

Too bad for him I'd already had his chest in my sights, my finger poised on the trigger. I squeezed.

The gun's recoil vibrated in my shoulders, the smell of smoke and gunpowder hitting my nose as the assassin ricocheted backward, landing on his back. He tried to sit up, but couldn't quite manage it. He ended up wilting against the tile, unmoving.

"Careful," I said as Cole rushed over, his crossbow extended.

As he crouched, intending to roll Benjamin over and tie his hands behind his back, Cole's legs were kicked out from under him. He launched another arrow as he fell, nailing Benjamin in the chest. But he cracked his head on the tub and was either knocked unconscious or silly, allowing the assassin to lumber into a sitting position—and aim his gun at Cole's chest.

Instinct. Rage. Panic. I'm not sure what powered me. I squeezed off another shot, hitting Benjamin in the hand, sending the gun flying. His narrowed gaze settled on me. I squeezed the trigger, a death shot this time, but heard only a *click*.

Out of bullets, when Cole constantly reloaded? Or another faulty gun? What were the odds of *that*...unless someone was tampering with our stuff? Whatever. No time. I hopped to my feet. Benjamin and I had faced off before. I'd won. I could win again.

Besides, someone in the house had to have heard the thump of falling bodies. He—or she—wouldn't know where, exactly, the sounds had come from. Or what room Cole and I were in. A search would ensue. Benjamin had time, but not a lot.

"Obviously you escaped your cage," I said. "Where are Frosty and River?"

He wiped his mouth, smearing the blood trickling from the corners. "Wasn't hard to palm a key. Then the second they left me alone..." He smiled, all *here I am.*

"Kill anyone along the way?" I tried for a breezy tone.

"And risk raising an alarm? No. I decided to wait for my prey."

Me. Clearly.

I didn't ask why, but he answered anyway. "A month ago, I was hired to bring you in or kill you. You got away, and now there's a stain on my spotless record. It's nothing personal, sweetness, but I want that stain wiped away."

"Good luck with that."

Despite being arrowed twice, and shot, he was surprisingly steady as he swiped up a couple of daggers and a short sword from the bathroom floor.

He grinned slowly, coldly. "I don't need luck. I have skill." Moving so swiftly I had trouble keeping track, he tossed one of the daggers. The blade sliced the underside of my wrist, nicking the vein. My pain receptors acted on autopilot, causing my entire hand to flinch. The already useless gun dropped to the floor.

Advantage—Benjamin.

Just. Like. That.

He stalked toward me, menace in every step. I backed away, rounding to the right and moving toward the door. It was closed, probably locked; I wanted it open and unlocked. Wanted to lead Benjamin into the hallway, away from Cole— *please be okay*—where we were more likely to be seen and heard. But he angled, too, forcing me to go in the other direction or be stabbed. Eventually, the backs of my knees hit the edge of the bed.

He stopped a few feet away, his smile returning. "Poor Ali," he said and tsked. "Nowhere else to go."

I knew it would be suicidal to try to kick the knife out of his hand. That was all Hollywood and stupid. My dad once told me to use whatever was nearby as a weapon. Anything. Everything.

"I'm going to enjoy this," Benjamin said. And then he did it. He swung the short sword at me. I arched away from the blade and grabbed his wrist, stopping his momentum. Then, with my free hand, I punched him in the throat.

Gasping for breath, he stumbled away from me.

I used what was nearby—a candle. I flung the hot, melted wax over his face. He grunted, wiping at his eyes, temporarily blinded. *Then* I kicked the sword out of his hand. Like this, I didn't have to kick as high, which meant I had a better chance of staying on my feet if he dodged.

He didn't dodge.

As the blade skidded across the floor, I moved in for another strike and kicked him in the nuts. He growled low, like a wounded, angry animal, but didn't hunch over. Somehow able to work past the pain, he drove me to the bed. I bounced on the mattress until his weight bore down and pinned me.

I could have panicked, but I knew emotions were my worst enemy right now. So, I stayed calm, even when he delivered a solid punch to my jaw.

Pain. A burst of stars. In a flash of violent motion, I bucked, creating a gap between our bodies. He was forced to grip the headboard to remain upright. Without his hands holding me down, I was able to clasp him by the hips and pull myself between his legs, sitting up behind him and turning.

I flattened my hand on the back of his head and shoved. His forehead banged into the headboard, the entire bed rattling with the force of the blow. But again, he wasn't as injured as he should have been. A slayer ability?

He grabbed my arm when I reached for him and flung me to the floor. Impact escorted the air right out of my lungs.

Benjamin jumped to his feet.

"Ali!"

I looked. I didn't mean to, but finding Cole whenever he called was habit. Absolutely essential. Our gazes met as he raced from the bathroom, and the world faded away—

—suddenly Cole was striding down a narrow corridor. I was hanging over his shoulder, beating and kicking at him.

"Let go," I demanded.

"Never again," he countered.

"You keep saying that. What do you want with me? What do you want *from* me?"

"What I've always wanted. Everything."

"Well, you can't have it. I don't know you, don't want to know you—"

—*what!* I almost screamed.

The scene instantly morphed—

—we were standing nose to nose, shouting at each other.

"Yes! Dang it, yes!" I stomped my foot. "You remember what the pages said. One person will give her life to save many."

"That person isn't going to be you."

"It is!"

"No," he repeated more firmly—

—the second vision vanished, and again I wanted to scream. Because I might be the one, the "she." We'd lost track of the assassin, and I probably had knife wounds all over me.

I blinked rapidly and looked down at myself. I was on my feet, warm blood trickling from my neck. My gaze found Cole. He stood a few feet away, his hands clutched at his sides, his expression murderous. He fought to reach me, but Bronx held him back. There was a smear of crimson on his temple.

"Cole."

"He's fine." Frosty moved in front of me, studied my features.

"The assassin—"

"Dead," Frosty replied with relish. "He was a split second away from cutting through your jugular. I wasn't taking any chances and shot him between the eyes."

One mission…over…almost died…wouldn't have had…chance to say…goodbye. Something was wrong with me—and only getting worse. I struggled to breathe, my thoughts derailing.

Every ache and pain I'd received during the fight roared with new life, driving me to my knees.

"I think...Cole...concussion," I managed to say. My eyelids became heavy.

"I don't care about me," he said, and I knew he was beside me now. He'd probably shoved Bronx and Frosty out of the way.

Sharp pains exploded through my head. "Something... wrong." I opened my mouth to say more, but I didn't have the strength.

"Ali?" he demanded. He sounded far away. "Talk to me. Tell me what's going on."

I floated away from him, going higher and higher, no longer able to hear him or feel him. It sucked. But it also didn't suck. Up here, I felt nothing.

"Alice."

The familiar, beloved voice called to me, and eyelids no longer weighed down fluttered open. My little sister stood a few feet away, white mist dancing all around her, creating a magical haze.

"Am I dreaming?" I asked.

"No." She looked worried and adorable at once. "You're hovering somewhere between life and death."

Death? I instantly recoiled. "I'm not ready to die. There's too much to do." I had to save Justin, as promised. I had to destroy Anima. I had to spend time with Helen.

I had to create a safe world for Cole and Kat and Nana.

"Then fight," she said.

I wanted to shake her. "That's what I'm doing."

"Fight," she repeated. "Alice. Fight!" The last was screamed.

No, Emma wasn't screaming. I was. Agony consumed me,

and my back bowed off the floor. Floor. Yes. That's where I was, not the clouds. I was lying flat on my back, fire burning me up, sweat pouring from me. Something hard beat at my chest, nearly cracking my ribs.

Finally, though, the fire died and I sagged against the wood planks, boneless. But still the beating continued.

"—must have poisoned her somehow," Frosty was saying.

I pried my eyelids apart. Cole straddled my waist, his hands flat on my chest, pressing.

CPR?

"Cole," Bronx said. He knelt beside me. His spirit, not his body. He glimmered so beautifully. He lifted his hands from *inside* my arm, the fire in his fingers dying. "Cole! She's alive. You can stop now."

Cole stilled, his eyes meeting mine. Agony ravaged his features. He pressed two fingers into the side of my neck and encountered the slow but steady *thump, thump.*

"Your heart stopped," he croaked. "It actually stopped."

And yet, I experienced no pain. Not now. Not even in my jaw, where Benjamin had hit me.

Even as fogged as I was, one fact became clear. We were getting stronger. All of us. We'd come through things that would have broken anyone else. We'd done things we'd never done before.

We would *do* things we'd never done before.

One life for many.

Even better, we were capable of things Anima probably wasn't equipped to handle.

"Ali," Cole said. "Talk to me."

"Thank you," I said on a sigh and closed my eyes. I was grinning as I drifted to sleep.

I woke gradually, luxuriating in the warmth surrounding me…and the strong chest underneath me.

I lifted my head, my cheeks heating when I realized I'd kinda sorta drooled on Cole's bare chest. I wiped away the humiliating damp spots as gently as possible, brushing against the piercing in his nipple.

His long lashes parted, and those lovely violet eyes crinkled at the corners as he smiled at me. "Morning, sunshine."

Gonna play the name game, were we? "Morning, sugar puff."

His grin widened. "I'm sugar puff now?"

"Well, it's better than monkey butt, isn't it?"

"And monkey butt is what you really wanted to call me?"

"Maybe." I smoothed the hair from his forehead, waiting for a vision that never came. I glanced at the clock on the nightstand—11:13…in the afternoon? That meant we'd already had one today, weren't due to have another one until tomorrow.

And in came a flood of memories. The assassin. The gunfight. The extended vision we'd already shared. Emma.

"I died," I said, blinking in surprise. "Kind of."

A pallor took root under Cole's skin. "Your heart stopped, yes, and that's the most scared I've ever been. But Bronx lit up like a Fourth-of-July rocket, providing the fire while I performed CPR. You came back to me."

I fell on him, hugging him close. "Always."

He hugged me back with gusto. "Ankh looked you over while you were snoozing and said you're as good as new."

Now I just had to stay that way. "Oh, hey. I just remembered. Emma told me I share my abilities with other slayers every time I use my fire. Like passing on spirit cooties, I guess."

He thought for a moment, nodded. "That explains why Frosty and Bronx had a vision."

"They did?" Seriously? "If you tell me Frosty saw himself in bed with Bronx, the way Gavin saw himself in bed with Jaclyn, I will absolutely, one hundred percent…want front-row seats when it happens."

He laughed as he only ever laughed with me, genuine and carefree. "Sorry, Ali-gator, but they actually saw themselves in a fight. Bronx was trying to drag Frosty away from something, and Frosty was trying to get back to it—whatever it was."

Mind twister: What could possibly make two best bros fight, when they'd never fought before? "Why don't the visions show us more?" I grumbled. "Why do we get mere glimpses?"

"Maybe what we see is all we can handle. Maybe they aren't meant to change our paths but to prepare us for what we face."

Yeah. Maybe. I sat up, my hair tumbling around my shoulders. "We've got a lot to do today."

Cole toyed with the end of a curling lock, as if he wouldn't tolerate a total separation from me. "Yes, we do." Then he gave the lock a gentle tug, disturbing my balance. As I fell on his chest, he rolled, pinning me to the mattress.

I glared up at him. "We are *not* doing what the fake people in books and movies do."

"And that is?"

"Kissing before we brush our teeth. I don't want you anywhere near my morning breath."

"You trying to deny me my prize? I saved your life. Now I own it."

"Well, the prize needs a good scrubbing."

"But I want it prescrub."

Not in a million years. "If we're going to get technical, I owe Bronx a prize, too. We should call him in here and let him collect."

"He prefers fruit baskets," Cole replied, deadpan. "Ali?"

I went soft and dreamy. "Yes, Cole."

"I'm about to do something you'll claim you don't like, but we'll both know you're desperate for more. Won't we?" Then he pressed a hard kiss on my lips, and I squealed.

Laughing again, he jumped up and threw a cell phone at me. "Kat's been texting all night. You can deal with her while I shower. And no, you aren't invited. Last night was too much of a temptation and right now we're too pressed for time."

Did that mean he would have *given in to temptation* if we'd had time?

Good glory!

His gaze remained on me, hot and needy, as he shut the bathroom door. The lock clicked.

Groaning, I sat up and looked over my phone's text-riddled screen. There were twenty-three messages. In an effort to save my sanity, I responded to only my top five.

1. WHAT'S THIS I HEAR ABOUT U DYING? U've got 2 tell me about things like that. A good friend keeps her friends informed, even in the afterlife.

My response: I'm alive & well—promise!

2. Ali Bell. U have 5 secs 2 contact me or I'm stomping N2 UR room & killing U 4 reals...slight change of plan. Frost tied 1 of my hands 2 my bed. NEWS FLASH: that might have stopped me from leaving the room, but it won't stop my convo w/U. UR welcome. But now he's giving me dirty look. I'm thinking he has bondage fetish.

Response: Having read all UR texts before responding, I know what comes next, U lucky girl.

3. What has 2 thumbs and just died & went 2 heaven herself??? This girl! Frost gives good argument. He uses his hands!!

Response: THAT.

4. Srsly, tho. R U OK? Because I've just broken up w/Frosty as punishment 4 keeping me away from U.

Response: I really am OK. Promise!

5. UR the most annoying friend ever. Except 4 Frost. He's worse. He keeps trying 2 take away my phone. Says I need 2 leave U alone & let U rest. As if! He doesn't realize U'd B lost w/out me.

Response: I really am sorry about the delay! I was sleeping off the death thing ☺ But now I need U 2 suck it up, take one 4 the team & put Frosty N a good mood. He's gonna B w/me later, helping w/enemy, & he's always a beast when U break up w/him.

My phone beeped, signaling a new message.

Kat: Fine. But only because U asked. UR lucky I heart U so much!

Me: I know!

Kat: UR also lucky I'm such a good friend. THE THINGS I DO 4 U! I guess I won't give Frost the poem I wrote about him. Check it: Roses R red, violets R blue, I have five fingers, & the middle 1 is 4 U.

I chortled. Then I read the lyrical genius to Cole as he came out of the bathroom. He wore a clean black T-shirt and ripped-up jeans. Leather cuffs circled each of his wrists, and a chain hung from his waist. He looked good enough to eat.

Put that on the to-do list.

Grinning, he rubbed a towel through his damp hair. "That girl is a hot mess."

"Yeah, but she's loyal and sweet and funny," I replied, "and if I wasn't in love with you, and I was into girls, and she was into girls, I'd be all over her. Guaranteed Frosty wouldn't stand a chance. She's already assured me I'm irresistible."

He stopped rubbing to peer at me with excitement. "Let's pretend. Just for a day. You're into girls."

"Dude. You'd never win me back." I gathered clean clothes and shouldered my way past him.

"But I'd have fun trying," he said as I shut the door.

SWEET SAVAGE LOVE

I showered, brushed my hair and teeth and dressed in a tight black shirt with long sleeves and hip-hugging jeans. Cole had left a stack of my weapons in the corner. Had even polished the daggers and loaded the gun. Maybe he could win me back after all.

When I exited, there was a note on the nightstand.

I've got to speak w/Ankh before we canvass the apartment building—he's been secretly buying properties all over the state. Our new safe houses. Why don't you eat breakfast and hang w/the girls? I'll come get you when we're ready to go.

Love, Cole.

P.S. You should probably give Kat a kiss when you see her. You know, to apologize for making her worry. Use tongue. I would.

Ha! In ColeHollandville, my lips belonged to him and him alone.

I made my way to the kitchen. Juliana and Camilla were there, chatting easily as Camilla buttered a piece of toast.

"—not fair," Juliana was saying. "She's nothing special."

Great. "She" had to be me.

"That's not for you to decide," Camilla said, and the show of support threw me. "Besides, guys like Cole Holland do not date girls your age."

"I'm only two years younger than Ali!"

"Yes, but teen years are just like dog years. To Cole, you're nothing more than a newborn."

Harsh.

Juliana thought so, too. "I am not!" she snarled. "You take that back."

"Do you hear yourself? How immature you sound?"

The younger girl glowered.

"Anyway, you just need to wait it out," Camilla continued blithely. "It's not like those two are going to get married or anything. High-school romances never last."

And that was more like the Camilla I knew.

I cleared my throat, and both girls turned to face me. Juliana flushed with embarrassment and anger, while Camilla blanked her features, revealing nothing.

"Leave everything out when you're done," I said.

"I've suddenly lost my appetite." Juliana tossed her hair over her shoulder and flounced out of the room.

Brat.

"I'm in total breakfast mode," Camilla said. "Why don't I just make you a slice?"

A peace offering? "Thank you."

"Strawberry or grape jelly?"

BC—before Cole—I would have said grape. Now? "Strawberry." He'd addicted me.

As she worked, she said, "I've been trying to decode the rest of the papers, but even when I read while in spirit form, I can only make out a few words. So I was thinking," she added before I could reply, "maybe you could use your fire on me and share the ability."

"How do you know about the fire-share?"

"There's been talk."

Already?

She was still an unknown entity, and I wasn't comfortable sharing my abilities...or my secrets. "I'll think about it," I said, accepting the piece of toast she offered.

A flash of irritation she couldn't hide. "You do that. Meanwhile, I'm going to give myself a tour of the grounds."

She headed for the back door. I ate my toast and took off in the opposite direction. Destination: Reeve's room. That's where Kat would be. But I made it only halfway before I spotted Helen. She waited at the top of the steps.

Startled, I tripped. *Good one, Ali-gator.*

Great. Now even I was using that ridiculous nickname. Mind had to be misfiring. Which was understandable. This was the first time I'd seen Helen since I'd learned who she was to me—who I was to her.

Cole would insist I get rid of her. But I couldn't. I just... couldn't.

"You know who I am," she said, hesitant.

"Yes," I whispered, not wanting to draw attention to myself. I looked left, right. No sign of a slayer. Still. Better safe than sorry.

I motioned for her to follow me to my room. What should I call her? Helen? Or Momma, like before?

I closed my eyes against a rush of pain. Would calling her Mom be a betrayal to the woman who'd raised me? Who'd loved me as her own?

Get it together.

"I'd hoped you would remember," she said after I closed the door.

Her words reminded me of the last dream I'd had. "Did you wipe my memories when I was a little girl?"

Anyone else might have blanched when faced with my anger, but not her. She held my gaze. "Yes and no. Like you, I was born with several abnormal skills. One allows me to reach my spirit inside a person's head and cover their memories. Like I'm placing a blanket over their mind. It's a defense mechanism, I guess, in case civilians ever see something they shouldn't."

"You covered mine." That look in my eyes… I'd gone to my dad as a blank slate.

She nodded, seeming shamed but resolved.

"Uncover them. Now." They were mine. I wanted every single one. I'd *earned* them.

"Ali—"

"You had no right," I growled. "No right." Those memories would have helped me. Then and now.

"I'm sorry, but it only works one way. I can cover, but not uncover."

I ignored the rising tide of bile. "How am I remembering, then? Are the memories uncovering on their own?"

"Again, yes and no. I've been sitting at your bedside, telling you stories. Sharing *my* memories. It seems to be thinning the blanket, for lack of a better description."

It was better than nothing, I supposed. She was trying.

There I went, seeing the best in her again.

I eased onto the edge of the bed. "What do you want from me? Why are you here?"

"I've been watching over you. *Am* watching over you."

"I've never seen you, but I've always seen Emma."

"Do you remember how Zombie Ali was able to cloak herself from prying eyes? Well, she inherited the skill from me."

Why hadn't I? "Just how many of these skills do you have?"

"A handful of others. And no, I wasn't born with all of them. I used to…steal from slayers."

In other words, she'd tormented and killed to get what she wanted.

"Stealing is teachable." She reached out her hand. "I would allow you to practice on me, but time isn't on your side. Let me give you the ability to cover memories. That way, you can rest assured I'll never use it again."

You can't trust her, Cole had said.

After everything Helen had just told me, I *shouldn't* trust her.

And yet, I stretched out my hand, letting it hover under hers. I wished I could tell myself it was because we were at war with Anima and we needed all the weapons we could get, but that would have been a lie. Bottom line, I was overcome by a desire to connect with this woman on any level.

"I'd give you everything all at once, but I fear it would be overwhelming." She closed her eyes. A stream of warmth hit my palms, seeped past my skin and zinged through the rest of me.

The transfer was easy, no burning pain, no urge to scream the roof down, and in seconds we were done, our arms returning to our sides.

"There," she said. "Just swipe the hand of your spirit through a person's mind. The only drawback is you will cover *all* of their memories. There isn't any selecting or picking and choosing this one but not that one. Everything is hidden."

I couldn't imagine needing the ability. Or allowing myself to use it.

"I didn't want to screw up your life all over again," she said, "and I would have continued to remain in the shadows, but Anima killed your friends, and I realized they were going to come after you hard. I knew I had to act. For you. I will do anything for you, Sami."

I was quick to snap, "That's not my name."

"Ali," she corrected softly.

Deep breath in...out. "Why did you help Anima kill Cole's mom? By that time, you knew how corrupt they were and planned to leave."

She whipped around, giving me her back. "I had a choice. I made it."

When she said no more, I asked, "What choice?"

"After I gave you to your dad, I went a little crazy. Anima assumed I was in mourning over your death and gave me time. I could have left. I should have left. But I opted to stay for two reasons. I thought I could destroy them, and if that proved futile, I wanted to know if any suspicions about you arose. Because I stayed, I had to obey orders or come under suspicion myself. It was as simple as that."

Something Veronica said niggled at the back of my mind. "What about Veronica's mom? Did you wipe her memory?"

"Yes."

No remorse. Only cold, hard facts.

Was it bad that I thought, *At least she didn't kill the woman*?

The door swung open, and Cole strode inside. Panic instantly chilled me. He would see her; he would know what I'd been doing.

But he stopped and casually said, "Just heard from my dad. He did a little digging into the life of the mysterious Ms. Smith and discovered that outside the boardroom, she is most well-known for her interrogation techniques. Anyone who ends up strapped to her table dies. If they tell her what she wants to know, they die quickly. If not, slowly."

I looked to Helen—gone. The panic eased, leaving room for frustration. I wanted so badly to tell Cole what I'd learned, what I'd been given.

I couldn't.

"Tell me about the safe houses," I said.

"We now have one right by River's place."

"That's good." But my frustration wasn't going away. "You and I haven't gone head-to-head in a while," I said and punched him in the shoulder. The one that had taken the bullet. When we sparred, we *sparred*. There were no rules. No holding back or going easy.

"In need of practice, Ali-gator?" He liked to be on the receiving end of our scuffles and didn't flinch, didn't miss a beat…just grabbed my arm when I made to punch him again, twisted me around and pushed me to my knees.

Actually, I needed an outlet.

I kicked back and out, knocking his feet together. His hold loosened and I swung around, punching with my other arm. But he knew me and expected the sucker move; he managed to block.

"You can do better than this, love," he said with a grin.

Yeah. I could. I latched on to his arm to spin him away from me, but he held on tight, taking me with him. We ended up turning in circles before he purposely tripped me. Down we fell. On impact, we rolled. When we stopped, he was on top of me.

I wrapped my arms around his neck and lifted my hips, rubbing against him. Instantly improving my mood.

He hissed in a breath. "You're fighting dirty now."

"That's the only way to fight, Coleslaw."

He positioned his knees outside my hips, straddling me. Meaning to take control and turn the wrestling into a make-out session? I cupped the side of his neck and shoved, sending him to his back. Then *I* straddled *him*.

"I must say, I adore seeing you like this," I said. "Totally at my mercy."

His eyes softened. "I'm at your mercy no matter what position I'm in."

My sense of triumph vanished, replaced by guilt and need… always need. How could I keep a secret from him?

I jumped off him.

"Where are you going?" he asked, grabbing my ankle and sending me crashing face-first. Rat! He moved on top of me. "We're not done. There are things I want to tell you…do to you."

"Uh, am I interrupting something?" Jaclyn stood at the open door, blinking at us.

I thought, *Yes. No. Gah!* Calm, steady.

Cole climbed off me, helped me to my feet and scowled at the girl with murderous intent.

"Your parents let you come back?" I asked.

She shook her head, saying, "Nope. They think I'm resting in my room."

"Your timing is… Yeah. We're headed out to search for Justin." Cole drew in a heavy breath, met my gaze. What was going on inside that gorgeous head of his? "By the way, Kat's coming."

"What!" No way Frosty would allow it.

"Apparently she's got some live-life-to-the-fullest list and Frosty can either go along with it or lose her. He's decided to go along, and it's making him crazy, so try not to even make eye contact with him. You'll regret it. Trust me."

Well, okay, then.

As our big group was about to pile inside two different SUVs, Juliana came marching outside, draped in more weapons than Cole and I combined.

Veronica jerked her finger to the front door. "Back inside."

"Kidney girl is a freaking civilian and she gets to go," the younger teen snapped. "*I* can actually help."

One donkey-punch, coming up.

Cole held me back. "I'll talk to her." He closed the distance, whispered something in her ear.

She softened, muttering, "Fine," and trudged back into the mansion.

"What'd you say to her?" I asked as I settled into the backseat of our SUV.

He took the seat next to me, clasped my hand in his. "She'll get to spend a few hours every day training with Mackenzie."

Mackenzie wasn't one to care about age, and she would utterly annihilate the girl.

"As soon as Mackenzie deems her a good enough fighter," he added, "she can start coming with us."

"Mackenzie won't deem her good enough for, what? Two years?"

"At least."

River claimed the driver's seat, Camilla shotgun and Jaclyn the middle. Gavin moved behind her, practically shoving Bronx out of the way to get there. Oh, no. That could mean only one thing...

I rolled down my window, stuck out my head and said, "Kat, change places with Gavin. Stat."

"Already planned on it." She trotted over, only to be grabbed by Frosty midway and carted back to the other car—but not before he flipped me off.

The fifteen-minute ride was both awesome and pure, unadulterated torture. Cole kept his arm wrapped around me, his fingers toying with the ends of my hair, but Gavin and Jaclyn snipped at each other the entire way.

"You gonna try to kill me again, sweetness?" Gavin began.

"Why don't you save your breath?" she snapped. "You'll need it to inflate your date later."

"True. I will. Do you want to know what the sad thing is?" He didn't give her a chance to respond. "She'll still be better company than you."

Jaclyn shook her fist at him. "If you don't shut up, I'll help you swallow your own teeth."

"Even then, you'd still want me. Because that's what all this animosity is about, isn't it?" He wiggled his brows at her. "Why don't you do us all a favor and admit it? After all, everyone already knows you're going to end up throwing yourself at me. That's the only way I'll take you to bed."

Her snort of derision echoed. "Me? Throw myself at you? Sugar, you couldn't get laid in a whorehouse with a fistful of twenties."

"I totally could. And when I sneak into your mom's room later tonight, I'll prove it."

No. No mom insults. "Enough," I said.

"Do you dream about all the ways I'll satisfy you?" Gavin asked Jaclyn conversationally, ignoring me.

She bared her teeth at him in a fierce scowl. "The only way you would ever satisfy me in bed is if you left me in mine—alone!"

"Seriously. Enough!" River said with a lot more volume than I'd used. "I'm usually a big fan of sexual tension, but this is like an X-rated kindergarten class, with two little jerks crushing on each other, both too stupid to admit it out loud."

Blessed silence.

Until Jaclyn said, "I do *not* have a crush on him. He refers to girls as candy. And guess what? This candy store is closed. Forever."

Gavin yawned, then peered out the window, as if bored. "I've decided girls are like diseases. You happen to be Ebola. That causes vomiting, right?"

"And massive internal bleeding." Jaclyn huffed and puffed, waiting for him to say something else, and despite everything, I was glad to see a little life to her.

"Silence is easy," River said. "Try it."

"If it were easy," Camilla said, "it'd be your mom."

"My mom is your mom."

"So? I never liked her."

"When we get back," Cole whispered to me, "I want to take you on our second date."

"How romantic of you," I replied with a grin.

"Romantic...desperate to get you alone. Same thing."

"And what are we going to do on this second date? It'll be hard to top the near-death experience."

He glowered at me. "You love premature joke-ulation, don't you?"

"What can I say? It's one of my many charms."

"Well, tonight you'll see one of *mine*."

He'd basically just thrown a match inside me. Suddenly I burned and ached in the most delicious way. Had he just assured me that he would—that *we* would finally go all the way?

Concentrate! "You keep hinting about your plans for me. Tell me—"

"Nope. Too late," he interjected a little evilly. "You'll have to wait to find out what I meant. We've reached our destination."

Dang it! He was right.

River parked in the east lot, out of view of the warehouse. We planned to start at the bottom of the apartment building and work our way to the top, knocking on every door we came across.

"We'll take floors one and two," Cole said to Gavin and me. To Jaclyn and River he said, "You'll take floors three and four."

"What about the rest of the gang?" I asked.

"They'll be patrolling outside to make sure we aren't ambushed."

Or, in other words, keeping Kat out of the building and Frosty from going cray-cray on some poor, unsuspecting witness.

The building was a bit run-down, with paint peeling and threadbare carpet. There was also a musty smell in the air. Old dust, as if cleaning wasn't always a priority.

The first floor proved unfruitful. On the second floor, however, we knocked on a door at the end of the hall, with a window overlooking the warehouse. An angry-looking man answered. He was a little shorter than me, his sandy-colored hair shaggy and unkempt. His eyes were bloodshot and his lips chapped. He wore a stained, wrinkled T-shirt that read Always Give 100% Unless You're Giving Blood and pants way too tight for his bulky frame.

We hadn't asked the man about the night of the murders, yet still he thrust a phone in my direction. "Here," he snapped, "it's for you." And then he shut the door in our stunned faces.

A jolt of confusion. I tried to make sense of what had just happened.

Cole tensed.

Gavin palmed a gun, as if he expected the phone to explode at any second.

Tentative, I held it to my ear. "Hello?"

"Ali Bell. It's nice to chat with you again."

Shock blasted through me. "Ethan?"

"The one and only."

Cole didn't need to hear any more. He slammed into the

apartment door, wood shards raining to the floor as the thing ripped from its hinges. He and Gavin marched inside.

I leaned against the wall to maintain my balance. "What do you want?" And how had he known I'd show up?

"My sister."

Isabelle, a fifteen-year-old girl dying of cancer. "We don't have her."

He laughed bitterly. "I know. But Anima says they will bring her back—*if* I bring you in."

Wait. "Bring her back. As in…"

"She died, Ali," he said, his pain crackling over the line. "It was horrible. Painful."

My shoulders drooped. Another loss. "I'm sorry, I really am."

He continued as if he hadn't heard me. "But not from the cancer. Killing her was the only way to save her," he rushed to add. "We injected her with the zombie toxin. Her spirit rose, as we knew it would. But we controlled the environment and captured it. Now we're keeping it locked away and her body preserved."

We, he kept saying. As if he and Anima were one. How was I supposed to respond to that? To any of this?

"So…" Ethan cleared his throat. "This is the part where I admit that I have Justin and some slayer we caught trying to rescue him."

Knew the first. Hadn't known the second. My heart sank all the way to my feet.

Cole and Gavin stomped out of the apartment, their expressions equally dark. Cole shook his head, and I knew what he was telling me. The guy had somehow escaped.

"I'm willing to do an even trade," Ethan said. "You for the boys."

Please. He'd double-cross me in a heartbeat. "There's no way—"

"Think about it. Keep the phone, and I'll send you proof of life. We'll talk again tomorrow."

Click.

FOLLOW THE
BLOOD-SOAKED ROAD

As we ransacked the Anima guy's apartment, I told the boys about Ethan's trade suggestion. Their responses?

Cole: "Sure, we'll trade you. In never."

Gavin: "Going to kill that boy so dead."

Now that I'd had a little time to think about it, my answer waffled. I valued my friends' lives above my own, and if it was within my power to save one, I would.

Yes, Ethan would double-cross me as suspected. But I'd be aware of that going in and have ways to circumvent him. And even if he came up with ways to circumvent *me,* it could still be a win for my team. If I ended up in an Anima facility, I could free the boys and possibly damage a branch of the company.

Torture and death were the only downsides, but I was in danger of the latter every day, no matter where I happened to be.

We searched the apartment. Besides a few pieces of furniture and a TV, the place was empty. There were no secret compartments or hidden cubbyholes that we could find—just a chair and a few empty bags of chips and cans of soda. It looked like the guy had been holed up, just waiting for us to show up.

We finished canvassing the building, and it wasn't long before we found the clue we'd so desperately needed. A forty-something woman had gone outside to smoke the night of the attacks, and she remembered seeing a teenage boy being put inside a dark sedan and hearing two guys in black talk about where to take him. Dr. Hodad or Dr. Rangarajan. The men in black had laughingly decided on Hodad.

Hopefully he was listed.

But when were things ever that uncomplicated?

Darkness had fallen by the time we finished, and the proof-of-life photos still hadn't come in.

"What's next?" I asked.

Lines of tension framed River's eyes. "You're welcome at my place."

I looked to Cole. We could go to our new safe house instead.

But he shook his head at me and said to River, "Sounds good."

Well, okay, then.

"My boys will work a little computer magic and learn everything they can about this Dr. Hodad." River smiled without humor. "The more we know, the more likely we are to hit him where it hurts and get the answers we need."

Agreed.

We met up with the other group. Cole pulled Frosty aside, and the two engaged in a heated conversation.

I couldn't hear what was being said.

"I told Frosty we wouldn't have any problems, and I was right," Kat said, beside me. "Now he's even more ticked, thinking I'll want to accompany him on *every* mission."

"Is he right?" I asked.

"Hardly. This kind of sucked."

Good.

The boys returned, but Cole wouldn't meet my gaze.

O-kay. Clearly he had a problem. Thinking about me offering to trade myself for Justin, perhaps?

Yeah. Definitely. In other words, date night had just become lecture night. Great!

Everyone climbed into the cars. Ours claimed the front of the line and Frosty's the rear. All of us kept our attention on the streets, searching for any sign of zombies. And, even worse, the detectives.

"Feel free to hang in the courtyard," River said as we entered the building. "I've got to tell my tech nerds what we need. I'll be out in a few." He stepped away, only to pause. "Veronica, why don't you come with me?"

"I'd love to," she said, smiling as she bounded to his side.

"I'm going with them." Cole brushed his fingertips over my cheek and took off.

"But—"

He was gone.

Goodbye to you, too.

"No courtyard for us. We want a room," a very tense Frosty said, his arm slung around Kat's shoulders.

She blew me a kiss. I winked at her.

"Toni," Camilla shouted, and a young girl rushed over. "Show those two to a room."

"A good room," Kat corrected. "The best."

The threesome headed upstairs.

Camilla glanced at me, sighed and led us to the courtyard, where another death match was taking place on one side and a party with dancing on the other. There were around fifty other slayers present, and all were in their late teens or early twenties.

For a single girl, this had to be a slice of heaven.

My friends might not understand the cheers and boos surrounding the zombie pit, but they gravitated to the action.

"Introduce me." A boy stepped in front of us, stopping us, and nodded to Mackenzie. He was my height and on the lean side, Asian, with hair colored green. He had three teardrops tattooed underneath his right eye.

"Hiroaki, these are Cole and Ali's friends." Camilla rattled off their names. The boys nodded stiffly. The girls smiled in welcome.

Hiroaki kept his attention on Mackenzie. "Nice to meet you."

"You, too," she replied formally.

I waited for her to curtsy.

Two other boys approached and flanked Hiroaki. One of them was Knuckle Scars, and he, too, focused intently on Mackenzie, as if he'd just spotted his next—and last—meal.

"Who do we have here?" the other one asked. He was black and rugged, pure sex appeal. But he couldn't have cared less about the girls. He peered at Gavin with come-hither intent. "I could just eat you up one tasty bite at a time."

Gavin puffed up like a peacock. I think he totally expected

everyone to be sexually attracted to him, no matter their gender, so, to him, this was just confirmation that he was right.

"I seriously hate to break it to you," he said, "but I'm the buffet of choice for girls, and they don't like to share me with the other team."

"Figures." The boy shrugged, an I-had-to-try gesture. "I'm Joshua. Josh to my friends, but you can call me anytime," he added with a wink.

"I'm Chance," Knuckle Scars said, and, oh, wow, his voice! He probably made angels weep.

He took Mackenzie's hand, while she stood frozen. "We've met," she said.

"I know."

As Chance turned his attention to Jaclyn, Gavin moved behind her and crossed his arms, staring at Chance with more menace than I'd ever seen from him. It was almost comical.

The muscular Chance wasn't intimidated and dared to take Jaclyn's hand.

She blushed, the added color only making her prettier.

A low growl broke from Gavin's throat. Gasping, Jaclyn spun. When she saw how close he was, and exactly how aggressive his stance, she backed away from him.

"Was that necessary?" Mackenzie asked Chance.

"No. Fun? Yes."

"Our definition of *fun* differs."

His smile was brief, but no less spectacular. "I've shown you mine. Why don't you show me yours?"

"Seriously?" she said. "You don't speak to me the first two times we see each other, and this is how you lead?"

He shrugged, unabashed.

"Why don't you two fight in the pit?" Camilla suggested to Gavin and Chance. "The rest of us can place bets."

"Pit?" Gavin asked, clearly intrigued.

"This way." She marched forward, my group blindly, happily, shadowing her.

They watched the current fight for several minutes.

"Twenty dollars on the girl in the jogging pants," Gavin called, and Josh patted him on the back, as if he'd just said the most brilliant thing ever.

Jaclyn clutched her middle and backed away.

Chance noticed and sidled up to her. "Come on. I'll take you somewhere quiet."

She nodded, and the two soon disappeared inside. Gavin watched their departure through narrowed eyes. "She's supposed to be with *me*," Gavin spat.

Wow. He really did like her. "Are you sure? The visions don't always mean what we think they mean. You and I saw ourselves kissing, but that wasn't what happened at all."

"I still got a little action, didn't I?"

I rolled my eyes. "You should be nicer to Jaclyn."

"Girls don't want nice," he grumbled.

"Who told you that?"

"No one. But I pay attention. I know girls want what they can't have, and they want to be the special exception responsible for taming the boy no one else can, even though they probably won't be."

He was…kind of right. "Jaclyn isn't like other girls. She's fragile and—"

He gave a short, sharp laugh. "She isn't fragile, Ali-cat. She's tough as nails."

"No, she isn't."

"Yes, Ali, she is." His gaze leveled on me. "Like the visions, what you see is not always the truth. You focus on the hurt she projects and never dig past the surface to see the rage bubbling deep inside, desperate for release."

"No—"

"You baby her," he continued, "and that's the last thing she needs."

I stomped my foot. "You didn't see her during our capture or after the attack."

"Doesn't matter. I see her now."

Mackenzie patted his shoulder. "You gonna stand here all night, Gav, or go get your girl?"

Meaning, she wanted Chance away from Jaclyn.

What a night.

As the zombies continued to fight in the pit, I noticed Camilla had wandered to the far edge of the courtyard to drink a cup of beer in private.

I joined her. "How do you capture them?"

She pressed her lips together and pretended I wasn't there. But I didn't go away, and finally she sighed. "We patrol every night, and on the occasions zombies come out, we collar as many as we can and kill the others. And if you dare tell me we're being cruel to zombies, I think I'll smash your face."

"Emotionless husks of evil will never get my sympathy."

"All right, then," she said. She looked over my shoulder and nodded. "You'll have to excuse me. I'm needed elsewhere." She took off for...wherever.

I wasn't alone for long. A boy-man hybrid bounded over and handed me a cup of beer. I thanked him even though I knew I wouldn't be drinking the contents. My dad had been an alcoholic, and I'd hated watching his decline; I'd always (mostly) avoided alcohol like the plague.

"Can't have you feeling left out," he said with a grin. He had at least ten long, thick scars on his face, making the plainness of his features hauntingly tragic.

"Thank you," I said again.

"No prob. Hey, I saw your fight the last time you were here. Not that it was really a fight. You were too hard-core for it to be fair. But, man, I was blown away. Never seen anything like it." He peered at me from under a thick fan of lashes. "So…how'd you do it?"

"It's just something I can do."

"Well, you should think about getting in the pit tonight. We've been talking about you, and the guys that missed it will do just about anything for the chance to watch you work."

"Maybe another time," I said. To me, zombie killing was a business—a privilege—not a sport.

Cole appeared at my side, glaring at the boy—who held up his palms and backed away.

"We found out what Hodad means," Cole said the moment we were alone.

The reprimand I'd been about to deliver died in my throat. "Well? Tell me."

Motions clipped, he took the cup of beer and set it aside. "Hands of death and destruction."

Oh…crap.

"River's guys found Dr. Rangarajan, too," he added. "We're sending a team to pick him up and bring him here. He might be able to tell us where the boys are being kept."

Glancing over his shoulder, I watched as River spoke to Gavin and Bronx, probably explaining the situation. Well, no *probably* about it. The three guys plus two others stalked from the courtyard.

"You're not going with them?" I asked.

"I delegated. Come on." He led me out of the building and across the cold, night-darkened street.

"Where are we going?"

"The safe house."

Alone? Together? For the lecture…or something else?

The building was smaller than River's, a little more run-down, but safety measures had already been taken. Cole had to punch in a code to open the front door. Inside, what had once most likely been a hotel lobby had been transformed into a rocking living room, with a large-screen TV, two couches and multiple recliners. There was a beautiful hand-knotted rug in front of a cracked marble hearth.

"It's been furnished," I said, surprised.

"Only this room." He built a fire. "Look. I know you, and I know you're thinking it'll be okay for you to trade yourself for Justin."

Lecture. Great. I got comfortable on the rug.

"But it's not okay. Not now, not later. And don't even think about arguing. I lead the slayers. Hence, I lead you. I make the decisions, and you do what I say."

He'd met me, right? "The only reason I'm not knocking you to your knees and making you beg for mercy right now is because I know you're speaking from a place of deep concern for me. But, Cole? You are seriously irritating the crap out of me."

He sat in front of me. I yanked at the collar of his shirt and let the material snap back into place.

"You're either my boyfriend or my boss," I said. "You can't be both. Pick one."

He scooted closer to me, so close I basically had to straddle his lap to remain upright. Big hardship. His chest brushed against mine, and whether accidental or intentional, it thrilled me.

"If it means keeping you safe," he said, "I pick boss."

As different emotions played havoc with my heartbeat, the scent of strawberries teased me. "Best-case scenario, I don't have to trade myself. I make Ethan think I'm willing and strike at him. And yes, he will attempt to double-cross us the same way we'll attempt to double-cross him. But you're acting like we can't win." I tried to mask my breathlessness as he traced his fingertips over my spine. "There's a chance we can save the boys and deliver a major blow to Anima at the same time."

"A chance you could be tortured and killed."

So I'd had the same thought. So what. "But at least I'll have done something." I *had* to do something. "And what if I'm the one, huh?" The girl who would sacrifice herself to save many. "What if I *need* to die?"

"You don't. What we read might be a counterfeit."

"It isn't. It was part of the journal."

He lowered his head, and his nose pressed against mine. "What if you're not the one? You would have put yourself in harm's way for nothing."

He had an argument for everything. "Not for nothing." But, okay, fine, I did get where he was coming from. "No matter what, we have to get those boys back. That's priority one."

A moment passed, the tension heating me up inside.

"You're right," he said and nodded. "But we'll do things my way."

"Agreed. If your way is my way."

He snorted. "Forget the right way—my way—for now."

"Already done. Now, enough talking. I've got a better use for your mouth." I brushed my lips against his and pushed his shoulders, easing him back on the rug.

He quickly rolled me over. His movements were as sleek as a panther's as he spread himself over me and pinned me down. "This your way of distracting me?" He kissed the line of my jaw, and my veins became a conduit for tingling warmth. "Because it's working."

"You did promise me a second date, did you not?"

"I did."

"Well, *this* is what I want to do."

"Lie here…talking?" He unveiled a slow, wicked smile.

The blood in my veins flashed white-hot. "Kissing…touching. More. *Everything.*"

Expression growing pained, he said, "Ali—"

"I almost died yesterday," I interjected. "I could die tomorrow or even an hour from now. I want to be with you, Cole."

"Ali—" he repeated.

"No. You are under the impression that this decision is yours. Or your dad's. Well, news flash. It isn't. It's ours. I'm ready. I've been ready. *You're* ready."

A battle seemed to wage in his mind. "I've talked myself into and out of this all day."

So he *had* contemplated it. "What are my eyes saying?"

He pressed his forehead against mine. "Too much."

"And I'm sure every word is riveting. Listen to them."

I tangled my fingers in his hair and placed scorching kisses along his jawline. It wasn't long before he angled his head, meeting my lips with his own, stealing my breath.

"You're sure?" he rasped, hands beginning to wander.

He got his answer when *I* maneuvered him to *his* back... and made my move.

A MIND IS A TERRIBLE THING TO WASTE

I wanted to stand on a rooftop and shout. *Hey, world! Cole and I finally had sex!*

The big event ended over an hour ago, but we hadn't moved from the rug. Well, I hadn't. He had, but for only a moment, when he'd disposed of the condom. Then he'd returned and gathered me close. I was glad. I was still utterly overwhelmed. Me and Cole. Cole and me. The two of us. Together.

Was it stalker-clingy to think our souls were now melded together?

Probably. But I didn't care! We'd had sex!

As much as I belonged to him, he now belonged to me. Not just in word, but in deed. There was responsibility. Accountability. And yes, those things had been a part of our relationship before, but…everything just felt different now. More intense.

He held me in his arms, as if I was a precious treasure. Considering what we'd just done—melded souls!—I had better be. I could feel the *thump, thump* of his heartbeat, a riotous pound in sync with my own.

"You okay?" he asked.

I propped my chin in an upraised palm and peered down at him. His dark hair was rumpled and sexy, his eyes at half-mast. His lips were slightly swollen from the force of my kisses. Honestly? He'd never looked better.

"I think so." A deep sense of vulnerability washed over me—it wasn't the first time. "What about you? Wishing we'd waited two more years, as planned?"

"I think we both know that plan was destined to fail. And stupid. And a crime against nature."

I kissed the spot just over his nipple ring. "You gave it your best shot."

"That's all a guy can do, really," he said as he played with my hair.

"Well, A for effort."

"Oh, are we scoring each other now?"

"No!" I blurted...then nibbled on my bottom lip. "Yes?"

He chuckled. "You are off the charts, love. The best. My favorite. No one compares."

"Obviously," I replied, my tone imperious.

His chuckle morphed into a snort.

Another wave of vulnerability washed over me. "You love me, right? Now and always?"

"Of course I love you. And you believe me, because you trust me to always be honest with you."

Just like I would always be...honest with...

Oh, crap. I hadn't been honest with him. I hadn't told him about Helen. I'd had sex with him, but hadn't freaking told him about Helen.

I knew how devastating a single lie could be. How it could destroy a lifetime of trust. And this *was* a lie. A lie of omission. But I couldn't tell him now. Not while our clothes were scattered around us and we were basking in the warmth of the fire.

So...when?

Tomorrow. Yes. And he would forgive me. He would understand. Because of what we'd just shared, we would work things out easier now, each more willing to compromise.

In a desperate bid to change the subject, I said the first thing that popped into my head. "Have you ever been with someone like me before?" And then wanted to slink away and hide.

The thought of him with another girl—even girls who'd come pre-Ali—did something to me. Something it hadn't done before. I wanted to put each one in the hospital. Just for a few days. Just as long as blood flowed.

"Someone like you? There is no one else like you."

"Inexperienced."

A sigh. "One," he hedged.

"Did you love her? How did she act afterward?"

He sighed. "Do you really want to talk about this?"

"Yes."

Tracing his fingers down my spine, caressing, he said, "No, I didn't love her. That was my do-anyone-who-agrees stage. And I don't know how she acted. Her parents came home and I had to sneak out the window."

I still wanted to make her bleed, but maybe I'd also bring

her flowers. I didn't like the thought of her all alone, vulnerable, like I was now. "How did *you* feel?"

"Do you care, or are you really asking how I feel about us?"

I gulped. "Us."

He held me tighter. "I want all of you, forever, you and me, every day."

Um. "Did you just quote Nicholas Sparks? Or rather, Ryan Gosling from *The Notebook?*"

A pause, a chuckle. "Was hoping you wouldn't catch that."

Too bad. "And you're not dying of shame for memorizing something from a chick flick?"

"Baby, that movie isn't a chick flick. It's the best wingman of all time. Any guy can get laid afterward. Besides, the thought of Ryan Gosling made you go all dreamy and crap."

It had. It so had. *Well played, Cole Holland. Well played.* "Have you ever had a one-night stand?" But I was back on track now.

He kissed my temple. "Where is this coming from?"

"I don't know," I admitted. "I feel so out of control right now, like I could pull out my hair, and then pull out yours, and then hug you and kiss you, and maybe eat a big stack of chocolate-chip cookies."

"That's… Okay, wow. You are weird in the most perfect way."

"That doesn't answer my question."

A pause. A sigh. "Yes. I've had a one-night stand."

"With who?" I asked, already jealous of the faceless girl. Or girls.

"To be honest, I don't even know their names."

Names. Plural. Just how many girls did I need to hospitalize?

"So…what do you want to be when you grow up?" he asked. "Assuming all zombies have been wiped out by then."

I grabbed on to the distraction this time. It was a lifeline. "Seriously? *That's* how you phrase it?"

"Why not?"

"*When I get older,*" I said with emphasis, "I want to… Don't you dare laugh! I want to be a counselor or something."

"Why would I laugh? You'll make a great counselor, helping people blubber about their—"

I twisted his nipple ring.

"Ow!" He pried my fingers loose. "You've been through so much," he said, serious now. "You can understand people and pain in a way so many others cannot."

"What about you? What do you want to do?"

"I've got it all figured out. On my downtime, I'll be a survivalist, taking people out in the woods and teaching them how to thrive."

"And telling them what to do."

"That's just a bonus."

"Well, it's perfect for you. But what about your up time?"

"Law enforcement."

Even more perfect. "You'll get to deal with punk kids with secrets."

He flashed a dazzling grin. "Karma."

"The cow." I yawned, a wave of fatigue sneaking up on me. "Sleep."

"No. Talk." But his warmth was lulling me deeper and deeper into a sea of darkness, and I soon drifted off.…

I'm not sure how much time passed before he woke me up with a kiss.

"We've got to head back to River's, love. I need to find out if anything new was learned."

"Mmm, 'kay," I said and rolled to my side to sleep some more.

Chuckling, he gave my butt a light tap. "Up or I start tickling."

"And I start punching."

"Let's hold off on the foreplay until we're where we need to be."

Cole met with River, and I went back to bed. When I awoke, however long later, Cole was sitting at the side of the bed, watching me, his expression soft and tender.

"Good morning," he said with a grin.

I sat up, mumbled, "Yeah, yeah." I was sore and my mind was screaming one word over and over—*sex, sex, sex.*

"Hope you're hungry." He placed a tray piled high with pancakes over my lap. "They aren't chocolate-chip cookies, but I thought you'd enjoy them anyway."

I'm not sure how he'd managed to climb in and out of bed without waking me, but he had, and now he was encompassed by the bright light of a new day, looking sexier than ever while I probably sported a major case of bedhead.

"You're blushing," he said.

Because we just had sex! "Well, you're annoying me," I muttered.

He gave me the laugh reserved solely for me. "Note to self.

Ali-gator turns into an Ali-cat when she doesn't get enough rest."

"And you're about to have the scratches to prove it."

"Oh, no," he said, holding up his hands. "I'd *hate* to have your nails embedded anywhere on me…again."

I stuck my tongue out at him.

He rubbed his knuckles into my crown.

"Stop!"

"Eat."

"Fine." I ate, showered—alone—and dressed in clean clothes that actually fit—thanks, whoever!—and tried not to think about everything we'd done in each other's arms. It was as I towel-dried my hair that I realized Cole and I hadn't yet had a new vision. I tried not to panic. The last time we'd stopped having visions, we'd broken up.

"Cole," I said, frantically moving in front of him as I fastened a leather cuff around each of my wrists. Anything that made it harder for zombies to bite down became a vital part of my wardrobe. "We didn't have a vision."

He frowned but said, "It'll be all right." He bent down and pressed a soft kiss into my lips. "We'll have one—"

—and suddenly we were in a narrow corridor. I was slung over his shoulder, and for the first time, I could actually feel the bone pushing into my stomach, cutting off my air. I could actually smell antiseptic, the tang of old pennies and smoke.

In the distance, gunfire and grunts of pain echoed, making me cringe.

"Let me go!" I snarled.

"Never again." As I beat at his back and slammed my knees

into his torso, he lifted a gun and shot every single man brave enough to approach. *Pop. Pop. Pop.* Bodies fell.

Human bodies. Not zombies.

"I mean it. Let go," I demanded.

"Never. Again."

"You keep saying that. What do you want with me? What do you want *from* me?"

"What I've always wanted. Everything."

"Well, you can't have it."

At the end of the hallway, he could go left or right. To the left, Frosty was shooting his way through a group of men, his arms moving so quickly, from one target to another, I could hardly keep track. Bodies fell around him, too. *Boom, boom, boom.* Blood sprayed over the walls.

I'd never seen him look quite so fierce. His eyes were wild and glazed with hatred.

To the right, a sea of zombie collars lay on the floor—without zombies.

In both directions, fires crackled.

Cole went right, away from Frosty, surprising me. He—

—a knock at the door jolted us from the vision.

I blinked and found myself back inside the bedroom, the air clean and fresh, sunlight pouring in through the window.

"Rangarajan is here," Camilla announced. "If you want in on the action, you need to get to the courtyard."

Cole and I peered at each other, silent. Tense.

"That was more vivid than ever before," I said.

"I know. Our stronger connection must affect our visions, too."

"But why the delay in having one?"

"Because we have more control now and actually wanted it to happen? I don't know." He tangled a hand through his hair. "We'll put this on hold for a while."

All right. Okay. Because it wasn't life or death.

Was it?

"Hey," he said, gently chucking me under the chin. "This isn't a bad thing. The visions are our friend, not our enemy. They've helped us in so many ways."

True. "But they've hurt us, too."

"Only because we didn't know how to interpret them."

"This one seemed pretty cut-and-dried."

"Someone's a downer today, isn't she?" he asked with a growing smile.

I patted his cheek. "She is. And don't you forget it, or you'll lose something precious."

"If you're talking about my penis, I'd like to think it's precious to you, too."

Oh, good glory.

He laughed as he escorted me out of the room and to the courtyard. Only a handful of kids remained. River, Camilla and Knuckle Scars—I mean, Chance—plus all of our crew. The sun was high, a warm caress that contrasted nicely with the chilly air.

Someone had dragged a wide wooden circle to the center of the yard. Inside it had to be Dr. Rangarajan; his arms were shackled overhead and his legs shackled below, so that he formed a perfect X. He was a short, thin man, probably in his mid-sixties, with salt-and-pepper hair and tanned, deeply wrinkled skin. Next to him, slayers looked like Vikings of old.

The doctor had been stripped to his underwear, and the

cold air had to be chomping on his exposed skin. Tears had chilled in his lashes and on his cheeks, and snot had dried on his nose.

Kat raced across the way to step in front of me. She didn't say a word, just looked up at me, and I knew what she was thinking. We should protest. I'd been tortured before, and she'd gotten an up-close-and-personal look at the results. If we did this, we would be stooping to Anima's level, fighting evil with evil.

But just like with Benjamin, I didn't know another way. And if the doctor knew where Justin was, we had to do something.

"P-please," Dr. Rangarajan begged. "Just let me go. I have a family."

"So did the kids you've killed." River paced in front of him, twirling a dagger at the end of his index finger. Blood dripped from a wound the action caused, but he didn't seem to notice. "I'm very close to losing my patience with you. You work for Anima, and I will hear you admit it. Every time you refuse or lie, I will carve an *X* in your flesh. When I run out of room, I'll carve one directly into your heart."

Dr. Rangarajan licked his lips as he nervously eyed the crowd of onlookers. One of his eyes was swollen and discolored, and there was a lump on his jaw. He'd already been beaten, but clearly hadn't given away any secrets.

"Where's my brother?" Jaclyn stomped over and punched him in the gut.

Gavin grabbed her by the waist and pulled her back. She struggled for freedom, even delivering a punch to Gavin, but he never loosened his grip and finally she tired out, resting her head on his shoulder and sobbing. He ran his fingers through her hair, treating her as tenderly as he would a lost child.

River grinned at the doctor. "So," he said, waving the blade in front of Dr. Rangarajan's face. "Admit you work for Anima."

A tear rolled down Kat's cheek.

I found my feet moving forward of their own accord. Cole placed a hand on my shoulder in an effort to stop me, but Kat batted it away, and I kept going. I gently pushed River aside and faced the doctor.

Silently he pleaded with me.

What the heck was I going to do?

"Ali?" Camilla said.

"I—"

Helen appeared just in front of me. I gasped, and behind me, several people demanded to know what had happened.

Cole did his thing and jerked me behind him.

"Cool down on the protection detail," I said, moving around him. "Nothing happened. Nothing's wrong."

He grudgingly returned to Kat and Frosty, and I scanned the crowd. No one seemed to realize Helen stood next to the doctor. She was cloaked.

Facing Helen, while seeming to direct my attention to Dr. Rangarajan, I said, "Can you help us?"

"I lost track over the years," she said, "but since the first night of the attacks, I've been researching, just like Holland. Here's what I've learned. Dr. Rangarajan works directly under Rebecca Smith. I know her, worked with her. She is now the one in charge, the one you want. Her father started Anima, and when he died two years ago, Rebecca took over. If ever you meet her, trust nothing she says. Dr. Rangarajan's colleague, Dr. Wyatt Andrews, is the one referred to as Hodad."

"Dr. Wyatt Andrews," I said loudly. "That's who we need to look for next."

Dr. Rangarajan widened his eyes. "H-how did you know that?"

Rustling clothes behind me, footsteps. Clearly, someone had decided to search *now*.

Helen continued, "Justin is still alive, but not the other boy. He died last night."

With a heavy heart, I made the announcement.

Curses. Cries. Jaclyn's sob of relief.

Dr. Rangarajan struggled against his bonds. Did he assume I could read his mind? Fear me more than River's blade?

"Anima wants you, Ali," Helen said. "They took your blood when you were captured last month and ran some tests. You might have killed the guy responsible, but you didn't destroy his samples. Anima knows who you are. They know you're my daughter, the girl with the special zombie-destroying spirit. They want you back, and they'll stop at nothing."

I announced most of the rest, and Helen vanished. Gone as quickly as she'd come.

I was about to turn, when a thought occurred to me. The moment I was gone, Dr. Rangarajan was going to be killed. We couldn't afford to let him run to Anima and tattle on us, and that's exactly what he would do if we allowed him to live.

Could *I* live with his death? Especially when I could save him *and* stop him with my new ability.

An ability I'd yelled at Helen for using.

Did I really have another choice? I was backed into a corner, and I knew it. As she must have been.

Licking my lips, I placed my hands at the doctor's temples. He thrashed in an effort to dislodge me, but I held steady.

"What are you doing?" he demanded.

Helen said all I had to do was wave my spirit-hand across his mind. So, I did it. And it was...weird. Not cold, not hot. But warm. Little zaps pricked against my fingers—electrical?

He stilled, frowned. Intelligent eyes glazed over.

I jerked away. Had it worked?

"What's your name?" I asked.

His frown deepened. "I—I don't know. Why don't I know?"

It had. It really had.

Behind me, the slayers went quiet.

I faced my audience, shoving my hands in my pockets.

"How did you learn that stuff?" River asked. "What did you do to his mind?"

My gaze locked on Cole. Curiosity stared back at me—maybe a hint of anger. Did he suspect the truth?

Shifting guiltily, I said, "A Witness told me. And I used an ability."

Different reactions. Shock. Confusion. Only Cole's mattered. A magnification of the anger.

Oh, yes. He suspected.

A kid came rushing through the crowd and stopped at River's side. "Two detectives are here, and they want to speak with you and Cole."

"Again?" River groaned. "This is becoming tiresome."

Cole massaged the back of his neck. "How did they know I was here?"

Everyone came to the same conclusion. They had followed us last night.

I stiffened. Last night, we'd seen no sign of them. So...what had they seen us do?

"Get rid of Rangarajan," River instructed, "and tell the underage to hide. The rest of us will go have a chat with the detectives."

ZOMBIES WERE PEOPLE TOO

Could this day get any worse?

Wait. Scratch that. Bad things tended to happen whenever I contemplated that question.

The detectives *had* been monitoring us—and had readily admitted it—but if they'd seen us doing anything illegal, they hadn't alluded to it or even asked questions about it. In fact, they'd seemed downright leery of us. As if their eyes had finally been opened to the truth, and they knew we were slayers, the only thing standing between them and a zombie apocalypse.

They'd come because a corpse had been found. A teenage boy.

They showed River and Cole a set of photographs, hoping to get an ID, and River finally said, his tone hollow, "That's Cary. He's mine. No other family."

The detectives offered little information about the boy's murder and soon left with a cryptic "Be careful."

What did they know? And did it affect us?

"Let's get back to Ankh's." Cole wrapped his arm around me, and for the first time, it wasn't a gesture of affection or comfort, but an intractable hold to prevent me from bolting.

To River, he said, "I'll call you in the morning and tell you our next move."

River disguised his anguish with an irritated expression. "You'll *tell* me?"

"We'll decide together," I offered. We needed everyone's mind programmed to only one setting: attack. We had to be smart about this, all head, no emotion. Justin's life depended on it.

Cole led me away. "Helen," he said quietly.

Wanted to lie. "Yes." Couldn't.

"And the memory thing?"

"Helen," I whispered.

His fingers bit into my shoulder. "I thought you knew better. She's a liar, Ali. She's a betrayer."

"She's my mother, Cole."

He sucked in a breath. "Is that *affection* I detect in your tone?"

No. Yes. "Maybe."

"I can't believe you're doing this. She abandoned you. She betrayed our kind. Killed my mother! Ensured she was turned. Because of Helen, I had to watch my father ash my mother— *after* she attacked me, her own son."

Aching for the boy he'd been, and the man he'd become, I whispered, "I'm not disagreeing with you. What Helen did was wrong, no matter her reasons."

"Exactly. There's no reason good enough."

And still I said, "What you don't know is that she was desperate, felt she had no good choices." The words sounded lame, even to me. "But she's different now."

"People don't change, Ali."

"They do."

"She's going to get you killed. Get us *all* killed."

"Cole—"

"No. Don't you dare try to talk me into forgiving her."

"That's not what I'm doing." I tried again. "Cole—"

Again he shut me down. "Did last night mean *anything* to you?" Cursing under his breath, he let me go and quickened his pace, moving ahead of me.

Realization hit. The boy I'd trusted with my body, and given my heart to, had just left me in his dust. There had been no talking it over. No compromise.

Things weren't easier after sex, I realized. They were far more complicated.

"Anything to me?" I called. "What about you?"

He ignored me.

I'd hurt him. I knew it. But he'd hurt me, too. And now… now I was on my own. Confused, more vulnerable than ever before.

I trudged behind with the rest of our crew. This wasn't my fault. Cole was wrong to make me pick between him and my mother. Wasn't he? Gah! Or was I wrong for expecting him to accept her?

Kat came up beside me and linked our fingers. "I get the feeling your boy is being as lame as mine."

"I don't know what to think." I glanced up at the clouds— saw a rabbit cloud and sighed.

Had definitely gotten worse.

"Always blame the guy," she said. "That's my new motto. And I've been plotting revenge. It goes a little something like this. We run away together, get married the way I know you want to, and then, just for grins and gigs, we send the boys a postcard that says, and I quote, 'Are you still planning to murder your postman?'"

This girl… Light. Of. My. Life. "I'm in!"

Halfway to the car, Cole stopped, his nose wrinkling as he sniffed the air.

"Rot," he announced.

Surely not…but I sniffed, and yep, encountered the telltale scent of rot. "But it's daylight."

"Could be a dead animal." Even still, he withdrew his crossbow. "Jaclyn, let River know what's going on. Frosty, get Kat inside."

As Jaclyn raced back into the building and Frosty hefted Kat over his shoulder like a sack of potatoes, the rest of the slayers withdrew their weapons, preparing for battle. I searched the area, expecting to find…maybe a family of slaughtered raccoons. May they rest in peace. I could even visualize what had happened. They'd crossed the street, hoping to start a new life in River's front lawn, but some hit-and-run driver mowed them down. What I didn't expect to find was—

Zombies.

There.

At least twenty of them raced out of the warehouse next door. No slow amble, but a sprint, their arms flailing as they reached for us. Steam curled from saggy skin, the bright rays of the sun like an oven.

I spotted collars. Someone was controlling them.

Slayers began stepping from their bodies and throwing themselves into the fray. Me? I looked around the area. I wanted to know who was responsible. Street—empty. Parked car—empty. Another parked car—empty. Two people striding along a crosswalk, each carrying a briefcase. Unaware. Parked car—two people in front...facing this direction.

My targets.

I raced toward the car, my dagger hidden by my forearm. The pair didn't seem surprised as I neared. They didn't pull a weapon on me, either. Instead, they dropped the remotes and sped away just before I made contact.

Cowards!

Less than two minutes later, the zombies fell to the ground— the control must work only from a short distance. The spirits writhed, the sun continuing to bake them like Christmas hams. Darkness never had been able to handle light.

As slayers ashed zombies and returned to their bodies, I wondered what Anima had hoped to accomplish. If they'd actually hoped for a battle, the men would have stuck around.

"Anyone hurt?" I asked.

"No." Cole sheathed his crossbow. "The zombies were unable to focus on a specific target. They were simply flailing."

Jaclyn and River rushed from the apartment, ten of his fighters not far behind. The group noticed the ash floating through the air and stopped abruptly.

"What happened?" River demanded.

"We won," Cole responded.

I explained about the guys in the car, and a heavy silence descended.

"We've got more to think about than we realized," Cole said to River, and the boy nodded.

★ ★ ★

At Mr. Ankh's, Cole bounded from the car without a word to anyone. Even me. Or maybe a better way to phrase that was *especially me*. Still mad. Got it.

Frosty tailed him, adopting the same M.O.—still mad.

"I thought I was dating a guy, not a baby," Kat muttered as we trudged inside the house. "Clearly, I thought wrong."

"Frosty's worried about you, that's all."

"And what's Cole's problem? Because, gator, that boy's temper puts the others to shame."

"He isn't getting his way." And that, right there, was the truth of the matter.

"Figures."

When we hit the stairs, a text came in from Nana. I slowed my pace.

Are you safe? No matter how you feel about me, I deserve an answer.

Me: I am. No worries.
Nana: Good. That's what I like to hear. Or, see.
Me: And how I feel about U? Nana, I love U.

I remembered my vulnerability with Cole, how much assurance I'd needed from him. I figured Nana was in a similar riotous state.

Nana: Still?

I imagined her trembling.

Me: Always.

I got it now. I really did. Why she hadn't told me. For the

same reasons I'd kept Helen a secret from Cole. Fear of the unknown. How could I blame her for it?

"Ali! Kat! How cake." Reeve leaned on the banister railing. "I thought I heard your voices. Did Bronx come back with you?"

"Yep," Kat said, "but don't expect to see him anytime soon. He's with Cole and Frosty, throwing a temper tantrum."

For a moment, Reeve was the picture of disappointment. Then she shook it off and said, "Why don't you two come to my suite? We'll protect each other from their negativity."

She led the way. In the sitting room, tarp covered the couch and coffee table, but everything else had been moved out. The edges of the wall were taped.

"You're painting?" I asked.

"Yes. To distract myself from the horror of waiting for you guys to return from a mission, I decided to renovate."

We moved through the little kitchenette and into the bedroom, where the computer screen flashed a picture of Frosty. I did a double take. He wore a formal gown, as pink as Reeve's walls used to be, complete with ruffles and bows.

"Do you like it?" Kat asked, noticing the direction of my gaze. "It's a little something I threw together for Frosty. Had it blown up and framed. Best Christmas present he's ever received. Classiest, too. I couldn't *not* share its beauty with Reeve—and half the kids at our school—to use as a screensaver."

Priceless. "I'd like one of Cole in the same outfit. Only sleeveless."

"Done!"

Reeve giggled.

My phone beeped, and I expected to find another text from Nana. But when I checked the screen, it was blank. I frowned—until I remembered I still had Ethan's phone. Trembling, I withdrew it from my other pocket. Justin's face stared up at me. He was alive, just as Helen had said, and holding this morning's paper. One of his eyes was swollen shut. His lip was cut in two places, and there was a knot in his jaw. He needed medical attention ASAP. No, he needed our fire.

Below the photo, Ethan had typed, My apologies for the delay. We lost the other boy. We're still willing to trade—are you?

My hands clenched so tightly the sides of the phone cracked. I forwarded the text to my cell and from there forwarded it to Cole.

Cole: Tell him U'll give an answer 2morrow. We need time 2 plan.

I did as commanded.

Ethan: Until then.

Me to Cole: It's set. Where are U? I'll help w/planning.

Cole: I'll find U later.

I gnashed my teeth. Did he think I'd tell Helen our plans? Did he not trust me anymore?

I sent him one more text: We need 2 test the new vision development.

Cole: Later.

"What is it?" Kat asked, concerned.

I put both phones away with more force than necessary. There was no way *anyone* would allow Miss Mad Dog to participate in what was to come, so there was no reason to argue about it now or alarm her over Justin's condition.

"Cole and I had sex," I announced, switching gears. "In other news, I want to smash his face!"

In an instant, everything else was forgotten.

"What!" the girls exclaimed in unison.

"How was it?" Kat asked. "Totally cake?"

"Yes. Frosted and sprinkled."

"Last I heard, you weren't ready," Reeve said. "What changed?"

Everything!

I flopped onto the bed and covered my face with the comforter. "I almost died when Zombie Ali showed up, and that affects a person, you know. I wanted to live and basically begged Cole to make the next move. He wouldn't, until I almost died again, and now it's changed things between us, changed me. I feel closer to him than ever, so of course his anger is harder to take. I mean, I hated his anger before, but it's like a thorn in my side now. I can't get past it. Can't think about anything else. I'm confused and upset and, okay, even more angry with him than he is with me. How dare he get mad at me! Sure, he has a good reason, but I'm his girlfriend. Shouldn't he focus on me rather than the past?"

Silence.

"I don't think I've ever heard you string so many words together at once," Kat said. "But let me see if I got the gist of what you were saying. Cole needs to be castrated?"

Knows me so well. "Exactly!"

We spent the next few hours dissing boys, wondering what the world would be like without them. Final conclusion: magnificent. We'd never have to shave our legs or style our hair. If we wanted to gain a hundred pounds, big deal. No one would accuse us of being unreasonable, because all the stupid people would be gone!

Reeve patted my hand. "What's Cole angry about? What does he think you've done?"

"I…" How could I explain? "My mom…wasn't my birth mother. My real mother worked for Anima and even helped arrange *his* mother's death. That's why the guys were so freaked about my ability. It came from my mom. And I… I've been talking to her, like I talk to my little sister. I *trust* her. Cole wants me to stop."

"Oh," she said, a thousand emotions dripping from that one word. Clearly, she agreed with Cole.

"Not helping," I said on a sigh.

Should I apologize to Cole?

Answer was immediate. No! Helen was my mother. The only one I had left. I didn't want to lose her the way I'd lost everyone else. I would talk to her—believe her—if I wanted.

Kat tapped her chin and said, "Let's look at this situation like a math test. There are four possible answers. *A*, Cole's wrong and you're right. *B*, Cole's right and you're wrong. *C*, you're both wrong. And *D*, you're both right. You've selected *A*, and he's selected *B*. Meaning, you've both flunked. The correct answer is *D*, and if you guys are too stubborn to see that, you're going to lose each other."

I rolled to my side, sighed. "I need to think."

"My genius usually has that effect. Take all the time you need."

Kat and Reeve switched topics, and I might have joined… if I hadn't seen Helen kneel beside the bed. The source of my problem.

Actually, no. That was Cole.

Our eyes—so identical in color—met and I found I couldn't resent her. Couldn't even work up a spark of upset. She was here. For me. Part of me loved her for it.

She reached out as if she meant to smooth the hair from my forehead, smiled sadly just before contact that would never happen and dropped her arm to her side.

"Close your eyes," she said.

"Why?" I asked.

"Why what?" Reeve replied.

Note to self: *must guard my tongue.*

"I'm going to close my eyes for a bit," I said, attention locked on Helen. "You guys continue on without me."

Kat patted my shoulder. "If you insist."

"When you were five, I made molds of your hands...." As she spoke, the scene began to crystallize in my mind.

I sat at the edge of a red-and-black rug playing with a toy car, rolling it over dolls. Bowls of powder and water circled me. Helen was in front of me, a black ink pad and several towels beside her.

"I made molds of your hands," vision Helen said, "and now we're going to add your fingerprints to the ends of the fakes. That way, I can upload your prints into Anima's system." She smiled at me. "One of their greatest flaws is their cloak of secrecy. The medical side is never told what the security side is doing, and so on and so forth, so that no one can ever reveal all of their schemes. I'll create a fake name for you, call you an agent, give you the same security clearance I have, and they'll never know, never remove it, because you'll never be reported as missing or dead."

She cleaned my hands, smiling triumphantly, almost mani-cally. "If ever they capture you, you'll be able to free your-self. Just hold your palm to their scanners. Hopefully, I'll have destroyed Anima long before anything like that can happen. But if not…" She pressed each of my fingers into the ink pad. "I want you taken care of."

Thoughts raced through my mind. Helen *had* loved me. Did love me. Cole was wrong about her. She wasn't here to harm me or betray me. She would die first—as she'd proved.

Because of her, I could get in and out of Anima. I could free Justin, keeping my promise to Jaclyn.

I just had to find him first. But Ethan would help me with that.

Thank you, I mouthed.

"I'm sorry I didn't appear to you sooner," the real Helen said. "I'm sorry you were captured and tortured, and the way out was within your reach, you just didn't know it. They have ways of blocking Witnesses from their buildings, and I couldn't get to you. Knew you wouldn't believe me even if I could. People don't listen to what they're not ready to hear. Now you know everything, and if you want me to leave and never return…for you, I will. For you, anything."

Never see her again?

It's what Cole wanted.

"Stay," I said.

ZOMBIE SEE, ZOMBIE EAT

I thought about Helen—my mother...my *beloved* mother—all night. Alone. Cole never snuck into my room.

In his defense, I never snuck into his.

The next morning, however, he banged on my door. "Ankh's office. Now."

That's it? That's what I got from him? Where was the cuddler I'd left at River's?

I rushed through a shower, brushed my teeth, dressed. Cole, River, Frosty and Bronx were already assembled in the office.

Cole wouldn't meet my gaze. "Call Ethan. Set up the trade."

Bleeding inside.

But I'd made my choice, hadn't I? I'd have a relationship with Helen, no matter what.

I gulped and dialed the number. The phone rang over and over, but Ethan never answered.

I texted him, and though we waited five minutes...twenty... forty....he never replied.

It made me nervous. Was Justin okay, or had he—

No, don't go there.

We spent the rest of the day on a hunt for Dr. Wyatt Andrews. The name Helen had given us. But we found absolutely no hint of him.

It was as we were stomping back into Mr. Ankh's house that Cole finally looked my way—and I really wished he hadn't. His violet gaze proclaimed: *Told you so.*

He was certain Helen had lied about the doctor's identity.

I stopped hurting, stopped bleeding and got angry all over again.

A day passed, then another and another. Still no word from Ethan.

Cole and I barely spoke, the tension between us like needles in my skin. He felt as if I'd betrayed him, and in a way, I had. But he'd betrayed me, too. We were supposed to put each other first. Right now, we were closer to last.

Every night I climbed into my big bed, alone, and cried. We weren't even having visions anymore.

By choice?

If so, it was his, not mine.

Helen came to see me only once. I suspected she was keeping her distance, even though I'd asked her to stay, in an effort to make things easier for Cole and me. I was relieved—and angrier.

I asked her how she was able to visit, when Emma struggled more and more to do so as the bond between us weakened. She said it was the slayer side of her—used to operating in the spirit realm, she could do more than the average dead girl.

She also told me where one of Anima's laboratories was

located. I told Cole. He knew where I'd gotten my information and dismissed it. So, I did the only thing I could. I called River and made plans to raid the building with him.

When Cole found out about *that,* he utterly lost it.

He stomped into my room, slammed the door. "You don't go to River for *anything.*" He was savage, intense. "You come to me."

I was in the process of gathering my things, expecting River to arrive at any moment. I stopped to glare. "I did. You ignored me."

"I've *never* ignored you. I just didn't mention that I told my dad about the lab and intended to do a stakeout tonight."

Wait. "You were going to do a stakeout without telling me? Why?" Did I really need to rack my brain? "Never mind. You didn't want me to warn Helen."

A muscle ticked under his eye.

Bingo.

Blood boiling, I pointed to the door. "Get out. Now."

Features as cold as ice, he planted his feet. "Make me."

I pushed him.

He didn't budge.

I pushed again, harder, and finally, movement. He stumbled back a step. I could feel his heart racing under my palm. It was the only thing that kept me sane. He was affected. He might not want to show it, but he was.

"I'm only trying to protect you," he said through gritted teeth. "Helen is going to betray you, and if it doesn't get you killed, it's going to break your heart."

"I don't need your protection, Cole. I need your support." Why couldn't he see that?

"You can't have it. Not in this. I will always give you what you need, even if it's not what you want."

"Need, according to *you*."

"You aren't objective."

"Neither are you!"

He wrapped his fingers around my wrist, squeezing just enough to hold me steady. At first, I thought he meant to bring my knuckles to his lips and kiss me. Wishful thinking. He let go, severing contact.

"I'm going with you to the warehouse," he said.

Calm. "Fine. I can't stop you." Didn't want to stop him. "Dress in black. We're not stopping with a stakeout."

He opened his mouth to say more, but closed it. Then he said, "Let's try to force a vision. See what happens."

Now he wanted to try? "No," I said and turned away. I didn't want to see our future. Not anymore.

He left the room without another word—and *he* was the one to break my heart.

Compartmentalize.

No. Just…no. I wouldn't start that again. At best, it was a temporary fix. I'd pour my anger and hurt into destroying Anima.

I finished arming myself and marched to the foyer. River, Camilla and Chance were already waiting. As were Cole, Frosty, Bronx, Veronica, Gavin and Mackenzie. How had Cole gathered the troops so quickly?

I can do this. I kept my attention trained on River. "Bring everything we'll need?"

"More than."

Good.

We headed outside.

Frosty threw his arms around my shoulders and whispered, "This is hard for Cole. The situation scares him, that's all."

"He's not the only one," I muttered.

"Yeah, but you're a girl. The braver species."

"This is true."

The lab was just outside of Birmingham. We parked down the street, watching the front doors, taking pictures of the employees who entered and left the building. River told Cole our strategy, and though the muscle below his eye started ticking again, he agreed it was sound.

Finally, darkness fell. Time to get to work. My adrenaline jacked up as we took our places around the building. Only two guards manned the reception desk.

"In five...four...three..." River's voice whispered through the tiny bud in my ear. "Two. One."

Camilla approached the glass doors in front and knocked frantically. Her shirt was soaked with fake blood, and she clutched the "wound" as if she was in terrible pain and even wavered on her feet as if she was about to faint.

Guard Number One popped to his feet. Guard Number Two grabbed his arm to hold him in place. From the shadows outside, I watched as One and Two engaged in a fiery conversation. Ultimately, Two picked up the phone to call...911? His boss?

Taking it up a notch, Camilla fell to her knees, then tumbled the rest of the way to the ground, where she sprawled, still as death. One ignored his buddy and rushed to the door. The moment it was open, and he was leaning down to help her, Camilla shot him point-blank with a tranquilizer gun.

Cole did a mad dash from the shadows to the doorway, leaping over Camilla and the guard to shoot Two with a tranq. He collapsed, and Cole swiped up the phone to listen.

"Hadn't finished dialing," he said.

Frosty and Bronx dragged One inside. The rest of us came in behind them. I made sure to lock the doors. As we tiptoed through the narrow corridor, part of me expected a million guards to rush out of hiding and Frosty to go bat-crap crazy and kill them. When would the visions come true?

We reached a thick, red door without incident. The ID pad on the left was like a neon sign flashing the words *You'll. Never. Get. Past. This. Point.*

Could I? Even though Helen had said my prints would not be wiped from Anima's system, eleven years was a long time. Anything could have happened.

Chance withdrew a bunch of equipment I didn't recognize, hooked this to that, and that to this, pushed buttons, rewired and *boom*, it was Open Sesame. No fingerprint ID necessary.

Which was probably for the best. Cole would freak, and everyone else would claim Helen had done it to trap me in some way. To trap *us*.

We found offices and, under Camilla's direction, copied the hard drives. We found rooms with medical equipment and a vast array of medications and, again, under Camilla's direction, took samples. "We need that. And that. And that," she said, expecting us to grab the items.

As River's sister, she was used to taking charge. I got that. But I wasn't her lackey, and she wasn't my boss. Her commands scraped my nerves raw.

In the back was an unlocked door. I checked behind me.

No one paid me any attention. I breezed through and found myself in a hallway. Alone. At the end was another door, but it was locked. Licking my lips, I performed another quick check before resting my palm on the ID screen. Lights glowed between my spread fingers. I waited with bated breath—

And the lock disengaged.

I couldn't... It was... Wow. Just wow. It had worked.

"Ali," Cole barked.

I jolted, guilty.

I raced around the corner, chasing the sound of his voice. Everyone had gathered in the back of the building, where at least fifty cages with grunting, collared zombies lined the wall. We ashed the creatures and stole their collars.

We checked the rest of the building, found nothing, no one, and dragged the unconscious guards outside. Then we did what we'd all been waiting for. Destroyed. Everything.

River claimed to be something of an explosives expert and set a charge. The entire structure imploded, tumbling down, dust pluming in the air without any debris flying out to harm a civilian. A sense of triumph.

At Mr. Ankh's, we poured into the entertainment room to celebrate.

I lost interest, my mood dark.

Cole stood off to the side, chatting with Camilla.

Jealousy prickled at me as I strolled over. I placed my hand on his shoulder. Rising on my tiptoes, I whispered, "Guess Helen wasn't lying after all" straight into his ear.

He stiffened, giving his back to Camilla to glare at me. "Not this time."

"Not ever."

"Why can't you see the truth? She is the spider, and you are the fly. She's just lured you into her web."

My hands tightened into fists, and I looked pointedly at Camilla. "I could say the same to you. Enjoy your time together."

I walked away, hating him…hating myself.

Over the next few days, a routine developed. Mr. Ankh tested the samples we'd stolen, becoming increasingly frustrated with the results. Everything was useless. The more tech-savvy people dissected every word on every computer file pulled from the slip disks, but again, there was nothing of value.

It was as if Anima had known we were coming, removed everything incriminating and *let* us have the lab. Let us waste our time searching for answers that weren't there, either to pacify us or distract us.

If that was true, we had a mole in our midst—which might also explain how Benjamin the assassin had gotten free, despite what he'd said.

The idea sickened me. I trusted everyone in my group; we'd fought together, bled together. And I wanted to trust River and his friends. But could I? I mean, they supposedly had spies inside Anima, and yet, there was never any new information to report.

Cole would say Helen was to blame for all of this. Only Helen.

My stomach twisted, wringing out bile. *Oh, glory.* What if he was right?

Can't doubt my instincts now. In too deep.

Every morning, the slayers worked out in the gym. Our job was physical; we had to stay in shape. On more than one occasion I noticed Camilla eye-stalking Cole, making it (more) obvious she wanted a piece of him. Today, she even trailed him when he finished on the treadmill. It took every bit of my willpower not to go after them.

Stupid fight. And stupid Cole!

Stupid Camilla!

At least he glanced over his shoulder, meeting my gaze. Every cell in my body lit up. I almost cried his name. Almost. I wouldn't crumble first.

He looked away and continued on. Still no spontaneous visions.

I wasn't sure how much more of this I could take.

Though I wanted to chase after him, I hopped on the treadmill he'd just abandoned, letting my mind explore the visions the other slayers had been having. Just this morning, Frosty had seen himself digging through a pile of rubble, and Bronx had seen himself holding Reeve while she cried.

Gavin had seen himself fighting to reach an injured Jaclyn and an unconscious Justin, and Jaclyn had seen herself taking a bullet to the leg.

Bad, but at least we knew Justin was still alive despite Ethan's lack of communication.

Another point in our favor: no more daylight zombies. However, they *did* come out every night and cluster around Mr. Ankh's property line. Every night but yesterday, that is, and I wasn't sure why. Still… The frequent attacks had allowed me to practice using the push-ability. I was getting good. I would focus, drawing energy into the center of my being, and then imagine it shooting out of me. And it would! I allowed myself one push, and that was it. So far, I hadn't experienced another leak.

But the frequent attacks were also the reason more and more of River's slayers were moving into the mansion. We needed backup.

The new females were all over Cole. Not just Camilla, but most of her friends, too. A sly touch here. A suggestive remark there. I was no longer sure of my position in his life, so I kept quiet. But deep down, rage simmered.

I wasn't just going to make them bleed; I was going to cause permanent damage.

Needless to say, tensions were high. And not just mine. All of the slayers were exhausted. Our current schedule was grueling. Too much so. We kept this up for much longer, and we'd collapse.

But maybe that was Anima's plan. Exhaust us, and after we collapsed, pick us off one by one.

The conversations around me ceased abruptly, jarring me. I focused. Cole had just returned to the gym, his expression dark. My heart rate quickened, and not because of my steady jog.

He stopped beside me. "You've got a phone call."

I wiped the sweat off my brow, smoothed my damp hair from my face. "Who is it?"

"Ethan."

Finally! I jabbed my finger at the machine, and the belt froze. I hopped down and raced out, only to realize I didn't know where to go.

"The cell is still in Ankh's office," he said. Mr. Ankh had it hooked to some kind of tracing device.

I picked up speed. Mr. Ankh was at his desk, and he did not look happy.

"Ethan will only talk to you," he said.

We'd all prayed this day would come.

Just this morning, Kat had patted me on the back, smiled her most wily grin and said, "Let them think we're going their way, while we really go our way…the best way!"

Now threads of nervousness slithered through me; I had to cut them with mental scissors as I reached for the cell phone.

Mr. Ankh donned a set of earphones so that he could listen to the entire conversation. He gave me a stiff nod.

"Hello, Ethan," I said, proud of my seeming calm.

"Hello, Ali." He displayed the same calm.

"Where have you been? Why the delay?"

"A few things came up. Nothing you need to worry about, though. Justin hasn't dropped dead or anything like that."

Sweet confirmation. My gaze scanned the room. Cole had come in behind me and Veronica and Juliana behind him. River strolled in next, with Frosty and Bronx close on his heels.

Jaclyn raced inside, her gaze wide, hopeful.

Word had spread.

I gave everyone a thumbs-up.

"—there?" Ethan asked.

"Yes, I'm here." *Steady.* "I still want to do the trade," I said. "But I'll need new proof of life."

"You'll get it. But first, there's someone who'd like to speak with you."

Static. Then, "Hello, Miss Bell." A woman's voice. Unfamiliar.

"You have me at a disadvantage. You seem to know me, but I have no idea who you are."

"My name is Rebecca Smith. You may call me Rebecca."

The head of Anima herself. Why not call her Becky?

Or Satan.

"You've caused me so much trouble," she said, "I've decided to deal with you myself."

"You'll understand if I don't wish you better luck, *Ms. Smith.*" My gaze found Cole—his expression darkened further. This was the woman his father and Helen had warned us about. The one known for her interrogation "technique."

She chuckled, as if she'd expected no other reply. "A born rebel. Just like your mother."

As if she knows me.

"We did some jobs together, you know," she continued. "Not the one with your boyfriend's mother, of course. That was all Helen. But others that were equally successful. I'd be on the field now if the antidote hadn't stopped working for me."

Bile…burning up my throat… My features remained relaxed. I wouldn't give anything away to the onlookers. "Why don't we concentrate on the here and now, hmm?"

"Very well." I heard fingers tapping on a keyboard. "As I'm sure you've guessed, you are the key to our success. With you, we can capitalize on all the good zombies provide while discarding the bad."

"How?"

She ignored me and said, "I'm sending Ankh an email. There's a video attached. You'll want to watch it. It's your proof of life."

Okay, good, we were moving right along. "So, how would you like to do this?"

She didn't hesitate. "I would like to send Ethan to your door and make the exchange that way, because it's the easiest solution, but we both know you'll only kill him and take the boy. Instead, I'll expect to see you at—"

"You know what?" I interjected, as rehearsed. "You don't get to arrange this. You'll be at Hearts, the nightclub downtown, in two hours, with Justin, because he's your ticket through the door. Fail to comply and my mission will be the destruction of everything you hold dear." Actually, it already was.

Click.

I wanted to hunch over and vomit. Had I just made a huge mistake, insisting Ms. Smith meet us at Hearts, rather than playing the game by her rules? I hoped not. Mr. Ankh owned the nightclub, and our slayers were used to the building's layout. We'd have the advantage.

We needed every advantage we could get.

"Did you get a trace?" Cole demanded of Mr. Ankh.

"No," he snapped. "They rerouted the signal a thousand different ways. I'm guessing there'll be no way to trace the email, either, no matter how many people I put on the task."

Great.

We waited with bated breath for the telltale ding to sound, signaling the email had arrived. And when it did, we crowded behind Mr. Ankh's desk as he pushed Play on the video.

Justin appeared on the screen—and Jaclyn would have collapsed, if Gavin hadn't held her up.

Justin was huddled in back of a cage. He had on a pair of underwear, nothing more. Around him was a toilet, a sink and a twin bed. He'd lost so much weight, his ribs were visible. There were bruises under his eyes, track marks up his arms.

Was Anima pumping him with drugs, sedating him? Or taking blood?

Heck. Probably both.

Beside his cage were two other cages, and in those were countless collared zombies.

The camera moved away from him, the screen going blank, and Jaclyn cried, "No!"

I blinked back tears.

"I doubt they'll really try and do an exchange," Cole said, checking the magazine in his gun. "We've got a fifty-fifty chance. They'll either try to capture us all or kill us all. Flip a coin."

He was right. I'd known it all along, and yet, here, now, with slayers I'd only ever wanted to protect standing around me, it seemed wrong. "I'll do it, then. I'll trade." No double cross.

"No!" He spun around, glared at me. Except, it wasn't anger I saw. It was anguish. "No."

"Yes! Dang it, yes!" I stomped my foot. "How many times do I have to remind you? One person will give her life to save many. This is what I'm supposed to do."

He got in my face, yelling, "And how many times do I have to remind you that you can't know that for sure? That I refuse to lose you?"

"You have a funny way of showing it!"

He backed up a step, drew in a breath.

I squared my shoulders. "I'm making the trade, Cole."

"No." He shook his head. "Even if you are the one, I won't

let it happen. None of us will. So. Not another word from you. Go weapon up. We'll do the same. Everyone meet in the foyer, ten minutes."

"Cole—"

"Not another word! We'll go as if they plan to make the trade. We'll fight, kill as many of them as we can, finally put a dent in *their* forces." At the end of his control, and with a final glare aimed at me, he left.

AT THE CORNER OF MURDER AND MAYHEM

The countdown had begun.

Five minutes, and I was armed and ready.

Six minutes, and I gathered in the foyer with the other slayers and hugged Reeve and Kat goodbye.

"You come back to me, Ali-cat," Kat whispered. "You're nothing without me."

"Um, I think the saying is actually 'I'm nothing without you.'"

"Exactly what I said."

I smiled despite the tense situation. "Love you."

"Love you, too. And you had better be careful, Frosty," she called. "Or else."

"Always, baby."

They'd made up. Good. Heart squeezing, I peered at Cole. To my utter shock, his gaze was already sealed on me. Narrowed. Intense. As always, shiver-inducing. There were a thousand things I wanted to say to him, a thousand more I wanted to do.

Look away.

Somehow I managed it.

Eight minutes, and the slayers were striding toward the two SUVs outside.

I headed for the car in front, reached for the handle of the back door. My wrist was grabbed and I was spun around, a hard weight pushing my back against the cold metal. I gasped.

Cole!

My heart squeezed harder.

He cupped my cheeks, his hands warm. His gaze was pure violet fire. "I'm sorry. I'm miserable without you. Haven't been eating or sleeping. Just wanting. And there is no way I can let you head into a situation as dangerous as this one without telling you."

I trembled, overcome. Finally, one of us had breached the wall between us. The stronger one, I realized. "We—"

"I'm not done. I love you," he continued. "I've missed you. I don't like that you're talking to Helen. I'll never like it. I don't trust her, and I'm so afraid only terrible things will come of it. But I trust you and your instincts, so I'm taking it on faith—in you. I'm backing off."

I clutched the collar of his jacket. "I'm sorry, too. I handled things poorly and—"

He shook his head. "Still not done, love. There's one last thing, and it's a bit of a topic switch, so try to stay with me. Ready? Camilla made a play for me. You're just going to have to trust me when I say I turned her down and nothing happened."

"What!" I exploded.

He pressed his mouth to mine. I melted against him. The

kiss was a balm. The pain I'd felt these past few days melted away. The sense of rejection. The anger, the bitterness, too. I was swept up in our connection, the heat of him forging me into something greater.

Catcalls. Grunts of irritation. Prods to hurry. They penetrated my awareness as Cole lifted his head. I was too dazed to move, so he spun me around, gave my butt a smack and helped me into the car. He climbed in beside me. We held hands the entire drive.

Camilla was lucky she was riding in the other car. Later we would be having a chat. Maybe with knives. I wouldn't allow her to walk away—she'd have to crawl.

Once we pulled into the club's parking lot, my internal clock kicked back on. We had a little less than an hour and a half before the exchange was to take place.

I'm not sure how Mr. Ankh had managed it, but he'd already cleared the lot. We strode inside, our booted footsteps echoing off the walls. I'd been here a few times before, but it had always been overcrowded. Now we were the only occupants.

Frosty and River took positions at the front door, and the rest of us marched to the center of the dance floor. Chance and Mackenzie kept going, a team, taking posts at the back doors, making me wonder if something had happened between them. All the others formed a circle around me, each one facing a different direction. Mr. Ankh had cameras outside and in. Cole, Frosty and River each wore an earpiece, allowing the males to stay in constant contact.

Twenty minutes passed without incident. Thirty. Forty. This could go down so many ways, my head spun. Anima could bring Justin or leave him behind. Could come in the front door or try to ambush us through the back. Or both! They could be no-shows. They could send one man or a hundred.

If worse came to worst and they came in hot, without Justin, we would fight, as Cole had said. We could cripple their forces and even take hostages. Do a little interrogating of our own. I'd give River free rein. I was past the point of caring.

Suddenly, Cole stiffened. "Two girls heading toward the front entrance."

Girls? Without Justin?

I waited, fighting for breath, every second agony. Then Frosty stomped around the corner dragging Wren and Poppy behind him.

You've got to be kidding me. I pushed my way through the circle. "What are you doing here?"

"Some guy called me," Wren said, anchoring her hands on her hips. She was a smart, beautiful black girl, with a stubborn streak a mile wider than my own. "He said I had better get here quick or I'd miss Justin."

"And you believed him?"

Poppy, a model-pretty redhead, looked around. "What's going on?"

We had to get these girls out of here. But we couldn't send them off on their own. Anima could be waiting to grab them. We couldn't spare a solider to escort them. We needed all the manpower we could get. But then, Anima had known that and had hoped to thin the herd.

"Take them to the back office," I said. "Lock them in."

Both girls stared at me with wide eyes.

"It's for your own protection."

"Seriously. What's going on?" Poppy demanded.

"You walked into the middle of a war." I waved Jaclyn over. "Whatever you hear, you aren't to leave that office. And if someone you don't recognize busts in, shoot." I placed a .38 revolver in Wren's hand. It had a manageable recoil for a novice. "Have you ever fired one of these?"

"N-no," she stuttered, "and I never want to."

Too bad. "It doesn't have a safety, so if you squeeze the trigger, you're firing. But it does have a double-action trigger, which means it won't fire unless you squeeze all the way. Do not point the barrel at yourself or Poppy, understand?"

Jaclyn grabbed both girls by the arms. "Come on."

"Guns? A war?" Poppy cried, digging in her heels, wheezing. I think she was having a panic attack. "What kind of war?"

"We don't have time for this." Camilla rushed over and flung her arm around Poppy, forcing her into the hallway.

Boom!

The entire building shook. A blast of white-hot air knocked me across the room, and something hard smashed into me.

Every inch of me throbbing, I fought to sit up. My ears rang. Smoke billowed, nearly choking me. I coughed, trying to make sense of what I was seeing. Little fires, everywhere. An entire wall of the club, gone. My friends, scattered across the debris-laden dance floor.

Gavin was crawling to Jaclyn, who appeared to be unharmed as she helped Wren and Poppy to their feet. Also unharmed. Thank God!

River and Frosty were lifting a piece of plaster from Veronica's chest.

Camilla was trying to tug River...toward the front door? He kept shrugging her off, determined to help Chance, who had an unconscious Mackenzie in his arms.

Bronx lay on the ground, struggling to rise.

Cole...where was Cole?

I spun, searching, desperate. "Cole!"

A wall of smoke cleared, and I expected to see him run through it.

Instead, I saw zombies.

More than I could count. No collars.

"Zombies!" I shouted and split in two. I withdrew my axes and hacked through a zombie's spine, then another and another, staying in a constant state of motion. The creatures came at me from every angle. I fought, fought so hard, landing more blows than I took. But the fact was, I did take them. A lot of them. Considering I was already battered, every strike hurt more than it should have.

Whoosh. An arrow soared past me and sank in the eye of a zombie that had been preparing to bite me.

Cole was there a second later, covered in soot. He punched into the end of the arrow, sending the tip deep into the zombie's brain. Then he withdrew a short sword and sliced off its head.

"You're okay," I exclaimed.

"Yeah. Just got thrown outside."

Two zombies rushed up behind him. I tossed my axes, nailing the offenders between the eyes. They soared backward, and when they landed, Cole was there, removing their heads, too. Yet, even without bodies, the mouths snapped at us.

Fingers tangled in my hair, jerking me down. I fell, rolling backward with the motion, kicking the zombie responsible. He stumbled, and I straightened, swinging my arm, cutting his throat. Black goo oozed.

I went to get my axes, but a hand reached out, tripping me. I crashed face-first, stars winking through my vision. Before I'd recovered, a hard weight dived on top of me, shoving the air from my lungs. But as quickly as the weight landed, it lifted. Cole jerked me to my feet.

He kicked the zombie reaching for me, then stomped on the creature's hand, shattering the bones. Feeling no pain, the zombie leaned over and gnawed on his boot. He stabbed in the center of its skull, then, with the skull still attached to the blade, tossed it across the room.

I drew in a deep breath—mistake. Hacking cough. Watering eyes. Still too smoky in here.

In an effort to regain my composure, I rolled my shoulders, shook out my hands. If we were going to win this, I needed to push. I had the faith to do it, could even feel the energy gathering inside me, preparing. I could do this. I *would* do this. The zombies would lift, and they would ash, and that would be that.

Now! I raised my arms…and every zombie catapulted into the air.

A sense of triumph surged through me, strengthening me further.

Bronx and Mackenzie were on the ground, each writhing in pain. Frosty ran halfway, then slid on his knees the other half, reaching Bronx's side. Hands flaming, Frosty punched into Bronx's chest. The boy jolted, his back bowing.

Chance crouched beside Mackenzie and, after a slight hesitation, copied Frosty.

Movement at the corner of my eye. I switched my attention, saw two men wearing hazmat suits carting my body out the giant hole in the wall. Good glory. *This* had been Anima's plan all along. Distract us with zombies and steal my body. Wherever one went, the other would always be forced to follow.

"Cole," I shouted, running forward. All of the zombies fell, thumping against the floor. Grunts and groans sounded, and not just from the creatures.

One second I was far away from my body and the next I was right next to it. One touch, and the two linked up.

I grabbed the unsuspecting men by the neck and slammed their heads together. They released me and stumbled back; I fell.

One of the men recovered quickly and moved to punch me. I braced to take it, even as I withdrew a minicrossbow from my boot and worked it between us. Before either of us could strike, Poppy appeared out of nowhere and whacked him in the face with a piece of wood. Blood sprayed his mask. Despite the dizziness he must have been battling, he remained on his feet and snarled at her.

I squeezed the trigger, shooting him in the neck, cutting through his suit. His eyes widened as he slumped forward, over me, pinning me down. Cole was there a second later, helping me stand. He must have linked up, too, because we were solid to each other.

"Thank you," I said.

There wasn't time to say more. Two other Hazmats rushed out of the darkness. I pushed Poppy at Cole.

"Get her inside." If I did it, the Hazmats would only give chase, and she could be hurt. I was the target. I would be the one to fight.

Cole obeyed, gone in a blink.

Both men swung at me. I blocked their punches with my forearms. Impact hurt, and I lost my grip on the crossbow. As soon as I had the opportunity, I kicked the first guy in the kneecap—he howled with pain and dropped—then spun and punched the other guy in the throat.

Victory...not quite yet. Someone grabbed my hair from behind and jerked. I lost my balance and fell. Dang it! Before the culprit could do any more damage, Camilla was there—

No, Camilla *was* the culprit.

Surprise! She smacked me in the jaw, then the gut, calling, "Come get her before it's too late."

Another Hazmat sprang toward me.

What the—

Before I could fight through my shock, he stuck me in the neck with a syringe. The sting... I cringed, a chilling tide sweeping through my veins. I moaned and shivered, unable to fight, my muscles freezing into blocks of ice as I was dragged away.

Camilla watched with a smile of satisfaction. "Buh-bye now."

Betrayed...mole... My thoughts broke apart.... Everything faded to black....

"It's okay. It's all right. I won't let them take you."

The soft voice whispered through my head. Helen's voice.

"I can do more than give, Ali. Remember when I told you I can steal?"

The ice melted, my thoughts realigned, and colors returned to my line of sight. Even as I was being carried away, my mother walked through me once, twice…a third time…passing through me, as Emma had once done, but each time, Helen's features became a little more pinched, her lips a little more blue…as if she drew the cold out of me and into her.

I tried to move my fingers— Yes! Success! My toes. Again, success.

Helen dropped to the floor, spent. Our eyes met, and I think she began to smile encouragingly. I might never know; she vanished.

Disappointment? Yes, I felt it. Rage? Yes, that, too. And I had a target in mind. Camilla. She would pay for this.

My drug-and-dragger propped me against his thigh as he opened the door of a van.

Twisting, I sucker punched him in the groin. As he hunched over, too agonized to do more than grunt, I straightened and elbowed him in the back of the head. He crashed face-first into the ground. As I attempted to race inside the club, he wrapped his fingers around my ankle, tripping me. *I* crashed. He was on me in a snap, squeezing my neck so tightly I knew I'd carry the bruises for days.

Rather than try to pry his fingers loose, I reached back… patted my hands over his waist…felt the hilt of a dagger. All I needed. I unsheathed it and stabbed his thigh.

He released me, writhing against the ground.

Suddenly I could breathe. I got up. He didn't follow.

Heart pounding, I rushed back into the decimated club.

Camilla was helping her brother subdue a trio of zombies, as if she hadn't just tried to sign my death certificate.

My rage magnified. I pushed out another stream of energy and lifted my arms, zombies catapulting into the air. Camilla paled, scanning the club until her gaze found me.

I stomped toward her. Above me, zombies exploded as I passed. Ash rained like snow. And then all the bodies were gone, the battle over.

But not the war.

"You." I kicked the gun out of her hand—screw being wise—then kicked her in the chest. She tripped backward.

"What are you doing?" River snarled, stepping in front of his sister. He raised his fist, as if he meant to hit me. "Stop."

Cole moved in front of me. "I wouldn't, if I were you."

"She's a traitor," I spat. "She gave me to Anima."

She shook her head. "No. No, you're mistaken. You were drugged, didn't know what was happening around you."

"How do you know I was drugged, huh? Unless you were out there with me?"

She blanched. "I saw one of the men in the hazmat suits inject you."

"The man *you* told to come and get me." I shouted, "*You* are the reason the zombies made it onto Mr. Ankh's property without detection. *You* are the reason we found nothing but useless junk at the lab. *You* are the reason the assassin got free." Dark realization pushed me to add, "*You* are the reason my weapons have been jamming."

Her head-shakes became more violent.

Shock registered on River's features, then fury. "You don't know what you're talking about, Bell. My sister isn't a traitor. You're mistaken, just like she said."

"I'm not!" I screamed. A wave of fatigue hit me, but I battled through it. Pushing the energy a second time had been a mistake, but I couldn't regret it.

"You don't even look drugged," River pointed out.

"Doesn't matter," Cole said. "It happened exactly as Ali said it did."

"You didn't see," River insisted.

"I didn't have to. What she says, I believe. End of."

It was less than a minute later that the club was divided into two camps. Theirs—and ours. River, Camilla and Chance chose one side. My friends and I chose the other. The show of support nearly undid me, because I hadn't always had it.

"We're done here," Cole said. "From this moment on, our association is over. We don't want information from you, and we're not offering any."

River's hands fisted at his sides. "You're being unreasonable. Your girl makes an accusation and suddenly there's no other side to the story? Did you ever stop and think that maybe little Miss Bell is just trying to get my sister out of the way? *Your* way?"

I pointed at Camilla, my finger trembling. "You're making a fool of your brother and we both know it. At least love him enough to be honest with him."

Pain and regret played over her features. Indecision.

But that's all it took. River looked at her and then had to do a double take.

He shook his head and said, "No. It's not true. Tell me it's not true."

Her resistance crumbled. "I did it for you. You remember how, a year ago, they were closing in, and you were a major target. They wanted to take you out and almost succeeded. So I went to them. Told them I'd give them information in exchange for your life. They agreed. And they kept their promise, Riv." Her expression was so hopeful, begging him to say she'd made the right decision. "You haven't been injured in all this time."

"No. No!" River stumbled back, as if he'd just received a major blow. "That's impossible. You know our rules. You know what we do to traitors."

What did they do?

Camilla fisted his shirt. "I did it for you," she repeated. "For us. You're all I've got."

"We have friends," he spat. "Kids we're supposed to protect, who are dependent on us. Helping Anima puts them in danger."

"But keeps you safe," she screeched. "Why can't you understand that?"

River scrubbed a hand down his face. His dark eyes were glassy, his breathing labored. "Did you know what was going to happen tonight?"

She gulped, licked her lips. "N-not all of it."

He laughed without humor. "And rather than warning us, helping us organize a counterattack, you led us straight to a slaughter."

"They just wanted her. Once they had her, the attacks were going to stop."

He gave another shake of his head. "Ali's right. You've made a fool of me. But *they've* made a fool of *you*. Now you'll pay for it." He palmed a SIG and aimed the barrel at her chest.

Horrified gasps rang out.

Camilla's jaw dropped. "Riv, you can't be serious. You can't mean to kill me. I'm your sister."

She stepped back, but Chance blocked her way, refusing

to budge. In fact, he grabbed her by the arms and held her in place. Making her the perfect bull's-eye.

They were going to kill her. Effective, but unnecessary. Despite my anger, I didn't want her death on my conscience.

And, despite everything, neither did River. He couldn't see that now, but one day, he would. "Wait," I said. "I can take away her memories."

I became the center of attention.

I ignored everyone but River and said, "I can. Like I did with the doctor. She won't remember who she is, or who you are, but she won't remember Anima, either."

Hope blazed, then anger, and I figured River was considering the pros and cons of both actions. Death versus erasure.

Ultimately, he nodded. "Do it."

"What?" Camilla spluttered. She struggled as I closed in, and she might have escaped, if Chance hadn't placed her in a choke hold. Not squeezing hard enough to knock her out, but just enough to make her still. "Riv, you can't let her do this to me. Please."

He turned his back, but not before I saw the tear trickle down his cheek.

My knees knocked together. I fit my hands at her temples, my chest throbbing. Today's life lesson? One bad decision could mean a lifetime of consequences. "It didn't have to be this way," I said and closed my eyes.

FOREVER IS A
SINGLE SECOND

The rest of the night passed in a daze, and I came to awareness only for the highlights—and only because Cole shared his fire with me, patching any leaks, strengthening me.

It took a toll on him; he'd absorbed some of my weakness. I owed him. Big-time.

We escorted Wren and Poppy home. They were scratched up and bruised, but otherwise okay, babbling about how we'd each seemed to freeze in place.

They hadn't seen the zombies, or our spirits, and when Cole had tried to explain, they'd both shut down. It was too much to compute.

Tomorrow, after they'd rested, they'd either convince themselves we were crazy or accept the truth. There were no other options.

A despondent River and seemingly unaffected Chance returned to their home with Camilla. The erase had proved successful, and she was now a blank slate. It was sad, really.

She'd done everything in her power to save her brother, but because she'd done it the wrong way, she'd lost him anyway.

On the way back to the mansion, Cole received a text from his dad with a possible location for Justin.

Even though we were tired, and ragged, and pretty much beaten to a pulp, we changed directions and drove so fast I'm sure we broke sound barriers. I said a quick prayer for safety.

As I said "Amen," red and blue lights flashed behind our vehicle.

Tense, Cole eased to the shoulder of the road and stopped. The sun was in the process of rising, casting muted rays of gold, and I wasn't surprised to see Detective Verra illuminated as she approached the driver-side window.

"Where you guys off to in such a hurry?" she asked.

"We might have found Justin," Cole admitted, and for a moment, I was shocked.

But really, what better way to get the boy out of Anima's clutches than with a police escort?

Verra asked only one other question. "Where?"

As soon as Cole told her, she said, "Well, all right, then. Follow me. I'll radio for backup along the way." She returned to her sedan and, with her lights still blazing, darted in front of us. We tailed her all the way to the building.

Only, it had already been emptied out.

Papers and test tubes were burning in an incinerator, and cages were open and vacant.

"I don't know what you guys are into, exactly," Detective Verra said, running a fingertip over a debris-ridden worktable, "but I can tell you I've been watching you, and I've seen things

I can't explain. Things I don't want explained. So take what you need and go home."

What had she seen?

Was she part slayer?

I was too tired to care.

We salvaged as many papers as we could and headed home. Mr. Ankh was awake and stressed to the max. The security system had been giving him fits, and while he suspected Anima was responsible, he couldn't figure out how they were doing what they were doing. He was giving himself until dark to fix it, then moving us all to one of the new safe houses.

Kat came flying down the stairs and threw herself into Frosty's arms.

Reeve wasn't far behind, and she did the same with Bronx.

Juliana, also not far behind, ran to Cole, only to stop midway and glare at me.

I wondered why—

The next thing I knew, I was yelping as Cole swept me off my feet.

"Easy, Ali-gator."

I rested my head on his shoulder.

Veronica grabbed her sister by the arm and pulled her away as Cole carried me up the stairs, to my room. He set me on the bed.

"You awake enough to try for a vision?" he asked.

No, but that wasn't going to stop me. "Let's do it."

"How should we start?"

"Last time, we thought about having a vision and looked at each other."

"Easy enough." He peered into my eyes.

I peered into his, getting lost in the violet. Several minutes passed.

He smiled. "This isn't working."

"What do we want to see?"

"Each other naked?"

For sure. "Besides that."

"How about our next battle with Anima?"

"Perfect. Let's think about that and nothing else."

He nodded, and we once again peered into each other's eyes. A moment passed...and nothing happened...but before disappointment could settle in, the world began to fade.

It was working—

—and then we were in the forest. Cole was on his knees, soaked in blood. I walked past him, my gaze vacant. Smoke was thick in the air. So thick I nearly choked on it. I could hear sobbing behind me. Masculine sobbing. The kind that didn't happen often. When a big alpha male had just lost something precious.

The sound of it made me increase my speed, leaving Cole farther and farther behind.

All around me, fires raged. White and black ash mixed, floating through the air, dancing in the light cast by the flames. Cars were crashed into trees. Odd. Human bodies littered the ground, lifeless, skin bubbling black from zombie toxin. Sad.

But I kept walking, unfazed by all of it.

And yet, in the present, the scene faded...faded...until the forest vanished and I was back inside the bedroom.

Why had it faded?

I must have asked the question out loud because Cole said, "Could be a turning point. A moment when you will have to make a decision."

"So the future isn't set." But what about the rest of it?

"The good news is, we finally have control of the visions. We can decide when, where."

"Bad news is, that's next," I said, fighting a tide of fear. "How do we get there?"

"I don't know."

Could we use the visions to find out?

"Think about how we get to that point." I yawned, even as I locked my fingers behind his nape, peering at him…peering so intently…but all I saw was a flash of Juliana's face, which I didn't understand.

Unless she wasn't part of the vision, and I was just remembering our trek to the room?

Or she had her own decision to make?

"Whatever happens, we'll deal," he said, "just like we've dealt with everything else."

"How can you be so sure?"

"Because I've won you back. I can deal with anything. Now go to sleep." He gave me a gentle nudge, and I offered no resistance.

"What about you?" I asked after my jaw nearly cracked with another yawn. My eyes were already closing.

"I'm going to help Ankh, and then I'll be up."

"We'll snuggle," I think I said.

He chuckled warmly. "There's nothing I'd like more."

I had. I'd said it. Though I would have been mortified if I'd been more alert, I drifted into a deep sleep, smiling with anticipation.

Hovering somewhere between awake and asleep, my mind got stuck on my great-grandfather's journal. He'd written every passage in past tense, except for the one about the "she" who was supposed to die for the well-being of many. So, the girl had obviously come along after him.

But he'd made it sound like she was coming right away. If so, I wasn't her. She had already lived and died.

But that couldn't be true, because the well-being of many hadn't yet been established.

Had it?

Was there some piece of the puzzle I hadn't yet seen?

Something hard and warm settled on my shoulder, shaking me. I came up swinging.

The person responsible ducked, barely avoiding a black eye. "Whoa!" she said, frowning as she straightened.

"Juliana?" I rubbed my eyes, a thread of unease winding around me. "What are you doing here?"

"There's a problem," she said, and she *did* sound worried. "Cole needs you outside."

Cole? I checked the bed. No indentation to prove he'd ever returned. "What problem?"

Her eyes narrowed to tiny slits. "Like he'd really tell me. I'm a baby, remember?"

Good point. Did this have anything to do with our last vision?

Juliana backed away from me. "I had a message and I delivered it. Cole wants you out back ASAP. Like, five-minutes-ago ASAP. But go ahead. Take your time. Maybe he'll finally wise up and kick your scrawny ass to the curb." She stomped out of my room, the door slamming behind her.

Brat.

"You're sweeter than sugar. Said no one. Ever," I mumbled.

As I threw my legs over the side of the bed, my phone rang. If Cole thought to command me to hurry…

I picked up, barked, "What?"

"Get everyone out of the house!" River's frantic voice registered. "Now! Don't waste time doubting me. What's the worst that could happen if I'm lying? Just get everyone out. I went through Camilla's papers. They've rigged bombs, Ali. They're set to go off sometime *today*. I'm on my way. We'll help you find and deactivate them. Okay? All right? Trust me on this. Please."

Bombs? My heart raced. Was this why Cole wanted me outside?

No. Couldn't be. He never would have sent Juliana back inside.

I rushed to the window. The sun was high, bright. I had a view of the massive backyard but saw no sign of Cole.

"Did you hear me, Ali?" River demanded.

"Yes. You wanted to know what was the worst that could happen if you're lying. Well, you could have Anima waiting outside, ready to ambush us."

Did I really think he would do that, though? That he'd help Anima like his sister?

No. No, I didn't.

"Ali," he said, and he sounded agonized.

"Okay, I'll—" The rest of the sentence died in my throat. Helen had just come strolling out of the house, and two men in hazmat suits had just stepped from the bushes, clearly intending to grab her, not realizing she was spirit rather than flesh.

If they could see her, they were slayers, and she had dropped her cloak. But why would she do that?

I beat my hand against the pane, but of course, no one glanced up. I turned, raced for my door.

"What's wrong?" River demanded.

Boom! The entire house rattled on its foundation. Plaster crumbled. Dust and smoke thickened the air, and I coughed as I stepped into the hall.

Boom!

Boom!

Good glory. The bombs!

"Ali!" River said.

"It's happening." Trying not to panic, I tripped my way to the staircase, looked down. Countless zombies ghosted through the walls, entering the mansion. They had somehow breached the Blood Lines.

Or Camilla had wiped away the Blood Lines before we'd left for the club.

My throat went dry. The zombies wore collars, as usual, but today, small packs of explosives were hooked to each one.

Lord, save me. Anima's actions the past few weeks began to make sense. The reason they had sent zombies out in the light of day that first time—they'd been testing to see how long the creatures could withstand the rays of the sun. They'd been testing us, too, to see how we would react. Then they'd waited until we were too exhausted to fight and ambushed us.

We'd been outplayed.

Boom!

The house shook against the force of another explosion.

Either Anima had stopped caring about keeping me alive, deciding to eliminate us all, or—

Oh, no. Not *or*. Please not *or*. Or Juliana had been working with them. Had attempted to lure me outside so the Hazmats could whisk me to safety while my friends died. Helen must have seen them and gone to check things out so that she could learn what was going on and warn me.

I dropped my phone and sprinted down the hall. "Cole!" The smoke thickened in the hallway, and my coughing intensified. "Kat!" I had to get them out. Now.

Screams of pain, moans of agony. But when I attempted to descend the staircase, the foundation underneath my feet... just...collapsed. I flailed as I tumbled down...down...down....

Landing, I lost what little breath I had. A dark spiderweb wove through my mind; pain slashed me from head to toe.

As many abilities as I had, I was currently helpless.

No! Never helpless. "Cole! Kat!" My eyes burned and watered. Dust and rubble enclosed me, pieces pinning different parts of me. Bleeding parts. Where were they? "Cole! Kat!" Panic...closing in... "Someone! Please."

Movement to the left. I struggled to free myself, calling, "Over here!"

Red eyes swung to me, and I froze. A zombie. He was struggling underneath the rubble, reaching for me, chomping his teeth. I yanked with all my strength, finally gaining my freedom, and scrambled backward. A sudden high-pitched ring made me cringe. Pain...more pain... I curled into myself, my hands flattening over my ears.

Boom!

Guts and shattered bones became shrapnel, hitting me, cutting me.

The zombie had just exploded.

At least the noise had died, too. I stood on wobbly legs. "Cole! Where are you?" I stumbled forward. Shock held me in a tight grip, nearly cutting off my airways. Destruction...everywhere. "Kat! Please. Talk to me." I couldn't distinguish furniture from plaster or room from room. There were only piles and piles and—

A hand!

My heart hammered against my ribs. I dropped to my knees and heaved away different-sized rocks, each one heavier than the last. *Please be alive, please, please be alive.* Finally, pale hair came into view. A face I loved.

Gavin! His eyes were swollen shut, his lips parted on a moan. He was alive!

His pitiful condition angered me, and another dose of strength lanced through me. Anima would pay.

I left my body behind and fired up. As injured as I was, I managed to produce only the smallest flickers of flame. Still, they were enough. I pressed them into Gavin's cheek and his moan morphed into a bellow. Within seconds, the swelling drained from his eyes, allowing him to blink into focus.

"What happened?" he asked.

"Zombies are here, and they're loaded with explosives." The two parts of me joined and I helped him to his feet.

"The other slayers?"

"You're the first I've found."

A small cry for help caught my attention.

I snapped to, heading toward the sound, stumbling over the rubble, closing in. "Kat? Kat, is that you?"

Boom!

Boom!

More rattling.

More dust.

How many explosions would I have to endure before I found all of my friends?

Boom!

A gust of molten air threw me backward. I landed, losing the breath I'd only recently regained. Gavin and River rushed to my side and helped me up.

This wasn't happening. Couldn't be happening.

"You okay?" River asked.

Not even close. "You made it," I said.

"Brought five of my best," he replied. "Would have brought more, but I wasn't sure who I could trust. We've already found Reeve. Chance is taking her to our van. Come on. I'll take you there."

"Forget it. I stay. I search." I protect. "By the way, there were two guys from Anima in the backyard. Zombies aren't our only threat."

"Got it."

My nails cut into my palms, and I realized I'd fisted my hands. "Have you seen Cole or Kat?"

"No. I'm sorry."

Okay. Okay. No time to waste. "Help us search."

River moved forward. Gavin and I lumbered after him, closing in on the cries—except, all went quiet.

"Kat! Kat, where are—" Another zombie, headed our way. "Incoming!" I shouted, dragging the boys to the ground.

Boom!

The moment the rattling stopped, we raced through the rubble. Too much dust. Hard to breathe. Hard to see—but I noticed movement, a spill of dark hair... Mackenzie, I realized, my heart skipping a beat as she clawed her way up from a pile of concrete and slumped over.

I quickened my pace, but the boys beat me to her.

Gavin felt for a pulse, then hefted her into his arms. Her head lolled against his chest. "She's alive."

For how much longer? She was bloody, already black-and-blue. "Take her to River's van," I said, "and heal her with your fire. I'll look for the others." I wouldn't stop until everyone was found.

We branched apart. "Cole! Kat!" I headed in the direction of Mr. Ankh's office. Smoke parted with my movements—

And finally, blessedly, I saw Cole!

He held a babbling Juliana in his arms, Veronica limping beside him.

"Ali!"

My knees almost buckled, so great was my relief.

"I'm s-so s-sorry," Juliana said. "M-Milla said they'd take Ali. Only A-Ali. Just wanted t-time to show Cole h-he could live w-without her."

Her words registered, and I flinched. I'd already guessed the truth, but the confirmation stung. She'd helped Camilla, and together, they'd helped Anima do *this*. Just to get rid of me. Was I really that bad?

"You did *what?*" Cole almost dropped her.

She squeezed her eyelids tightly closed, no longer able to face him, tears leaking out.

He opened his mouth to blast her.

"Don't," I said. There was time enough for that later. "Let's find Kat and the others. Stay away from zombies. They explode."

Frosty must have heard our voices. He jetted from around the corner. Blood poured from his temple and soaked his shirt. His wild gaze scanned our faces, noting our identities. "Have you seen Kat?"

"No." *Lord, help us.* Of everyone, she was the most fragile. "Kat," I shouted.

Boom!

As the ground shuddered, Cole thrust Juliana at Veronica. "Get her out of here. Now. I can't even stand to look at her."

Juliana sobbed. Veronica gave a weak nod.

"There's a van at the end of the driveway," River said. "Gavin and Mackenzie are there."

"Reeve?"

The frantic voice came from behind me.

I spun. Bronx rushed toward us, features smeared with blood and soot.

I pointed in the direction of the front door, or what used to be the front door. "River's guys found her. And before you flip out, they're on our side, here to help. At the end of the driveway, there's a van. She's there."

Bronx didn't stick around to ask any more questions.

Dodging zombies and explosions, Cole and Frosty helped me pick through the rubble. I'm not sure how much time passed before sirens erupted in the distance.

Boom!

I continued working, hot tears streaking down my cheeks.

Besides Kat, we were missing Jaclyn and Mr. Ankh. They were okay. They had to be okay.

But how likely were all of us to survive this much carnage?

I wasn't good with numbers, but even I knew the answer to that.

TOO LATE! TOO LATE!
VERY IMPORTANT DATE!

Anima must have done something to divert authorities away from the house, because, despite the sirens, no one but River and his boys ever showed up to help. We were on our own, becoming more desperate by the minute.

The van, our fastest means of escape, had just been bombed. Thank God everyone inside it had exited in time.

"I've done triage before." River motioned for Bronx and Veronica to place their charges on a flat plot of land. "Keep zombies at a distance, and I'll take care of the girls."

The two, plus two others from River's crew, formed a protective circle around him. The rest of us continued digging, fighting, ducking, digging again. I pushed myself hard, harder, screaming Kat's name until I grew hoarse. By the end of the first hour, I was trembling so violently, I probably looked like I was having a seizure.

"Ali, go over there and let River check you out," Cole said.

"No!" I threw a block of concrete to the side. I had to find Kat.

"You have to stop. If you keep this up, you won't be on your feet much longer, and we need you on your feet."

"I'm not going to pass out." My gaze caught on something sticking out from a pile of rocks. I dug faster, saw…Mr. Ankh's hand! "Help me free him."

Everyone crowded around me. Together, we managed to clear the debris. His eyes were open, and—

Staring straight ahead, I realized. At nothing. My excitement withered. His mouth was parted on a pained gasp he'd never gotten to finish. His chest was crushed, flatter than it should have been.

He was dead, and there was nothing we could do to save him.

Razors in my chest. Reeve had just lost *everything*. Her father, her only family. Her home and refuge. All of her possessions.

No. Not everything. She still had Bronx. But I knew how badly she was going to hurt. How horribly she would suffer. How she would blame herself, and hate herself, and relive what had happened.

Can't break down. Not now.

Kat needed me.

I threw wood and plaster and glass over my shoulder, screaming, "Kat. Kat! We're here. We're not leaving without you. Hold on, okay. Just hold on."

Pop. Pop. Pop.

"That's gunfire," River called, holding a rag against Juliana's wound. "Anima sent in the troops. We're screwed if we stay here."

I didn't care.

Pop. Pop. Pop.

"Weapons?" Cole demanded.

As the slayers told him what they had on hand, a low moan caught my attention.

"I'm staying behind to—" Frosty began.

"Shut up!" I screeched. Still as a statue, I listened. More gunfire. The hiss of flame. The crackle of burning wood. I ignored the sounds, concentrating. Then…

Another moan, soft but sure.

I rushed over to where I thought they had come from and heaved pieces of wood and glass out of the way, ignoring the sharp stings in my palms. And then I saw her. My sweet, sweet Kat.

Her collarbone was broken, the end cutting through her skin. There was an angry gash over her pelvis, and one of her legs was twisted in the wrong direction. But her eyes were open, and unlike Mr. Ankh's, they focused. She was alive! Happiness and relief bombarded me.

Her arms were wrapped around an unconscious Jaclyn, providing a first line of defense, protecting. Even now. She smiled weakly, blood gurgling from the corners of her mouth.

"She's here!" I shouted.

"Finally," she whispered. "Had to be…last one to…arrive at party. Grand entrance…my thing."

"Shh, shh, kitten." Frosty shoved me aside to kneel beside her. "Save your energy, all right."

I rushed around to her other side, saying to Frosty, to anyone who would listen, "We need to get her to the nearest hospital. And someone call Detective Verra. She— No," I gasped out.

Kat had bite marks on her arms. The flesh was black, oozing.

Zombie toxin.

Frosty must have noticed, too; he sucked in a sharp breath.

You can sit here, panicking, or you can act. "Does anyone have the antidote?" As soon as I'd learned what the fire could do, I'd stopped carrying mine. But civilians like Kat couldn't tolerate the fire. They ashed as quickly as zombies.

Frosty and I waited, tense. Desperate.

No one spoke out.

"Anyone," he shouted. "Please."

Then we heard the sweetest words this side of heaven. "I do." Chance bounded over from triage, with a tiny plastic vial in his hand. "It's only half a dose. We didn't come with enough for everyone, so I've been doling out sips. It'll keep her symptoms at bay until you can get her a proper injection."

Frosty poured the contents down her throat.

"Kat," I said, doing my best to disguise my fear. Time wasn't our friend. Had just become slayer enemy number one. Just?

Her gaze shifted to me, and she offered a small smile. "My Ali. Helped me…live."

"And that's not going to change. Do you hear me? You're going to continue to live. I promise. And you know I never lie." I met Frosty's wild gaze. "Do it now."

He gently lifted her into his arms. The pain should have been excruciating for her, but she didn't even cringe. That wasn't good. I knew that wasn't good.

Chance extracted Jaclyn and carried her to River.

"Let's get you to the hospital, kitten," Frosty said.

"Cole's place is on the way." The words spilled from me. "We can get more antidote there."

He eased forward, careful not to jostle her. "You're going to be okay, kitten. I'm not going to let anything happen to you."

"Love you," she whispered. "Just wanted to…fix you… lunch…and live…you and Ali…made life worth…fighting for…thank you."

Killing me. "Don't thank us. Live! Keep fighting."

Pop. Pop. Pop. The gunfire drew ever closer.

Boom!

Boom!

More zombies, too.

"Frosty." I forced myself to put one foot in front of the other, maintaining the moderate pace. "We have to hurry."

"Shut up, Ali." His tone remained gentle, despite the heat of his rebuke. "I can't risk jostling her."

"I know." *But I can't risk losing her.*

Pop. Pop. Pop. The ground shook. Little fires blazed in patches of foliage, dark smoke mushrooming to the tops of the trees.

"Bronx, get everyone to the closest safe house." Cole's voice rang out. "Chance, give me two of your guns." Then he came up beside me and slapped one of the guns in my hand. "I'll guard the front. You guard the rear."

All business. Good. Exactly what I needed.

The deeper we traveled through the forest, the thicker the smoke became, the more obvious the scent of rot. It wasn't long before we discovered why the authorities hadn't made it to the house. Zombies had attacked their cars en masse and dragged policemen and firemen outside, where they'd become a spiritual feast.

Soon, they would rise.

Scratch that. No "soon" about it. Some of them were already crawling out of their bodies.

Multiple sets of red eyes landed on us and narrowed. And suddenly, it was like a starting bell rang out, zombies leaping into action and racing toward us. Some wore a collar…and a bomb—the new ones didn't.

"Run, Frosty! I've got this." I stepped out of my body and fired the gun. Bam, between the eyes. Bam, right inside the mouth. Bam, direct to the heart. I hammered at the trigger until I ran out of bullets, then used the butt of the gun to knock a few skulls around. Summoning flames proved ineffective.

I threw a punch at a zombie, then another, then ducked to avoid a chomp of teeth. I swiped out my leg and knocked a pair of ankles together. While I fought, I thought, *Screw the fire* and tried to push out a stream of energy, but failed at that, too.

Behind me, gnarled fingers locked on my shoulder. I was dragged to the ground. Multiple sets of teeth flashed in the moonlight. I rolled and kicked, nailing two zombies in the face, and then I twisted, using one hand to punch the zombie beside me and the other to brace my weight.

Gold star, Ali. The creatures were going down fast.

I popped to my feet, a high-pitched noise making me cringe. A noise I recognized.

"Bomb," I shouted, diving to the ground.

Boom!

Another blast of molten air whooshed over my back and might have even singed the ends of my hair. Bits and pieces of zombie pelted me. Coughing, I kicked decrepit limbs away from me.

Then I ran. I ran and listened. A grunt. Snapping limbs. There. I chased the sound, turning left, quickening my pace, darting through a canopy of brittle leaves. Frosty's features were bathed in panic as he bounded toward me, Kat flopping in his arms. Anima was coming at him from every angle.

Two of the soldiers raised their guns. Aimed.

"No!" I screamed, diving forward.

But I was too late. The bullets too fast.

One embedded in Frosty's thigh—the other in Kat's shoulder.

He fell, twisting midway to take the brunt of impact. Kat rolled from his arms. She stopped several yards from me. He stood, desperate to reach her, but he took a bullet to the chest and flew backward.

On my hands and knees, I scrambled to my best friend. Her eyes were closed. Dirt smeared her cheeks. "Come on. Come on! Mad Dog, you have to listen to me." I tore off my shirt, didn't care that I was left in my bra, and wrapped her bleeding shoulder. I trembled as I felt for a pulse.

Nothing.

No. I'd missed it, that was all. It was there. Had to be there. Maybe if I pressed harder, deeper. "You're going to wake up. Do you hear me?"

Blood streamed from her mouth. Still there was no telltale beat to signal her heart had started working again.

I choked on a sob.

Pop. Pop.

A Hazmat toppled at my left, another at my right. Whatever. The men were nothing to me. "Kat. Mad Dog. It's Ali. It's time to wake up now. Okay? All right?"

Silence.

Respond! "Listen to me," I screeched, desperate, so terribly desperate; there wasn't room for any other emotion. "This isn't cake. I need you to wake up. You've got a wedding to plan, the most horrid bridesmaid dress ever created to choose for me. Puke-green. With pink bows."

Miserable silence.

She...

She was...

I fell back on my haunches, fighting to breathe. Anima had done this, had hurt an innocent girl. Ruined an innocent girl. Kat was—had been—*no! I refuse to believe it*—she *was* a bright, beautiful girl. Smart and witty. Kind and caring. She wouldn't just...*die* out here in a forest, with zombies and fires and the enemy all around us. No, when she died, it was going to be on her own terms. In a blaze of glory.

Cole crouched beside Frosty and tried to tug him to his feet. The injured Frosty batted his hands away and crawled to Kat. My Kat, who still stared at nothing. He gently lifted her into his arms and settled her on his lap.

He croaked, "Kitten. Talk to me." He kissed her forehead, his tears dripping onto her face. If this had been a fairy tale, she would have healed then and there, true love awakening her. But it wasn't, and she didn't. She didn't smile, and she didn't tease us about acting like babies.

And...she wasn't going to, was she?

I *could* feel something else. Rage, sorrow and fury. So much fury.

"Tell me you're okay," Frosty demanded.

She couldn't. She was…gone. She was gone, and I was a liar. I'd never gotten her to the hospital, and she wasn't going to be all right.

Hot, stinging tears flooded my cheeks. I raised my face to the sky and screamed. Screamed so piercingly I could have shattered glass. But the sound, no matter how loud, could not drown out Frosty's weeping. He was a male in pain, his greatest love stolen from him.

I had to leave. I had to leave now.

A strange calm washed over me. I stood to shaky legs and wrapped my arms around myself. I stumbled forward. There was Cole. Maybe he'd been shot. He was on his knees, his arms resting on his thighs. His head was bowed, his chest soaked with blood.

The pose struck me as familiar. The vision had come true at last. I didn't care, wouldn't stop.

Cole faced me. "I tried." His lids squeezed tight, his lashes fusing. Tears welled between the strands. "I tried so hard to get them before they reached Frosty and Kat."

I kept trudging forward, no destination in mind. Anywhere was better than here. At the back of my mind, I knew I'd come to some sort of mental crossroads; I had a decision to make. Give myself time to heal, if that was even possible, or let Anima have me so the madness would end.

I knew what I needed to do, but it wasn't what I wanted to do.

I reached the street. A car was parked in the distance, two

men standing outside it, holding remote controls. They spotted me and stilled, as if shocked to find their prey had come directly to them—and wasn't bolting.

I could have shouted. Cole and Frosty might have come running. I could have raced away and hid. But I did neither of those things. Anima wanted me. Fine. They could have me.

Decision made.

They'd won. They'd taken another piece of my heart. One of the best. They could have their prize, shirtless as it was.

The rage burned up everything else. I would destroy them—even if I had to destroy myself in the process.

I headed straight for them…was almost within reach. "I'll go without a fight, but you have to stop. Now."

One of them grabbed me. The other shoved a black sack over my head. My hands were tied behind my back, and I was patted down for weapons. For once, I didn't have any.

I was picked up and thrown into the car.

LONG LIVE THE QUEEN!

As the car motored down the road, my mom whispered, "I'm so sorry, Ali. I heard Juliana talking to someone on her cell. She said she'd have you outside in five minutes, for the troops to wait in back. I hoped to lead them away from the house, didn't know zombies were coming…or that bombs would go off and you'd be trapped inside. I'm so sorry."

It was nice, knowing she was with me.

"Emma's frantic, trying to get here to see you, but I've made friends throughout the years and asked them to stop her. Gently."

"Thank you." I didn't want my little sis to see me like this.

"Quiet," one of the Hazmats snapped.

"I would appear to Cole," Helen continued, "and tell him where you are, what's happening and where you end up, but he wouldn't believe me."

No. He wouldn't.

And maybe that was for the best. I didn't want to be found.

"I'll think of something. Just...remember what I told you," Helen said, and then I think she left me.

Remember...what?

I didn't have to ponder long before the answer hit me. The fingerprint ID. How she had died protecting me. How she had made arrangements for my future. I couldn't let her down.

Like I'd let Kat down.

I'm not sure how far we traveled. Finally, the car stopped and I was hauled outside. The men dragged me inside a warm building, only to release me and push me inside...a cage, most likely. That was Anima's usual M.O. I stumbled, my shoulder brushing against a cold metal bar. Yep. A cage.

Footsteps. Angry muttering.

I sat. Something pulled at the ties around my wrists, and suddenly I was free. I removed the hood and blinked into focus. The cage was a four-by-four with bars on every side. The floor was made up of dirt and more dirt. I had a cot and a toilet, nothing more. *Been here, done that.* Anima needed new material.

The only piece of furniture outside the cage was a long metal table. Papers were scattered across the surface. A pen.

Weapon.

Fingers snapped at my ear.

At least there were no men in lab coats milling around, pretending not to scrutinize my every move.

The fingers snapped again. "Ali."

Slowly I turned my head, blinked when I realized Justin occupied the cage next to mine. Well, well. I'd finally found him. In the proof-of-life video, he'd worn only underwear. Today he was fully clothed.

He pulled off his shirt and handed it to me. I pulled the material over my head as he gripped the bars between us. The swelling in his eyes had gone down, revealing the desperation swirling inside.

"Tell me what's been going on," he pleaded. "Men come and rough me up, bragging about slayers they've killed, and I don't know what's true and what's not. How's Jaclyn? Is she okay?"

"She's..." I paused. Last time I'd seen her, she'd been unconscious. "Still breathing." It was the best I could offer. "Trina, Lucas, Cruz and Collins are dead. Have been since the night you were taken. Today, Anima bombed Mr. Ankh's house. We were all there. Mr. Ankh died." My chin quivered. "Kat..." I couldn't get out any more than that.

Had the antidote had enough time to cleanse her of zombie toxin? Had it been strong enough?

Would her spirit rise, dark and hungry?

Not knowing what was to come...

Being so far away from her...

In some ways, I felt as if I was falling into an endless pit of despair. No, not a pit. A grave. Falling, faster and faster, with no way to save myself. But the truth was, I'd already hit rock bottom.

Kat had wanted a life, had decided to fight for more time. Time, so precious. Every second mattered. And now she had no seconds left. They'd been taken from her. Every. Single. One.

I'd never get to tell her I was sorry. Or that I loved her. Or that she meant more to me than oxygen.

I'd never hug her. Never see her. The pictures we'd taken

that night in my room, when she'd made such hard-core love to the camera she'd created a baby, were gone. Lost in the rubble of Mr. Ankh's home.

Rage...stronger...

Justin sagged against the bars. "I hate myself. I used to work with these people. Used to help them strike at Cole." He laughed bitterly. "How stupid was I?"

"Save your pity party for later." Good advice. Wished I could take it. "How often are you left alone?"

"More often than not."

"Did the men who brought me here say anything about when we could expect a visit?"

"No. They were complaining about having to go back out and clean up the mess that was just made."

Good. I pushed to my feet, stumbled to the door and prayed this worked. Reaching around, I pressed my thumb into the pad of the lock. With slayers, Anima never used the kind that needed keys. Too many of us knew how to pick them.

The lock disengaged. So quickly. So easily. Almost comically.

Justin jumped up and rushed to his door. "How did you do that?"

"My mother," I said.

"I thought she was a civilian."

I wasn't going to explain. I walked to the door of his cage and pressed my thumb into the lock. The door opened, and he sprinted out.

"Let's go." He was halfway to the exit before he realized I'd merely walked to the table. "Ali! Come on!" He waved me over.

I stuffed the pen in my pocket. *Use any weapon, Daddy? Watch me.* Then I returned to my cage, shutting—and locking—the door.

He stumbled toward me, his dark eyes glittering with confusion. "You're not coming with me?"

"No." I was right where I needed to be.

"But—"

"No buts. Get out of here. Let Cole know I'm alive and that I've got a plan."

He gaped at me. "Ali, don't do this. Don't stay. They'll hurt you. And your plan, whatever it is, will get you killed."

I offered him a small smile. "It's already done. Now go. Before it's too late for you."

He took a step away, stopped. Took another step, stopped. Always looking back at me. I knew there was a battle waging in his head. The alpha side of him screamed not to leave the damsel in distress behind. Wanted to protect me. But the logical side of him knew he wouldn't get very far if I was fighting him every inch of the way.

"I'll gather the others. We'll come back for you."

"All right," I said, pretty sure I'd be moved by the time he made it to Cole, but knowing he needed some sort of incentive to go.

Justin disappeared beyond the door.

I breathed a sigh of relief. And waited.

Time passed. I'm not sure how much. Eventually, three Anima soldiers stepped into the warehouse. One was sipping from a coffee cup; all were relaxed. No hazmat suits.

Just T-shirts and jeans. The guys stopped when they realized Justin's cage was open and empty.

Cursing, they sprang into action, searching the makeshift prison for answers. Finding none.

They focused on me.

"Where is he?" one demanded.

Another male strolled inside the warehouse, and he, too, sipped from a coffee cup. He wore scrubs. He was on the short side and lean, with thinning gray hair. Was that a piece of muffin in his beard?

He was somehow familiar to me, but I was certain I hadn't met him. I would have…remembered….

Remembered. The word echoed in my mind, reminding me that Helen had covered my memory. That I'd spent the first five years of my life—no, six years—being tested by Anima. This man must have been there.

"Dr. Andrews," one of the guards said. "The boy is gone."

How nice. This man from my past was the mysterious Wyatt Andrews—Hodad. The one who'd hurt Justin. Perfect. Made my job a little easier.

Dr. Andrews stopped at the table, his gaze remaining on me. He set down his coffee and ran his tongue over his teeth. Focusing on me, he said, "We were going to do you both a favor and move you to a cleaner facility with better accommodations. Now we'll have to hurt you first." His attention shifted to the men. "Tie Miss Bell's hands behind her back and bring her over." He withdrew a small velvet pouch from the pocket of his shirt and unrolled it. Pieces of silver glinted. Weapons, I was sure.

The three males stomped to my door.

"How many Anima douche bags does it take to open a cage?" I asked, and I think my blasé tone startled them. "Three. Because they're scared of the little girl trapped inside."

One growled.

One smiled coldly, probably imagining his hands wrapped around my neck.

The other disengaged the lock and jerked open the door.

"Heard it before?" I asked, standing. The pen I'd taken from the table was already clutched in my hand, its belly pressed flat against my forearm, hiding it.

The first man stopped in front of me and reached for me. With lightning speed, I stabbed him in the neck. As his blood spurted, I twisted, giving the next guy the same treatment. Both tumbled to the ground, bleeding out. The other guard, the last one, was in the process of racing to the still-open door, but I dived on his back and stabbed him as we fell.

Just like that, all three were dead or dying. And I was without a single shred of remorse.

I stood, gaze locked on Hodad. He was paling, backing away from me. The table blocked him. It toppled over, crashed into the dirt and he darted around it. He reached for the phone in his pocket and dialed.

Ms. Smith?

Oh, pretty please with a cherry on top.

I tsked. "Look at what you made me do, Hodad. Use my own hands of death and destruction. But I haven't always been so hard-core, you know. I even cried after I made my first kill. Cried over a man who'd hurt my friends and me. But do you know what I'm feeling right now?"

Panicked, he shook his head.

"A desire for more."

He held out his hands to ward me off. "Stay back."

I spread my arms and dropped the bloody pen. I wanted him dead—and I'd see that it was done—but I needed him to do something for me first.

"Don't worry. I'm not quite done with you yet. Take me to Ms. Smith," I commanded.

MY SOUL TO OFFER

He *must* have dialed Ms. Smith from the warehouse and must not have hung up. Because by the time he parked his dark sedan at the security gate outside a magnificent chrome-and-glass building in the heart of Atlanta, Georgia, two and a half hours later, an army of guards waited for us.

My door flew open, and I was dragged outside. My wrists were cuffed behind my back. No rope, not anymore.

I didn't fight. Just let it happen.

I was shoved into another car already loaded with four hulking men dressed in black. No one said a word as we shot into an underground parking garage. I twisted, relieved to find Hodad motoring after us.

When we stopped and emerged, the hulks forced me into an elevator. Guns remained trained on me. All this for little ole me. "Really know how to make a girl feel special, guys. Kudos."

A bell dinged, and the doors slid open. I was shoved into a

foyer, a glass wall dead ahead—peering straight into a laboratory bustling with workers.

"Welcome." A beautiful woman in a well-tailored dress-suit stood in front of the wall, her hands folded demurely at her waist. I didn't have to wonder who she was. Dark hair, slicked back from her face. Pale skin. Bloodred lipstick. Professional. This was none other than Ms. Smith. "We meet at last. I'm Rebecca."

The murderous rage returned in a flash, and I barely managed to tamp it down. "You killed my best friend."

"Me?" Her hand fluttered to her chest. "I did no such thing. I've been here, in Atlanta."

"You ordered it done. So, no matter whose finger was wrapped around the trigger, you fired the shot."

She shrugged, unconcerned. "You say potato, I say we've won." Her lips curved in a perfect crescent moon, points up. "We have everything ready for you. Let's get started, shall we?"

Two of the guards hauled me past the glass wall and into the lab. At the back was a gurney with leather straps at the ankles and wrists. Finally, I erupted. I fought with every bit of my strength. I kicked. The moment the cuffs were loosened, I punched. I even bit into a guy's ear.

He grunted with pain and punched me in the jaw to pry me loose. But I maintained my hold and took a piece of his lobe with me. His grunts became howls.

I spit the bloody cartilage in his face.

But no matter how savagely I struggled, I was eventually laid flat and shackled. As I'd known I would be. Even with all of my amazing abilities, I had limits. But that was okay.

The saying was true, I decided. What didn't kill me would only make me stronger.

I wanted to be stronger.

The guards left, and Ms. Smith approached my side.

I glared up at her. "Tie me up, hold me down. It's not going to change what I do to you. I'm going to hurt you, and I'm going to kill you—and I'm going to enjoy every second."

She ignored me, saying, "Do you prefer Ali or Sami? Or what about Alammi? Samali?" She chuckled as she pulled on a pair of latex gloves and lifted a syringe full of clear liquid. "Here is what's going to happen. Over the next few days, I'm going to inject you with all kinds of goodies and you're going to suffer. If your spirit, and thereby your blood, possesses the properties we think they possess, you're going to become a walking cure for zombie-ism. If not...well, try not to let it bother you that all of our other subjects died during testing. We have higher hopes for you."

I smiled without humor. "Do it. Do whatever you want. I won't die until I've spit on your grave."

I guess my lack of fear finally got to her. She paled. "Perhaps you'd like to change your tone. I'm the only person capable of helping your friend Kat."

"Don't say her name! Don't you dare even *think* her name!"

Unperturbed, she said, "We were able to acquire and preserve her body, and we're now holding her spirit. Her *zombie* spirit. Yes. She was infected. If this treatment proves successful, we'll be able to bring her back to life. So do yourself—no, do *your friend*—a favor and don't fight me."

I—

Stopped. Thoughts raced through my mind. Hope flickered to startling life.

Bring Kat back to life? Yes, please. I'd give anything. Absolutely anything to make it happen.

But some of the flickers quickly dimmed. Could I do *this?* Could I willingly help Anima? I'd blasted Ethan for doing it. Hated Justin and Jaclyn for it. Took Camilla's memory for it. And yet, here I was, desperate to believe Ms. Smith was telling the truth. That Kat could be brought back. That dead wasn't really dead.

But that wasn't the natural order.

And if this was successful—that was a big *if*—would Kat even be Kat? The girl I knew and loved? Or would she be something else entirely?

My struggles renewed, and Ms. Smith sighed. "Very well, then. We'll do this the hard way." She jabbed the syringe into my neck.

Sharp pain. A cascade of fire, causing my blood to boil in an instant.

My back bowed, and I screamed. I'd been thrown into the fires of hell, was melting from the inside, my organs liquefying. Any second, I would ash. Ash just like a zombie.

An eternity later, the burn cooled. I sagged against the gurney. Sweat poured from me, soaking my hair and clothes. I was panting, couldn't quite catch my breath.

Ms. Smith could not contain her glee. "You survived round one, just as I'd hoped." She smoothed her hand over my brow, and I jerked away. Unaffected, she said, "Now, let's get you comfortable. You're going to be here awhile, and I don't trust you in a room of your own. I won't take any chances with my prize."

She moved away, and three men in lab coats came over to cut my clothes away. Everything. Bra, panties. Gone. I fought, but they managed to insert a catheter between my legs and an IV needle in my vein. It was humiliating, absolutely degrading.

A few seconds later, I was too pumped with sedatives to care, my eyelids becoming too heavy to hold up, my limbs too heavy to move.

Going to be so strong after this…hurt…kill…

My head lolled to the side, my thoughts losing focus, darkening… I drifted away….

"That's two injections she's survived," Ms. Smith said. "Two more and we'll be ready to test her."

"She's even more powerful than we realized." Hodad. "We've never been this close to a cure. Just think what we could have accomplished by now if Helen hadn't taken her."

"Helen," Ms. Smith scoffed. "She almost brought this company crashing to the ground. There's a perfect irony about her daughter being the one to build it back up."

Their voices faded….

The volume gradually increased….

"Who should we allow to bite her first?" Hodad asked.

"The girl, Kat," Ms. Smith said. "If all goes as I suspect, Ali will switch to our side. Then she won't fight when my father takes his turn."

Kat…a zombie… They were going to feed me to her. Let her munch on my spirit, taking my life bite by painful bite.

"Smith…hate you," I whispered, drifting away again.

★ ★ ★

"Miss Bell." A hand tapped at my cheek. "Miss Bell. We need you awake for this. Zombies can eat a sleeping spirit, yes, but it's not as powerful. It's like a lightbulb that hasn't been turned on."

I blinked open my eyes.

"Good girl."

Bright light streamed into a room…no, into another cage. I wasn't strapped to a gurney anymore. I was chained to the back wall, a metal ring around my neck, and I was now wearing a hospital gown. Still no bra or panties, though. I jolted upright, a wave of dizziness sweeping through me.

Hodad backed away from me and slammed the cage door, locking me inside—with a zombie.

Not just any zombie. Kat.

Instant game changer. My worst nightmare—my greatest hope.

A Hazmat outside the cage. He held a remote control, and she wore a collar. Her skin had a slight grayish tint. Her hair was tangled, her eyes pink rather than red, with dark circles underneath. Her collarbone was broken, still sticking out of her skin. Her leg was twisted at an odd angle.

Was any part of my friend in there?

Grunting and groaning, she reached for me. I hopped to my feet, swayed.

"Now," Ms. Smith said.

Kat tripped forward.

I couldn't bring myself to fight her. I just…couldn't.

As her teeth sank into my neck, I stumbled backward, hit the wall. Sharp pains, a fire burning through my veins.

Rather than push her away, I wrapped my arms around her, holding her closer.

"Take whatever you need," I whispered. Tears streamed down my cheeks.

"Enough," Ms. Smith said, impatient. "The barest amount should be plenty."

Kat was wrenched away from me. Her teeth took a hunk of my flesh with her.

I dropped to my knees, praying, waiting. Hoping.

"It's working," Ms. Smith exclaimed. "It's actually working. They're both healing from the infection."

The gray faded from Kat entirely. The pink washed from her eyes, revealing the hazel I so loved.

"The toxin is gone," Hodad said.

"She's a Witness," Ms. Smith said.

Their excitement was contagious. Toxin…gone. Witness… like Emma and Helen.

It was a miracle. More than I'd ever dreamed possible.

If I'd had this ability sooner, Trina, Lucas and Collins could have been saved, too.

Joy and despair…a painful combination. I gritted my teeth against it. I blamed Ms. Smith for what should have been. Her unconcern for collateral damage. Her lack of ethics. Her. Just her. She was more evil than the zombies I fought. They, at least, were mindless, operating on instinct. Her every action was a conscious decision.

She had to be stopped.

Kat's collarbone snapped into place. Her leg straightened out, and she looked around the lab with confusion. "Where am I? What's going on?" Her gaze lit on me and widened. "Ali! You're hurt."

"Move on to phase two," Ms. Smith said.

Using a remote control linked to Kat's collar, Hazmat forced her to exit the cage.

"What's going on?" Kat repeated, trying to dig her heels into the floor. "Why can't I stop?"

"Stop this!" My chains rattled as I struggled. "Let her go!"

Kat walked to a gurney off to the side. There was a body strapped atop it—hers. She reached out, touched it. When nothing happened, she reached out again…and again.

"Ma'am? Sir?" Hazmat asked.

"It's not working," Hodad said.

"Ali!" Kat said with a whimper. "Help me!"

"Let her go!" I shouted.

Ms. Smith sighed, ignoring me. "This is disappointing, but not devastating. We'll study the Witnesses, find a way to make use of them."

As determined and wild as she was, Kat managed to fight past the pulses, fight *Hazmat,* kicking and punching, using the skills I'd taught her, and he lost his hold on the remote. It shattered, and the collar separated in the center. Kat ripped it off, tossed it away. Suddenly my best friend was floating up… toward the ceiling. She reached for me, and I reached for her.

"Ali!"

Our gazes met for a final time—and then she vanished.

Sorrow ravaged me. I dropped to my knees. Gone. Again. But at least she was safe now. Anima would never be able to hurt her.

"Idiot!" Ms. Smith snapped.

"I'm sorry," Hazmat replied, inclining his head.

"Save your apologies. They won't bring back the girl." She flattened her palm over her forehead, as if feeling for a fever. "Just go get the next zombie, and be more careful."

He rushed off, soon returning with an older zombie. Male. The cage door opened, and the collared zombie entered.

He raced for me, and I had no compunction about punching him in the head. As he stumbled back, I kicked him in the chest. Again, he stumbled. I tried to step out of my body, tried to summon the fire, but failed at both.

"You're too weak, Miss Bell," Ms. Smith called. "And don't waste our time trying to use your other abilities. I took them. Helen wasn't the only one capable of stealing."

No. No!

When the zombie came at me again, I shoved my palm into his nose. Cartilage to the brain didn't slow him down. He snapped his teeth at me. I twisted, elbowed him in the temple, sending him to his hands and knees.

"Restrain him," she said, and Hazmat thrust a metal hook into the cage, grabbing the zombie by the neck.

He'd been dead a long while. His hair was gone, all of it. Eyebrows, eyelashes. No lashes. His eyes glowed redder than most, as if he was fed well and often. He was tall. Or would have been, if his shoulders hadn't been stooped. He wore an old suit, the cuffs and ankles frayed. I'd broken his jaw, and it now hung at an odd angle.

"Sedate her," Ms. Smith said. "Not enough to put her to sleep, but just enough to make her too weak to fight."

A fine mist sprayed into the confines of the cage. I held my breath as long as possible…my lungs, burning…*come on, come* on…not long enough; I sucked in a mouthful of air. It tingled going down, and I coughed. And whatever they'd laced it with broke the blood-brain barrier fast, removing the starch from my knees. I collapsed.

The zombie was released. I tried to push him away, but the dizziness distorted my vision and I missed. His teeth sank into my shoulder and gnawed. I'd hurt when Kat bit me, but this went beyond hurt. His teeth were like razors that had been dipped in salt. I batted at his head until I finally managed to dislodge him.

He convulsed on the concrete floor for one minute…two… and stilled. The gray tint faded from his skin, returning it to its natural tan—meanwhile, I lost the natural rose tint to my skin and turned gray. Fire spread through every inch of me, burning me from the inside out, and the gray left me, too.

Fire, and yet, I saw no flames.

I stayed on the ground, right where I was, stealthily looking over everyone in the room. A guard had joined the party. He had a .44 sheathed at his waist. Hodad had a pen in his pocket. Ms. Smith wore a necklace. If I could get my hands on any of those things…the rest would be history.

I moaned, collapsing and pretending to sink into a state of unconsciousness.

"Take my father's spirit to the special cage I had made, then take his body to the cooler," Ms. Smith commanded. I think she pressed a button. "I want the girl restrained."

She and Hodad returned to their conversation. I ignored them, listening for the telltale click of the lock, nearing footsteps…

There. My cue.

On your mark…

The guard toed me over. *Get set.*

He scooped me up in his arms. *Go!*

I grabbed his weapon, sliding off the safety as I shoved the barrel against his chest. A simple squeeze of the trigger, and his heart was shredded. He gasped as he toppled, taking me with him.

Hodad got with the program real quick and raced for the cage door, slamming it shut to keep me inside.

Mistake.

I raised the gun, squeezed the trigger again. *Click.* A bullet jammed. I quickly cocked, heard the problem shell drop to the ground. Hodad was now racing toward the exit, Ms. Smith to the counter at the right, shoving papers and pens to the floor as she searched for…what? A weapon?

I fired a shot in her direction, but she ducked. A miss!

Gritting my teeth, I aimed at Hodad, who was just about to fly through the door.

Boom! A bullet to the brain. He collapsed against the door, shutting it.

A sense of victory. One down, one to go.

Ms. Smith was crouched, keeping the counter between her and one of my bullets, while aiming a semiautomatic at me. Her grip was steady, reminding me that she was a former slayer. Battles to the death were part of her business.

"Do it," I said, smiling coldly, keeping my barrel trained in her direction. Was the room soundproofed? Unmonitored? Must be. No one came running in to protect her.

"Put down your weapon," she commanded.

"How about…not."

"I'll do it," she screeched. "I'll kill you, I swear I will."

"No, you won't. We both know you've spent too much money, wasted too many resources on getting me here."

I reached around the front of the cage and disengaged the lock.

She peeked out. Her eyes widened as I stepped free. "How did you do that?"

"Magic fingers. Need proof? Watch this." I shot the gun out of her hand.

She screamed as it went flying across the room. I fired off another shot, this one destined for her brain. She rolled out of the way.

Click. And now I was out of bullets.

Okay, then. We'd do this the old-fashioned way.

The thought kind of gave me a case of the happies.

I stalked across the room. Her hand bled as she backed away. The moment she was within reach, I swung my arm. She blocked my pistol-whip with her forearm and punched me in the sternum, as if to stop my heart. Maybe she did. I lost my breath, hunched over, and she kneed me in the jaw. Stars twinkled as I propelled backward.

She pursued me to the floor, tried to pin me. But I still held the gun and swung at her. The butt of the weapon crashed against her temple. She moaned and went lax. I flipped her to her back and straddled her. Hammered the butt of the gun at her temple, but she blocked. I tried again, and she blocked that, too. She bucked, dislodging me, and I had to catch myself with my hands to prevent a face-plant, losing my grip on the weapon.

She unleashed another solid strike to my sternum. Uncaring about the pain, I grabbed one of the fallen pens and aimed for her carotid. But again, she blocked. The tip sank into her forearm, slicing through muscle, hitting bone. Her scream echoed from the walls. I was able to settle back on my haunches, grab her injured arm and punch the pen, sending it deeper, all the way through.

Another scream bowed her back.

The perfect position, I thought with a grin. *Watch Ali whale.* Punch, punch, punch. Her face absorbed every hit, her un-injured arm pinned by my knees, unable to act as a shield. Punch, punch. But as I raised my fist to go again, my wrist was shackled by a vise-grip and I was yanked to my feet.

The cavalry had arrived.

I struggled with all of my might, but the male was joined by another, and another, and both of my arms were captured, my legs lifted. Someone helped Ms. Smith to her feet. One of her eyes was already swollen shut, and there was a gash in her lower lip. She limped toward me.

"I'll make you regret this," she snarled. Then she flattened her hand against my temple.

I frowned, confused. She really thought *that* would hurt me? Then I felt five little spiders crawling around in my brain, and I knew. They weren't spiders. They were fingers. She planned to cover my memories.

"Stop! Just stop! Don't do this! We can—"

I…had no idea where I was. I stilled, blinked. Why was there a battered woman in front of me? Why were men hold-ing me?

"There, that's better," the woman said.

Who was she? I couldn't remember. Couldn't remember

anything. Something was wrong. Terribly wrong. "Where am I? What's going on?"

She smiled without humor. "Don't worry. I'll get patched up and explain everything."

WHEN TWO MINDS COLLIDE

My name is Samantha Conway and I've been alive for eighteen days. Well, I only remember the past eighteen days. My friend Rebecca says I hit my head during a fight with slayers and the blow knocked a few screws loose, causing amnesia. She suggested I keep this journal, write down all of my feelings and any memories that surface. So far, I just feel frustrated. I've remembered nothing! The only thing I don't have to wonder about is the hole in my heart. I know it's there—there's never a moment I'm not aware of it. It's like a bottomless pit of despair and it's so not cake.

Ugh. Did I really just write "so not cake"? Clearly there's something more than amnesia wrong with me.

I'm supposedly some kind of bad-A enforcer. I capture and kill the people who slay my zombies. But I haven't gone out on a mission since The Incident—what I'm calling the world's worst brain fart—because cleansing zombies has kept me weak, but Rebecca says today is my last cleansing. For a while, at least.

Apparently, slayers are hunting me, determined to kill ME. I'm supposed to take them out first. I'm told I'll head out tomorrow. But the problem is, I don't remember how to fight! So how am I supposed to stop them?

Enough! I threw the pen and journal across the room and rose. I was sick of writing. Sick of not remembering. Mostly sick of this helplessness. I needed to…

I didn't know what I needed to do. Something. Anything.

A knock at my door. Rebecca strode inside without waiting for permission, as usual. And as usual, it annoyed the crap out of me.

"Excellent," she said. "You're awake. Your presence is required in the lab."

Her tone was clipped. But then, her tone was always clipped. I wasn't sure she liked me all that much, even though she'd claimed we'd known each other for ages. And to be honest, I wasn't sure I liked her. I looked at her, and the hole in my heart throbbed.

The same way it throbbed every time I looked at the tattoos on my arms and the one on the back of my neck.

"Come on." She waved me over with her good arm. Her other one had sported a thick bandage for the first week of my stay, and now that the bandage was gone, I could see a big black scab.

Anger pricked at me—not at her, but at slayers. They'd hurt her, same as they'd hurt me. A group of them had invaded our building, our home, hoping to abduct me, but she'd saved my life, taking a beating for me.

I could only guess why they wanted to stop us from cleansing zombies and making the world a better place. Their own gain.

She led me to the bank of elevators at the end of my hall.

There were thirty-two floors in the building, each a maze of hallways, offices and labs. My guards and me had an entire floor to ourselves. The one above us had rooms teeming with cages and zombies.

Zombies I would save.

That was the only thing I really liked about my life. Saving the lost.

"This is Ethan," Rebecca said as we entered an area with all kinds of medical equipment. "You met him before your accident. You adore him."

He was a little older than me, putting him at about twenty. He was only slightly taller than me and lean. He had dark hair and a weird expression. As if he was trying to say sorry without actually saying a word. Had we fought? We must have, because the hole in my heart was throbbing again.

I wanted so badly to remember.

"Ali," he acknowledged with a nod.

Ali? An image flashed through my mind, there and gone in the blink of an eye. But still it managed to arrest me. This boy, this Ethan, sat on a bench beside a stunning teenage girl with dark hair and eyes. He looked at her with such tenderness, such love. Beside her was another teenage girl. This one had lighter brown hair, straight as a pen, and mischievous hazel eyes.

She was looking at me and laughing.

The throb in my heart hurt so much I almost doubled over.

"Her name is Sami," Rebecca snapped. "And, Sami, I need you to get in the chair. Please don't make me tell you again."

"Or what?" I quipped. I hated obeying her. But I did it. I

sat. Because even though I hated it, I loved the results. Two men in hazmat suits strapped my ankles and wrists to the chair.

Rebecca and Ethan stepped into a protected chamber within the room. The walls were clear, allowing them to watch everything that happened outside it.

Both hazmat-clad men exited and then returned with a young zombie girl. She hadn't been dead long, I didn't think. Her skin was gray, but not dark, and she still had most of her hair. There was a metal collar around her neck.

The closer she came to me, the more she struggled, reaching for me. Her nails scraped over my thighs, and I flinched.

She lowered her head and gnawed on my arm. I sucked in a breath, the pain coming quick and hot. But soon after she started, she was jerked back. She sagged to the floor and began to seize. Her skin lost its grayish tint, and the red glow faded from her eyes. She lifted her arm to the light, turned it, studied it, and a slow grin bloomed.

Rebecca and Ethan exited the chamber.

A gloating Rebecca clapped. "Told you."

Ethan only had eyes for the girl. "Izzy," he said, rushing to her.

The girl gasped at him happily, excitedly. "Ethan!"

But one of the hazmat-suit men stepped between them, preventing a reunion.

"Out of my way," Ethan commanded.

The suited man remained in place.

Scowling, Ethan turned to Rebecca. "Tell him to move out of my way. Now."

"Your sister has been cleansed, just as I promised," Rebecca replied. "Now she's what we call a Witness. And we can't just let Witnesses run wild, can we? No. We have to test her, find out what she can do and how she does it."

Rebecca had said the same thing about all the others I'd cleansed. I'd protested more than once, to no avail.

Ethan shook his head. "I won't let you run tests on her. She had enough of that during her first life."

Far from intimidated, she said, "And how are you going to stop me?"

He tensed.

I struggled against my bonds. They were going to fight, and I— What? What was I going to do about it?

An alarm screeched to sudden life. I stilled, glanced around.

A paling Rebecca barked orders at the guards. "You, get the Witness into the cage I prepared. You, lock Ali in the safe room."

Ali, again. Why?

"And you," she said to Ethan. "If you want to leave this building alive, you'll shut your mouth and come with me. I'll expect you to watch my back—or I'll put a bullet in yours."

Wait. "Don't leave me!" I called.

But they'd already marched out of the room. One of the suited men took the collar-bound Witness through another set of doors while the other freed me from the chair. I made to stand on my own, but he grabbed me by the wrist and dragged me through the same doors the other suited man had used.

A computerized voice announced, "Intruders, first floor. Intruders, second floor. Intruders, third floor. Fire, fourth floor." On and on, the litany continued.

My heart raced, but not with fear, I didn't think. Was that... excitement? Anticipation? But why?

"What's going on?" I asked.

He jerked off the mask. "Shut up and walk."

I gritted my teeth, contemplated tripping him—and the impulse baffled me. We were on the same side.

Down a hall we raced, around a corner. We came to a group of teenage boys fighting guards and zombies at the same time and drew up short.

I watched, enthralled. *Throb, throb, throb.* I'm not sure I'd ever seen a more awesome sight. The tallest and most muscled of the boys had black hair—and were those *violet* eyes? Good glory. He was fearsome. A minicrossbow in one hand, a dagger in the other. He pushed his spirit from his body, took down a zombie, then turned in a circle, stepped back into his body and shot a guard with an arrow. His motions were fluid, a ripple of wind, as natural as breathing.

His gaze shifted—yes! violet!—and landed on me. He stopped. Just stopped—

—the world around me crumbled, and suddenly I was on a bed, flat on my back. The dark-haired boy was on top of me, pinning me down. He didn't mean me any harm. His hands gently framed my cheeks as I smiled up at him. He lowered his head with every intention of kissing me. I—

—lost sight of him and yelped. Hazmat-suit man must have decided it would be unwise to aid his friends, because he yanked my arm, tugging me away from the action. I turned back, needing to see the violet-eyed boy again.

"They're slayers," Hazmat said.

That meant… *Oh, crap.* They had come back to finish the job—to finish *me.*

Hazmat tripped and fell, taking me with him. Impact hurt.

As I crawled to my hands and knees, I realized he hadn't tripped on his own. He'd had help. Courtesy of an arrow through the back of his neck. Blood pooled around him. But the violence of the action…didn't shock me.

Heart pounding, I scrambled up to face the violet-eyed boy now stomping toward me. Every cell in my body sizzled. In fear. Had to be fear.

"Don't hurt me," I gasped out. Warning bells sounded in my head. Or maybe that was the still-blasting alarm. I backed away, came up against a wall. "I'll fight you. And I'll injure you. I will. I hear I'm quite good at combat."

He stopped a few inches away from me. Those gorgeous eyes danced with relief, happiness and confusion. He took another step toward me.

I held up my hands to ward him off. "Don't come near me!"

The confusion overshadowed the other emotions. "Do you know who I am?"

"Of course. You're a slayer. I've taken down your people, and you now want revenge. Well, it's not going to be easy." I raised my fists. I might not remember how to fight, but I wasn't going down easily.

Two boys came up beside him. One flashed me a toothy grin. The other, a blond with tragic navy eyes, never lost his scowl.

"Go," Violet told them. "I'll take care of her."

Off they went, and all too soon, I heard the pop of gunfire behind me.

"Listen to me," Violet said, drawing my attention.

I gasped. He'd closed more distance. I could feel the heat

of him now, smell the soap and strawberries of his scent. I swear my heart skipped a beat.

"My name is Cole, and I'm here for you. To take you away. I'm not going to hurt you. Would never hurt you."

I wanted to believe him, but Rebecca's warning blasted through my mind. I spat, "Liar!"

"Ali-gator," he said, his tone gentle. "Ali."

That name again… I frowned. It struck me with the same force as one of his arrows, my chest throbbing, throbbing so intently. "I'm Samantha." Wasn't I?

"You were captured, brought here. Took us a while, but we finally found you. I don't know what they did to you, but I can assure you they aren't your friends. We are. None of us would ever hurt you."

I edged around the corner, backing away from him.

"A lot of people are worried about you." As he spoke, he inched toward me. "Nana, my dad. Reeve. Do you remember Reeve?"

I racked my brain, came up empty and shook my head. *Chest…throbbing harder…*

"Emma, your little sister, has been helping us look for you. But Anima used pulses to surround the perimeter, so she wasn't able to get inside until after we'd disabled them. Then *I* wouldn't let her in the building. I knew you would be upset if anything happened to her."

Emma…Emma… The name made the throbbing far, far worse.

Could I trust this dangerous boy?

"All right. You've left me with no choice." Before I could

decide, he was on me, hefting me over his shoulder. "Time to make the vision come true. At least I finally understand it."

Answer: no, I couldn't trust him. "Let me go!" I beat at his back and slammed my knees into his torso.

"Never again." He lifted a gun and marched forward.

"I mean it. Let go," I demanded.

"Never. Again."

"You keep saying that. What do you want with me? What do you want *from* me?"

"What I've always wanted. Everything."

"Well, you can't have it."

There was something familiar about the scene....

Another flash of this boy kissing me.

A flash of this boy stripping me and touching me.

A flash of this boy smiling at me, violet eyes sparkling.

A flash of this boy studying his cuticles while I killed zombies.

Killed zombies, rather than healed them?

I must have. *If* these flashes were memories. But that would mean Rebecca *had* lied to me.

Why would she lie?

Cole stopped at the end of the hall. Smoke billowed, layered with the scents of rot, gunpowder and blood. To the left, the blond boy with the tragic eyes fought a handful of guards— on his own. He had a gun in both hands, aimed, shot, aimed, shot. Bodies crumpled around him.

"We've got slayers all over the building," Cole said. "River's team is with us, and we're taking every floor. There will be nothing left of Anima when we're done."

I twisted. Two men in lab coats raced around the corner.

They caught a glimpse of Cole and backtracked. Cole shot both in the legs. Then he returned to his easy pace, as if nothing had happened.

"Do you know where Smith is?"

Smith. Rebecca. My friend—who wasn't really a friend.

I gulped. I couldn't tell him. He'd kill her. And even though I wasn't sure I liked her, even though I didn't know if she was friend or foe, I didn't want her dead. Did I?

Throbbing again...

I'd never been so confused.

Another blond boy came tearing from the opposite direction. "Can't find Smith. But I see you found my cupcake."

"Mine," Cole snapped.

Uh, was the cupcake supposed to be me? Because it was a weird nickname for a supposed enemy.

"Ali," Cole said, "I'm going to set you down. Don't run. If you run, I will chase you, and when I catch you, I will spank you."

"Excuse me?" I hated the idea of being spanked. Really.

"Why would she run?" Blondie asked.

Cole eased me to my feet, and I did contemplate running. Now was my chance. But curiosity held me immobile. These boys could have hurt me. They hadn't. They had spoken to me with affection.

"I can help you," a woman said. A tall, slender blonde with eyes as freaky a blue as mine appeared out of thin air.

Throb.

Cole stiffened. "We don't need your help, Helen." He stepped in front of me...protecting me?

Throb, throb.

I…didn't like that he was upset. Why?

"Who do you think has been feeding Emma information all this time?" the Helen lady snapped. "Me. Now, do you really want to leave this building without taking care of Rebecca? Because the choice is yours. If it were up to me, I'd rather you did something. I love my daughter and never want to go through something like this again."

Daughter? *Throb, throb, throb.*

Cole cracked his jaw, nodded. "Fine. Lead the way. But if this is a trap…"

"You'll what?" she quipped. "Yell at me?"

He snapped his teeth at her. Mimicking a zombie?

She moved through a hall I didn't recognize. Cole maintained a tight grip on my hand. Up an elevator she had to hot-wire, since the fire alarm had shut off every cart. Down a flight of steps. Down another elevator.

Finally, Helen stopped at the end of a dim corridor. "Ali. Your hand."

What—

Cole moved me to the front, pushed my palm against the ID box. Warmth. A click. The door opened, and it wasn't long before we were in another room I'd never seen. One with the twenty or so Witnesses I'd cleansed, trapped in a special cage with electric pulses that rode the length of the metal bars.

Slayers stopped and stared, flabbergasted.

"What. The. Hell?" Blondie said.

"They were zombies. Like those." I pointed to the other cage and the undead. "But I cleansed them."

"Cleansed?" Cole repeated.

I yanked from his grip and went to the cage of Witnesses.

Another ID scan, and just like that, they were free. They floated out, thrilling with excitement and relief…rising…soon vanishing through the ceiling.

I went to the cage of zombies.

"No, Ali," Cole shouted, stomping after me. "Don't."

"But I can cleanse them, too," I said, turning to face him. Didn't want him at my back.

A zombie reached through the bars and grabbed me. Because he was collared, he was solid to me and managed to sink his teeth into my arm. It hurt, and I yelped, but it wasn't anything to send me to my knees. In fact, it was better this way, being free of the shackles.

Cole was suddenly in front of me, pulling me to safety. Scowling, he punched the zombie in the face.

He faced me, tenderly framed my cheeks with his big hands. Just like in the memory. "In a minute, there's going to be two of me. My hand will light up. I'll push the flames inside your wound. It'll hurt but—"

"There's no need," I said. The bite was already healing, the burn in my veins already cooling. "The toxin doesn't affect me."

"Impossible."

"Cole," Blondie said. "Look at the zombie."

Cole twisted in time to watch the gray fade from the creature's skin, the red dim from his eyes.

"I don't understand," Cole said.

"Hello. Anyone remember Rebecca?" Helen clapped her hands to gain our attention. "Zombies can wait."

But—

Cole tugged me down another hallway. We stopped in

front of a metal door. Ethan sprawled in front of it, motion-less, practically floating in a puddle of blood.

I wasn't sad, I realized, and that confused me all over again.

Helen waved her hand at the door. "When you stopped the pulses around the building, I went straight to Ali. When I re-alized her memories had been covered, I knew Rebecca had stolen her slayer abilities, and went after *her*. So, Cole, you've got another choice to make. Kill Rebecca now and end her reign of terror, but in the process, ensure that Ali will never get her abilities back. Or take Rebecca with you and cage her. When Ali remembers her past, she will be able to take her abilities back."

Stolen abilities? Covered memories?

"The code is…" Helen rattled off too many numbers to remember.

Cole glared at her for a long while before jabbing his fin-ger into the keypad. He extended his crossbow as the door slowly opened.

I waited, more uncertain than ever. What would we find on the other side? Rebecca, as promised? Or a trap?

Which did I prefer?

If Rebecca *was* in there, the slayers would win. If it was a trap, I might be able to get away.

But did I really want to get away?

A smile lifted the corners of Cole's lips. "Hello, Rebecca."

SEVERED HEADS
OR TANGLED TALES

I paced the confines of my new room. Well, not mine, but *his*. Cole. This was his bedroom. He was letting me borrow it, though I knew he wanted to stay here with me. Last night, when he'd brought me here, he'd said so, about a thousand times. I'd said no. Of course.

He was still an unknown.

Could I trust him?

Before, I would have given an unequivocal no. Now? I wasn't sure. When he wasn't gunning people down in a hallway, he was actually kind of sweet. And charming. And witty. And so hot he made my mouth water.

He'd brought me breakfast this morning. He'd pointed out the dresser drawer holding my things, so that I would always feel welcome. He'd said he was planning our "third date," that he wanted to take a knitting class with me, or something equally tame, because we needed less excitement in our lives.

And he was majorly concerned with my well-being. Like, obsessively so. He and Helen had argued heatedly last night.

He'd demanded that she fix me. She'd said that she was trying, and it'd be nice if he would, too. He'd said he was doing everything she'd told him to do, telling me stories about my past.

It was true. He had. For hours. But his stories were so far-fetched.

Or had been. When finally I'd fallen asleep, I'd had such vivid dreams....

I'd seen everything he'd described. Me, standing in a hall-way painted black and gold, catching a glimpse of him for the first time. He'd been leaning against a bank of lockers at school, goofing off with his friends. A hat had shaded his eyes, but then he'd looked up and we'd both been trapped, connected by a vision of the two of us kissing.

I shivered.

Then I'd seen us training in a boxing ring. We'd taken jabs at each other and argued good-naturedly, our hands roaming where they shouldn't, our sweaty bodies rubbing together.

Another shiver.

I'd seen us fighting zombies together, protecting each other. The concern on his face every time I was bitten—

Yeah. Another shiver.

I couldn't deny there was history between us. Or that my heart recognized him, even if my mind did not. I couldn't deny that the urge to throw myself into his arms, press my lips against his and cling to him as if my life depended on it—as if he was the only raft in a storm—grew stronger every second. But Rebecca was trapped in an underground bunker behind his house... Was I just supposed to ignore that?

Even if Rebecca was a liar and the enemy, I didn't condone violence. Did I?

The door swung open, and in stepped the woman I was supposed to call Nana. I liked her, a lot, and wasn't annoyed that she'd just barged in, like I'd been with Rebecca. She'd been here waiting for me when Cole brought me, and I'd enjoyed her too-tight hug.

"Ali," she said with a huge grin. "How are you, dear?"

"Well, thank you."

She embraced me again, and I awkwardly patted her back.

Her expression was a little sad as she straightened, and I hated that I'd upset her. "I'm here to escort you to the dining room."

Time for dinner, then. *He* would be there.

She hooked our arms and led me through the house. There were tons of visitors, but I didn't see any sign of Cole. Sharp disappointment. Tendrils of dread. A houseful of slayers—why? I'd been introduced to each one already, and they seemed to like me, but that didn't make them any less intimidating. Not that I'd ever let them know I was disconcerted.

"Hello," I said, nodding in greeting. I frowned when I realized there was no food on the table. Slayers, but no dinner?

Gavin winked at me.

Mackenzie blew me a kiss.

Reeve waved at me.

Bronx nodded at me.

Frosty stared out a window.

Justin and Jaclyn smiled at me.

River patted his lap, a silent request for me to sit.

That would be a big fat no, thanks.

He shrugged, unfazed by my refusal.

Mr. Holland, Cole's dad, motioned to an unoccupied chair. Nana led me forward and I sat.

Besides Cole, the only two people missing were Veronica and her younger sister, Juliana. Apparently, Juliana had done something to enrage everyone, especially Frosty, so the two had gone back home to Georgia, where they would stay.

At the far end of the room, Emma the Witness appeared. Like Mackenzie, she blew me a kiss. Once upon a time, Cole and I had been the only ones capable of seeing my little sister—was she really my sister? But now, because of some kind of fire-share, everyone could.

Helen materialized beside her, and everyone saw her, too. She had the ability to cloak her image, but wasn't doing that anymore.

What the heck was going on?

One by one, the slayers told me stories about the time they'd spent with me. There was a bit of disconnect between the first round of stories and me. I heard, but I didn't see. Then little Emma spoke, and the throb returned to my chest. Two sisters, deeply in love. Separated by a crash, yet able to find each other again.

The throb only grew worse as Helen spoke. A mother who'd given up her only child in an effort to protect her. A mother who'd mourned the loss every day for the rest of her too-short life. A mother determined to have a second chance.

When it was Frosty's turn to speak, he stood and walked out of the room. Without uttering a single word.

The throb...out of control now, consuming me, hurting me. I hunched over, gasping for breath. An image flashed through my mind. The dark-haired girl with hazel eyes. Helping me tie Get Well balloons on roadkill. Loving me when everyone else turned their backs on me. Laughing, always laughing. Living.

Where was she? How come I hadn't gotten to speak to her? Because she was joy, and she was love, and I wanted so badly to—

To bring her back.

Yes. To bring her back. But I couldn't. She was dead, gone. Her eyes, dull. Her body, immobile. Blood, all over her.

Kat!

The name screamed through my mind, the pain that came with it...too much. Tears rolled down my cheeks. "Kat." I said it. I had to.

"Her funeral is tomorrow," Mackenzie said with a sniffle. "She would want you there."

Her name. I'd gotten it right.

"We think Frosty has seen her spirit, that she's a Witness like Emma and Helen, but he won't confirm or deny," Reeve said, wiping away a tear.

I rubbed at my heart. Where was Cole? I needed Cole. I wasn't sure why.

As if I'd summoned him, he walked through the crowd. Maybe I *had* summoned him. There was a connection between us. His eyes never left mine. I reached for him, and he picked me up to carry me to his bedroom. He placed me on the edge of the bed. As my gaze lifted, the reason he hadn't been part of the storytelling party became clear. He'd been hanging poster-sized photos of us all over the room.

In them, we smiled. We laughed. We kissed.

My already raw nerves kicked up a fuss as he crouched in front of me and smoothed the hair from my forehead. "No more stories," I said. "Not now."

"Sorry, love, but we're going to bombard you until your memories are completely uncovered. And if it can't be done, well, we're going to start building new ones. And we're going to start now." He fisted his T-shirt at the collar and pulled the material over his head.

I gasped at the beautiful buffet suddenly displayed before me. Strength and vitality—life. He was bronzed and muscled. Tattooed—good glory! That was my name etched across his chest, stretching from one nipple to the other. Ali Bell, not Sami. And one of those nipples was pierced!

He could not be any sexier.

I reached out before I'd realized I'd moved and flicked my fingertips over the silver loop. The metal was cool, solid. His pec tightened up, and he hissed in a breath.

"Gavin has started calling you the queen of zombie hearts," Cole said. "And you know what, he's right. It fits. Before you, I wasn't really living. I was existing. Moving from girl to girl. Killing zombies. I was as good as dead, but you brought me back to life. And you are most definitely the queen of my heart."

Melting me…

"You know what else I realized?" he said. "You were never the 'she.' Your mother was."

The *she?* "I don't understand."

"Because of her, what she died doing for you, the rest of us had a chance." He fisted two handfuls of my hair. "I can't really regret the past, because I have you in my future."

"Cole."

He pulled me forward and kissed me. His lips pressed

against mine, his tongue thrusting into my mouth, and I tasted the strawberries I'd scented on him every time he'd neared.

I found my arms wrapping around him of their own accord, my head tilting to welcome him in and take him deeper, my legs even parting in a silent plea for him to scoot closer. A plea he must have heard. His hands lowered to my backside and yanked me forward so that the hardness of him was flush against the softness of me.

My blood heated…and heated…and I began to move without conscious thought. My fingers, tangling through his hair, then lowering, riding the ridges of his strength. My hands, playing at the waist of his pants, opening the fly and the zipper before I could process what was happening.

When I did, I wasn't frightened. I was excited.

Cole tore off my shirt, unsnapped my bra. He kissed the skin he'd bared—and I had a flash inside my head. Of a time before, when he'd stripped me on a rug, and I'd opened up to him, and he'd taken my virginity.

He'd branded himself on me. Spirit, soul and body. Had left no part of me untouched. I was his girl then, and I was his girl now. The knowledge bubbled inside me, unable to be covered for long.

"Cole," I exclaimed, and he stilled. "We've done this before."

I'd thought him still before. Now he didn't even seem to be breathing. "Yes."

I closed my eyes, ignoring the cool stroke of air against my skin. A live wire seemed to run through every inch of me, and his kiss had just used it to delve past a layer of dark clouds and into an ocean of memory. The good, the bad and the ugly. A storm in my mind. The first six years of my life with Helen. Coming to love my dad and Miranda. Emma. The crash. Meeting Cole. Falling in love with Cole. Being captured by Anima the first time, being tortured. Kat, oh, the joy of Kat. The heartache of losing her. Being captured by Anima the second time.

Finally, victory.

A tide of emotion. Happiness, regret, sadness, sorrow, more joy, more heartache, anger—triumph. The storm calmed. The dark clouds thinned…cleared.

"We won," I said, shocked to the bone.

Cole stiffened, as if he didn't dare hope. "You remember?"

"I do. I really do." Tears streamed down my cheeks. "I remember everything."

"Thank God!" He launched himself at me, throwing me back on the bed, wrapping his arms around me, pinning me with his weight. A kiss on my brow, the tip of my nose. Both of my tearstained eyes and, finally, blessedly, my lips. Kiss, kiss, kiss. Between kisses, he said, "Rebecca—has your—"

"Abilities. I realize that." Now. "I'll take them back… and then I'll take her memories." The decision solidified as I spoke. "She'll never be able to hurt us again. The war will be over." Once and for all.

And we could live, I realized. Really live. We could cleanse zombies. Have a new purpose. A greater one. Gift with life, rather than end with death.

A girl couldn't ask for more than that.

"I love you, Cole Holland."

"I love you, too, Ali Bell. And now…I think it's time we stopped talking and put our mouths to better use."

"Hey! I once said that to you."

"And it was definitely the smartest thing I've ever heard."

I laughed as he kissed me.

Here I was, at Kat's celebration of life. I'd lost her twice already and should have been prepared for the emotional turmoil. But I wasn't. I cried like a baby and didn't care.

Deep down, I knew it wasn't about how long we lived, but *how* we lived. And she'd lived well. She'd made an impact. She'd loved. She'd forever changed me for the better.

Detective Verra had found her body inside Anima's building, along with hundreds of others. She'd then made an official statement, saying the company had kidnapped people to illegally test medicines they hoped to sell on the black market.

The world was shaken.

And rightfully so.

Kat's dad stood in front of her casket, his shoulders shaking as he sobbed. Since the moment of her birth, he'd known he would one day lose her, but like me, he hadn't been prepared. A bright ray of light in a very dark world had been snuffed out. We needed more of those, not less.

Wren and Poppy were here. Both had hugged me, and though they'd said nothing about zombies, I knew they'd accepted the truth. They were on guard now, distrustful of those around them.

Though the sun was shining, the air was bitterly cold, a sharp wind slapping my hair against my cheeks. Breath misted in front of my face. I distantly heard people talking about Kat, about how she'd touched their lives, but none of it registered. I was too lost in my own memories.

How she and I had laughed and teased. How we'd bonded

to each other. Nothing and no one could destroy that bond, not even death. It was far too powerful. Too precious.

Even still, I missed her.

But one thought kept me from breaking down. We'd have all of it again. Her body was dead, yes, but her spirit lived on. She was up there, and one day, I would join her. I would hug her and never let go. It would be cake.

Frosty stood off to the side, separated from the crowd. He wore a pair of sunglasses, hiding his eyes. His head was bowed, his hands fisted at his sides. My heart broke for him.

But it was quickly put back together when I noticed the two girls standing hand in hand a few yards away from him. Emma and Kat. They were here!

I wanted to run to them but didn't. Disturbing the ceremony would have been so uncool. So I stood in place and waited, squeezing Cole's arm to hold myself back. He kissed my forehead, his comfort and support unwavering.

Finally, everyone ambled away from the site.

Kat watched Frosty, her expression concerned.

"Ready, love?" Cole asked me.

"Let's talk to the girls."

"They're here?"

"Yep." I released him and bounded over. Both Kat and Emma smiled at me, and I would have sworn the sun got brighter.

"Dude. Did you notice how many people were here? Tons!" Kat exclaimed. "I put the fun in funeral."

Only Kat.

She arched a brow and said something I'd said to Cole many times before. "Too soon to joke?"

"Forever will be too soon," I muttered.

Cole came up behind me, wrapped his arm around my waist. "Girls still here?"

"You can't see them?" I asked.

"Nope."

"Why can't he?" I asked the girls. "He's always seen Emma in the past."

"Helen taught us how to cloak ourselves," Emma said, clearly proud of herself. Then, in a whisper, she added, "We only have permission to speak with you."

I kissed Cole on the cheek. "Give us a minute, all right?"

He squeezed my hand and strode to the car. He didn't climb inside, but leaned against the side, waiting for me, ever the protector.

Kat's eyes twinkled up at me, only to quickly lose their sparkle. "I'm worried about Frosty."

Honestly? "I am, too."

"Take care of him," she said.

"I will."

"And take care of yourself." Her smile was sad, but also hopeful. "As much as I want to throw a welcome-to-forever party for you up there, I want you to live a long, long time. I want you to do what you were born to do. To let go of the past, the pain and the sorrow, because they'll only slow you down, and push forward. You, Miss Ali-Kat Bell, have the ability to do great things. And I'm not just talking about your slayer skills. You're going to change the world and lead zombies to the light. Don't let anything stand in your way."

Tears burned the backs of my eyes. "I'll try."

"Don't try," Emma said. "Do."

I nodded, because I'd suddenly lost the capacity to speak.

These girls knew how to cut through the crap and strike where it mattered.

They smiled at me one last time before disappearing from view.

I stood in place for a long while, missing both already. Again. More. But Kat was right. It was time to let go of the past and push forward. I had a lot to do—a lot to look forward to. And with Cole and the other slayers at my side, I could do anything.

Would do everything I'd been born to do. I still didn't believe in fate, that everything that happened was meant to be. But I did believe we each had a purpose, and it was up to us to get off our butts and do whatever was necessary to fulfill it.

I was ready.

I was smiling as I walked to Cole, and he smiled at me in turn. This wasn't the end for us, I knew, but merely the beginning.

A NOTE FROM COLE

Let me guess. You skipped ahead. You're reading this before you glance at a single word of Ali's tale because you're too impatient, have to know if there's a happily ever after for everyone.

Too bad.

I'll tell you nothing. I'm evil like that.

Or I was. Can you hear me grumbling? Ali's had a strange effect on me. She took a heart as hard as stone and wrapped in barbwire, and chipped away until she found some kind of gooey candy center.

I'll never be the same.

Don't want to be the same.

So, all right. Okay. You want answers. Here they are.

Did everyone get a happily ever after? Sorry, but no.

Welcome to life.

It's been four weeks since Kat's celebration of life, as Ali calls it, and Frosty is still a mess. Worse, even. His pain is... There are no words. I'm slain every time I look at him. He's turned into someone I don't know, his every action meant to destroy his life in *some minute way. I don't know how to help him, and I'm not sure more time will soothe him. He needs something I cannot give him.*

He needs peace.

He thinks Ali can give it to him. Every day he begs her to cover his memories.

Every day she refuses.

He's even started asking me...and if not me, the others. With her fire, Ali has shared all of her abilities with us. Even the ability to cleanse zombies. And it's weird, helping creatures we once fought so fiercely to destroy. But it's also kind of wonderful. They have a future, and so do we.

Ali cutting in here. We *do* have a future. Like, the greatest one ever.

Cole's been making plans. He'll graduate high school, and a year later, I will. We'll go to college together. He'll do the cop thing, maybe even go total bad-A crime fighter and become an FBI agent, and I'll do the counseling thing. We'll get married—he says he may lock me down *before* college. Can't have other guys getting any ideas about his 'gator or he'll have to give up his dream of being a crime fighter and become a felon. Bones will have to be broken. Blood will have to be spilled. I wouldn't mind the carnage, though. I know the beast I'm paired with and love him anyway.

Cole cutting in, reclaiming my letter.

You didn't want to write it in the first place.

Are you whining? That sounds like whining.

Fine. Take the pen while I show you my favorite finger.

Telling me I'm number one in your heart? Love, I already knew that.

Anyway. Smith didn't get a happily ever after, either. Ali covered her memory and sent her on her way. My girl admitted just how badly she wanted to kill the woman responsible for so much loss, but she knew she had to let go of the hate before it drove her into becoming someone she isn't. Someone like Smith herself. Cold, callous. Collateral damage something to be shrugged over.

I'm proud of her. Hate would have been easy.

I'm still struggling with mine. But that's okay. I've realized hate...and even love...are more than emotions, more than words. They are choices. I decide—what to say, what I do. And I've decided to bet on love. On Ali. She's always been, and will always be, the moral of my story.

Let your light shine,

~~*Cole and the future Mrs. Cole*~~

Ali and the future Mr. Ali

P.S. This letter will self-destruct in ten seconds.

★ ★ ★ ★ ★

ACKNOWLEDGMENTS

Love never fails. I know this to be true, more so now than ever before. To God, the One who blessed me, strengthened me and, no matter what was going on in my life, always made a way for me. Every day You say, "You are Mine," and I am honored to reply, "I am Yours. Always."

To Natashya Wilson, an editor who defies description— and yet I'm going to try to describe you anyway. Brilliant. Dedicated. Amazing. Magnificent. Genius. Fun. Witty. Talented. Cake. (← You know I couldn't leave that one out.) You have made this series a joy in every way, and I will be forever grateful for your insight and support!

To Book Rock Betty, a blogger who has rocked me in so many ways. There are only a handful of people I consider a divine connection, and you are one of them. You make me smile. You make me laugh. You make me happy. (Sensing a theme? LOL) I am blessed to know you! P.S. Cole + Betty = LOVE FOREVER

To T. M. Pennington, a man of many talents, a marketing director and writer who took time out of his own hectic schedule to give me masterful feedback. Thank you, thank you, a thousand times thank you!

To Katie McGarry, an amazing woman and author I admire and adore. You are an inspiration, and a treasure, and another divine connection. Thank you for your support!

To Jill Monroe, who has been with me every step of the way. When I'm sad, you cheer me up. When I'm happy, you laugh with me. When I'm working, you encourage me. My life is better because you are in it!

To Bo, Nikole, Isabella and Abrielle Pham and Brook LeFlore at Cafe Bella in Oklahoma City. Your coffees and lunches are so freaking delicious they should be considered a drug—I'm addicted!

And to everyone who fell in love with Ali, Cole and the rest of the gang. Thank you! Thank you for welcoming my characters into your home, rooting for them, sometimes even wanting to donkey-punch them in the throat, talking about them as if they are real people—because they totally are!— and taking this wild journey with them. May light always shine in your lives and chase away the darkness!

A NOTE FROM GENA

Hey, y'all! You voted for the scene you'd most like to see rewritten in Cole Holland's point of view, and the big breakup in chapter five of *Through the Zombie Glass* won. (The first time Cole and Ali meet and have a vision in *Alice in Zombieland* was a close second.)

You'll notice that while *Alice in Zombieland, Through the Zombie Glass* and *The Queen of Zombie Hearts* are all written in past tense, that is not the case with this scene. When I sat down to draft it, it came out in present tense, and I couldn't bring myself to change it. Let's face it. At this point in the series, Cole lives in the moment. Plus, he's my book boyfriend, and I pretty much give him whatever he wants.

As you can guess, this was a heartbreaking scene to write the first time around, but honestly, it was even more so this time. Cole does not hold back.

I hope you enjoy this peek into his head as much as I did!

Cole

War is all I've ever known. I was born into it, and I will die in the midst of it. I've accepted this. Hell, I wouldn't have it any other way. I'll take countless zombies with me.

And I'll do it with a smile.

Friends have died before me. Many friends. After a while, a sense of numbness settles in. I've thought: *Another casualty. Sucks, I hate this.* But then I've moved on.

I've had to. War doesn't take a time-out so I can deal. Slayers are better off without giving in to feelings anyway. I know this. I've always known this. Yet here I am, ready to tear down these bedroom walls with my bare hands. I don't care about the daily stresses I've been bombarded with lately. Not anymore. My girlfriend lies on the bed, and she is dying. This has been going on for days. Every minute, every second, I try not to lose hope.

What I am learning: I am strong, but my strength means nothing in the face of *this*.

What the hell am I supposed to do?

Ali kicks off the covers. When her teeth begin to chatter, I drape the heavy fabric over her once again. But it isn't long before she's too hot and kicks them off a second time. She even attempts to tear off her clothes.

"Ali." I grab her hands, hold them down. What little numbness I have left shatters. I am nothing but panic and fear.

She came into my life, a tornado I couldn't stop. Now I'm addicted to the violence of the wind. Deny my feelings for her? Impossible. She broke me down and put me back together, and I'll be damned if I allow her to be taken from me.

"Feed me." Her voice is a broken rasp.

If feeding her would actually help her, I would do it. Nothing would stop me. But her hunger isn't for food. She's infected with zombie toxin, and she wants my spirit.

I've experienced the effects of a Z-bite firsthand and know she's trapped in a bottomless ocean of pain and agony, trying to tread water but swiftly sinking. I would cut off my arms if it meant I could take her torment into myself and fight it for her.

She shivers, cold again. I release her hands to cover her. I stroke her cheeks in an effort to ease her in some way. Any way.

She jerks away from me. "No. Don't."

"Ali." Her name is a prayer, a demand. *Heal. You have to heal.*

She turns her head in my direction and attempts to bite me. Her eyes are closed. She's acting on instinct. *Zombie* instinct. I despise soul-eaters to the depths of my being, and yet still I battle an urge to give her what she craves; it's a need. Denying her is torture.

My dad strides into the room and, with a curse, pins Ali's head to the pillow. It's a terrible sight to behold. One person I love restraining another.

"She can't go on like this," he tells me.

I know. "I administered a double dose of the antidote hours ago." I tangle my fingers through my hair and yank at the strands. "Why isn't she better?"

A muscle ticks in his jaw. "Give her another."

Another? To my knowledge, no slayer has ever had so much in so short a time. We don't know the long-term effects. "Can she take it?"

His eyes are bleak. "Do we have a choice?"

No. No, we don't. If she continues along this path, she will die, and her spirit will rise from the dead, a shell housing absolute evil. Ali will be forever gone, forever out of my reach.

I imagine having to fight a zombie that wears her beautiful face and think I'd rather die. I grab one of the syringes resting on the desktop and plunge the needle deep into her neck. At first, she continues to writhe and snap at me. Finally, blessedly, she sags against the mattress, her head lolling to the side.

"Good. This is good. The worst is over," my dad says.

Relief is a surging tide inside me. I struggle to remain on my feet.

My dad places Ali's iPod in its dock. He pulls a chair behind me and I just kind of fall into it. He says something to me, but I am lost in my thoughts and the words are distorted. I think he leaves. I remain in place. I don't care how long it takes for Ali to wake. I will be here when she opens her eyes. I will hold her.

I need to hold her.

Things have been strained between us lately. I've been keeping secrets from her, meeting with a slayer I shouldn't trust, believing him when he says there's a spy among a group of friends I know. But then, his proof is irrefutable.

Ali knows me, knows something is wrong with me. I refuse to talk to her about it, and it hurts her. I've tried to stay away from her in an effort to ease the source of the hurt while I continue to dig for the truth. If she knows what I suspect, she will want to help me. Will insist on it. She's stubborn like that. But to investigate the wrong person is to invite their wrath, maybe even their hatred. It's happened to me, and I won't put her in that position. I'll deal with the consequences myself.

"Ali, I need you to wake up, okay?" I've never come so close to begging.

Her eyes begin to roll behind her lids. She is fighting with everything she's got.

"Good girl," I say. "That's the way. Come back to me, sweetheart."

Though she tries for a while longer, the effort tires her and she sags once again.

A hand roughly pats my shoulder. "I'll watch her if you want to take off and shower—and, dude, I highly recommend you shower."

I look up. Gavin stands beside me. I've known him a long time. Years. I've always liked him. We used to hunt brunettes together as eagerly as we now hunt zombies.

"No. I—"

—the world around me fades, a new one taking shape.

For the first time in our history, a vision ensnares us. I've only ever had visions with Ali, but there's no time to process why I'm suddenly having one with someone else.

Gavin and I are walking through a doorway in Ankh's house. This house. Downstairs. In the entertainment room. Details hit me like bullets. A celebration is winding down. Ali is several feet away from us. She is more beautiful every time I see her. Tall and slender with a fall of white-blond waves that frame a face straight out of a storybook. She is the princess who will save an entire kingdom. The girl with a purpose she's only just beginning to understand.

The one worth waiting for.

Ali is everything I've ever wanted, everything I never knew I needed. Not just in looks. She is witty. I want to kiss even the words that come out of her mouth. She is smart, and she is strong. Stronger than she has realized. Stronger than me. She is loyal, brave. Honest. She refuses to lie. Does she know what a gift that is? She is comfort, and she is peace.

In a lifetime of war, she is my first taste of peace.

She spots us and smiles with delight. She literally glows, and it stops me in my tracks. How did I ever live without her? But she rushes into *his* arms. His. Gavin's. Not mine.

She…chooses to be with him?

Will be with him?

I am struck dumb.

He wraps his arms around her. She frames his cheeks in her hands, as I've done so often to her, rises on her tiptoes and places a soft kiss on his lips.

Every cell in my body shouts in denial. I want to yank her away from him, wrap her in *my* arms, where she belongs, and demand she press her lips against *mine*. Only ever mine. I want to shake her. Shake her so hard the memory of Gavin is forever damaged. I want to tell her to keep her distance from the guy. To never speak to him. Never even glance at him. He is wrong for her. He'll break her heart.

But it won't do me any good. The visions are never wrong—

—the entertainment room washes away in a sea of black. I blink, and I'm back inside the bedroom. *We're* back inside. Gavin stumbles away from me. He is pale, obviously shaken. I know he recently had a vision with Ali. In it, they didn't just kiss; they made out. I'd heard about it from Gavin after

Ali refused to speak of it. I have tried to convince myself they misinterpreted what they saw.

I can't do that now.

"Leave," I snap, gripping the arms of my chair to stop myself from reaching for him. I want to kill him. And I have the skills to do it. I can even make it look like an accident. I know where to hide the body. Ali will never know what's happened. But she might miss him, might mourn him—and the thought of that maddens me. "Leave now."

He does. It saves his life.

I try to breathe. There are now a thousand land mines in my mind, and I'm stepping over every single one of them. Ali will leave me. Boom! Ali will fall for Gavin. Boom! Ali will kiss and touch Gavin. Boom! Gavin will win her, and I...I will lose her. Boom, boom!

I'm not used to helplessness. If there's a problem, I act. I fix. Things get better. But there's nothing I can do about this and I know it. I can't make someone love me.

She shifts on the mattress and her eyelids flutter open, revealing eyes the color of a perfect summer morning, clear and blue, startling.

"Hey there," I say. I reach for her hand, but stop myself just before contact.

She can't quite focus. "Hey." Her voice is different. Hoarser. "I'm glad you're speaking to me again."

I should smile at her, reassure her in some way, but I frown. She's glad I'm here now. But how long will that last? When will she rejoice over Gavin's presence?

"I wasn't ever not speaking to you," I say.

"You were avoiding me, then."

I can't lie to her—won't. "Yes."

Her gaze meets mine, and just like with Gavin, a vision kicks off—

—we are in Ankh's entertainment room. I'm standing across from her...smiling at something Veronica is saying to me. I'm barely listening, too consumed by the fact that Ali is in front of Gavin again, cupping his cheeks again.

Despite the distance, I can hear what she's saying to him. "You're a better man than I ever gave you credit for."

"I know," Gavin replies. He is total cocky assurance, and I want to slam my fist into his nose, smashing cartilage into his brain.

"And you're *so* modest," Ali says.

He chuckles. "Are you happy with the way things turned out?"

She glances in my direction, unconcerned by the fact that Veronica is at my side.

Unconcerned. As if she doesn't care that I'm with an ex. As if she doesn't care about *me*.

"Yeah," she says. "Yeah, I am—"

—the vision ends before she can say anything more, gone in a single, broken heartbeat.

I drop my head into my upraised hands, scrub my fingers through my already mussed hair. More proof. The end is near. The countdown clock on our relationship is running down.

Anger fills me. No. *Anger* is not a strong enough word. *Rage* fills me. It's dark, heavy and barbed, weighing me down, cutting at me. Why Gavin? Why him and not me?

"Gavin's a man-whore, you know." I infuse my voice with ice to hide the savagery of my rage. "Never been with the same girl twice. And he's never liked blondes. He won't stay with you for long."

"I'm not interested in Gavin," she rushes out. "Cole, you have to—"

"Don't say anything. Just...don't." Her reassurance will only make things worse. One day, I will have to watch her fall deeper and deeper for one of my friends. I will be shredded.

I *am* shredded.

I grab two pillows and work them behind her back. When she's comfortable, I take the glass of water from the night-stand and place it at her lips. "Drink."

Color blooms in her cheeks as she obeys. "Thank you."

I nod and set the cup aside. "Let's talk about what happened with Justin." It's the reason she's here. It's business. It will buy me time, allow me to get control of myself.

"Has he recovered?" she asks.

"Yeah, and a lot quicker than you." A zombie bit Justin, and the toxin worked in him so quickly, he then bit Ali. *He* infected her. But while a single dose of the antidote healed him, it required *three* doses for Ali. Why?

"Hey, don't blame me. I'm the victim here."

"Yeah. I know." I massage the back of my neck. "Sorry. It's been stressful watching you suffer and not being able to help." Among other things.

The tension drains from her, and I can't bring myself to tell her the rest. "Has a slayer ever bitten another slayer like that?" she asks.

"Not to my knowledge. Not while both are still human."

"Did I try to bite anyone while I was...out of it?"

"Just me," I say.

She pales all over again. "I'm sorry. I know I failed. Wait. I failed, right?"

Her need to protect me is one of the things I've always admired about her. I nod. "You did."

Her relief is palpable. "I'm so sorry, Cole. I don't know what came over me, but I do know I'm not going to do it again. I promise you."

There's something strange about the fact that she tried to do it in the first place, but I have no answers and shrug.

"I mean it," she insists.

"You tried to bite me more than once."

"I'm so sorry," she says again, clearly horrified. "I didn't realize…"

Yeah. "I know."

She swallows, the picture of unease. "Do you think Anima put Justin up to hurting me? Causing this kind of reaction, thinking we'd destroy each other?"

"Maybe, but like you, I don't think Justin knew what he was doing."

"Where is he now?"

"Ankh kept him below in the dungeon, as you like to call it, for a few days to make sure the antidote was working and he wouldn't try to attack anyone else. Tests were run, and a strange toxin was found in his blood. Not zombie, but actually antizombie. Different than what's in the antidote. We think it's what made him vomit."

Her brow furrows with confusion. "A few days? How long have I been out? Did you check my blood, too?"

I'm used to the way she fires off a million questions during any given conversation. Her curiosity is another thing

I've always liked about her. Maybe because I feel like a hero when I have the answers she seeks.

Today I'm resentful. Soon, Gavin will be the one to answer her.

I clench my hands. "About a week," I say. "And yes. You had—have—the same antizombie toxin, only you have a lot more of it, which makes us think you shared it with him when he bit you."

I'm not sure what this means for her...for slayers.

"How and where would I have gotten an antizombie toxin?" she asks. "And why is it in my blood rather than my spirit?"

I give another shrug. "Could be an ability, like the visions. And if it's in your spirit, it's in your blood. We have to test what we can."

She nibbles on her bottom lip. I want to stop her. I want to kiss away the sting she's caused. But I don't. I won't. If I put my hands on her, I won't be able to let go. I will cling. I'm sure of this.

"Just so you know, we told everyone you'd overdone it and reopened your wound." A wound I had accidentally caused. I have yet to forgive myself. "Both of which are true." She would have protested if we'd lied.

"Thank you."

I nod. I force myself to stand and move toward the door. I have to leave her. Now. It's becoming more difficult to maintain any kind of distance.

"Cole," she calls. "We need to talk."

"You need to rest."

"Cole."

Knowing her, she will chase me if I leave. I pause, draw in a fortifying breath. Slowly I turn and face her. I'm careful to keep my features blank.

"This has to stop," she says.

She is going to force me to make a decision. Here, now. Cut her loose, or hang on until the bitter end. I'm not ready.

"I tried not to push you, but you have to give me something," she continues. "Your silence is driving me crazy."

I cross my arms over my chest and have a fleeting thought that it is a defensive action meant to protect me from the blow to come. "Some things aren't meant to be discussed, Ali." *Let me go. Just let me go.*

"At Hearts, you couldn't spend time with me. Why?"

I spied on my friends that night, and I still hate myself for it. I'm glad I refused to entangle her in the mess then, and I won't do it now. "I've already told you all I'm willing to say on that subject."

She expels a heavy breath. "You asked me to trust you, and now I'm asking you to trust me with the truth. Why?"

The need to give her what she wants redoubles. I resist.

"You told me you wanted me to stay away from Gavin," she says, "and yet you have been the one to stay away from me. Why?"

At the sound of his name, my rage returns, and it is far stronger than my need. Gavin and Ali. Ali and Gavin. A couple. In love. Holding each other. Kissing each other. Touching each other. A growl brews inside my chest.

Ali bangs her fist against the mattress. "What we just saw in the vision—"

"Will happen," I shout. The words burst from me. I can't stop them. "You know it will. It always does."

"Maybe it doesn't mean what we think it means."

I want to hope. "What do you think it means?"

"I...don't know. What do *you* think it means?"

But hope is my enemy. Because I don't *think* anything. I know.

Cut her loose, or hang on until the bitter end. Let the wound begin to heal, or let it fester.

Choose.

"I think it means..." A crushing pain throbs in my chest. One I've never before experienced. My heart pounds against my ribs in an effort to escape it. I bite back the words that will be final nails in the coffin of our relationship, but it does no good. "We're over."

She flinches as if she's been struck. "No." She shakes her head. "No."

My instincts scream in agreement. No! I almost drop to my knees and beg her to forgive me for even suggesting such a thing.

The pain in my chest intensifies.

Who the hell am I? I'm supposed to be immovable. When I make a decision, nothing changes my mind. I'm supposed to be invincible. Zombies cannot hurt me, and yet this girl is *killing* me.

I'm helpless all over again. I hate it, hate myself. Even hate her a little. "Okay, let me rephrase. I *know* it means we're over." Every word is a dagger, cutting at me, but still I continue. "We have to be. I've almost lost you twice, and I'm going to lose you for good when the visions start coming true. I'm not going to hang on to a lost cause, Ali."

Panic radiates from her. "I'm not a lost cause. *We're* not a lost cause. I don't like Gavin."

I want to believe her. She is everything to me. A reason to wake up in the morning. A reason to fight for a safer world. A reason to breathe. If I do this, if I walk away from her, I will never be the same.

"But you will," I say.

"Don't do this. Please. You have to trust me. Please. There are some things you can never take back, and this is one of them."

Damn it, I know! Does she think this is easy for me? That I'm made of stone?

Before I realize I've taken a step, I'm across the room, slamming my fist into the wall. Dust plumes the air, almost choking me, as the skin covering my knuckles splits. Bones crack and blood wells. It hurts.

I'm glad. I prefer this pain to the other one.

Very gently, she says, "I'm not going to look at Gavin and suddenly start wanting him. You're the one for me. And this isn't like you. You never back down. You never walk away from a fight."

Exactly. Right now I'm fighting for my life. I'm the one trapped in the bottomless ocean, and I can't escape.

I press my forehead into the damaged wall.

"Cole," she whispers. "Do you want Veronica?"

"No. Not even a little."

"See!"

"Ali, I…" *Want to make this work. Will do anything to make it work.*

I straighten and face her. Deep down I know "anything" will not be good enough, and that hurts almost as much as this end. "Our feelings right now aren't the problem. One day I hope you'll forgive me. I doubt I'll ever be able to forgive myself." If I could press rewind on our lives and go back to before the visions, I would. I would stay with her, never let her go, the two of us lost together. I would be happy. Now I'm certain I will never be happy again. "But…we're done."

"Cole."

"We're done," I force myself to repeat. For her. For me. We both need to hear it. I back away from her, needing distance but hating it, too. "We're done."

Her eyes glass over, as if she's fighting tears. "I won't come crawling after you."

Do it. Come after me, part of me shouts. *Don't ever let me go.* "I don't want you to." The other part of me is self-preservation, and after all these years of battle, it's strong.

"I won't take you back even if you come crawling back to *me.*"

"I know," I say softly, and I can feel all the broken pieces of me withering. "And I won't… I can't…" I shake my head, try to gather what little strength I have left. "There's nothing I can say to make either of us feel better about this, and I'm sorry about that. You'll probably never know how much. But that's not going to change my mind. It has to be this way."

I leave her then. I leave her before I do it, before I drop to my knees and beg not only for forgiveness but for another chance. I've just severed the most precious part of my life. I'm not going to heal from this. I know it.

"Cole."

Frosty calls my name. He's at the end of the hall, waiting for me.

I stride past him without a word, without a pause.

"Cole."

Again I ignore him. My eyes burn. I must have something in them. Somehow I make it outside the house without drawing the notice of anyone else. I climb inside my Jeep, but I don't even get the key into the ignition before the rage and helplessness explode from me. I pound at the wheel with my fists. The metal circle bends, unable to withstand the fury. But I don't stop. I can't, even when I'm leaving smears of blood behind. I can't breathe, either, and I'm not sure I want to.

I should have ripped my heart out of my chest and given it to her. It would have been easier than this. Less painful.

We are done. We are really done.

Realization settles like a boulder. We are over. She's free of me, free to do as she pleases…and I will be forever lost *without* her.

DELETED SCENES

Gena Showalter and Harlequin TEEN are thrilled to share, exclusively for Barnes and Noble, the following deleted scenes from the original draft of The Queen of Zombie Hearts.

Hey everyone! Before we unveil the handful of deleted scenes, I thought I'd explain a little about my revision process. With *The Queen of Zombie Hearts,* I didn't do much plotting before I began the actual writing. I had a few key points and scenes in mind, but not much else. I hoped the characters would take me wherever they wanted to go. And they did. But there were a few places they led me astray—even fictional people are sweet like that. It was only after I'd finished writing my first draft, and talked things over with my editor, that everything fell into place and I realized the book would be a lot stronger with some changes.

I hope you enjoy these deleted scenes!

This is the original "Note from Ali," which I completely rewrote. I wanted something that hooked me from moment one, something that wouldn't let me go, and while I adored the imagery here, I knew that special "something" was missing. So, it had to go.

A NOTE FROM ALI

On your mark...

In my mind, I can see it. Runners take their place on the block, ready to begin.

Get set.

I watch as they inhale deeply, centering their thoughts, the rest of the world fading away. There's only here and now, a suspended moment of incredible peace as the sun shines and a cool breeze dances.

Go!

A gun fires. Adrenaline surges through the competitors' veins and in unison, they spring forward.

The race is on. Or, rather, the tour of duty. Victory is the prize, and it's worth more than gold.

Family and friends wait at the finish line, holding big bouquets of flowers. And sometimes, the person you least expect to see shows up.

Though you are tired and sore, it's a great day.

If you make it.

Some runners will give up somewhere along the way, too tired to go on. Some will be injured and disqualified. Not everyone presses through to the end, no matter what happens.

What a perfect analogy for my life.

The day I lost my parents and beloved little sister in a car crash, I was thrown into the middle of a good versus evil—slayer versus zombie—marathon. And yes. You read that correctly. I said *zombie*. These vile creatures live among us, invisible to the ungifted eye, and they emerge at night, hungry for spirits, the essence of human life. They feast, and they poison, and when you're bitten, *your* spirit rises from *your* body, just as hungry.

I've been running ever since. Mile after endless mile. Figuratively—sometimes literally. There have been times that fear distracted me. Grief tripped me. Betrayal blindsided me, and secrets weakened me. There have been times that regret weighed me down, turning every step into an agonizing chore. But I kept going. My friends were always at my side, running with me, cheering me on.

Until now.

The enemy snuck up behind us. And I'm not just talking about the zombies. I'm talking about the ones *controlling* the zombies. The people at Anima Industries.

Here's a cold pimp-slap of truth: Humans can be more dangerous than monsters.

The things I've seen Anima do...the horrors I've witnessed... the friends I've lost.

Oh, the friends I've lost.

Four in one night. Then, soon after, two others.

Part of me wants to drop to my knees, raise my fists toward the sky and scream, "That's it! I've had enough! No more! I'm done."

But I can't. Staying on my feet has never been more important. For the first time, I can see the finish line. I know it's time to sprint.

You see, we have a plan. With it, we'll either destroy Anima for good—or they'll destroy us. But one way or another, only one of us is walking away.

Until then,

Ali Bell

These next three scenes were part of the original backstory I wrote for Helen, Ali's mom. In the first draft, Helen was a drug addict, but when all was said and done, that didn't work for me because it removed Helen's sense of choice. I wanted her to own her decisions and face the consequences with courage—like Ali. So, without further ado:

I had the strangest dream. I sat in the middle of an old, ratty rug. Toys were strewn all around me.

"—has to stop," my dad was saying. And wow, was he young! Like, he was barely older than me. But I recognized his height. Not many people achieved six and a half feet. And his hair. Sandy blond. His eyes. Navy blue.

My heart lurched at the sight of him.

A plain but elegant woman stepped into view, her narrowed gaze focused on him. She was a little taller than average, and slender. Such a small bone structure made her look like some kind of fairy princess from a storybook. She had wavy shoulder-length hair the color of newly fallen snow, and eyes so pale they were freaky.

I'd seen those eyes before. *Many* times before.

Like, every time I'd looked in a mirror.

Was this girl a relative of mine? One I'd never met?

It was possible. But why was I dreaming about her?

"I will not stop," she snapped, and her tone held a razor's edge of hate.

And that would be why I'd never met her.

I wanted to punch her in the face. No one spoke to my dad that way, not even in a dream.

I stood up and put my hands on my hips, growling, "You have five seconds to apologize, princess, and then I get mad."

She ignored me, saying to my dad, "How can you do this to me? After everything I've done for you?"

"I'm grateful for what you've done. I am. But—"

"But that's not going to change anything," she interjected. She turned her back on him, and her expression was one of total anguish, as if her heart had been shredded inside her chest. "I have rights, you know. I could fight you."

"You won't," he said, not the least bit concerned by her threat—whatever it was.

"You don't know that."

"You're a junkie, and you know it. I know it. You put your drugs before everyone and everything. You can't afford to do anything."

His words must have felt like fists to her, because every sentence made her flinch.

Whatever her reply, I missed it. Something was tugging at me, luring me away from the dream. Farther and farther. And every several seconds, it felt as if someone had poked holes in me, draining my strength.

A sea of black washed over me. The tugging continued, worse now, pulling me down…down…down…and for a moment, I thought I sensed Cole. His pine and soap scent. His love. His intensity. I fought with all of my might, and managed to break the surface, dragging whatever was tethered to me…him?…with me. I gasped for breath.

Here is another scene that was cut when Helen's backstory changed. As before, this one is a dream Ali is having:

…I opened my eyes and found myself in a car seat, a pacifier in my small, chubby hand.

Uh, this had better be a dream, or I was going to have one heck of a freak-out.

Though he was parked rather than driving, my young dad sat behind the wheel of the car, and Helen sat in the passenger seat. Rain pelted against the windows.

"You can't do this to me," she spat.

"I can," he retorted. "You're using again, and we both know it."

Using?

"No." She latched onto his wrist. "No, I—"

He jerked from her touch. "Don't lie to me. You're using."

With a screech, she banged a fist against the console between them. A high-pitched cry reverberated through the car, and when she looked at me to apologize, I realized it had come from me. More gently, she said to my dad, "You can't blame me, Phillip. Look at what you're doing to me. Look at what you're putting me through."

He glared at her. "I won't feel guilty."

"You should," she whispered fiercely, casting me a furtive glance. "You've ruined my life."

The fight drained out of my dad, and he sighed. "I know, and I'm sorry. I'm sorry for the way things turned out. I never should have—"

"No. Don't you dare apologize. You aren't sorry for any of it. You got everything you could ever want. From me, and from your precious Miranda. But one day," she said, pointing a finger in his face, "one day it's all going to be taken away from you."

I stiffened. Maybe Cole was right about this girl.

"Is that a threat?" my dad asked.

She laughed without humor. "It's a promise. The monsters—"

"I don't want to talk about them."

"Too bad. Miranda doesn't see them. I do. She'll never understand you the way I do."

Miranda. My mother.

This *had* to be a dream. But…could it be a memory, too?

Had my dad known Helen?

If so, how did they meet? *When* did they meet? What kind of relationship did they have?

"Ali, baby, I need you to wake up."

Cole's voice startled me, yanking me from the car…the dream…and I jolted upright with a gasp.

Strong arms banded around me, tugging me back down, forcing me to lie against a warm, strong—familiar—chest. Cole's chest.

Another dream cut because Helen's backstory changed:

As they talked about everything and nothing, I began to drift away…

…and soon found myself standing beside my mother, holding her hand, tears streaming down my cheeks. I watched as my dad forcibly hauled Helen to the front door and shoved her onto the porch.

"You gave her to me, Helen. Did you hear that? *You* gave her to *me*. Told me you wanted nothing to do with her. Then, a few months later, you kidnap her. I didn't know where she was, or if you would return with her. Then you show up at my door twelve hours later to give her back, and you think I'll let you see her again? No!"

"She's my daughter!"

"Is she? Because she sure doesn't know you," he snarled, his tone crueler than I'd ever heard it.

I grimaced.

Helen cringed.

And then my dad's words finally sunk in. *You gave her to me. Told me you wanted nothing to do with her.*

Helen had given Phillip her child, Veronica had said.

Good glory. It was true. There was no more denying it.

Helen was my birth mother.

I wanted to sob. I wanted to scream. Both urges roared through me. I was the girl she'd given up, as if I were no more worthy than garbage. Threads of resentment wove from my mind to my heart, and like a spider's web, dark emotions began to stick. Hatred…anger…remorse…sorrow…

"You gave her to me," my dad repeated. "She's mine."

"I did it to protect her," she whispered, and I almost believed her. Almost.

"Then keep protecting her," my dad said. "Only, do a better job. She has a life with Miranda and me. Why don't you let her live it?"

Light blue eyes misted over. "Because I love her."

My heart clenched painfully, some of the threads falling away.

He remained unmoved. "You've said that before. You said you'd prove it, that you'd never shoot up again."

Shoot up. Good glory. *Helen is—was—a junkie.*

Shame coated her expression before she ducked her head to peer down at her feet. "I messed up, but it was just one time," she said, her voice begging him to understand. "It'll never happen again."

"And now you're lying," he barked. "I've had it, Helen. Don't come back here. Don't contact me. You do, and I'll move so far away you'll never be able to find me."

Her head snapped up and she clutched at his shirt. "Please, Phillip. Please, don't do this. I got help. I really did. They're helping me get clean, and they're helping me fight the monsters."

"Goodbye, Helen," he said, then he dislodged her and shut the door in her face.

This is the original version of the scene in which the slayers kidnap and question Dr. Rangarajan. When this scene was written, Ali possessed the ability to push her spirit into other bodies, but then I made adjustments to what she could and couldn't do—I didn't want her becoming all-powerful—so this scene had to be changed completely:

If Cole and I had control over the visions, maybe we could have visions with other people. Anyone we wanted, at any time. It was worth a shot, at least. Because, while a vision wouldn't tell me Dr. Rangarajan's secrets, it might reveal the kind of man he was.

"Don't fight this," I told him, placing my hands at his temples. Contact wasn't needed with Cole, but this wasn't Cole. I closed my eyes, breathing in and out. "It's going to happen one way or another." I hoped.

"Wh-what are you doing?" he asked.

I ignored him, concentrating on our connection, on my skin against his. Tremors vibrated from him and into my body, nearly shaking me off my feet.

"You won't have a vision with him," a sweet voice said from beside me. I didn't have to open my eyes to know Emma was here. "You can't. He's not a slayer, and already you have too many walls built against him. But you *can* get the information you want. You just have to push your spirit out of your body and step into his."

What! I stiffened. No one I knew had ever done—or spoken of—anything like that.

"Trust me, Ali," my sister said. "I've been working tirelessly to help your cause, talking to slayers who have died, researching the different abilities. Once you're inside his head, all you have to do is think about what you want to see and his memories will automatically go there."

I did trust her. Like Cole, it was so much a part of me that I couldn't question it. So, I did what she'd suggested. I pushed my spirit out of my body. The cold hit me as I continued to step forward—into his body. Then, a warm shield cocooned me. But it was odd, ill fitting, as if I'd picked a winter coat one size too small.

Now, at least, I could see the world through his eyes. The slayers surrounded me, staring at me with hatred in their eyes. Hatred and menace. I could feel the throb of pain in my face, wrists and ankles, and my heart drummed far too swiftly, the beat warped.

"—have to get out of here," I heard him cry. No, he hadn't cried—not out loud. I'd heard the words inside my head.

Justin, I thought, bringing his face to the forefront of my mind.

A second later, images began to flash. From a computer screen, I saw an unconscious Justin. Justin, inside a cell. Justin, pacing. Justin, strapped to a table.

Then, the computer disappeared and a room took shape around me. A large office. Cherrywood bookcases on the far wall. A massive desk with a thirtysomething woman behind it. She wore red. A lot of red. Red lipstick. Red dress. Her hair was black and slicked back from her face, pinned in a bun at her nape. Her skin was pale. Paler than mine, even, but flawless. Her eyes were as dark as her hair, and cold. So freaking cold. As if she'd never experienced an emotion in her life.

"The boy, Justin, has become a problem," she said. Her voice was as cold as the rest of her. "Dr. Andrews was unable to get him to talk."

"And the other slayer that was taken?" I asked. No, not I. Dr. Rangarajan. His voice was businesslike, indifferent.

"He's dead."

Poor River. He had another punch of bad news headed his way.

"What would you like me to do?" Dr. Rangarajan asked. "You know you have only to ask, and it will be done."

Say her name. Come on, come on.

"Just stay available. We have a plan in motion to destroy the rest of the slayers. All but the girl. She will be brought to you. You've read the results of her tests, yes?"

What plan? What girl?

"Yes. She's extraordinary."

"I still curse Ethan and his father for losing her. She will be our greatest asset—or theirs."

They were talking about me, I realized, shaking with dread.

The phone on the desk buzzed. "Ms. Smith. Your two-thirty appointment is here."

Smith—only like the most common name in America. But it was a start, I supposed.

Dr. Rangarajan stood and strode from the office without being told, and the memory faded. I tried to stay inside his head, to direct him into another one, but the invisible chain linked to my body was somehow being tugged, and I found myself being whisked back.

I blinked open my eyes and stumbled away from the doctor. I couldn't quite catch my breath, and my lungs were burning unbearably.

"—hear me, Ali?"

Cole's voice. Filled with concern. "Yes," I said, focusing on him.

"Thank God." He pressed his forehead against mine, and breathed a sigh of relief. "You were turning blue."

I looked around, but there was no sign of my sister. She was gone.

★ ★ ★ ★ ★

We hope you enjoyed these exclusive deleted scenes!
Thank you for reading
THE WHITE RABBIT CHRONICLES.
Look for Gena Showalter's new series coming in fall 2015!